MERCENARY

Rex Mangin

Published by Rex Mangin – 2021
Revised – 2026

Contact the author at: **rex.mangin@xtra.co.nz**

Also available as an e-book

Cover Design: Alexandra Taylor

ISBN 978-0-473-58847-2

Books By Rex Mangin

Available as paperback and e-book

Infidelity Gun Running & Other Tales

Cold War Warrior

Flying The Pacific

Mercenary

Albert McConachie's Bad Day

Carrie Gray

Travel Bites

Introduction

Rex Macare, fresh out of the military, a highly qualified pilot, his apprenticeship's finished, now he wants the real money. His quest leads to the mysterious Mr Roberts who makes him an offer too good to refuse. He meets, and falls in love, with the beautiful Kate, a high end fashion model.

He soon finds himself immersed in a whole new world, a heady mix of big money, huge money, dangerous flying, high end fashion, and unbridled sex. It does not last.

Contents

Author's Note

The *F* word, nice people do not use the *F* word; I have. It adds impact and intensity to some of the more erotic parts of this tale of high adventure and unbridled sex. If you find the *F* word objectionable then perhaps this book is not for you.

Mr Roberts

Bzzzz, I press the doorbell, 'Monsieur Robier?' no response. I knock, 'Monsieur Robier?' still no response, have I made a mistake. I'm sure it was two this afternoon, room 202. I push the door, it swings open and I recoil in horror, the place is a charnel house, blood everywhere. There's a body on the floor, throat slashed open. I feel faint, want to throw up, it's worse than a horror movie. I look closer, the body has been mutilated, clothing torn open, blood all over the place. It's Monsieur Robier. There's something on his chest, a note.

Rentrez chez vous Monsieur Rex, ne plaisante pas avec nous.
Go home Mister Rex, don't mess with us.

French, English, my name, it's meant for me, shit! There's something else, his genitals have been torn off and stuffed into his mouth; the FLN's brutal calling card.

Eighteen Months Earlier.
It's a bright autumn morning in Auckland New Zealand when the phone rings.

'Hello.'

'Is that Rex Macare?' A male voice heavy with authority.

'Yes this is Rex Macare.'

'Hello Rex, I would like to talk to you, something you might be interested in, perhaps I could come 'round and see you to…'

'Hang on, not another scammer, don't you guys ever give up?'

'No I'm not a scammer, it's aviation. I would like to talk to you face to face. Would it be convenient for me to call around later this morning, I think you will be interested in what I have to say.'

'What's it about exactly?'

'Not over the phone, needs to be face to face.'

What could it be, aviation, how does this fellow know I'm interested in aviation. I'd been sounding out the flying scene around Auckland, I needed a job, a flying job, perhaps he'd heard about me.

'Ok, I'll be home for a while, later this morning would be fine. Do you know where I live?'

'Yes, see you in an hour.'

'Alright, what did you say your name was?'

'I didn't.'

That got me thinking, wonder what this is about. I'd been back in New Zealand for a month after an absence of several years in Europe. A pilot on a specialist low flying outfit in Germany, latest jets, exciting stuff. It had been great, did not get much better for a pilot but the problem was money, the military were not great payers. The flying was terrific, the money was not and it was starting to look like it would continue unchanged into the foreseeable future. I was not getting any younger. I really needed to get into something that came up with a lot more cash. I had been sounding out the contract pilot world, perhaps mercenary would be a better description. The Congo, South East Asia, Middle East, South America, plenty of rumours about serious money but all high risk, the more the money the greater the risk. It appeared life expectancy was not good in most of these places. I came across a mate from the Air Force who had been involved, Air America, a CIA front. He'd secured a contract to fly supplies to the Meo people in the highlands of South Vietnam. The Meo sided with the South Vietnamese Government and the Americans in the war that was raging in that country. A contract was more lucrative than being employed as a pilot but you needed your own aeroplane. He had purchased a small Cessna and took up the contract. It was dangerous. Flying into the mountains in all weathers and being shot at. The Viet Cong and the North Vietnamese army did not like the Meo. The supplies were mainly rice and it was an advantage to land somewhere to get this to the right people rather than just drop the sacks out of the plane. Places to land were few and far between; and dodgy. He did this for six months and made a lot of money but he could see an early grave with his name on it and decided to get out. An American bought his Cessna, and the CIA contract. Two weeks later the American was shot down and killed.

This mate was a Kiwi, he too was back in New Zealand trying to sort something out, money again the driving force. He had been in contact with Mike Hoare, 'Mad Mike,' in the Congo, there was flying available. Rumour had it that Mad Mike had some armed Fouga Magisters, a small French jet aircraft; he needed pilots. The deal was if you were interested then you had to present yourself to Mad Mike in Kinshasa and take it from there. The money on offer was reportedly huge, so was the risk. My mate was not sure about this one, the vibes were not good. He would inquire further and keep me advised. There was South America, but getting information was difficult, the general feeling being that just about anything on offer would be drug related and very dangerous; serious money though. Middle East? mostly Arab Governments. Good money but all fighter pilot stuff. Most of the offers came via British companies who were selling their wares to the Arabs. They were tapping into the RAF for qualified fighter pilots about to retire, offering short term contracts to fly in the Middle East.

Interesting this mercenary business, it was possible to make some real money but getting all the facts was difficult. Most of it was just rumour, however, one thing did stand out, it could lead to an early grave.

As well as the mercenary world, I had been casting around the New Zealand scene, what's available? There were flying jobs going and a lot of pilots chasing them, all a bit mundane though. Small aircraft, charter flying, tourist stuff, nothing exciting. I had spent virtually all my flying career doing 'hairy stuff,' all that low flying in Europe had spoilt me for anything else. What was offering in New Zealand was not very interesting and the money was 'ordinary.' There was top dressing, that was good for a thrill or two but again the money on offer did not stack up against the risk. The airlines? I had an application in with two of the majors, but that was seriously boring, I was not ready for that. Mind you if you could crack the airline scene then it was a secure job for life. The money was reasonable, quite good actually, but boring. I needed a bit of excitement, I was not ready to settle down, would I ever be? *Then there was Kate.*

I met her on my first day back in New Zealand, in a pub of all places, bit corny really, but a pub it was. I was in there with another mate from way back, from the days when I lived in Auckland. We were having a drink to get reacquainted. There was this gorgeous creature closely escorted by what appeared to be a possessive boyfriend, I could not take my eyes of her. She was drop dead beautiful; how can I crack this one? A discreet word with the barman and he takes them a couple of drinks, *from an admirer.* It was interesting, their looking around, who? Boyfriend did not look impressed but her face lit up, she really scanned the customers. I caught her eye and winked. A little later a couple of drinks arrive at our bar leaner, there's a piece of paper, Kate, and a phone number. Wow careful, you could be treading on toes here. She was not looking in our direction in fact there was no further eye contact. The following morning, early, I phoned, it was answered immediately, *Kate.* That was the start of it, now, a month on, we are seeing a lot of each other, boyfriend? I don't know, I have not asked.

A knock on the door. It's just an hour on from that mysterious phone call. There's a middle aged chap in a suit, that distinctive authoritarian voice.

'Rex Macare?'

'Yes, that's me, come in, you've certainly got my interest, what is it you have?'

'I represent an organisation that does clandestine work for the British Government, we are always on the lookout for talent we can use and your name popped up on our radar.'

'You're kidding me, right?'

'Definitely not, I'm very serious, you have abilities we can use.' What am I hearing, who is this fellow? is this a sophisticated scam?

'Perhaps a coffee, tea?' I offer.
I need time to get my head around this, is this guy for real or am I about to be ripped off?

'Tea would be nice.' That voice, very distinctive, full of authority, this fellow's no mug, I think he could be for real.

'Good, I'll make a pot.' I disappear into the small kitchen I need some time to think.

'Here we are, a pot of tea; you're British?'

'Yes I am.'
I arrange a couple of cups and pour the tea.

'Well you've certainly got my attention, how is it that I popped up, as you say, on your radar?'

'Well we know you are a competent pilot highly regarded for your flying skills and not averse to a bit of risk taking.'

'Really, how do you arrive at that conclusion?'

'Classified.'

'Come on, what is this, you're just appealing to my ego, why?'

'I'm being serious, what I am going to offer you is serious.'

'Ok, fire away.'

'During your tenure in Europe you were involved in a few high risk activities, gun running, sabre rattling in Africa, and a couple of excursions across the border into East Germany.'

'Excuse me, you sure about all this.'

'Very sure, and there are people in authority around the place who would like to have a word with you about some of your past activities, the French in particular.'

Suddenly I don't feel so good, who is this fellow, how does he know these things, am I being threatened? Past memories start to surface, memories that were buried forever. The events he's just alluded to are true. I had been in the military at the time and you do as you're told in the military, you don't pass moral judgment on things. The French, how would this fellow know anything about that? As far as I had been able to find out the incident he was referring to never happened, officially erased. It was gun running, the FLN in Algeria. A transport aeroplane full of Thompson sub machine guns delivered to El Aouina in Tunisia in the dead of night. A secret British Government job. What game the British were playing I didn't know, didn't want to know. I was ordered to do it and in the military you do as you're told. The French were involved in a bloody conflict with the FLN in Algeria and El Aouina was right on the Algerian border. It was not hard to figure out who the guns were for. If this fellow was able to trace it to me had the French done the same?

The African business. It was 1962 and yes I had flown a fully armed warplane down to Southern Rhodesia from Germany. It was no secret, quite the opposite. The idea was to intimidate Mugabe and his nationalist buddies who were becoming a problem. As far as I was concerned I had been ordered to do it and I was only too pleased to comply, it was a great lark. I was young and bulletproof, what could go wrong? Now this fellow is implying that perhaps these things could bite me on the bum.

The East German border thing? That was supposed to be classified, no one would know anything. Now here on the other side of the world I am confronted with it. How much does this chap know? It's obvious he's got access to highly classified information so why is he so interested in me?

'Ok you've got my attention, tell me more.'

'Amongst other things you've done quite a lot of flying in Chipmunks, we would like to use that experience.'

'Chipmunks?'

'Yes, Chipmunks, the Rhine River Gorge.'

He was right I had flown Chipmunks, a lot. Most Air Force stations had a Station Flight that sported a variety of aircraft, Meteors, old Ansons, the occasional Auster, and invariably a Chipmunk. I went out of my way to endear myself to whoever ran the Station Flight wherever I was stationed so I could get to fly their Chipmunk. I loved it; after a fast jet it was almost therapeutic. Fully aerobatic, a delight to fly. I did a lot of aerobatics. When I was not doing that the Chipmunk was the perfect way to see the countryside and an area where I did a lot of sightseeing was the Rhine River Gorge, especially that bit from Bonn down to Koblenz, the picture postcard bit, all those castles on hilltops. I did a lot of low flying in the Rhine River Gorge, probably illegal, however, there were never any repercussions. My primary role in the fast jet I flew in Germany was low level strike, we were always practising low flying so when I found myself in the little Chipmunk it was just normal to fly low. You could poke its nose into places that would be unthinkable in a fast jet.

'You are fluent in German, right?'

'Ah, yes, you seem to know a lot about me, how come?'

'Well a couple of your girlfriends in Germany did comment on your German.'

'What? you're kidding me? how could you know that?'

'We like to know all about the people we are interested in and we are interested in you. We want you for something in Germany, short term, you will be well rewarded. I believe you are casting around for something that carries substantial remuneration.'

'Who would be employing me?'

'The British Government, however, it will be via an agency, there will be absolutely no official connection.'

I was starting to feel a bit faint, this was all a bit overwhelming. I certainly was looking for something that would carry substantial reward and so far it seemed that high reward carried high risk. What this fellow was on about appeared to be government backed, and in Europe, a much better proposition than some dodgy African operation.

'Take your time, have a think about what I have said. I'll get back to you in a couple of days.'

'Hang on a mo, what exactly would you be requiring me to do in Germany?'

'I'll give you more detail at our next meeting. I'm sure you will find what we have to offer appealing given your adventurous nature and flying experience. There is the possibility it could be an ongoing commitment. There's the money of course, it's substantial. And now I must be going, I'll contact you in a couple of days; oh yes, you can call me *Mr Roberts*.'

And with that he got up and headed for the door.

That was incredible, was Mr Roberts for real or am I delusional. What he hinted at was something I had been trying to get onto for some time and he just walks in and practically makes me an offer, and where did he find out so much about me? Obviously he has access to classified military information but the mention of low flying in the Rhine River Gorge, how could he possibly know about that? Girlfriends? I had dated a couple of girls in Germany but would that be known to higher authority? Suddenly a thought, the girlfriends, a clue, was Mr Roberts really a government rep, or something more sinister.

16 Mr Roberts

When I was on that strike squadron in Germany what we did was classified; we were nuclear armed; serious stuff. We were aware that the East German authorities were always trying to find out about what the NATO forces in West Germany were up to. Most military bases could expect to be infiltrated by East German agents, usually civilians employed on the bases with relatives in the east. They were blackmailed. The 'spying' was at a low level, not considered a real problem however we were made aware that it did go on and to be discreet in our contacts with the local population.

Contact with the local population!
I was young and single. My mates and I were not averse to patronising the local pubs and taverns, chasing the girls, I mean what's wrong with that? Some of the girls we encountered were lovely. I did take up with a couple of them during my tenure; were they agents of the East? I don't think so, get real, but now Mr Roberts has raised doubts.

What to make of this? At first glance it appeared to be something I could get into and make some money, that was the whole purpose of the exercise, but Mr Roberts? Was he a British spook or was he on the 'other side' and how could I ever find out. Think, think, a lot of what he divulged could only be from British Government sources, how would anyone else know these things? The low flying and the girlfriends? how did he obtain that information? Did I talk about my low flying? Possibly. Had he tracked down the girlfriends? also a possibility. Could I look up those girls, discuss it? no not possible. Here I am on the other side of the world, those affairs were in the past. Perhaps the best thing I can do is string Mr Roberts along, find out as much as I can about what he's offering. It could be a good deal but there could be a downside, there will be a downside. He's offering good money and in the mercenary business that means risk.

Kate; put Mr Roberts on the back burner, if that's possible, think about Kate, the lovely Kate, the ray of sunshine that's suddenly come into my life. I've taken Kate out several times since the pub encounter, she seems to enjoy my company, has never mentioned the fellow she had been with in the pub. I assume he was the boyfriend, could be wrong, I won't ask, she will tell when she's ready, but she's never mentioned him. Kate shared a flat in Parnell with another girl, another gorgeous girl, Ali, Ali Fischer. Little unusual, in my experience, 'lookers' tend to hitch up with 'plain Janes,' is it a female competition thing or my imagination, whatever. There was a man in Ali's life, Jeff. On one occasion we made up a foursome and went along to a local restaurant, it was great, we all clicked. Kate is really nice, a model, fashion and photography, Ali did the same. They worked for the same agency in Parnell. Their careers were on the up and up, both in demand. Suddenly my life in Auckland was pretty enjoyable, Kate in particular, she seemed to like me; how lucky can you get. But I had no job, no income, and my meagre bank account was looking decidedly sad. I really needed to sort something out sooner rather than later and right on cue a call from Mr Roberts.

'Hello there, can we meet, I have a proposal for you.'

'Of course, what did you have in mind?'

'Not over the phone, perhaps I can come around.'

'Yep, suits me, when?'

'How about in an hour?'

'Sounds good, tea again?

'Yes that would be nice.'

The Proposal

Right on time, a knock on the door, Mr Roberts.

'Hello Rex, I can call you Rex, is that ok?'

'Fine with me,' a pregnant pause, I expected him to come up with something I could call him by other than Mr Roberts, but he didn't.

'Tea, I've just boiled the pot.'

'Yes, that would be nice.'

I poured a couple of cups and sat down, what is he going to tell me?

'We are interested in your low flying experience in Chipmunks, we would like to make you an offer.'

Chipmunks, the least of my qualifications. I could compile a CV that would include things a lot more interesting than a little Chipmunk. There were clandestine things however, things I could not divulge, but I was beginning to think that Mr Roberts would know this already. My CV would read something like this.

Pilot, New Zealand born, Royal Air Force trained. 4000 hours, mainly on jets, including multi jet aircraft. Considerable LABS (low altitude bombing system) experience using nuclear weapons. Experienced in ground attack on Canberra B(I)8 twin jet aircraft, cannons, rockets and bombs. Very familiar with low flying techniques both day and night. Familiar with Africa, the Middle East, and Europe, particularly Germany. Competent aerobatic pilot on jet and piston aircraft. Fluent in German, experienced SCUBA diver, distinguished marksman with many trophies for small bore shooting.

Then there would be the things that perhaps I could not include. Gun running experience in North Africa and the Middle East. Carried out 'intimidation' flying in Southern Africa, completed several covert missions into East Germany, familiar with NATO's tactical targets in Eastern Europe and well-practised in how to strike at them. Involved in long range flying in the Pacific, Christmas Island, Britain's nuclear testing programme, Operation Grapple.

There's more but what's the point, could hardly trumpet all my clandestine experience in a CV. Most of this flying did not appear in my log book, probably not recorded anywhere, it could get me into trouble. In the military you are sworn to silence, unable to divulge anything that's not already public knowledge. This legal restriction carries on into civilian life, however, the mysterious Mr Roberts seems to know about these things.

'We would like you to do some flying in Germany, low level stuff at night, something you are experienced in. It will be a Chipmunk and it will involve some cross border flying.'

'Really, sounds interesting, how much flying and when?'

'One night flight into East Germany two weeks from now.'

'One flight?'

'Yes; however depending on what you think about it and what we think about you, there could be an ongoing commitment.'

'What's the reward?'

'Not so fast. I know you are interested in the money however let me fill you in on some detail. There will be an upfront payment that you will use to get yourself to Germany. You will check into the Schapers Hotel and Restaurant in Celle, that's a town just to the north of Hanover, you know the area, you've done a lot of low flying there.' Mr Roberts has certainly done his homework on me. 'You will be contacted at the hotel and given the detail of what's required but briefly it involves flying a Chipmunk across the border into the DDR at night and photographing a building. The Chipmunk will be fitted with low light infrared gear. That's it, just one flight then you will return directly to Auckland. You'll make your own travel arrangements and the reason for your visit to Germany, should anyone ask, will be to tidy up some loose ends from your previous period of residence there.'

'Ok, got all that. I'm on for it.'

'The money. We will give you NZ$30,000 upfront and a further NZ$40,000 on successful completion, cash, paid in New Zealand.'
I'm gobsmacked, that's a lot of money. It's what I've been trying to get onto and here it is dropped in my lap. The risk? money like that comes with risk.

'Eh, that's a lot of money, there must be some risk involved?'

'Yes, there is. The East Germans will not like you crossing their border at night and taking photographs. You've been there before, same area, similar role. This time it's a little piston aeroplane not a fast jet, they will not be expecting that. Low and slow at night, very hard to detect, but you already know all about that, familiar territory.'
Mr Roberts never ceases to amaze with his knowledge.

'One more thing, and I think it goes without saying, tell no one, absolutely no one, zipped lip, not even Kate.'

'Kate?'

'Yes, she's a lovely girl.'
Again I'm gobsmacked, this Mr Roberts really does know everything, it's extraordinary.

'I cannot stress it enough, you must not confide in anyone about what you have been told and try not to ask questions. You will be told what you need to know, what you don't know you cannot divulge.'

'Divulge to who?'

'Well you have on occasions commented on some of the more dubious things you got up to in the military and if I were to be pedantic you could be taken to task under the Official Secrets Act, something you are party to, remember?'

'Mr Roberts you amaze me.'

'This time you will be told very little, it's nothing new, you've been there before.'

'Excuse me?'

'Well what did you really know about some of those dubious activities you got up to in the past?'

He had a point, precious little. I was just having a great time, young and bulletproof. The reality was I had been doing the sorts of things that a mercenary would do. Gun running, threating African nationalists, classified operations into Soviet Bloc countries, all for peanuts, no money in it, just risk. But those sorts of thoughts did not cross my mind at the time, just do as you're told, don't need to know why and besides, it was great fun. What could possibly go wrong? In Africa it was Southern Rhodesia, Robert Mugabe and his sidekick Joshua Nkomo had become a problem. What might have happened if they had got their hands on me? Never really thought about it, I was just having an exciting time. I did a couple of those missions into Africa. On one occasion we spent a few days with our warplane at Entebbe in Uganda, had a great time. It was not long after we had left that the place descended into terror, Idi Amin. As Mr Roberts pointed out, I really did not know the reason why I was doing those things, did not need to know, just do it, and for peanuts. This time 'round it's for serious money and when I thought about it the risk factor will probably be a lot higher as well.

'To wrap it up, you have two days to make up your mind, I'll get back to you for a 'yes no' response, ok?'

'Yep, ok,' and with that Mr Roberts was off.

Later the same day my mate, who had been casting around for some flying, got back to me with some information about Mad Mike's African operation, it was not the greatest. A lot of Cubans were getting involved and things had deteriorated. Apparently Mike Hoare's 5th Commando, as his mercenary army was called, had taken to collecting human heads, nasty business, and one of his Fouga Magisters had been lost. The pilot, an Irish chap, was involved in strafing operations against Simba Rebels in Katanga province in the Congo. He had been shot down, apparently by rifle fire; he survived the crash but was captured. The Simbas strung him up by his feet and butchered him, cut his liver out, something the Simbas liked to do. Forget Africa, suddenly Europe had a lot more appeal.

Two days to make a decision that could determine my future flying career, my future life. Should I commit to the world of mercenary flying? It appears I may have tapped into something good. The money appeared to be very good but in the back of my mind that nagging thought, *big money, big risk!* If this Mr Roberts thing worked out and led to further work it could be a good thing. No way to tell until I had accepted his offer and 'done the job.' What to do? what indeed, I'll have to give it some serious thought, just forty-eight hours to decide.

'Kate, how about dinner this evening?'

'Love to.'

On the dot, two days later, Mr Roberts is on the phone.

'A simple answer Rex, yes or no?'

'Yes.'

'Good, that's what I wanted to hear. I'll come around, how about an hour from now, is that convenient?'

'Yep, I'll put the kettle on.'

Exactly one hour later.

'Afternoon Rex, made the tea I see.'

'Let's get down to the business in hand.'

'Ok.'

'You will fly to Germany sometime during the next ten days, be in Celle on the 25th, it's now the 9th. Celle is just north of Hanover. Schapers Hotel & Restaurant, you will be contacted there.'

'Ok, got all that.'

'Here's an envelope, $30,000, make all your own travel and accommodation arrangements. The reason for the trip, if anyone wants to know, is to tidy up some loose ends from the time you lived in Germany, that's all you need to know. Arrange to leave Germany on the 29th and fly directly back to New Zealand. You can break the trip going north if you want. How does all that sound?'

'Pretty straight forward.'

'Well then, I'll be off.'

'Just a minute, what if I want to contact you?'

'You can't, you're on your own, however we will be watching. If you appear to be in difficulty we'll be in touch.'

That was it, Mr Roberts was gone.

That was extraordinary, it's what I'd been looking for, now it's right there on my plate. I felt overwhelmed, where will this lead? A continuing commitment perhaps, a regular income, a substantial one. The risk? what about the risk? I have no idea, no idea at all, perhaps this initial job will answer a few questions. It appears to be simple enough, it's an area I'm familiar with. Low flying at night is not ideal however. I had done quite a bit of it around northern Germany and it had always been nerve wracking. You can't see at night, that makes it really difficult. We used to cheat a bit, the 'low' was not that low but this time around it will need to be *low low,* there will be people trying to stop me, that will introduce additional risk; *big money, big risk.* A chipmunk, low and slow will not be quite as challenging as low and fast in a jet. Bit different to what I was used to. I had not flown a Chipmunk at night, why would I, it's not the sort of thing anyone would want to do. I'm sure I'll adapt, some fast on the job learning. Life is a learning curve, a favourite saying of mine. The curve was about to trend uphill, steeply.

'Kate, how about dinner this evening?'

We go along to what is becoming our favourite restaurant; it's in Parnell.

'Kate, I'm going to be *out of town for a while*, some loose ends to tidy up.'

'Oh, that's a bother, there's a party this weekend, I was going to show you off. My inner circle is all abuzz, who's this new man Kate? they're giving me a hard time.'

I was thinking furiously, *don't divulge*, already it's intruding into my life. Am I going to string Kate along with some mistruths, that's a departure from what I've done all my life, never tell a lie, it will bite you on the bum eventually.

'When are you leaving town?'

'To-day's Monday, not sure but it could be Friday, will know in a couple of days.'

Better get right onto it, keep it close to my chest, what do I have to do, a return airfare to Germany and a hotel booking, it's not rocket science, I've got fifteen days to get there. Might be a good idea to arrive a bit early and get the feel of the place again. Could make a stop on the way, Singapore perhaps, forget America, their transit visa requirements, and that Los Angeles airport, have killed it. It's Germany I want so go via Singapore, simpler. Just a minute, do I really want to be gone by the weekend? a few days in Singapore instead of going to a party with Kate, it's a no brainer, forget Singapore.

'Hang on, it can't be Friday, there's a bit to do here first, you're tempting me with a party as well, it will have to be after the weekend.' Kate's face lights up.

Being a bit fast and loose with the truth here, careful. I'll need to come up with a cover story, they will be asking. 'What do you do Rex?'

Kate knew I had been flying in Europe, Air Force stuff. I had not said too much about it and she has not asked. What am I doing right now in Auckland? again she has not asked. I suspect her friends will be a lot nosier, I need a story. Don't tell lies, *and do not divulge.* Contract pilot, that's it, I'm a contract pilot with connections in Europe, that's a true statement. It's a contract I'm off to fulfil in Germany. You will need to be a bit vague though.

'What are you doing living in Auckland?'

'It's my home town, I like it here.'

'What, you travel to Europe to work?'

'Yep.'

It could give me an advantage with Kate's friends. They will probably be advertising and sales types, possibly big noters, big egos perhaps. Contract pilot, sounds a bit exotic, works in Europe, that would be right outside their world.

'Definitely be here at the weekend Kate, love to go to your party.' She leans over the small table and plants a big kiss right on my lips.

'Can I come home with you to-night?'

That was the start of it, she was fantastic, I think I am falling for her. It surprised me. I had known quite a few girls over the years and I sort of thought I had become a bit 'case hardened,' wrong, very wrong, Kate has got to me big time.

A flurry of activity and I had a return flight to Hanover with stops at Singapore, Dubai, and Frankfurt, and a booking at Schapers Hotel & Restaurant. Along to the bank, some German currency, and I am good to go. The flight out is on the 18th, this gives me four days in Celle before I'm required, it also gives me another eight days in Auckland. Suddenly this assumes some significance. I want to spend a lot more time with Kate.

Germany

The big jet lifts off the runway, I'm off to my first 'contract.' It's going to be a long flight, straight through. A few days in northern Germany, springtime, the countryside around Hanover is lovely, especially in the spring. A few days to psych myself for what could be the first of many such 'contracts.' Hopefully, my new life.

The party at the weekend was interesting. The beautiful people were all there, some big egos on display and some really beautiful girls. Mainly advertising and sales types plus a few design and manufacturing people, the girls were all from the modelling world. Kate stood out, what have I found, she was an absolute knockout. As I had guessed they were curious about Kate's new man.

'Hello, we've not met, I'm Marty, friend of Kate's.'

'Well hello Marty, nice to meet you. I'm the stranger here, don't know any of these people, I move in a different world.'
I bite my tongue, careful, don't want to invite questions. Quick as a flash Marty comes back.

'And what world would that be?'
Damn, did not really want that but I guess the question was going to be asked anyway.

'Aviation, I work in aviation.'

'Interesting, what exactly do you do in the aviation world?'

'I fly aeroplanes.'

'A pilot? Airlines?'

'No, contract flying.'
This could be tricky, my cover could be tested here, remember don't tell any falsehoods, they'll catch you out sooner or later.

'Contract flying, not heard of that one, tell me about it.'

Bugger, could be digging a hole here.

'Well if you want a flying job done I could be your man, with reservation of course.'

'Reservations?'

'Yes, if you want a ton of meth smuggled into the country then I'm not your man.'

Perhaps I can burn him off, don't want him to lock on, make me tell some little white lies. Get real Rex, a lie is a lie, what's this little white lie nonsense.

'I like that, a ton of meth, but it does happen, right? not your scene though?'

This Marty was becoming a pain, he seems to be trying to trip me up.

'No Marty it's not my scene but tell me what do you do in this big world.'

I don't think he was expecting a counterattack. I'm beginning to think he's a smart arse. I wonder if my being Kate's new man has anything to do with it?

'Err, sales, I'm with one of the majors.'

Gotcha, he's just a functionary, a pipsqueak with a big ego.

'Rex, my adorable man, there you are.' Kate lands a big kiss right on my lips, Marty evaporates.

'Thought I had better rescue you, that Marty can be a nuisance. Let me introduce you to some nicer people, males, better keep you away from the maneaters, don't want my lovely man to be tempted.'

The party continued on, a great bunch of people, apart from Marty, the sharp end of the fashion business. There were some smart cookies amongst all the beautiful people. I did notice the fellow who had been with Kate in the pub that first evening, he seemed to be paying a lot of attention to several of the girls, the beautiful girls, they were all beautiful girls at this party. Kate appeared to be ignoring him, oh well.

'A drink sir?' it's the hostess. I was drifting, away with the fairies, Kate, she's right there in my dream world, in my bed, god she's beautiful.

'Ah, yes,' where am I, yes I'm in an aeroplane, 'a beer would be nice, thank you.'
'Coming right up sir.'

Be careful, a long time in an aeroplane, alcohol is no help; perhaps one beer then stick with the water.

Kate, I've fallen for her, she's way ahead of the field, I think I want her in my life but what's that life going to be? Is it the mercenary world, sorry, contract flying world, or do I need to get into something more acceptable, something that the kids at school can be proud of, 'my dad's a ….'

'Here you are sir, and some nuts.'
I'm snapped out of my day dream.

'Thank you, it will be just one beer, don't let me have anymore, I'm my own worst enemy at times.'

'Very wise sir, you're right about that, we do have problems at times with some of the customers, particularly on long flights.'

The beer hits the spot, sends me off dreaming again. Can't get her out of my mind, where is this going, how can I reconcile a life with Kate and contract flying, is it fair asking her to accept that I'm getting into a risky business, possibly a dangerous one. Right now she has no idea what I'm involved in. I have not told her that I'm off to Germany to do something dangerous, just that I will be *out of town for a while*. I told Marty I was a contract pilot, that snippet will get back to Kate. I have not said anything to her about being a contract pilot, let alone a mercenary. That's not good, you're not being honest with Kate.

A realization that I'm not managing my life very well is taking shape. My obsession with money is leading to dubious decisions, affecting relationships. I'm contemplating asking Kate to share my life, what will that life be? Is it something I can ask her to be a part of? Would this in fact be my life? I have not done any dangerous flying for big reward yet, but it's close. Will it be my thing? Will I be hankering for more? The money, perhaps it's a corrupting influence. Perhaps I should call Kate and tell her what I'm up to? no, *do not divulge.* Telling Kate is not an option, how am I going to handle that. The deal with Mr Roberts is one of secrecy, nobody is to know what I am up to, not even Kate, how am I going to live with that? I doze off, it's the beer. Aerobatics, chipmunks, rolls, stall turns, loops, barrel rolls, tail slides, down low, scrapping the ground, it's a fast jet, blasting along low down, what! what! I wake with a start, where am I? In a big aeroplane going to Germany, yes, that's right, Germany, going to do something covert, remember.

The long flight goes on and on, broken by stops, walks around airport transit lounges, Singapore, Dubai, Frankfurt, finally we are at Hanover. I'm beat, that was a long time jammed in a small seat. A bus ride and I'm at Schapers Hotel, bed.

The Briefing

Ring, ring, the bedside phone. I glance at the small clock, 8.30, must have been really tired.

'Hello.'

'Reception here.'

Good English, they're on the ball for their New Zealand guest.

'A gentleman called to say he would be around to see you in two hours, he did not leave his name.'

'Vielen dank.'

Out of bed, shower, shave, down to the dining room and an excellent breakfast. I certainly slept well. It had been a long flight, several flights in fact.

'There's a gentleman to see you, he's in the lobby,' it's the waitress.

'Vielen dank.'

'Mr Roberts,' the last person I expected.

'Yes it's me, how was the flight?'

'Good, good, did not expect to see you here.'

'I get around, we like to keep the circle small, fewer tongues to wag. We need to get down to business, perhaps we can go to your room.'

'Yep, that's fine.'

'Right, here's the detail. We want you to fly a Chipmunk across the DDR border and seek out a building near Brandenburg. It will be low level at night. The aircraft is set up with some sophisticated camera gear. The target building is at the head of a lake. It's a large water feature that will assist in determining your exact position when approaching the target. We want you to fly over the lake inbound from the south west to the target then turn around and fly back over the building a second time, then it's a matter of getting back here. When you are approaching the target switch on the camera gear. There's just one switch, switch it off when you have cleared the area. The camera gear is fully automatic, no input required from you. Ideally we would like you at 500 feet over the target, however, there is some height tolerance. You will take off at dusk tomorrow. There will be some daylight for the flight in and the setting sun will be behind you, it will make map reading a bit easier. Memorise everything you see going in, it will help on the return flight in the dark. Here are some maps covering the ground between Celle and Brandenburg, you have one day to study these and figure out just how you will proceed. Note, the DDR border is just east of Wolfsburg. I will be here tomorrow morning and go over what you have planned. Don't mark anything on the maps, you will commit your track in and out to memory. You can take the maps with you, however, I say again, do not mark anything on them. There are numerous water features and roads en route. I know you like these, they show up quite well, even with just a little bit of light and there will be some, a rising moon, it will be behind you on the way back, there should be little cloud.'

What does Mr Roberts not know?

'The target building is on the left bank of the Silokanal canal that runs off the north east tip of Quenzsee lake. There's a bridge where the canal joins the lake and the target is immediately beyond the bridge. Here's a photograph taken from the bridge. Note its distinctive shape, how it stands apart from the other buildings. It should not be difficult to recognise. Here's an envelope with some East German marks, take this with you. You will leave all your possessions, including what you have at the hotel, with our man at Celle airfield, passport, wallet, etc, and all your clothing. We will give you some clothes to wear at the airfield. You will not have anything that can identify you. Do not check out of the hotel, tell them you will be out with friends for the night. Now then, I have to tell you this. You may have figured it out already. If things don't work out and you find yourself stranded in East Germany then you are on your own. The British Government will deny all knowledge, however, assistance will be offered to a New Zealand citizen, or perhaps I should say someone who claims to be a New Zealand citizen, who appears to be stranded in the East.'

Big money, big risk. I was told! The envelope he just gave me, there's a fair bit of money in there, I wonder what that could be for? Questions? yes I do have a couple but I won't bother, I'm sure Mr Roberts will have told me all he's going to, *only what you need to know, remember*. The target building? probably just that, a target should hostilities break out, that implies that it has some military purpose, is it defended? I remember target photographs from my Air Force days in Germany, they came in many forms, some ground level, bit like what I'm being provided with in this case, some taken from a low flying aeroplane. Perhaps they were obtained by people like myself doing what I am about to do, but hang on, they were daylight pictures and some of the targets were right over on the Polish border, a long way into Eastern Europe, hardly low slow aeroplane stuff. I recall asking about some of those pictures once, *'don't need to know.'*

The envelope? What sort of scenario would require the use of East German marks? Perhaps best if I did not give that one too much thought.

'That's all for now, there's plenty there to keep you busy for the rest of the day. I'll be around tomorrow morning to go over it all, good luck.'

'Ah, there is one thing. I would like to have a look at the Chipmunk. Perhaps a short flight before I crack off into the dark, can that be organised, perhaps later today?'

'Yes, I should have offered that, bit remiss of me. Come out to the airfield around two,' and with that Mr Roberts was off.

Well this will keep me busy, reminiscent of my Air Force days, target planning and I definitely want to have a short flight in the Chipmunk.

I spend the rest of the morning scrutinising the maps Mr Roberts has given me, water features, roads, power cables, pylons, yes, there is a line of pylons, they are some distance off to the south of my intended track, I can give them a wide berth. The trouble with power cables is they are at the same height as a really low flying aeroplane, then there are the pylons, they stick up quite high. Hitting either will bring down a Chipmunk and flying high enough to avoid them makes the aircraft vulnerable to detection by radar. The whole idea of going in really low is to be under the radar, lost in the ground clutter. In my Air Force days flying in the same area in a B(I)8 Canberra, and a lot faster, power transmission lines were a real problem. We flew as low as we dared, 50, 40 feet. We had a radio altimeter that measured the exact height above the terrain, it was very accurate, however, most of our flying was daylight and our eyes were the safest guide. Doing it at night was a whole lot different, you can't see at night!

I poured over the maps and planned a route that maximised the water features. There were a lot of small lakes, that was good, and main roads. My big concern, power cables, only one line of cables, were there more? Going in, the setting sun would be behind me, that was in my favour, make it easier to see things and make it hard for people on the ground to see me coming. Coming back in the dark would be different, follow the same route, try and remember everything I saw on the way in.

It was now half past one, better get out to the airfield. Reception got me a taxi and I was on my way.

I front the main gate. Celle is a joint RAF, German Air Force airfield. They knew I was coming, Mr Roberts is certainly thorough. I'm directed to a tarmac area and there's a little Chipmunk parked all alone. Something's different, no markings, no registration numbers, no air force roundels, nothing at all. A fellow approaches and tells me he's my helper, German chap, good English. I look around the aircraft then strap myself in. It was then that I notice it, no radio altimeter, oh dear, this is going to make it more difficult. Chipmunks are not normally equipped with radio altimeters, in fact the instrumentation is very basic, pretty much a seat of you pants type of aeroplane. There was an altimeter, a standard one found on most aircraft but that type of altimeter is nowhere near accurate enough for the sort of flying I was about to do, but when I had a think about it the very accurate radio altimeters I had been used to were only used during an actual strike when an exact height above the surface was required, all the other low flying was pretty much eyeball stuff and most of that was daylight. When we did do it at night we were not that low and the radio altimeter did get a lot of attention on those occasions, hmm. I guess this could be a bit challenging but then the Chipmunk is a lot slower, cruises at around 100mph, that will make map reading and height judgment a bit easier than the high speed jet stuff. I think the fastest a Chipmunk could go was about 135mph. The camera gear? There was a fitting under the fuselage and a single switch in the cockpit, all pretty simple. I had never done any really low flying in a Chipmunk, perhaps right now might be a good time to have a go. If my memory serves me right there's a low flying area just to the north of Celle. In my heyday in Germany the whole of the northern part of West Germany was covered with low flying areas where the NATO Air Forces could practise the art of low flying without raising the ire of the local population. The locals did indeed get very angry about it. Fast jets thundering overhead very low make an incredible amount of noise, however, the low flying was officially sanctioned; if there was going to be a war then the potential defendants needed to hone the required skills, pilots nirvana!

I start the engine and make contact with the tower, callsign, what callsign will I use?

'Chipmunk;' the word was hardly out of my mouth when the tower comes back with.

'Is that you Kleiner Chippie?'

'Err yes, Kleiner Chippie.'

And that was it, my callsign. I advise the tower I will be doing some flying in the local area, about half an hour. All cleared, off I go. I make no mention of low flying. The little Chipmunk is a delight, it always was, I head north. There are no low flying areas marked on the map I have, the Mr Roberts one, however, I vaguely remember there was one just north of Celle. Down to about 100feet, eyeball stuff, the altimeter's no use, down a bit further. It's not difficult estimating height at this slow speed and map reading is easy. But it's daylight, be a different story at night. But even a bit of light, like the moon, will be a huge help and there's going to be some moon. I wonder if that's intentional? Ok, got the hang of it, up we go, 3000 feet, couple of loops and a barrel roll, that will do, back to Celle. My German crewman is there to meet me.

'Thanks for the help, guess I can leave the Chipmunk with you, see you tomorrow.' I wonder how much this fellow knows?

Along to the main gate, taxi back to Schapers, some more time with those maps, think, think, just how am I going to do this thing. Memorise the water features, imagine flying back along the same route when it will be a lot darker, the roads, there are a couple of rather prominent ones, forested areas, there are quite a few of these as well, all good aids to map reading. The big worry is things that poke up like church steeples, tall trees and the cursed power pylons.

The route I've planned is free of any obvious obstacles and there are plenty of good ground features. The power transmission line is away to the south. I plan to cross the border east of Wolfsburg then it's pretty much a straight line to Brandenburg. That will do for now, dinner. I'll use the hotel dining room then into bed, need to be at the top of my game tomorrow.

The following morning up early, breakfast.

'There's someone to see you Herr Macare.'

That'll be Mr Roberts.

'Morning Rex, all set for it?'

'Yep.'

'Show me how you'll do it?'

I show him.

'I have one question, power lines. I've noted the one on the map, are there others?'

'As far as we know, no, and I'm 90% sure of that. I appreciate that power cables are the achilles heel of low flying at night, hard enough to see in daylight, but no, pretty sure there are no more.'

It's possible to spot most things that poke up, a little light, and some practise, and you can confidently get around at night low level, and I will be low, no sneaking up a bit as we used to do in the fast jet, this time it's for real. The one thing that could get me would be a pesky power cable. The pylons are not so bad, they do show up, in fact the technique we used to use was scanning ahead for pylons then allow for the cables that were strung between them. Being confronted with cables right in front of you, same height, when travelling at speed was scary and that was during the day. The Chipmunk's slow speed will be a big plus on that one but still a potentially deadly problem.

'Well I see you've applied your mind to the task in hand, I'll leave you to it, aim to be airborne about 7pm. The same fellow will be at the airfield to help. Maintain complete radio silence, the tower will be aware of this.' That was it, Mr Roberts was off again.

I had the rest of the day to refine my plan, this was spooky stuff, there was risk involved, *big money big risk.* What could go wrong? Sounds a bit corny, *what could possibly go wrong?* Well everything, I could end up dead.

What will I be up against? Radar detection, if radar can detect me so can a surface to air missile. Radar's no good at low level, any return is lost in ground clutter so stay low, really low. Missiles? they are used to defend important military targets, is this building an important military target? Guns, ineffective at low level. A low flying aircraft, even a slow moving one, is difficult to track and fire at, and really difficult at night.

What if it does all turn to worms and I finish up in the hands of the East Germans, what will they do. I'm an unknown, no identification. Would the STASI, the East German secret police, pull my fingernails out? It would not take them long to figure out I had been taking photographs, so what, hardly something they would not be expecting. Unmarked Chipmunk, obviously English, and the camera gear. I wonder what they would do? If they made the connection between me and my old outfit, NATOs 2nd Tactical Air Force, it might be different but how would they manage that, no ID, it might be the fingernails, the STASI are a nasty lot by all accounts.

The STASI? The word was they're not the brightest. When I was in the Air Force I spent some time in Berlin. We went there to play rugby against RAF Gatow, the airfield that gave the British a token presence in the divided city. It was before the wall but even then it was a very divided place. Part of the attraction was being allowed to cross into East Berlin. NATO military personal were allowed to do this. The crossing point was at the Brandenburg Gate. Why this was I could never understand. Here was me, a NATO strike pilot with valuable target information in my head wandering around East Berlin at the height of the Cold War. The STASI could have picked me off the street at any time, why didn't they? Another thing that was cause for concern, well not really, was the STASI's apparent fixation on keeping files on potential adversaries. When I was on the squadron at Geilenkirchen we were told that the STASI would have individual files on each of us containing all sorts of personal information with an emphasis on anything sexual. Should we find ourselves in their hands then this personal information would be used to extort military information, interesting. How in hell would they get the personal information in the first place and did they really think it would be that intimidating? Fingernails, much more effective.

I enjoyed wandering around East Berlin, fascinating!

It was now early afternoon, a nana nap might be a good idea, I will need to be wide awake later on. Set the alarm for four, up, light meal, then out to the airfield.

What have I let myself in for?

A Building Near Brandenburg

I'm down low, really low, over the lake, relatively safe over water, nothing sticking up to fly into, Bright lights ahead, there it is, all lit up. There's an illuminated perimeter fence, yep that's it, just like the photograph. Why the fence? must be something important. Concentrate, don't let the mind wander. I'd taken off from Celle at 7pm and flown east dropping down low close to the border by Wolfsburg, radio silence, nav lights off. An ugly wire fence flashed by under me, the DDR border. Down a bit more, I was going to need all my skills from here on. There was still some light from the setting sun, the border guards would have seen me. I was happy in my mind about the track to follow, the memorised ground features started appearing as planned. I still kept a nervous lookout for pylons, didn't expect to see any but there was this nagging doubt. Map reading was not difficult at this low speed, a lot easier than I had been used to in the past. As the sunset faded into blackness it became more difficult. A first for me, seriously low level at night. Things went as planned, small lakes, wooded areas, roads, all appeared as expected. It was not long before I was nearing Brandenburg. The thing now was to spot Quenzsee lake. There were three fingers to it stretching out to the west; 'bingo' there's water and yes it's Quenzee. Ok, camera on, flick the switch, height's around 100 feet, careful, there's that bridge, nudge it up a bit, 500 is the ideal, bit exposed at 500, won't be for long. Two passes then back down to whatever height I reckon I can get away with. The escape route is back over the lake. In the fast jet of yesteryear low at night was about 500 to 600 feet, anything lower was just too dangerous, not enough time to avoid those power cables and their pylons, that's if you were lucky enough to see them. Snap out of it, this is no time for daydreaming. Lined up, 500 feet, right over the top, hard left turn, line the building up again. The illuminated fence makes it a bit easier, running in for the second pass. What? Suddenly darkness, the perimeter lights have gone out, I've been detected, damn! Keep going on this heading it will take you over the top again, then straight out over the lake. What's that, shit, muzzle flashes, I'm being shot at. *Ping, ping, bang,* that's small arms fire striking the aircraft, shit, I'm in trouble! Ok, clear of the target at the edge of the lake, down, down a bit more, probably about a 100 feet now, you're over water, down some more, moonlight is glistening off the smooth water, that water is very close. Good, nature is on my side, it won't last, at the other end of the lake I'll have to come up a bit, be back over the countryside. There will be obstacles, trees and the like, those cursed power cables should be away to the south, did not see any on the way in, but you never know. That ground fire, probably small arms stuff, sentries guarding the place, must have been something sensitive. The aircraft was hit, any damage? Check the engine instruments when you can, don't go looking inside right now, you're dangerously low. Keep your eyes on that water surface, look for the end of the lake, you'll have to come up a bit then. There it is, trees, the end of the lake, nudge it up a bit, visibility's not great. I can make out the tree tops, hope that's all there is, trees, looked ok on the way in. Just above the tree tops, hold it steady, quick glance inside, engine instruments, all normal, get the eyes outside, concentrate on the map reading, you want to start seeing the same things that featured on the way in. Quick glance inside at the compass, should be indicating about 245 degrees, shit! the compass glass is broken and the compass rose appears to be stuck, must have been hit by that small arms fire. *That fire must have come dangerously close to me.* About then I noticed I was shaking, shaking a lot, shock, fear, or both, snap out of it, no time to lose it, get yourself together.

A flashback to yesteryear. The nervous tension of low level strike flying gave me a twitch, a shaky right hand, soupspoons became the bane of my life, needed two hands to control the spoon. Occasionally, if the flying was stressful, it was always stressful, my right foot would shake uncontrollably but I seldom noticed it, too preoccupied with the task in hand. What's that? Something flashed by close on the port side, a bloody pylon, shit, where are the cables? I'm off course. There was that transmission line to the south of the route I'd planned, the pylons you had carefully avoided in your planning, I'm off course. Ok, where's the moon, right behind me, turn a bit right, should take you back towards the track you want to be on. No compass, use the moon, won't be for long, probably cross the border to the south of Wolfsburg. Perhaps a bit more height, you're in unknown territory right now. Patches of woodland, there are lots of patches of woodland and they all look the same, small lakes, quite a few of those too, right now none of them look familiar. My foot, my right foot, it's shaking, the bogey has resurfaced. Keep going, this heading is taking me towards the border, I think! I'm paralleling my intended track a little to the south of it. Keep the moon in the same relative position behind me, should not be for long. What was that,? A black shadow passes overhead going the same way; shit, it's a Mig. There it is, the border, not hard to spot, the ugly wire fence with the occasional tall watchtower, a bloody prison for everybody in the East. It shows up as a long straight line crossing my track at right angles, stretching away as far as I can see on either side. A surge of relief. How's the foot, still shaking a bit and the hand, no that's not shaking, not had the handshakes for quite a while, not since leaving the Second Tactical Air Force right here in Germany. Ok, safe, gain a bit more height. The whole countryside opens up, map reading becomes easier and there's plenty of ground lighting, towns, villages, all lit up, very different to the drab darkness of the East. Turn north, moon on the right look for Wolfsburg and there it is. The foot stops shaking and I feel a lot better. It's relatively simple to find my way from Wolfsburg to Celle, nav lights on, in a safe place now. Shall I call the tower, no, radio silence was the deal, just land. The airfield's lights are on, probably for me. What now, do I get out and go back to the hotel? I park 'Kleiner Chippie' on the tarmac where I had started out from and climb out, nobody's there. I have a good look around the aircraft and find four bullet holes, two of them in the side of the cockpit; jees that was a bit close, probably an AK47, a sentry at the building perhaps, an armed sentry, why would that be? One of the holes was the entry point for the bullet that had broken the compass, it must have passed dangerously close to me, suddenly I do not feel so good. Still nobody around, what do I do? guess I'll go back to the hotel, I need to lie down. Bit odd though, nobody here. I guess whoever is running the show knows what they're doing, my role was the flying and getting shot at bit, hmm! I walk along to the main entrance and the guard calls me a taxi, no questions, all a bit strange.

A bad night's sleep at Schapers, a very bad night. I had just put my life on the line, for what? money. Realisation struck home, I was now a mercenary, a hired gun. Get up, walk around, back into bed, sleep evades me. Is this my future life? *big money, big risk*, is this what I want? can I have a life with Kate? What did I tell her? I'll be *out of town for a while*. What will she be thinking? somewhere in New Zealand, Australia perhaps? Would she be able to comprehend that I was far away in Europe doing dangerous life threatening stuff. How would she deal with me not reappearing *after a while*, after a few weeks, a few months, just disappeared out of her life, a short sharp affair and he vanishes. Then a rumour, killed in East Germany! How would she deal with that? no confirmation, nobody knows anything, Government agencies know nothing, how could she deal with a scenario like that? Is it fair for me to put her in that position? switch off, try harder to sleep.

Suddenly the sun is shining through the bedroom window, I did sleep. Oh shit, what happened last night, was it a dream perhaps. *Ring, ring,* 'Herr Macare a gentleman has dropped off a bag for you, he did not give a name.'

'Danke, I'll be right down.'

My bag, the things I had left with the fellow at the airfield. I still had the clothes he had given me, guess they're mine now. I have a closer look, pretty good quality, not a label in sight, curious.

Breakfast, will anyone be contacting me? Bus down to Hanover tomorrow and the long flight back to Auckland. I've got the whole day to myself, what to do? Well something that's relaxing, seriously relaxing, last night seems like a nightmare, a real bad one. A walk in the fresh air, into Celle, have a look around. Celle is very old, a thousand years old, a lot of timbered buildings. A café just off the main street, a coffee out on the sidewalk in the sunshine. What will Kate be doing right now? what will she be thinking? I earned a lot of money last night, put my life on the line, got myself shot at. I wonder if this is a good career choice, a career with a future, or just an early grave? What would Kate think about it if she knew?

I find a pub, a pub with character, they all have character in this part of the world. I can have a couple of drinks now, my responsibilities are over for a while. A big stein of draft Becks with just a touch of yeast, perfect. Have a seat, a secluded alcove, peaceful. A lovely place Celle, but a place with a dark history, terrible things happened in this area during the war, terrible things. Don't dwell on that, think about Kate, think about all that money.

The rest of the day passes by, another couple of steins and a weariness comes over me, understandable. There's a small restaurant in the pub, I take advantage of it, sausages and sauerkraut, it's good. Home to Schapers, no messages, no calls, nothing at all, into bed.

Home

The long flight home, the very long flight, scrappy meals, stops, transit lounges, careful with the alcohol. Dozing, a lot of dozing, never could sleep sitting in an airline seat, the mind wandering. All sorts of scenarios come and go, crawling along in a little aeroplane, zipping along in a fast jet, being blown to pieces, finger nails, my past sexual exploits being paraded before me by an ugly fellow in a black uniform, swimming in a sea of dollar notes, stumbling around on crutches with only one arm, it went on and on my mind tormenting me.

'Breakfast sir?'

A voice, a loud voice.

'Breakfast sir?'

Where am I, whose asking, an aeroplane, I'm in an aeroplane, that's right, I'm on my way to Auckland. A rush of memory, the past few days come surging back, I'm going home to New Zealand, the hostess is inquiring whether I would like breakfast.

'Yes, yes please, excuse me if I was a bit abrupt there, not sure where I was.'

'Not a problem sir, you were very polite, now then we have,' she rattles off a string of breakfast options.

'Yes please,' was all I could manage, unable to comprehend it all, too tired, this mercenary business has knocked the stuffing out of me.

'I'll bring you something nice sir, you just stay there.'

Well yes, I will be staying right here. She's trying really hard to be nice, good looking too. The breakfast is good, I'm awake now, daytime outside, sunshine, the mind kicks in, what did I do back there? You flew into East Germany and took photos of a building and that's all you know, all you need to know; yes, but I got shot at, why? Don't need to know, yes, but I want to know. The question will not go away, it's haunting me. Why would I put myself in a position where I could get killed and I did not even know what for? Money Rex, remember, you're a mercenary, you've sold your soul for the big dollars, you've put a monetary value on your life. Stop it, you make me out to be some sort of low life, a hired gun, an assassin, I don't kill people. No you don't, not yet. What if Mr Roberts comes up with a big money offer that involves you in something where someone might be killed and you become aware of that possibility, what would you think then? I don't know. I do not have to accept every proposition Mr Roberts might put forward do I? Sure of that Rex? Money can be addictive, lots of money, heaps of it, money to spend on Kate, really show her a good time, tempting isn't it? Shit, I don't know, go away, leave me in peace, I'll purge my mind of everything that's just happened, it never happened, I don't remember; that's it, it never happened.

But it did happen Rex you cannot just erase the whole thing. That dark shadow that passed over you nearing the border, was that a Mig? where did it come from? were they up looking for you? pretty quick off the mark, what would it be, fifteen, twenty minutes after the shooting, could a Mig get you? probably not, flying too slow, but they were trying. How good is your luck, can't always be lucky, it'll be an early grave for you my boy! Stop it, stop it right now, my mind's tormenting me.

Auckland, taxi home, phone Kate at her agency.

'Ah, Kate Fontaine is down in Christchurch at the moment, be back tomorrow afternoon.'

'Perhaps you can tell me what flight she will be on and I can pick her up at the airport.'

'Sorry sir, personal security, company policy, cannot tell you that. What did you say your name was?'

'Rex, Rex Macare.'

'Oh Rex, Kate's Rex. She'll be on NZ538, 2pm tomorrow.'

'Thanks, you're an angel, don't let her know, surprise.'

Get some sleep, nothing needs doing right now, save yourself for tomorrow.

Buzzz, the doorbell wakes me from a deep sleep.

'Courier sir, package from the Flint Agency, sign here please.'

The Flint Agency, who could they be, open it, holy shit, banknotes to burn. I count it, $60,000, no note, no explanation, Mr Roberts! Wide awake now, what's with the 60,000, perhaps I did not hear correctly, I thought it was 40,000. Have a coffee, back into bed, it's starting to rain, bed's a good option.

NZ538 passengers are coming out of the arrivals tunnel, there's Kate, she's not spotted me, she's probably thinking about a taxi home.

'Hello Kate.'

An incredulous look on her face, she throws herself at me, kisses all over the place.

'Rex, Rex, Rex.'

Home to her place. I have a car now, an ordinary car, could be in for an upgrade. Inside and she drags me to the bedroom, drags me right into her big bed.

'Rex, Rex, Rex.'

She's all over me, clothes go flying, hands everywhere, I'm mightily aroused. It happens. I'm bursting into her, she responds vigorously, passionately, god I'm in heaven. It goes on and on, into the early evening, we just can't get enough of each other, eventually we are spent and lie back exhausted.

It was not the first time. Kate had come back to my place that evening just before I went off to Germany, we had made love, a first.

It was tentative, both feeling each other out, not wanting to get it wrong, not sure of each other's sexual needs, desires, there was no indication then of what was to follow, the sexual frenzies that were further down the track.

I'm dozing, there's a noise, I open an eye, there's Ali, Ali Fischer, Kate's flat mate, at the foot of the bed, she's taking her clothes off, what? I have to be dreaming. Ali is gorgeous, she's down to her knickers, her tiny lace knickers. A wave of lust engulfs me, my manhood roars back to life hard as a rock, I look across to Kate, she's awake, I cannot tell what the look on her face portrays.

'Can I come into bed with you two?'
Kate glances at me and responds.

'Yes you can Ali.'
I'm shattered, what is happening?

It's beyond anything I could imagine in my wildest dreams, two absolutely wonderful girls and they both want me, want to have sex with me. Ali is going at it like she had a pent up backlog of desire, and Kate? she did not appear to resent the fact that Ali was having sex with her man, if anything it seemed to spur her on, two insatiable females. It goes on way into the night, an absolute orgy of sex with two beautiful girls, everything was on, every imaginable variation. Eventually, exhausted, we collapse into sleep.

I wake up with a start, what happened last night? Kate is asleep beside me, no sign of Ali. Was that real, that sort of thing only happens in fantasyland, where's Ali? Kate opens her eyes.

'Morning darling.'
She rolls over close to me and her hands go down to my manhood, it comes alive instantly hard as a rock again, oh god!

'Let me,' she's on top of me in a flash. I respond, it's just incredible, it's absolutely marvellous. We make love for quite a while then Kate collapses back onto the bed.

'Where's Ali?' I ask, a touch of guilt in my voice.

'She had to go to work, out of town shoot, don't worry about what happened last night, Ali just wanted sex. I'm not sure her man is up to it in that department and I know you like me, so I do not really mind you satisfying Ali, she's a good friend. It saddens me sometimes to see her going without, becoming frustrated. Look at it like this, I shared you, now she's probably envious, don't want to make a habit of it though, but it was fun eh!'

'That's a very understanding way of rationalising it Kate, as for me, well I'm a male, the sight of Ali in her knickers was just too much, I felt guilty for a bit but when you invited her into the bed, well that was it!'

'Again Rex and then we should think about getting out of this bed.'

We are up and dressed.

'Let's go along the road to that café for breakfast Kate.'

'Good idea, I'll just unpack my bag, need a couple of things, where is it, oh yes over by the door, last night's lust disrupted things,' she gives me a big wink.

'Indeed it did and it was an out of this world experience being disrupted. I love you Kate.'
I move close and kiss her passionately.

'Stop, stop, not again, we need breakfast.'
Up the road, eggs benny and cappuccinos.

'Kate Fontaine? Fontaine, that's a Huguenot name?'

'Yes it is, the old olds came from Berlin, big French Huguenot population there a few centuries ago, came to New Zealand via Ireland.'

'Bingo, we could be related, Macares, Huguenots, from Metz,

Berlin, Ireland, then New Zealand, small world.'

'Related? DNA check, genes perhaps, whatever it is they do, would not want mongoloid children would we?'

'What are you saying Kate?'

'Just a thought Rex.'

Kids in my business, hardly compatible, food for thought though. Kate is obviously thinking way ahead; me, I'm blindsided by all that money, where it's leading? I have no idea.

'Let's change the subject. Ali's man has a boat, a big Rivera, they're off up north in a couple of weeks, Whangaroa, bit of game fishing is the plan. Ali's suggested we join them for a couple of days, would you be interested?'

'Would I ever, but how are you fixed, can you get time off?'

'The arrangement I have with the agency is partly contract and partly freelance. I'm pretty much my own master when it comes to time off, it will not be a problem.'

'Well let's say yes right now.'

'Your *out of town for a while* will not get in the way Rex?'

'Kate, I wish I could tell you more about that but I can't, I think you understand, you seem to have a good grasp on the ways of the world. Certainly a good grasp on what goes on in the bedroom, I mean Ali, not many girls would go along with what happened there. I don't know how a girl can rationalise that, only what I've read.'

'Sure Rex.'

Careful, don't tell a lie. It had happened before, a long time ago, and it was a fantastic experience on that occasion as well.

'I'm sure my *out of town for a while* will not interfere with a trip up north in a couple of weeks,' neatly sidestepping her awkward question.

'I'll check with Ali and come up with some dates in the meantime I think we should go back to my place, I need a shower, not had one since I arrived home.'

'Your place Kate?'

'Yes, my place; you don't want to go home to your lonely abode right now do you? Don't worry Ali will not be home today, she's got a job in Hamilton, be away for a couple of days, no temptation Rex.'

'Come on Kate, I love you not Ali, it was your idea to invite her into our bed, surely you don't think I could not go along with what happened, not meant to be a test of faithfulness was it?'

'Stop worrying Rex, of course not, just good sex and it was marvellous.'

We're in the shower, gel everywhere, Kate's legs entwined around me, I am deep inside her, hot water streaming down is adding to the sensual atmosphere. This girl has a voracious sexual appetite and I'm loving it. She does not take long to reach orgasm, her nails raking my back, we stumble out of the shower onto the bed, so much great sex.

'Kate here's what I thought we might do. Drive to Dargaville, stay in the Central Hotel for a night, then on to Mangonui. The old pub there has heaps of character, warrants a visit. Could be at Whangaroa say three days out from Auckland. The Marlin Hotel In Whangaroa is a must. I know the place, used it years ago when I did a bit of game fishing. Ali's man, what's his name, ah yes Jeff, we'll time it so they'll be at Whangaroa at the same time, could spend a couple of days on their boat, chase the big fish, what do you think?'

'Darling, whatever you say, I love you, but really, yes, all that sounds good to me. I'll put it to Ali.'

It happened, but before it happened I traded up the car. The beat up Holden Wagon became a mid-size BMW coupe, a sporty one, Kate was impressed. If I continue making money at the current rate who knows, I could surprise Kate with something exotic as well.

We left Auckland bright and early and drove up to Dargaville. The Central Hotel, a real oldie, two storey, wooden, big veranda right around, tin roof, high ceilings and big ceiling fans, character to burn. Checked in, first floor room, veranda right outside, toilet and shower down the hall, that could inhibit our bedroom activities. We order up a couple of drinks and sit out on the veranda in the afternoon sunshine observing small town New Zealand. Small town indeed, nothing much moved at all. A Fletcher topdressing plane droned overhead. Northland supported a big topdressing industry. That could have been me if Mr Roberts had not made that call and put me on a very different course. Have I done the right thing, depends on what the right thing is. Flying around Northland in a Fletcher dropping fertiliser for peanuts is very different to getting your balls shot off in Germany for mega bucks.

'Another drink Kate? it's very peaceful here on the veranda in the sunshine, you're being here makes it perfect, I love you Kate.'
I can feel the passion rising. This girl has an extraordinary effect on me.

'Yes please, then perhaps we could check out that big old iron bed in the room behind us.'

'You're a devil Kate.'

'Rex, I can't help myself, I just want you to make love to me all the time, it's weird I know, but that's how I feel; I love you, I just want you inside me so much.'

The Hokianga, it's a fantastic sight. As you drive around the last corner on state highway twelve at Omapere the whole length of the harbour opens out right before you. We stop for a while, take in the incredible view, it really is something, then along to Rawene. There's a ferry across the upper reaches of the Hokianga. We take the BMW across and continue on to Mangonui. The Acacia Hotel, another big old wooden affair from yesteryear, big veranda, tin roof, ceiling fans, and a modern touch this time, an en suite. There's a café in Mangonui that's a must visit. The Mangonui Fish Shop, it hangs out over the water, serves fish meals to die for. It's now late afternoon, we go along to the Fish Shop and settle ourselves into their dining room for some serious eating and drinking. It goes on for quite a while, mussels, John Dory, crayfish, and several bottles of good white, expense no longer matters, I have money in my pocket, a lot of money!

It was the first time I had enjoyed a drinking session with Kate. When the alcohol got to her she was a real character, great sense of humour, even more beautiful when under the influence. The meal is seriously good and it's late when we eventually decide that perhaps it's bedtime, into bed, out like a light.

It's Kate, the sun is coming through the window, her hands are under the duvet caressing me, the effect is immediate, hard as a rock, I'm off in fantasyland again, will this ever stop, I hope not!

We drive along to Whangaroa, the Marlin Hotel this time, another oldie from yesteryear, high ceilings, tin roof, veranda, and this one is steeped in history as well. Ali and her man are due to arrive that afternoon, they'll use a berth at the Whangaroa Gamefish Club's marina, one of the oldest in New Zealand. We front the Club. 'Can we use your bar and sundeck, lunch perhaps?' they are very accommodating and when I convince the receptionist that I used to be a member, and that was true, it was no trouble being allowed in. A beer on the sundeck overlooking the marina, great.

Late in the afternoon the big Rivera arrives. We go down and greet them, it is a big Riv, two state rooms. I wonder what Jeff does, this boat would not be cheap. A drink out in the cockpit, good idea. There's a well-stocked bar, all the trimmings, very nice boat. We get to talking. I had met Jeff just once, the four of us had gone to a restaurant in Parnell some time ago but I did not really know him. The plan is to go out off the coast the following morning and spend the day dragging lures. It was not the season for marlin but you never know, probably be plenty of skippies, a yellowfin perhaps, a mako, you just don't know until you drag a lure. Spend tomorrow night up in West Arm, it's a branch of the harbour that features some spectacular rock cliffs, very impressive, good anchorage. Another day of fishing, then back here to the marina.

'Sounds great Jeff.'

'We'll be heading off after that, three days to get back to Auckland, work calls.'

'How about we have dinner at the Gamefish Club this evening, from past experience I can recommend it, the food is really good. Well it was, but that was quite a while ago however I hear it's still good.'

'Why don't we have another drink then I'll take you across to the bar in the Marlin, you'll not have experienced anything quite like it before, believe me, it's something else.'

'Done.'

It's a bit rough and it's inhabited by some extraordinary characters. Some elderly Maori women are sitting on a bench seat, their wizened faces something from a Goldie painting. Mokos, no teeth, smoking pipes, shawls, pints of beer, something from last century. It was hard to comprehend, something I had not encountered anywhere else in New Zealand. They were locals and they spent a lot of their lives sitting on that bench seat.

We have a couple of beers. It's hard not to look at these locals, they were straight out of the bush, don't stare, but it's hard not to.

'Hey you fellers, Auckland eh!'

A hard case Maori boy.

'Yep, JAFFAs, we are quite nice really.'
A big slap on the back.

'Ah, don't worry, you guys are ok, hey want a beer?'

'That's kind of you but we can't impose like that.'

'Don't worry you're not imposing, just get me a couple of rounds later.'

'Ok.'

Caught, can't leave here for a while. Our new friend fronted with four beers, good lad but there will be no getting out of here anytime soon.

'That your boat, the big one that came in this afternoon.'

'Yep, that's the one.'

'Nice, what you going to do with it?'

'Bit of fishing hopefully.'

'Wrong time of year for the big stuff but they are around, want to know where?'

'Do tell, not pulling our leg?'

'Here, got a bit of paper, I'll give you a couple of co-ordinates, they're straight out from the entrance, about five miles, just drag your lures along between these two points, you'll get something.'

'Thanks, we'll do that, now then what's your favourite?

'Beer.'

'Yes, but which one?'

'Any beer will do, all beer is good, no fancy craft stuff up here, just beer.'

It took a while and a few more beers before we could extract ourselves and go across to the club's restaurant. We finished up having quite a few beers with our Maori friend however he had come up with the goods, we'll see tomorrow.

The following morning, up early, bit of a sore head, no dawn breaker although I did sense Kate's hands caressing my manhood during the night, no real arousal though, too much beer. I think Kate had a bit of a sore head as well, that beer last night, bit rough. The meal at the club however was superb. Along to the boat.

'Morning, anyone home?'

'Yes, all up and running, just having breakfast, want some?'

'That'd be good, the Marlin don't do a breakfast, well not this early.'

It was good. Jeff, the captain, Ali's man, the fellow who apparently was not giving her the sexual satisfaction she craved, was the cook, he was good, eggs benny and coffee, another Parnell restaurant.

There's fog in the harbour. Whangaroa is long and landlocked with hills all around, it's very prone to fog. We sneak down the harbour paying close attention to the radar, a real pea-souper, can't see a thing. Nearing the entrance the fog starts to lift and soon after that the sun shines through and disperses it completely.

'Look, look at that.'

The harbour's boiling with kahawai, big ones.

'Jeff, got some lures, no:3 green?'

'Sure have.'

We run a couple of no:3 greens, a standard lure for kahawai, they're hit immediately, two big ones. There are a couple of tuna tubes rigged on the transom, in they go, they will spend the day standing on their heads. If we don't use them as livies they'll make great kokoda later, kahawai's a good fish for that. Out through the harbour entrance, head for the first of the two waypoints the Maori boy had given us. He'd given us some bearings from prominent landmarks as well that allowed us to determine just where the co-ordinates were. 'Rig the heavy gear.' Jeff's boat is well set up for serious fishing and he seems to be up with the play.

Four brightly coloured lures streaming out behind, popping occasionally in the wake, perfect, how can the fish resist? Well they do and it's half an hour before there's any action. *Bang,* one of the lines rips out from the tag line, nylon peeling off the reel, it's a skippy. *Bang,* a second strike, another skippy. We let the girls bring them in, two big fat skipjack tuna, great snapper bait. Run the lures again, nothing happening, then *bang,* a big bang. One of the outriggers bends back then springs forward as the main line rips free from the tag, the big Penn reel is screaming as line is ripped out, it's a big fish possibly a marlin.

'Ok girls, who's it to be?'

'Let Ali show us how.'

'Ok Ali, harness on, go for it.'

Ali's obviously done this before, no mucking about. She has the harness on and takes control of the big game rod in a flash.

'Go Ali.'

This girl knows how to do it, pretty obvious. About ten minutes and the fish shows, ten exciting minutes of long runs, screaming reel, and Jeff alternately gunning the boat or slowing it down as the fish tries to outwit us, they are a good team, Ali on the rod, Jeff on the helm.'

'Wow, look at that.'

It is a marlin, a stripy, a big one. It's up out of the water tail walking, shaking its head violently, trying to shake the lure. Ali winds furiously, Jeff guns the boat.

'Get that head down, get the slack out of the line.'

Suddenly a slack line, it's spat the lure, bugger, *released untagged!*

We continue dragging lures and pick up four more skippies, great bait, then just as we are about to come into shallower water for some bottom fishing another powerful strike.

'What is it, another marlin?'

'Don't think so, too fast, look at that, trying to outrun the boat, could be a yellowfin.'

Jeff is having to work hard on the helm, gunning it, slowing down turning, trying his best to stay ahead of the fish, definitely a yellowfin, worth landing, seriously good eating. Kate is on the rod this time and she's doing well.

'Go Kate, that's sashimi on the end of your line.'
Kate goes for it, I think she's done this before. We spot the fish, yep a decent size yellowfin tuna.

'We need this one Kate, dinner, how are the arms holding out, I can take over the rod if you want.'

'No way, this one's mine, my ego demands it, but yes, my arms are feeling the strain.'

Kate battles on, it's not easy, yellowfin are notoriously hard to land, you need a gun helmsman otherwise you've got no chance. Jeff is a gun and Kate has got a chance. It goes on for twenty minutes and eventually the fish is nearing the boat, Kate looks buggered but determined, good girl. Success, a flurry of activity, crash it's in the cockpit, a seriously big yellowfin, around forty kgs.

It's one in the afternoon, we decide to go in close and try some bottom fishing, snapper, perhaps a gurnard if we are lucky. In we go still dragging lures. *Bang, zing*, line flying off the reel again, another yellowfin perhaps. The girls point the finger.

'Your turn Rex, give us a master class.'
It's another yellowfin, smaller this time but still very elusive, all Jeff's helming skills are required again. I'm in my element, it's been a few years, serious fishing like this did not feature during my tenure in Europe.

'Go Rex, let's see some style, can you handle it, got the balls to deal with the big fish?'

'Cheeky things you'll get yours.'

'Oohh lovely, that's what we want to hear, can't wait.'
Another flurry of activity and a second yellowfin is boated, around twenty kgs, we've got a lot of yellowfin. Inshore we go, bit of bottom fishing.

The skippies are great bait. It's not long before we've pulled up several big snapper and two good gurnard.

'That's it, we've got enough for today, cocktail hour.'
Jeff helms the big Riv back through the entrance to Whangaroa and turns right into the magnificent West Arm. We motor along towards the top end, select a likely spot and drop the pick, it's all ours, no other boats are here, great.

'Right, first up, before we get into cocktail hour, give me thirty minutes and I'll deal to these fish, they're our dinner.'

I used to do a lot of this years ago. We have kahawai, a lot of yellowfin, some snapper, and a couple of big gurnard. Right, into it. Messy business filleting fish, get it over and done with then get cleaned up. First up the two kahawai in the tuna tubes. Been standing on their heads all day, plenty of life left though, kahawai are very robust. Only need one, let the other fellow go, we'll catch him again in the morning, no:3 green, they can't help themselves, works every time. One kahawai over the side, *boy have I got a story to tell*, the other one, throat cut, bled, reduced to small cubes all ready for marinating, the yellowfin, four huge fillets, we'll use some for sashimi and freeze some, the rest? Well my choice would be lightly pan fried in butter, could bake it, there's a lot of it. The snapper and gurnard are also reduced to fillets.

'That was exhausting work.'
I clean up the mess whilst downing a beer, then over the side to get myself cleaned up, the water is warm, refreshing.

'Come on girls.'
They do, the devils, anything goes, they're sporting G strings and nothing else, what a beautiful sight. I can feel a swelling in my swim shorts. How will Jeff react? No sign of him, must be in the cabin. I fool around with the girls in the water. Better be a little circumspect The girls don't make it easy pushing their lovely breasts up against me and what's this? hands on the bulge in my swim shorts.

'Easy girls, what about Jeff?'

'Stuff Jeff,' from Ali.

Whoops, things can't be going too well there.

'Right cocktail time, everyone out.'

Better get these two out of the water before it gets too embarrassing. They're both tugging at my shorts, trying to pull them off, whatever do they have in mind, what about Jeff? I lead the way back aboard.

We are standing there in the cockpit, myself and the two girls, all they have on are these skimpy G strings. Jeff appears, the sight does not appear to faze him in the slightest, I just feel embarrassed. There's a fresh water shower in the cockpit, we crowd together under the shower head, Jeff has disappeared back into the cabin. It's quite an erotic scenario, two almost naked girls and me all crushed together, hands going everywhere, the bulge in my swim shorts, which I have managed to keep on, comes in for a lot of attention.

Kate and I are in the front stateroom drying off, two big fluffy beach towels engulf our bodies, it's too much. Kate hops onto the bed and drags me on top of her, a short sexual interlude before dinner.

'You devil Rex, you've just fucked her haven't you?'

Ali has a cheeky look on her face.

'If only, later perhaps,' she sighs.

'Why don't you folk retire to the cockpit and knock off some of that white, I'll stay here in the galley and deal with today's catch, I enjoy cooking, it will be my pleasure to serve dinner.'

'You have a way with words Jeff, that is such a good idea.'

And it was a good idea sitting in the late afternoon sunshine in West Arm would have to be one of life's better moments. The place is spectacular, the huge rock formations that form one side of West Arm are unique, nothing even approaches it anywhere else in New

Zealand, the bush, the bird sounds, it's just a wonderful place, and there's a bonus, the place teems with whitebait; so? Well what you do is around nine or ten at night, if sobriety allows, you put a light over the side and millions of whitebait will magically appear swirling up in a great spiral from the muddy bottom. Jeff will have a whitebait nett I'm sure. Just scoop them up until you have enough for whitebait fritters in the morning, good idea? We'll see how we go, see if the wine gets in the way.

Jeff's efforts in the galley are quite magnificent, he certainly knows his stuff when it comes to seafood. First up, kokoda, perfect, we sit around the cockpit, chilled sav and kokoda, next up, sashimi, yellow fin sashimi, how good can it get, finely sliced, a touch of wasabi, a little soya, some more of Jeff's chilled sav, what a good host. Jeff vacates the galley and joins us, 'the main meal will be along in a little while.'

I wonder about him, how can he not be turned on by Ali, she's beautiful, very sexy, very good in bed, insatiable, how can he knowingly condone Ali having sex elsewhere, well perhaps he doesn't know, what's she going to get up to tonight?

We continue on, sashimi and sav, and Ali rubbing her leg up against mine. Christ Ali back off, don't bugger the whole evening, the whole trip, what's Kate thinking?

'Right, dinner, I'll be in the galley for a bit,' Jeff gets up and disappears into the cabin. Had he noticed what Ali's been doing, did he care, it's a strange situation.

'Stop worrying Rex,' it's Ali, 'Jeff does not mind me fooling around, he's gay, well not really gay, he's bi-sexual.'

'Oh dear, what's the attraction then Ali and do we need to keep our voices down?'

'No, he's fairly open about it, it's just that you didn't know Rex. I've not really told Kate either but I reckon you've guessed, right

Kate?'

'Yes I have Ali, it's certainly not fair on you, why do you stay with him?'

'Well he's very good to me, a real gentleman but the sex thing is a problem, we do have sex occasionally but it's a real let down, I just can't get him going.'

'Ali you need a real man, someone who will give you satisfaction, you've got a strong sex drive, suppressing it's not a good thing.'

'I don't know, right now I find myself in this odd situation. Kate has shared you with me Rex, bit different, bit odd really, where this could lead I've no idea.'

'Ali, I don't have a problem sharing Rex, bit weird perhaps, I've only just discovered this in myself when we all had sex together a while back. I find sharing intensifies my arousal, heightens my enjoyment, perhaps it's a good thing all 'round.'

This conversation is getting me aroused. I'm starting to wonder what the night ahead has in store when Jeff appears out of the cabin and saves the day.

'Dinner folks, first up cold avocado soup then snapper, pan fried in butter, followed by gurnard marinated in a little milk then lightly pan fried, then there's yellowfin, baked, can you manage all that? There's a selection of salads and plenty of wine, be my guests.'

The meal is superb, the setting perfect, the wine chilled and plentiful, the atmosphere? well, laid back, relaxed, but there's an underlying tension. How is this evening, this night, going to play out?

'Whitebait, let's do the whitebait thing, Jeff, you've got a net right?'

'Yes, and a light.'

'Oh yes, a light,' I slur.

The words are a bit jumbled, the wine, Jeff's very good savvy blanc. The problem with whitebait is they are not very cooperative about what time of day they present themselves.

'Wow look at that.'

Thousands of tiny fish rising up to the surface in a great swirl, a couple of scoops with the nett and we've got a bowl full, a big bowl.

'Whitebait fritters for breakfast folks, how good is that.'

We stow the gear, the whitebaiting had not taken long.

'Time for another vino perhaps? Jeff we are making a hole in your wine cellar, I feel a bit bad about that.'

'Not a worry Rex, I don't have a problem sharing what I have, as long as people enjoy, appreciate, have fun.'

Jeff is looking straight at Ali as he says this, Ali is looking a bit uncomfortable. I catch her eye but she looks away, oh dear!

We sit out in the cockpit for quite a while, there's a full moon and it lights up the surrounding cliffs with an eerie light, a spectacular sight. Jeff's efforts in the galley have set the standard. We enjoyed his meal, really enjoyed it and he's promised to do fritters in the morning as well. Kate is rubbing my foot with hers and holding my hand, the atmosphere is becoming intimate. There does not appear to be any interconnect between Ali and Jeff, bugger.

'I think I'll turn in, want to come now Ali, or another couple of savvies perhaps?'

'A bit later Jeff, it's too nice here right now, I'll be along in a while.'

Ali gives me a wicked look, winks, and pushes her pelvis up suggestively in her seat. Looking straight at me she silently mouths,

'I'll be along Rex.' Oh shit!

She has on a small tight fitting singlet that only just covers her breasts and finishes just below her navel, nothing else, it's incredibly sexy. My manhood springs to life and I feel guilty. Suddenly all I want to do is fuck her.

'Can I get into your bed, please Rex, will you?'

Am I hearing correctly? I glance at Kate, how will she respond? Kate had indicated a while back that she would not have a problem if Ali wanted to have sex with me, but really? Kate looks straight at me.

'Darling I will enjoy it even more if you fuck me right after you've fucked Ali.'

This conversation is having an incredible effect, the frequent use of the *F* word has aroused me, it's aroused the girls as well. My erection has become so hard it's almost hurting, I desperately need release, Ali, Kate, anyone!

'Yes Ali, you can get into our bed.'

I sense desire in Kate's voice, an urgency, a desperation. Ali jumps into the bed, it's not very big, we are all very close together. Ali is pressed up against me her full breasts pressing against my chest, my monstrous erection pushing against her tummy, it's very arousing. She starts kissing me with a passion, pushing her tongue all the way into my mouth. Kate's behind me, her breasts are pressed hard against my back. I slip my hand down over Ali's tummy, down past my huge erection, on down to her thighs. I stroke her pubic mound and slip my fingers all the way in, she starts to moan, it's obviously giving her great pleasure. Her hands find my burgeoning erection, she starts massaging it tenderly, the sensation's unreal, incredibly erotic. I push her onto her back, slide on top and guide my erection deep into her. The moaning increases. She starts pushing her body up at me, arching her back. Her moaning becomes quite loud as I thrust deeply, vigorously. Ali's on fire, gasping with pleasure. Kate is right there, her body rubbing up against ours, she's moaning, Kate is close to climax. It's surreal, having sex, with another female while the one I love is in the same bed. It had happened before when Kate had invited Ali into our bed. Her presence on that occasion had stimulated Kate and the subsequent sex with Kate had been extraordinary, the sensations more intense, the pleasure even greater.

I would never have imagined in my wildest dreams that having sex with two girls in the one bed could be this good, surely there would be some fallout, some jealousy, but apparently not. Kate seemed to be a willing partner in this arrangement and it satisfied Alis' sexual cravings. Me? well I was in heaven, how good can it get!

Kate is beside us lying on her back completely naked making little gasping noises, the sight is too much. I push Ali away and mount Kate thrusting deep into her, her back arches and she cries out with pleasure. Kate had come close to orgasm watching Ali and I, now she has a mighty climax almost immediately, I burst into her at the same time, it's absolutely beautiful.

The three of us lay back drained, there's a moon shining in through a side hatch, the sight of the two girls lying there naked in the moonlight is something else, there's a stirring in my loins, my erection's returning.

Sunshine is streaming through the side hatch onto Kate's naked body lying beside me, no sign of Ali. We must have dropped off to sleep after the sexual frenzy the previous evening. Kate's asleep, a beautiful sight, I'm a lucky man. It's going to be awkward facing Jeff, well I think it's going to be awkward. He will obviously be aware that Ali was in our bed last night, I just hope he did not have to endure the moaning, the rather load moaning that accompanied Ali's love making, oh well, that's the way it is, stop worrying.

'Fritters, whitebait fritters,' it's Jeff calling from the galley.

'Breakfast out the back, come on, out of the sack.'
How can Jeff be so chirpy when someone else has been fucking his girlfriend, it's completely weird. Kate and I front and there's Ali looking like a million dollars in a pair of brief shorts and a flimsy open blouse that does nothing for her modesty.

'Thank you Rex, that was just great last night, look forward to a repeat sometime.'

God Ali you sure know how to embarrass a fellow, can Jeff hear this conversation I wonder, hope not, he's in the galley, the fritters.

'Here we go folks, whitebait, spoil yourselves rotten.' Jeff does not seem to have a care in the world.

Back along West Arm, pick up a couple of kahawai, out through the entrance and head for that spot on the chart again, the Maori boys' spot. Drag the lures, and drag and drag and no action, no action at all.

'Over there, way over, can you see it?'

'Yes I can, get over there, quick as you can Jeff.'

The air way off in the distance is filled with birds, thousands of birds. As we get closer we can see all the diving and splashing, the sea is boiling with activity, a huge work up, a fisherman's dream. Gannets, terns, skippies, albacore, dolphins, a billion small bait fish, there are a couple of Bryde's whales in there as well. Every few minutes all these millions of fish explode up out of the water, marlin after an easy feed, an extraordinary sight.

'Let's take a run through this lot, got to be marlin even though it's not the season,'

Two lures are hit immediately, reels screaming. There's a big stripy tail walking not far behind the boat shaking it's head violently. The girls are on the rods and Jeff's fully extended driving the boat. A double strike, this will be a real test. Kate's got the tail walker and it's really going at it, desperate to shake the lure. Suddenly the second line goes slack, a mako perhaps and it's bitten through the trace.

'Go Kate, we want this one, none of this released untagged nonsense,' and Kate does go at it, quite the expert.

'Ok Ali, it's just you and me to get this fellow on board, you put those big gloves on and trace it when Kate gets it alongside, I'll get the gaff into the shoulder, ok?'

'Yes Rex, anything you say, you know how it is, anything,' that cheeky look again.

' Ali you want me to screw you right now?'

'Yes.'

Kate plays her big fish for another fifteen minutes, it's not easy, eventually it's alongside. Jeff and Kate are a good team, they've beaten the fish's best efforts to escape. Ali demonstrates her considerable ability. She traces the line like an expert and grabs the bill, she's done this before, I get the big gaff into the shoulder and there's a mighty effort by Ali, Kate, and myself to wrestle the fish in through the transom door. There's a heap on the cockpit floor, one huge fish all tangled up with Kate, myself, and Ali, and Ali's clothing is in disarray, her blouse, her flimsy blouse has been torn off, christ I'm getting a hard on.

It's a big striped marlin, we reckon about 130 kgs, that's big. Ali's topless and happy. There a frenzy of self-congratulation, hugging, kissing. Kate's ecstatic, the first big fish she's actually boated.

'Champagne, well some savvy perhaps?'

'No, there is champagne.'

'Really Jeff.'

'Yep I'll break it out.'

Jeff produces the goods, we pop the top and Ali wants to pour it over her semi naked body.

'You can lick it off, Jeff lick it off, please Jeff.'

'Jeff, Jeff, yes Jeff, do it Jeff, lick it off Jeff.'

Kate, Ali, and myself are egging him on, where this is leading I don't want to know. Ali grabs the bottle and tips quite a bit over herself, it runs down over her exposed breasts, her lovely sexy exposed breasts, I've got a hard on.

'Go Jeff, go, go.'

And he does, he grabs Ali in a big embrace and starts to lick her breasts, really licks, then he's pushing her shorts down, then her lace panties, Ali is naked, Jeff is aroused, where is this going. Ali is tugging at his pants, they come off, he's got a huge erection. Ali is gasping.

'Yes Jeff, fuck me please.'

'Go Jeff go,' from Kate and myself, this could be a turning point. Jeff pushes Ali down onto the cockpit floor and mounts her, really mounts her with a passion and they go at it furiously. I can sense Kate's arousal, my erection is rock hard. We stumble into the main cabin, tearing off what cloths we do have on. Kate goes down on her hands and knees and I enter her from the rear pulling her lovely body hard back onto my bulging erection.

Sometime later. 'About that champagne Jeff, any left?'
We're out in the cockpit, Jeff's pulled on a pair of shorts and I've wrapped a towel around myself, don't know why, the two girls have not bothered, beautiful in their nakedness, Ali looks happy.

'Yep, and there's another bottle, I'll get it.'
Ali smiles, 'thanks you two, you've awoken the lust in the man, I suspected it was there somewhere, thanks again.'

'Ali your nakedness is awakening the lust in me as well, perhaps you can put those panties back on, make it a bit more than just panties or else I'm going to be embarrassed under this towel.'

'Oohh, your right, what's that sticking out?'
We settle down, it's been a watershed moment. Looks like Ali's relationship has taken a quantum leap in the right direction, let's celebrate. A big fish and Jeff's return to the heterosexual world. We demolish the champagne. I feel really happy for Ali, we've achieved something on this fishing trip.

'Now then I think we should head back to the weigh station at the Gamefish Club, *the winners circle,* a privileged place. Don't want any more fish, we've got heaps, there's a lot of yellowfin in the freezer already. A celebratory dinner at the club might be appropriate don't you think so Jeff?'

'Yes I do Rex, I've got a bit of catching up to do.' He gives Ali a loving look as he says this.

'125 kgs,' the weighmaster announces to the assembled onlookers, tourists, locals, club members, there's a lot of picture taking. Kate's up there with the fish, the rod, and the display board detailing the facts, sepia tinted photos for future generations, *grandma Kate with her big fish*. The fish is lowered onto the local smokies truck. We will see it next in Aucklsand, smoked, chilled, and vacuum sealed into two kg packages, the Whangaroa smokey has a very good delivery service.

'Kate I think we should check into the hotel for the night. Ali and Jeff want to head south in the morning. I think it would be a good idea if we fill them up with wine at dinner then leave them alone on the boat to reinvent their relationship, what do you think?'

'Good idea, give Ali free reign with Jeff, no temptation from our bed. I don't need Ali's presence to turn me on.'

'Done deal, Ali will be a new girl, that will be nice.'

'Jeff, Ali, Kate and I are checking into the Marlin for the night. You want to be away early in the morning so that will make it a bit easier and the other thing, you don't really want us on the boat when you're running around tearing each other's cloths off do you?'

'That's very considerate of you Rex, no, we don't want any gang banging to-night, I want Jeff all to myself, to have him do whatever he wants with me, that ok with you Jeff?'

'Yes Ali, that is definitely ok with me.'

'Oohh, Jeff, a night of sexual excess.'

Dinner in the club, it's another good one. I have happy memories of many excellent meals over the years, great place. Our subtle plan to fill Jeff in results in us all getting filled in, hope it does not detract from Ali's expectations. When Kate and myself hit the sack in the Marlin we don't last long, it has been a long and enjoyable day, particularly for Ali. I wonder if the big Riv is rocking a bit down on the marina?

The Missiles At Fulder

We're just back from Whangaroa when Cathay Pacific contact me, they'll be recruiting pilots in a few months, am I interested?

Cathay, big airline, security, boring but secure, good money and much better life expectancy. Have to live in Hong Kong, that does not appeal, no contest with Auckland which is where I am established now. Some travelling to Europe, but basically living in Auckland, and there's Kate.

I've just made all that money for a weeks work, but what about long term? Do it for a while, then Cathay, the Hong Kong thing's a bit of a downer though. Right now I'm flush and I like it. A first for me, been on the bones of my arse since leaving home. Always having a great time, champagne tastes, beer income. But Cathay? need to consider it, don't let the opportunity slip by. I respond to Cathay's offer with a 'yes I am interested.' I hope they don't push it along too soon, I think I want to go along with the one I've got for a while, see where it leads.

A couple of weeks later, nine in the morning, *ring, ring.*

'Hello Rex, Mr Roberts here, I've got another proposal for you, cup of tea say around ten?'

'Yep, see you then.'

On the dot, Mr Roberts is at the door.

'Morning Rex, enjoying life?'

'Yes I am, certainly different.'

'We're pleased with your performance the other week in Germany, good pictures.'

'Thank you, hope the Chipmunk was not too badly damaged.'

'Yes, there were a couple of holes and the compass looked a bit sad. The boffins reckon the bullet that wrecked the compass missed your right knee by about a centimetre; we added a small bonus for your troubles.'

'Thanks, I really need to know that. I thought kneecapping was an Irish thing, thanks for the bonus. I was wondering about that, wondering if someone had made a mistake and you might want it back.'

'We don't make mistakes Rex, don't think too much about it. There's an element of danger in what you're doing for us, we are reimbursing you accordingly. Now then to the business in hand.'
I pour the tea and mentally prepare myself for what I suspect will be another flying job involving danger.

'Another job in Germany, bit further south this time. It's not so much your low flying skills we need, rather your ability to fly along valleys below hill top height at night.'

Different, valley flying, yes I had done a bit of that in my fast jet. Fjords way up north in Norway with the mountain tops invisible in cloud and me down low over the water, spooky stuff, not enjoyable at all.

'You have done a bit of it, the Norwegian stuff and that Ulm Cathedral business.'

What does Mr Roberts not know, how could he possibly know about Ulm, I don't think we mentioned it to anyone at the time, too embarrassed. What had happened at Ulm? We were looking for a target during a war games exercise near Ulm which is on the banks of the Danube. It was a very murky day and we were down low in the river valley when suddenly, right in front of us, the very tall spire of Ulm Cathedral, we only just missed it.

'Mr Roberts your knowledge is amazing, I bet you know my great grandmother's maiden name.'

'No, I don't Rex; not yet.'

'Now this job will require you to fly along some wooded valleys.

It's not so much the ground hugging aspect but your ability to stay below the level of the hill tops, radar won't be able to see you. There will be very few water features, I know you like them, however, there will be roads, mostly along the centre of the valleys. There are transmission lines, the pylons are on the hills with the cables strung across the valleys. The transmission lines will be marked on the maps we'll give you, we are fairly certain we've got them all. The cables will be your main problem, about 600 feet above the valley floor. There are numerous towns and villages along the way, their lights will help you pinpoint yourself.'

'Well that all sounds a bit different, what's the target?'

'Not now Rex, don't need to know at this stage.'

'Ok, I'll buy into it, worth my while perhaps?'

'We'll give you $40,000 now and the deal is the same as before. Get yourself to Germany and back and pay for your accommodation, just another happy traveller.'

'And?'

'$60,000 on completion, paid back here in New Zealand.'
Geezz that's huge money, *big risk, big money!*

'I'll give you a day to think it over. I'll get back to you, ok!'

'Ahh, I think I've decided already.'

'No, no, you have a good think about it overnight, don't say a thing to Kate.'

Don't say a thing to Kate. Very perceptive our Mr Roberts. Kate had been curious about my *out of town for a while* explanation after I got back from Germany, she had been probing. Can I sell her the *out of town for a while* again, possibly, but at some stage I am going to have to come up with a cover and it will probably involve telling a lie, that's a worry, I don't tell lies. I'll have to put my mind onto this one, give it some serious thought; in the meantime?

'How about dinner tonight Kate?'

'Yes please.'

We front what is now our favourite restaurant in Parnell for a romantic dinner. A strong bond has developed between us after getting back from Whangaroa. Those big hotel beds and the 'action' on Jeff's Riv has brought us closer together, very close in every sense of the word. I'm in love, a first for me. There have been girls, quite a few, but nothing like Kate. At the Irish Coffee stage I broach the subject.

'Kate I might be out of town again next week; business.'
Her face falls, she looks disappointed.

'I'll miss you, what's taking you out of town?'
It had to happen, the question was going to be asked sometime. Don't tell a lie, if you tell a lie then you will find yourself telling more lies to cover the first lie and you'll trap yourself with inconsistencies because you will not remember what you have said. The truth you don't forget; the truth sticks in the mind, lies do not.

'Kate this is hard for me, I want to be straight up and honest with you, no secrets, but this, this business I'm involved in, well it requires secrecy. It's pretty unusual and the returns are substantial. It's not anything dishonest, believe me, I'm not doing anything naughty, it's just that I can't tell anyone about it and not being able to tell you hurts, it's putting a barrier between us and that's not nice.'

Kate says nothing, a puzzled look on her lovely face. I feel awful; is this the sort of thing I want to have in our developing relationship? is the money worth it? I don't know, don't know at all.

'Rex, I'm not sure what to say, I don't want to go prying into that part of your life that you don't want me to, or cannot tell me about, I'm lost for words.'
I need to give her something, not a great big silence, but what? what can I divulge that's not going to compromise things, what?

'You know I was involved in flying before I met you, the Air Force in Europe, well this is really just an extension of what I did then, something the military cannot do but a civilian can.'

'But that was in Germany.'
'Yes it was.'
'Were you in Germany the other week?'
'Yes.'
She looks shocked, having trouble comprehending.
'Are you going back to Germany again?'
I said nothing, just sort of looked a bit blank, this was not very nice, not good for a relationship.'

'You're going to do some flying in Germany and it's covert, secret, and it's going to get you a lot of money. Ok Rex, I think I can get my head around that, whatever it is nobody is to know about it, not even me, have I got it right?'
What can I say, I can't tell a lie and I can't divulge anything; between a rock and a hard place, bugger! I just sit there and say nothing.

'Relax dear, I understand; I think! You look like a naughty boy right now and I love you!'
A great wave of relief sweeps over me and I lean right across the table and give Kate a really serious kiss.

There's clapping, cheers, it's the other restaurant diners, suddenly we're the centre of attention. Kate is smiling, she looks happy, I think I've just surmounted a huge hurdle. The rest of the evening is a bit fuzzy, I'm overwhelmed, Kate loves me, life is complete. We order up a bottle of champagne, the good stuff, Dom Perignon, after all I am no longer on the bones of my arse, no indeed, and it's looking like there could be a lot more coming my way.

'I do love you Rex and I can keep a secret, I won't be asking any more questions, I think I've got it figured, Germany again, you don't need to answer.'

The following morning it's tea at ten with Mr Roberts.
'Have you decided Rex?'

'Sure have, sounds interesting, different.'

'Yes it's different, here's what we want you to do. Make your own travel arrangements to get to RAF Gütersloh, you know where that is, you've flown out of the place quite a bit.'

'Yes I have Mr Roberts, you are all knowing. About my great grandmother's maiden name, that's on my father's side?'

'Ok, ok. I want you at Gütersloh by Friday next week. You are booked in at the Officers mess for three days, you're a Reserve Officer so you get full entitlements, they will be expecting you. You've got a couple of days there. On the Monday you will fly a Chipmunk from Gütersloh down to Fulder, just north east of Frankfurt, it's an American airfield in their zone, it's small and close to the DDR border. Book yourself into the Bader Park Hotel for three days. At Fulder you will be given the details of what we want you to do, it won't be me, it'll be an American fellow, this job is for the Americans. Book yourself back to New Zealand from Frankfurt on the Friday. Here's an envelope with your first payment, you'll need it to pay the travel bills if you've blown that first lot on Kate already.'

'Come off it Mr Roberts, but you're partly right and I cannot think of a better way to spend it.'

'Just keep in mind, this business is all covert, Kate cannot be told anything, I must stress that, not even in the heat of the moment in some place like the Marlin Hotel.'

'Mr Roberts you are something else,' and with that he was gone.
I put my mind to the travel arrangements. Fly Auckland, Singapore, Frankfurt, Hanover, then a bus to Gütersloh, book the Bader Park Hotel in Fulder. Leave Auckland next Wednesday should put me at Gütersloh on the Friday, depart Frankfurt the following Friday.

Fulder, in the American zone, I'm working for the Americans. Fulder? Fulder Gap, tanks. The big worry in that part of the world, particularly for the Americans, is a surprise tank attack by the Warsaw Pact into the Frankfurt am Mein area through a pass between the Vogelsberg and Rhön mountains called the Fulder Gap. There's a long history of armies using the Fulder Gap. It's an important place strategically.

How to break it to Kate, dinner again or just a coffee somewhere, perhaps coffee then dinner, a good one, upmarket, remember you're flush these days.

Kate accepted my leaving town next Wednesday for two weeks when I put it to her over coffee, did not ask questions, however, there was a sly look on her face when she did comment.

'Sausage and Sauerkraut again Rex?'

'Something like that Kate, how about dinner, Number 5.'

I front the main gate at Gütersloh, give the guard my name and ask him to advise the Officers Mess that I'll be there shortly, a phone call and it's done. I get the impression I'm expected. I have been here before, Gütersloh was a forward fighter base for 2TAF, NATO's Second Tactical Air Force, home to several NATO fighter squadrons. The Officers Mess was one out of the book, built in the nineteen thirties for the Luftwaffe, a favourite place with Reichsmarschall Hermann Goering during the war. Everything was on a grand scale, excellent accommodation, superb dining room and a big cellar bar that was accessed via a grand staircase, a really grand staircase. At the head of the staircase was a large copper bowl, really big. The story was that if you were not feeling so good after too much beer you could bound up the stairs and unload into this bowl, very Luftwaffe. The place survived the war intact, the British took it over the thinking being 'what a great place, better keep it on.'

It was now late afternoon, I'd checked in, been given a good room and, just for something to do, I wandered down to the bar, I'd been there before in my Air Force days.

'Rex!'

'Scruff! Scruffy Jacobs.'

It was an old mate from Geilenkirchen down by the Dutch border. Scruff had been a pilot on a Javelin night fighter squadron when I was a strike pilot on B(I)8s, had not seen him for quite a while.

'Rex, last I heard of you you'd left the Air Force and disappeared off home to the South Seas to make your fame and fortune.'

'Yep, that's true Scruff, not sure about the fame and fortune bit though.'

'So what are you doing here?'

Careful now, you'll need a cover story that Scruff will buy.

'I've secured a short term contract with Airwork in the UK, ferry pilot, delivering and picking up aircraft around Europe.'

'That's not fame and fortune?'

'No it's not, hard world out there, still working on it though, what are you doing here at Gütersloh?'

'Another three year tour on Javelins down at Geilenkirchen, up here for a couple of months on detachment, four aircraft. We are doing a lot of night patrols along the border, somethings up. Usual story, they don't tell us why, just do as you're told. Bit unusual though most of it's down low, not our usual, we're looking for low flying Migs. Same old bogy, Mig 21 'Fishbed'. Why the low level bit I can't figure, a fast Mig's not much cop down low. There's a bit of provocation involved as well, they've had us across the border a couple of times, I think the boffins want to test the Warsaw Pact's reaction time, don't know really, just my guess.'

'Exciting stuff Scruff, when's the war starting?'

'Back off, don't want that but there must be something going on, we are fully armed these days. Been doing a bit of live firing up on the coast at Sylt, now there's a place, go to Sylt. Wall to wall German girls, all 'wannabees,' a wild night club scene and, wait for it, a big nudist beach. We get to do five days at a time up there, all aerial gunnery stuff, it's wildly popular.'

'I bet, what's your take on the low level Mig stuff?'

'Hard to say, there are rumours there's a bit of cross border covert stuff going on at night and we are providing cover.'

'That's sounds serious Scruff, what else do you know?'

'Can't tell, sworn to secrecy, you know the drill.'

'Come on Scruff, I won't tell, what's going on?'

'Well a few weeks back I was doing a bit of patrolling at night, low level, up by Wolfsburg I was vectored across the border and asked to keep a close lookout for a couple of low flying Migs. We did get radar contact on two aircraft, probably Mig 21s, flying quite slowly towards the border, the instructions were to identify and engage if they crossed, they didn't cross, turned back right at the border, apparently it was going to be a live engagement, that would have stirred up a hornets nest.'

'That's interesting Scruff, very interesting, what's with the low slow Migs?'

'Hard to say, my take is that they were chasing, or trying to chase, a light aircraft.'

Shit, that first job I did was up by Wolfsburg a few weeks back.

'What about a beer Scruff, let me.'

'No, no, I'll do the honours, unless you've got a mess account you have to use a voucher system, it's a pain, what's your preference?'

'If I recall the mess here had Becks draught.'

'Yep, still do, a good drop.'

Two Becks and we settled down in a couple of big leather arm chairs, very well set up the Reichsmarschall's bar.

'Scruff, I'm surprised to see you still here on Javelins, what do you intend doing, staying on in the Air Force?'

'Don't know, there's good work on offer out in the Gulf for ex Air Force fighter pilots, excellent money by all accounts, way more than here, you must know all about that Rex? Right now I'm committed to another two years on Javelins here in Germany then I've got the option of leaving or signing on long term, don't know which way to go, you left for greener fields, is it working for you?'

'Ah well, not quite as easy as it seems, there is work available but getting all the facts can be difficult, a lot of it's a bit dodgy. The Arab States are always taking on fighter pilots, probably a good option for you, you're experienced and that's what they want. By all accounts they pay big money for jet jocks.'

'Why aren't you doing that Rex, what's with this ferrying for Airwork?'

Careful, don't blow your cover.

'Not quite my scene Scruff, remember I was the fast and low nuclear strike pilot, the fellow doing the real serious stuff, you were the glamour boy way up high flitting around in your flash jet fighter. What I had to offer was not quite what the Arabs are looking for, probably could have cracked it if I'd tried.'

'Why didn't you try Rex?'

'Well, there's a girl back in Auckland and there were other offers.'

'I see, the old ball and chain, girl, wife, come on where's the old Rex I used to know; ferrying for Airwork, that's not going to make you rich, or famous.'

'I have my fingers in other pies, the Airwork thing is just temporary.'

'So what exciting and mysterious job for Airwork brings you to Gütersloh Rex, excuse my sarcasm but it's just not you.'

'There's a light aircraft they want delivered down to Fulda, a Chipmunk.'

'Geez, that's riveting stuff, think I'll stay in the Air Force, more exciting, is this what you really want to be doing.'

'No, it's just temporary as I said.'

'Another beer, I want to pick your brains some more.'
Scruff's no fool, I don't think he's buying my story, careful. What I'm up to is covert, nobody is to know anything about it.

'A Chipmunk you say. A couple of nights ago we taxied in and parked in the dispersal area around midnight, been up on the border again, there was this Chipmunk, I think it had just landed. What's a Chipmunk doing up at night? We went over and had a look, it was quite badly damaged, bullet holes and what looked like a 20mm shell hole as well, a couple of fellows were helping the pilot, there was blood, I think he was unconscious. A security guy fronted and moved us on, *you've seen nothing, got it!* He was quite forceful in his manner. The next morning, early, I got down to dispersal, not a sign of the Chipmunk, checked a couple of hangers, no Chipmunk, so now then Rex, what's with the Airwork Chipmunk delivery?'
Scruffs definitely no fool, but he never was.

You must keep your cover, give absolutely nothing away, and perhaps ask Scruff to zip his lip.

'I have no comment Scruff, I've no idea what could have been going on.'
'You speak with forked tongue Rex, no fame, yet, but I suspect you may have cracked the fortune bit.'
I need to stop the rot right here, now.
'What about dinner Scruff, the dining room here used to be seriously good.'
'Yes, it still is. Let's put the Chipmunk to bed, trust me, I won't be saying anything, after all I could come begging at your door in a couple of years asking how you cracked the 'mercenary world,' how you have become so fabulously wealthy, that's if you're still alive!'

The next morning I'm up early, a free day. The following morning I'm to fly a Chipmunk down to Fulder. I'll be contacted there and be given the detail of what's required from me.

It had been a restless night, a shot up Chipmunk, blood, an injured pilot, there were others in this business. I've been lucky so far, how much luck do I have? is luck rationed? That chap Scruff saw, was he alive? could that have been me? Killed in Germany, how would Kate handle that? would she even know, or would I just disappear? An excellent breakfast, a walk into town, I need some quiet time. What am I doing? have I become obsessed with money? will I live to enjoy all the money? have a life with Kate? a quiet life. Cathay, there's an offer on the table, it's good money, not like what I'm into right now but a good steady income, no risk, long term. How about when you're hitting fifty? do you want to be putting your life on the line every time you go to work? will Kate put up with that? She will know of course, no way in the world are you going to keep her in the dark about what you do. Right now fifty is a long way off. Will you see fifty? Hang on aren't I going to make a lot of money quickly, then get out of the business? Nice thought but you'll get obsessed with the money, can't stop, you'll not have a life with Kate, you'll finish up dead and it won't be long, that fellow the other night!

It's not far into town, Gütersloh, it's old and it's lovely. I wander around soaking up the late spring sunshine, the medieval atmosphere, a pub on the banks of the Dalke, a beer, it comes in a stein, draft Becks again, *life is complete*, I wish! Nothing could be further from reality. Why am I doing this, why? You know the answer, the money thing, it's dominating your life and there's every chance it will be the end of you, perhaps in the not too distant future, Kate, think of Kate.

'Ein anderer stein, danke.'

I enjoy another stein of beer, the sunshine, this little pub in Germany, money is not the be all and end all, perhaps I've got my values all screwed up. I'll pass on the bar back at the mess, don't particularly want to expose myself to anymore questioning.

Parked on the tarmac, a chipmunk, looks new, perhaps it is, let's have a look. It's not new, just been spruced up, it's the same one I had flown out of Celle several weeks ago, I could see the camera gear mounted on the underside. When I looked closely I could see some repair work, patches, where the bullet holes had been. There was a new compass in the cockpit and registration numbers on the side, they were peel off stickers not permanent painted ones. There was an RAF fellow to help me and I was off, map reading my way to Fulder. I could not resist old habits. A low run along the Rhine, something I did quite often in my Air Force days. I dropped down low just south of Bonn and flew down the picture postcard bit of the Rhine River Gorge to just north of Frankfurt, turn left, look for Fulder, great fun, easy during the day.

Next morning a good breakfast in the Bader Park Hotel. I'm back in my room when there's a call from Reception.

'A gentleman to see you Herr Macare.'

'Good send him up.'

An American in civilian cloths.

'Rex Macare? Hello I'm Major Yallop, I'm here to brief you.'

'Right, hit me with the details.'

'Ok, we want you to do a photography run over a target just outside Eisenach, that's across the border a little north east of Fulder. It's a tank assembly area and we have reason to believe the East Germans have some new equipment there including nuclear artillery. Normally we would do this ourselves, however, the area is defended, SA-3 surface to air missiles and we …'

'Wow, stop right there, are you trying to tell me it's too dangerous for your own people so you have gone out and got me?'

'Doesn't sound the best I know Rex, however let me explain.'

This will be interesting, too bloody dangerous for the American military so get a mercenary, expendable.

'You have come to our attention because you are an experienced low level pilot and you have recently completed a similar job. The thing we like about you is the Chipmunk, something you like flying. The SA-3 that the East Germans have at Eisenach is a radar directed system. Our intelligence people tell us that it's not very effective below about 3000 feet and below 1000 feet it's radar system just does not work. Your little Chipmunk will be no match for the Soviet's SA-3 provided you stay below 1000 feet. Another thing that makes the Chipmunk ideal for this particular target is the approach and departure route. It's along some valleys that have turns, corners, in them and the hill tops will be above you, your speed will be around 100 knots. You will be able to fly along these valleys completely out of sight of radar. Our intelligence tells us your Chipmunk will be relatively safe from any hostile fire.'

'Major Yallop you have filled me with confidence but why haven't you used you own small slow aeroplane and experienced pilot?'

'Rex you come highly recommended, we want results not a stuff up.'

'Well that's nice to hear, good for the ego, but shit, this sounds bloody dangerous.'

'Not if you stay below 1000 feet. You spent all that time as a strike pilot and seldom did you reach those dizzy heights above 1000 feet.'

'Yeah, ok, perhaps I'll buy it, bit late to back out now, tell me some more.'

'Well as you know this will be at night. Your little Chipmunk has some pretty sophisticated gear on board that takes good pictures at night, probably better than we've got. The track in is marked on these maps here, it's all valley flying, the Fliede and Kinzig valleys. There are power transmission lines strung across the valleys at three points, the pylons are on hilltops and the cables are all about 600 feet above the valley floors.'

'Sure about that, 600 feet?'

'Yes, very sure, we've had our man in there to check, nothing under 600 feet so you will need to be around 300. The valleys are clear of other high obstacles and there's a road running along the valley floors, should be easy to follow at night There will be a moon and little cloud cover. The last transmission line on the route in is just as you turn the valley corner for the final run to the target. I suggest you go under this cable, then up a bit. The ideal for good pictures in 500 feet. The tank assembly park is illuminated and should be easy to spot. Two runs, one in, turn, one out, back into the valley and run for home. Once back in the valley they will not be able to see you.'

'Ok, got all that, so when's kick off?'

'Tomorrow night around eight. Leave all your clothing, wallet, passport, etc, in a bag with our man at the airfield, he will give you some clothes to wear, nothing identifiable on you.'

'You do inspire confidence. About these maps, they've got the route marked on them.'

'Yes, here's a second set with nothing marked, take these with you. Destroy the marked ones once you've absorbed the detail. One last thing, here's an envelope containing some East German marks.'

'When do I get to spend these?'

'Come on Rex, you know the ropes, we try and provide for all contingencies.'

'Here's a question, any top cover, any fast jets looking after me?'

'No comment on that.'

'Well thank you Major Yallop, plenty of food for thought, should keep me occupied for the rest of the day. Tell me what happens when it's all over?'

'Tell you what, on Thursday afternoon when you've had a good sleep and settled down, come over to the Officers Mess, a beer or two may be in order.'

'Yes please, that would be nice, all I've got to do is stay alive till then.'

'Come on now, you New Zealanders are the right stuff, of course you'll be alive.'

Hope the good Major is right.

I spend the rest of the day studying Major Yallop's maps in detail. The power transmission lines are the real threat, more so than the SAMs. What he had said about the SA-3 system was true. It had been around when I was in the Air Force and it was not considered a real threat; no good low down.

Around five in the afternoon I look in on the hotel bar and have a beer. I intend to have dinner in the hotel dining room then an early night, need to be at the top of my game tomorrow evening. There was an old fellow in the bar, German, having a drink, he spotted my passable German.

'Englander?'

'No, New Zealand.'

'New Zealand, really.'

His English was good, he seemed to want to talk.

'New Zealand, great fighters, real hard buggers.'

He really could speak the lingo, swearing and all.

'Crete, your lot got me in Crete, great soldiers. Our bastards shot prisoners, your lot treated us like, well prisoners, even gave us chocolate and that's while our lot were beating the shit out of your lot.'

'Well small world, I'm Rex, you are?'

'Lutz, Lutz Wolf. I'm still alive because of you New Zealanders.'

'Really, how come?'

'I finished up a prisoner of war and that was good for me, I'm still alive, doubt I would have survived the war otherwise. It also allowed me to learn all things English, including your terrible language.'

'Well Lutz that's nice to hear. My father was at Crete, killed at

Maleme during the invasion, but that's war, those things happen.'

'Oh shit, we killed your Dad. I was one of those paratroopers, and your people were so good to me, nothing's fair in war, not fair at all. Here, what's your drink?'

This could be a problem, don't want to be drinking tonight, definitely not, but can't be rude either.

'That's kind of you Lutz, just a small beer, have to be on the ball in the morning, not too much to drink tonight.'

'Ok Rex, just one drink eh!'

'Yep, thanks Lutz.'

'I've got a nephew in New Zealand, Ali, Ali Fischer.'

Ali Fischer, Kate's flatmate?

'Ali Fischer, is that what you said Lutz?'

'Yes, Ali Fischer, she lives in Auckland, lovely girl, in her twenties.'

I'm dumbfounded, Kate's flatmate and I meet her uncle here in Fulder, this small corner of Germany right on the DDR border and me about to put my life on the line tomorrow for money. Kate must never know, Ali must never know, god life can throw up some weird situations. Careful Rex, don't let on to Lutz that you know his nephew in far off New Zealand he would be overwhelmed but it could get back to Auckland and compromise your cover.

'Really, sure is a small world Lutz. I'm going to have dinner in the hotel here soon, have to be up really early in the morning, let me get you another beer.'

'No, no, but thanks anyway, have to get home to the ball and chain or risk a tongue lashing.'

Bit of a character Lutz, good command of English, got all the expressions sorted, glad he has to go home, gets me out of what could become an awkward situation. *Ali in far off New Zealand.*

Next morning, good breakfast in the Bader Park, the dinner last night was excellent as well, sausage and sauerkraut *was* on the menu. What to do with the day? A lot of thought about tonight's mission, there are far reaching ramifications. How come the Americans had heard about me? They were rather flattering but did they mean it? Weasel words perhaps, anything to keep me happy. Have they divulged everything? How dangerous is this going to be? Need to memorise just where those transmission lines are, need to go under not over, don't want radar to spot me. Safe under 1000 feet? possibly, probably, the map reading? follow the roads. Ok, need a bit of relaxation, a walk around Fulder then a nana nap.

It's very old Fulder, Baroque buildings, a lot of history, several museums, a lovely town. I spend some time wandering around soaking up the atmosphere. It's late spring, there's warmth in the air, summer is not far away. I find a small café with tables out on the footpath and enjoy a coffee and some apple strudel, 'apfelstrudel.' Back to the Bader Park and a nap. Around six I get up, a light meal in the hotel restaurant, then I pack everything into my bag and get a taxi out to the airfield where I'm reunited with what I now think of as my Chipmunk. It's been stripped of all registration markings. Nothing's been said about radio contact so I decide to maintain a listening watch on the tower frequency and say nothing, I'm sure they'll let me know if contact is required. There's a young American chap there to help me get airborne. He gives me some clothes to wear and I leave my bag with all my things with him. Shortly before nine I start up and taxi out to the runway, all the airfield lights are on. My Chipmunk appears to be the only aircraft on the airfield. I run over in my mind for the umpteenth time just what I am going to do and off I go. Up to the northeast of Fulder I soon find the entrance to the first of the valleys that lead to Eisenach. I estimate my height above the ground to be about 400 feet, I note where this point is on the altimeter. The Chipmunk's altimeter is no good for measuring exact height above ground at low level however once a reference point is established on the altimeter dial then it can be used. My actual height above the ground will simply be above or below my 400 foot reference mark. The road on the valley floor shows up quite well in the moonlight, navigation should not be a problem, the real problem, the cables. Well along this first valley is where the first of the three transmission lines should be and yes there they are exactly as marked on Major Yallop's map. I drop down to 100 feet below my reference point on the altimeter and fly under the cables, bit spooky but ok. I'm happy in my mind that I'm on top of the cable bogey. The valley takes a couple of turns then suddenly ends, I'm out over open ground then almost immediately the road I'm following enters another valley. Another transmission line is marked about half way along this one, keep a sharp lookout, stay at 300 feet, where is it, where the hell is it? There it is, cables right in front and just above, barely visible in the moonlight, it's scary. Stay at 300 feet, bloody cables. Now then the last lot of cables are just before you fly out of the valley into the target area. The idea is to go under, climb up a little, 100 feet above that reference mark, over the target at 500 feet, turn around, over the target again, down to 100 feet below, back into the valley, under the cables and scoot for home. The valley turns right just before it ends, this will keep me hidden during my approach, it will also allow me to disappear from sight when vacating the target area. My heart is pumping, I notice my right foot is doing a dance on the cockpit floor, twitchy! There they are, the last lot of cables and a turn in the valley, this is the business end of the mission. Under the cables, turn right, up a bit, there it is, a huge open area covered with tanks and big artillery pieces all brightly illuminated. Camera switch on, over the target, turn back, over it again. Suddenly the lights go out and there are multiple muzzle flashes from amongst the parked tanks and guns, some of the flashes are big. Shit, shit, I'm in trouble. Down to 100 below, race for the valley entrance, 'ping, ping, thump,' I'm taking hits, keep going, everything's still working. *Whoosh,* a loud noise and the shock wave of a missile passing close overhead rocks the little chipmunk. I see the glow of its rocket propulsion system racing away ahead of me, shit, shit. *Whoosh,* another missile goes over the top, races ahead of me, then an explosion, it's taken out a power pylon up on the hilltop over on the right, there's some sort of justice there, but shit, the cables will come down, up quick, how far up, make it 400 above that reference point until you're past the transmission line and then down again. *Whoosh,* shit, another one passes overhead dangerously close this time, and almost immediately another explosion, on the left this time, it's the other pylon. I'm into the valley where it turns left, I'm past the cables, down, right down, just about put my wheels on the road. Concentrate Rex you're not out of the woods yet. Follow that road, bit of cloud cover, the moonlight is not so good, can still make out the road. Took some hits back there, everything seems to be working. What's that smell, petrol, I can smell petrol, I've got a leak, shit. Just keep going, there's nothing you can do about it, just hope. Seems like an eternity, did not take this long flying in. There it is, the end of the valley, back in friendly territory. There's Fulder airfield, shit the engine's starting to misfire, fuel starvation. Break radio silence, call the tower, the response is immediate, perhaps they were waiting, probably as tensed up as I am.

'Fuel leak, the fire tender might be a good idea.'
I land, the motor keeps running albeit misfiring badly. I feel faint, it's shock, no wonder. I switch off the engine and clamber out, everything is hazy. Surprise, Major Yallop is there on the tarmac, the Americans offer a better service than Mr Roberts.

'Hello Rex, what did you think of that?'

'Shit,' is all I can say.

'Here I'll help you, stiff drink perhaps, your little Chipmunk has some holes in it, one of them is pretty big.'

'Stiff drink?'

'A cold beer would be nice.'

There's some quick talking and an ice cold Becks appears.

'Thanks, I need this.' It was then that I noticed it, my right hand could not hold the beer bottle steady, could not even find my mouth, the old right hand twitch had returned.

'You did a good job Rex, we had an observer at Eisenach, he's already let us know what happened.'

'Really, perhaps he could have taken a few pictures for you.'

'Would not have been as good as yours, that's pretty sophisticated gear in your Chipmunk.'

I was knackered, completely exhausted.

'I need to lie down.'

'I'll run you back to the hotel, get some sleep, we'll talk tomorrow, here's your bag.'

And that was it, back to the Bader Park and bed, sleep? no way was I going to get any sleep.

Whoosh, whooosh, whooooosh, kerumph, bang, no sleep for Rex. Dozing, turning, restless, *whoosh,* there was no let up, my brain was terrorising me. That was the most frightening thing I have ever experienced, people had been trying to kill me, shit! *Big money, big risk, bloody big risk!*

Next morning, sleep in, very tired, did all that actually happen last night? too surreal, can't be true. Get up, have something to eat, come back into the real world. Hang on this is the real world, the world of the mercenary, the hired gun, the big money, what have I got myself into? Down to the dining room and another excellent breakfast spoilt by the return of my twitch, cereal, milk in a spoon, forget it, the only way it will work is to use both hands and look like a retard, bugger.

I don't need this, perhaps it will go away? don't think so, remember Geilenkirchen? as long as you flew fast and low in your hot jet anything in a spoon was off the menu. Remember those lovely soups they served in the Officers Mess, and you struggling with two hands, the only fix is a career change.

The crisp morning air, a walk into town, have a relaxing coffee at that café, some apfelstrudel perhaps. A lot has happened since the last apfelstrudel, you could be dead. Think about Kate, that's nice, I wonder what she's doing today. I wonder what she would think if she knew what I had been up to? Is there a life for us together? Major Yallop invited me out to the Mess later today and tomorrow I'm booked back to New Zealand. That business last night, I need to get it into perspective, it's the life I have now. It's making me a lot of money that's why I've elected to do it, will it be long term? I don't have an answer to that, is there an answer? will I just keep on doing it to the point where it's too late to change, too late to give away the ability to make big money, too late to enjoy a fulfilling life with Kate? What if there was no Kate? no reason to think about settling down to a more mundane life, something secure, something boring. *Whoosh, boom, you're dead*, that's definitely not boring! Enough of this, go out to the airfield.

'Major Yallop, he's expecting me.'
'One moment sir, I'll locate him.'

'Hello Rex, all relaxed are we?'
'I wish.'
'Let's go into the bar and talk, pretty private at this time of the day.'
In we go, it's empty, mid-afternoon.
'Well Rex, we've had a look at the pictures, we are pleased with what you achieved, excellent intelligence.'

'Bloody hard on me Major, it was a lot easier in the Air Force.'

'Our man at Eisenach tells us they fired off four SAMs and as you are aware they all went over the top.'

'Four, I saw three, they scared the shit out of me. Two of them must have locked on to power pylons, there were two explosions that appeared to be near the hilltops.'

'Yes, it appears the Soviets have tweaked the SA-3's performance.'

'Is that what you really wanted to find out Major Yallop?'

'Come on Rex, don't be like that, what do you think we are, you did a great job and we thank you for it.'

Careful Rex, zip your lip, don't question their motives, you're just a mercenary, expendable. They will not be impressed if you start asking questions.

'Yes of course, thoughtless of me, last night's events have screwed my judgment, I'm still shaking a bit, no more jobs like that please.'

'Rex, we like what you did for us, could be we might want to borrow you again, by the way, here's a little bonus, don't tell Mr Roberts, it's our little secret.'

He hands me an envelope.

'5000 US for your troubles last night, you earned it.'

$5000, the value put on my life so the Americans could find out if the SA-3 had any capability below 1000 feet!

Careful, don't say anything, don't even think about it, you've no idea what these people are capable of. You're in dangerous territory, you're a mercenary remember, mercenaries get killed, *big money, big risk.*

'A drink sir?' the hostess is offering.

'Yes please, a Becks.'

Nice and cold, it hits the spot. I'm going to be cooped up in this little seat for many hours winging my way back to Kate. Perhaps I should have booked first class, didn't think about it, not in the habit of booking first class, still mentally penny pinching.

What's my life worth? depends who you ask. I think it's priceless, perhaps Kate thinks the same. People who buy my services however have very different values. That picture taking was bullshit, a story for my benefit, their man on the spot could have taken all the pictures they could possibly want but that was not his role. He probably had some sophisticated laser height measuring gear, had to determine my exact height when a SA-3 missile knocked my little Chipmunk out of the sky. How successful had the Soviets been in tweaking their SA-3's low level performance?

Major Yallop was probably very pleased when he saw me arrive back at Fulder, he would not have to explain away the loss of an aircraft and most importantly he had confirmation that the Soviet's SA-3 was still ineffective below 1000 feet.

Cold realisation was setting in. I had been a human target to enable the Americans to gather intelligence on the Soviet's SA-3. I was expendable. Well they got what they wanted, my survival was a bonus. The two pylons the missiles took out would have been around 900 to 1000 feet above the valley floor, they would be all metal, probably presented a similar radar return to that of a Chipmunk. The missiles went over the top of me. I would have been at 300 feet or less when the first two went over however I was higher, about 800 when the third one passed over very close, so there's a bit of intelligence that I have about the SA-3s low level capability. Unable to lock on at 800 feet but apparently can at 900 to 1000, geez that was bloody close. Perhaps Major Yallop was remiss in not quizzing me about that but then his man on the spot would know all this, he would have had all the good height measuring gear. The more I think about it the clearer it becomes. The picture taking was definitely a cover for my benefit, the true purpose was a live test of the Soviet's missile system. Using me, a mercenary, would divert attention should the test aircraft be lost, no public outcry, the public would never know, Kate would never know, how would she, I would simply vanish. How can I even contemplate doing that to her? do I really want to be in this brutal business? no one gives a stuff if I get killed. That fellow that Scruff had seen at Gütersloh being dragged out of a Chipmunk, did he survive? did anyone even know? I start to drift off, the fatigue, the one beer, the worrying thoughts crowding my mind, sleep, a first, I can never sleep in an airline seat.

Kate my lovely Kate, I'm floating way up in the clouds with Kate, high in the sky, floating in a sea of fluffy white, floating, floating, Kate I love you, I love you, aahhh I'm falling, falling, there's a big black hole and I've fallen in, down, down, blacker and blacker, falling, falling, ever faster, whoosh – BOOM - I'm dead. Kate, Kate, where are you, can I ever see you again, no you can't, you're dead, dead, dead!

'Rex, Rex', Kate throws herself at me, hugging, kissing.

'Oh my darling, you've survived the sausage and sauerkraut.'
Yes I have, no thanks to those who give me all this money but I'm not going to burden my lovely Kate with any of that, she must never know, it would destroy her. My bloody dangerous career choice is tuning out to be just that, bloody dangerous.

We're in the terminal building, I'm knackered, long flight, very long flight, but it was what preceded it that knackered me.

'The car is over in the car park, I got your message, could not wait to get out here, let's go home my darling. I've got the day off, let's go home to bed, you must be tired.'

'Not that tired Kate.'

'Oh god I can't wait.'

Next morning. I need to say something to Mr Roberts, put him in the picture, let him know what I think about being deliberately used as a target. How do I make contact? There will probably be a package from the Flint Agency but I doubt that's an avenue for contact. I know, a notice in the Herald, find out how vigilant Mr Roberts is.

Mr Roberts, phone me.

I need something to counter that Fulder thing, a holiday with Kate, get my mind right away from my brush with death. Yes a holiday with Kate, a truly romantic one, something I have never really done before, an island paradise, I know, the Club Med on Moorea.

'Kate I want to take you on a holiday, a romantic South Seas holiday in Tahiti, interested?'

'You're kidding me, interested? are you serious Rex? interested? Tahiti with my man and you ask am I interested? come here, it's a no brainer.'

Kate throws herself at me. Why do I put all this at risk for money? big money sure, but still just money, I don't know the answer.

Tahiti

We're on a big French DC8, UTA, Union de Transports Aériens, winging our way to Papeete, off to the Club Med on Mo'orea, jewel of the South Pacific, the perfect holiday spot. We're traveling first class, why not, getting my arse shot off in Germany does have advantages, going to Tahiti for a week with a beautiful girl is one.

The Med on Mo'orea, it's been there quite a while, one of the early Club Meds established just after the war.

'Two singles or a double monsieur?'

It's the Club Med receptionist, an attractive French girl.

'Excuse me?'

'Monsieur I have to ask, head office, Catholics.'

'Really, double, big, super king if you can.'

'Of course, silly me monsieur, but when guests check in and their surnames differ, and that's a lot of our guests, we have to ask. Macare et Fontaine, Huguenots oui? Est-ce que tu parles français?

'Afraid not, English only, and that's not the best.'

'Ah monsieur, French, English, who cares; faré 112, honeymoon special, super king. It's along at the end, private beach.'

'Mercie madame, you're very kind.'

'Monsieur a handsome couple like you two, definitely lovers.'

Here it is, faré 112, private beach right outside the door, looks great, there's a wine cooler with a bottle of bubbles on a little table in the centre of the room.

'Let's.'

We take the cooler and a couple of glasses out to the beach, we're in heaven. It's secluded, private, the sun warm on our bodies.

'Why are we wearing these clothes?'

Off they come, Kate down to her lace panties her full breasts magnificent in the sunshine, me in my boxers, it's very sexy. We just laze there in the sun, sipping champagne, enjoying each other's company. It's not long before the bubbles are gone and we're just dozing, very relaxed. I'm idly stroking Kate's breasts, she has a hand on the bulge in my boxers. It doesn't take long, the warm sun, the gentle stimulation. Kate starts breathing heavily, it becomes too much, inside, onto the bed.

Late afternoon, the sun's streaming into the faré warming our naked bodies. We're sprawled on the bed luxuriating in the afterglow of sex. I'm stroking her pubic mound, she has a hand on my thigh, it's relaxing and peaceful.

'Darling, perhaps we should tear ourselves away from this for a while, have a look at their bar, what do you think?'

'Yes, let's do that.'

'Your beads monsieur?' The barman takes the string of coloured beads from around my neck and pulls some off.

'Merci monsieur.'

They are tall 'cocktails of the day' and they're great but they've made inroads into my beads. There's no cash or credit in the Club's bar, just strings of beads purchased at reception. The different colours represent different values, the barman just helps himself. A string does not last long, the bar's pricy. Big-noters can flaunt their affluence with a sizeable bead display. We move out to the deck, the perfect place to enjoy a drink in the late afternoon sunshine. There's music, the distinctive sound of a clarinet. There's a fellow playing one wandering along the beach, he stops in front of us, the sound of his clarinet creates an amazing atmosphere, makes it feel like he's playing just for us. Kate is radiant, she's so beautiful, I feel a wave of love washing over me. I'm in love, I really am, it's a first, I've never felt this way, ever.

Dinner, a Club Med dinner, a unique experience. The dining room is huge, an open sided thatched affair. Along one side there's a smorgasbord to die for, everything, absolutely everything you could imagine is right there. At one end there's a big glass fronted fridge full of carafes of wine, red, white, and rose, help yourself, no beads required, how good does it get. The seating arrangements are a little different. All the tables seat six. As the diners enter they're directed to a specific table the idea being to mix it up a bit, and it works. We find ourselves seated with a French couple and two Italian fellows, this could be interesting; language, how's it going to work? Stop worrying, they all speak English, probably better English than ours, plus French, Italian, Spanish and who knows what else, Europeans are invariably multi lingual, unlike people from New Zealand, except for me, German, I've got German. Introductions and it's soon apparent the French couple, she's gorgeous, are honeymooners, the Italian fellows are gays holidaying together, this will be an interesting dinner, it is. Soup is served then it's the smorgasbord, help yourself to the wine. It eventuates that we all have similar tastes, three reds! The carafes don't last long, over to the fridge, another three reds, where is this leading? The meal is just so good, there's salmon, crayfish, prawns, yellowfin tuna, smoked marlin, wahoo, mahi mahi, every sort of cold and hot meat, salads I've not come across before, quiches, little pies, plenty of things I cannot recognise but which all taste good, it just goes on and on, and the wine, could be trouble here. The French couple and the two Italians are hard cases, they certainly like their red, I too am very partial to red, Kate's into it as well. There's dessert, a whole new smorgasbord of desserts as only the French can do it, completely over the top. We pig out, hard not to, a week of this could alter the body shape. The Italian lads are impressed with Kate, murmuring words of approval, saying nice things in Italian, right over the top of my head. The French couple, however, pick up on this and are rather amused. They whisper to me in English that both the Italians are smitten with Kate, they really fancy her but they fancy each other more, no need to worry Rex they chuckle. More wine, we are getting really friendly now.

The diners thin out, soon there's just a hard core of wine drinkers remaining, a bit of consolidation, a gathering of like minds, a drift towards a couple of the tables, one of them ours, more carafes, mostly red, the atmosphere's really friendly, many languages, everyone's multilingual. I just make the cut with my German, I think Kate feels left out, cultural cringe, only the one language, but who cares a girl with Kate's looks does not have to worry about trivialities like that. The party degenerates, it's the red wine, the Algerian blacktooth, what? Algerian blacktooth, cheap red, found wherever the French go. It's produced in Algeria, shipped abroad in forty four gallon drums, decanted into plastic flagons, then into glass carafes at Club Meds. It's cheap, however there is a downside. It has a high iron content and this gets into tooth enamel and stains it black, but who cares, 'pass the carafe.'

'That's it folks the shows starting, let's go.'
There's a rapid dispersal of happy wine drinkers. We head for the auditorium, it's a feature of all Club Meds, the evening show, they are always good.

'Morning darling.'
We're enjoying sex, wonderful sex, the sun coming through the opening in the side of the faré that passes for a window, the sound of the surf in the background, we're in paradise, life does not get any better than this, just let it go on and on. Kate, beautiful in her nakedness, moaning quietly, it's just so lovely.
'Breakfast Kate?' I say this quietly in her ear.
'Hmmm you feel so good inside me, don't stop, not yet.' She

arches her back a little and pushes up gently, god how can I stop? I'm in heaven.

Breakfast; a replay of dinner, it's just the banquet on offer is a little different. Keep this up for a week and we'll definitely be stretching the waist.

'Monsieur et Madame, you two beautiful people must go over to our île d'amour, only the beautiful people are allowed there.'

It's a motu, on the outer reef, transport is one of the Club's small boats, they'll pick us up later in the afternoon. It's very private, a favourite spot for honeymooners and the like. I'm becoming aroused on the trip over and I suspect Kate's feeling the same, this place looks idyllic, who knows what could develop.

'Pick you up around three messieurs; behave!'

It's paradise. We find a spot on the beach and spread out some big beach towels we've brought along. The warm sun, the sound of the surf, the shear sensual pleasure of it all. Kate rolls over and gives me a passionate kiss. She's taken her bikini top off and her lovely breasts are pressing on my chest, I can feel my manhood stiffening. In no time at all I'm rock hard, a massive erection. Kate notices it, her hand goes down onto my swimming costume, she gasps, and starts tearing at the bottom part of her bikini. I rip my own swimming costume off. The sight of my mighty erection is too much. Kate grabs it with both hands and pushes it deep inside herself. I start thrusting gently, she responds vigorously. I'm beginning to wonder just how obsessed with sex Kate is, it's fantastic, she really is enjoying it. Orgasm comes quickly and the intensity abates somewhat, into the water, we really do need to cool off.

'Rex, I've never done it in the ocean, let's.'

We're standing in waist deep water, she wraps her legs around me and we go at it with renewed vigour, it's fantastic.

Totally spent we collapse onto the towels and drift off, the warm sun on our naked bodies is just so nice, it does not last, my erection returns, nurtured by the sunshine, larger than ever. My eyes are closed, drifting off, suddenly an extraordinary sensation, she has her head down there and has taken my swollen manhood into her mouth. I'm transported to heaven. She's moving her head up and down, my erection's bursting, Kate's head is moving rapidly and then she's on top of me her lovely body rising and falling, the tempo increases, suddenly I explode just as she reaches a moaning climax, god this is just so magnificent.

The Club's boat picks us up around the middle of the afternoon.

'Messieurs you will be needing some food and wine after your Motu experience.'

The fellow has a knowing look in his eye, I guess he's seen this before, probably many times. Kate and I just cuddle each other all the way back to the beach at the Med.

'I love you Rex.'

'And I love you Kate, it's not just sex, I really love you.'

It was not all sex, we swam, snorkelled with the myriad reef fish, walked right around the little motu, did some sun bathing, marvelled at the little crabs that hid under every bit of corral. There were a couple of times when I felt the urge returning and I think Kate experienced the same however that initial frenzy just after we arrived had sated our appetite for now, how long would it last?

While we were lying in the sun recovering we got to talking.

'Tell me Rex, if you can, just a little bit, just a clue, what exactly is it that you do when you are *out of town for a while.* I know you've been in Germany, and that's about all I know.'

'Kate, it's hard, real hard. I'm in love with you and people in love do not keep little secrets from each other, well not if they want a lasting relationship. I have sort of been going along hoping you would never ask the awkward questions, bit unrealistic I know but I was hoping, and now you are asking and I feel honour bound to give you some answers.'

'Rex, I'm female and…..,' I interrupt her.

'You're certainly that Kate, an extremely sexy and attractive female and I'm madly in love with you, that's love, not lust, well perhaps a little bit of lust.'

I could feel my erection returning, *not now, please.* We are still naked, I can't help myself, I lean over and kiss one of her nipples, tickle it with my tongue. Kate shudders, my erection is now huge, Kate reaches for it, caresses it, I mount her, she moans, arches her back and I thrust into her. It's does not take long, orgasm comes quickly and we collapse back onto the towels, when will this end?

'Do you think there's something wrong with us.'

'Don't think so Kate, just good old sexual attraction, nothing wrong with that.'

'Hmm, guess you're right, I was beginning to think I had a problem. I've never felt like this before in my life and then you come along and set me on fire, I absolutely love it, I think I could make love with you forever. Now where were we before lust intervened? ah yes, what can you tell, or not tell, about being *out of town for a while*?'

'Kate I'm in a business that's really an extension of what I did in the military, it's covert. I don't know that much about what I do myself, don't need to know. There's an element of danger involved and the returns are huge but the whole thing has to be kept under wraps. If it became known what I do then my role, even my life, could be compromised and I could be out of a job.'

'Jeepers Rex, serious stuff and all this happens in Germany?'

'Kate, I'd rather not say anything more, I'll never tell you a lie but I'm sure you'll put two and two together and get an idea of what I do, all I ask is that you keep it to yourself, tell no one, not even your closest friends. The people who employ me have eyes and ears everywhere, nothing escapes them, nothing.'

'Big money, high risk, *and secrecy* Rex?'

'Yes it is Kate, can you take all that in?'

'Yes I can my darling, I understand, and yes I can keep a secret. I'll not ask questions, you'll tell me in your own time.'

'Thank you Kate, that's very understanding, and yes, when it's safe to tell, I will.'

Happy hour, we're on the deck outside the bar, the clarinet playing faintly in the distance. Kate is looking even more beautiful if that's possible. She's wearing a pareo she found in the club's boutique; on her it's a real knockout. There's a hei upo'o, or flower crown, on her head, straight out of Vogue, she looks absolutely stunning, heads are turning. Cocktails of the day, and another raid on the beads.

'Monsieur Macare,' it's a hard looking French fellow.

'Yes, that's me, Rex Macare.'

'Bonjour monsieur, parley-vous français?'

'Afraid not monsieur, English and poor German only.'

'English then, can I get you another drink perhaps?'

'No no, thank you but no, saving myself for dinner, the wine.'

'Yes, bit over the top I agree but nice. I've got something I would like to talk to you about, in private.'

'Really, what's it about?'

'Not now, how about we meet in the morning.'

What am I hearing, this fellow is sounding a bit like a French version of Mr Roberts, do I want to meet him, might as well, hear what he has to say.

'I could do that, what did you have in mind.'

'Shall we say ten tomorrow in my faré, number 67, come alone please, tear yourself away from the lovely Kate for just half an hour, can you do that?'

I glance at Kate, she's been party to the conversation and is looking a little puzzled, how come this fellow knows Kate's name?

'That ok with you dear,' I ask.

'Ah yes I suppose so, half an hour you say?'

'Oui madame, just thirty minutes of your man's time.'

'What did you say your name was?' I ask.

'Joubeit, Jacques Joubeit.'

'Well then see you tomorrow Monsieur Joubeit.'

With that the mysterious Frenchman gets up and wanders off.

'Out of town for a while, France perhaps?' there's a hint of sarcasm in Kate's voice.

'No idea Kate, have to hear what this fellow wants to talk about.' Bugger, my mercenary life is starting to intrude, what the hell does this fellow want, he's obviously sought me out. French, not sure about that, my mind flashes back to that gun running, shit!

'Morning darling,' we're enjoying each other's bodies in the early morning sunshine that's flooding into the faré. I'm running my fingertips over Kate's body teasing her nipples, tickling her tummy, gently stroking her pubic mound, running my hand down her thighs, she's stroking my hardening erection. Kate rolls onto her back and spreads her legs. 'Please Rex.'

'Monsieur Joubeit, good morning.'

'Ah, Rex, morning, sleep well? Thank you for coming along, how is the lovely Kate this fine morning?'

'She's fine, curious though.'

'Ah, the woman's intuition. What I have to tell you is for your ears only, Kate is not to know.'

'You make it difficult monsieur, do you want me to tell her an untruth.'

'Rex it will be for you to decide, I know you can handle these situations, you recent activities have not gone unnoticed.'
Oh shit, this guy's a spook, he probably knows all about me, and he's French, that's a worry, how much does he know, do I want to get involved?

'Rex we are aware you have done a couple of jobs for Mr Roberts, we too would like to utilise your particular skills. What we propose is not unlike what you have already done however it would involve Algeria, you are familiar with North Africa?'
Shit, he knows about that gun running, it's going to bite me on the bum. Who the hell is he? how come he's found me here on Mo'orea?

'Ah no, I'm not familiar with Algeria. Libya, Tunisia, Cypress, Malta, the Sudan, Iraq, yes, but not Algeria.'

'Come now Rex I am aware you were very young and following orders which is what you do in the military, I would not expect anything less of you however what you did was not in the best interests of the Republic, the DGSE have been keeping tabs on you.'

Shit, the DGSE, the French MI6, my worst fears are coming back to ruin my life, my wonderful new life with Kate. Something I did years ago when I was young and bulletproof, when I was in the military, when I did as I was told, how can this be held against me, and by a foreign power no less, France. How come it has caught up with me here in Tahiti? My name must be red flagged somewhere, French security tracking me, am I a threat to France? shit! All I did was help fly a load of Thompson sub machine guns to Tunisia in the dead of night, to El Aouina on the Algerian border. I was not even supposed to know what we were carrying but my curiosity got the better of me, I had prised open one of the boxes and discovered something I was not meant to know about. I wish I did not know about it but would that have made any difference, would the French know either way, how come the French knew about this in the first place?

'The DGSE may offer you some covert flying at a future date, nothing positive at the moment, this is just an initial contact to make you aware that we are interested, to give you time to consider it. Anything you do will be well rewarded. The DGSE would also like you to be aware that your involvement in the gun running incident in North Africa some time ago has not gone unnoticed. There are factions within the DGSE who would like you to be held to account.'

'Your threatening me Monsieur Joubeit, a bloody straight out threat, shit.'

'I'm not threatening you, merely stating a position, how you interpret it is your affair.'

'Ok, ok, got the picture, call me when you're ready, I'll think about it then.'

'Good, I'm sure you will do what they want, there could be considerable reward in it for you and remember, *you owe them.*'

'Excuse me, I owe your people nothing, *this is bloody blackmail,* now is there anything else?'

'That's it Rex, please try not to be upset, life can be like this at times, we all have a past. I'm sure you'll be able to turn this to your advantage.'

'Perhaps, right now I want to get out of here and find a beer, goodbye Monsieur Joubeit.'

I walked out of faré 67 shaken to the core, my high risk career has just ratcheted up several notches.

'Darling you don't look so good, what has our French friend done?'

'Kate, I don't tell lies, please believe me, I just don't and I'm not starting now. Monsieur Joubeit knows about things I've done in the past, covert military things, nothing I'm ashamed of, however, I'm not at liberty to talk. I just cannot tell you Kate and I'd hate this to drive a wedge between us.'

'Darling I do understand, I've figured out quite a bit of what it is you do, I'm keeping it to myself, not even telling you because it will only cause you worry. What I'm sensing here is blackmail, don't answer, don't compromise yourself, I love you Rex, I can handle it, now why don't we go down to the beach and enjoy a bottle of wine.'

Later in the day I call by the Club's office, I want to know more about Monsieur Joubeit.

'Monsieur Joubeit, oui monsieur he's just checked out, gone back to Papeete, he visits us from time to time.'

'Do you know what he does?'

'Non monsieur, I think he works for the Government.'

He's a bloody spook, the DGSE's man in Tahiti. When I passed through immigration at Faa'a airport the other day my name must have flashed up on a DGSE's computer in Paris, 'got him, he's on French soil, go over to the Med and lay it on him.'

The next four days of our romantic holiday in the south seas were rather overshadowed by what Monsieur Joubeit had said. I could not tell Kate, she was very good, did not ask. We immersed ourselves in everything the club had to offer, water skiing, snorkeling, a couple of picnics, one of them on île d'amour, on the very spot where we had enjoyed such wonderful sex, and the meals, the fantastic meals, those carafes, the shows in the evenings, we had a great time and I fell even more deeply in love with Kate, what am I going to do with my life? What?

Jacques Joubeit, a dark cloud on the horizon.

The Pick Up

A beautiful sunny morning in Auckland, I'm enjoying a lie in at my place. Kate's down country on a modelling assignment, *out of town for a while,* otherwise I'd be at her place, in her bed. Perhaps I should move in with Kate, or would that affect her blossoming modelling career?

Ring, ring, 'Roberts here Rex, how was Tahiti? You wanted to contact me?'

'Yes I did, just as well you didn't get hold of me earlier, I might have been a bit blunt with you.'

'Dear dear, that's not good, perhaps I could drop around for a cuppa I've got something I'd like to talk to you about as well, say in an hour's time.'

'Ok, in an hour.' I hang up.
My anger about the Fulder business has subsided somewhat, time and Tahiti have mellowed me a little. I'm still mightily pissed off about what happened, I need to set some ground rules for Mr Roberts.

Knock knock, right on time. 'Mr Roberts.'

'Rex, first let me tell you that the Americans were very pleased with what you did at Fulder, they've indicated they would like to use your services again.'

'What in particular are they so pleased about.'

'The pictures, excellent, brought them right up to date with what the Soviets have recently deployed in Germany.'

'And what is it in particular that they have recently deployed in Germany Mr Roberts?'

'Come on Rex that's classified stuff, you know the rules, don't need to know.'

'Well I do know. The Americans wanted an accurate assessment of the low level capability of the Soviets upgraded SA-3 and you apparently sold me to them as an expendable target, the picture taking was a diversion purely for my benefit. Their Johnny on the spot with the sophisticated laser height measuring gear could have taken all the pictures they could ever want, to put it bluntly, I'm mightily pissed off.'
Mr Roberts expression gives nothing away, he looks a little lost for words.

'Rex, perhaps a cup of tea.'

'Ok, just as well I'm making it, would not want to be served another poisoned chalice.'
I take my time making the tea, give Mr Roberts time to come up with some answers, see how believable he is.

'Rex you are reading far too much into it, imagining things that just do not exist, and ….,'

'Stop right there Mr Roberts, cut the bullshit. You sent me off on a job that could very well have been fatal and don't deny it, how big a mug do you think I am? I was in the military remember, a soldier in the Cold War. You know all this, you should have been aware that it would not take me too long to figure out what the stakes were. Pictures? rubbish, I was a live target and you know it. It's just fortunate for me that the Soviets have not been successful in upgrading their SA-3's low level performance.'

'Ok Rex, yes I was aware that the risk element was high, how high I didn't know, the Americans are pretty reluctant to give anything away, however, let me clarify things a bit here. You sell your services for cash and there's risk, how much risk? well we don't always know, that's the way it is. It's for you to decide if this business is for you.'

'Thanks for that, thanks for being honest, well as honest as you can be. I don't want to press the point about whether or not you knew the true purpose of Fulder. I hope you are not the sort of person who would tell a lie, so I am prepared to let the matter drop, however, from here on I want you to be selective about the tasks you offer me. Risky sure, I've bought into that scenario, but something that's stacked against me as this one was I want no part of. If I sense that there's little regard for my survival then I'll be out of the business, you'll have to find someone else.'

'I understand where you are coming from Rex and I'm pleased for you that Kate has got you thinking seriously about your life, to reassess how much risk you can manage rather than just ripping into it, gung ho, what the hell! I don't want to even attempt to make excuses for myself about the Fulder business. When it came up the Americans had no intention of divulging the true purpose. It was not until late in the piece that it became apparent to us just what was going on. I admit we were remiss in not pulling you out, however, you were already in Fulder. I guess we just crossed our fingers and hoped for a good outcome.'

'Ok, let's put it behind us, you'll be a bit more selective in what you offer me in the future; the tea, it's getting cold.'

'Now Rex I have another proposition for you, however, perhaps tomorrow might be a better time.'

'No, I'm ok, hit me with it now.'

'It's Germany again. There's someone across the border they want picked up. Don't know why they want an aeroplane to do the job, however, it must be a high value client, there's quite a bit of money on offer.'

'Tempt me Mr Roberts, massage my bruised feelings with cash, after all that's what I'm all about, a pilot for hire.'

'One hundred and fifty thousand NZ dollars, half now, half on completion. This person must be important and no, I don't know who it is, probably never will. The deal is across the border at night, pick up, and straight back, I'll give you until tomorrow to make up your mind, ok?'

'Ok, ten tomorrow, I'll have the pot on.'

Mr Roberts wants to shake hands, I think he's feeling bad about Fulder. Not as bad as me, I'm still pissed off.

'Put it there Mr Roberts, no more Fulders, ok!'

We shake hands and he leaves. Suddenly I'm lonely, no moral support, no Kate. I'm at a loose end, perhaps the Paddington later, I've been there a few times, could have a pub meal.

'Ali, Jeff, surprise, glad you're here, didn't really fancy drinking alone.'

'Would not be alone for long Rex, you're a girl magnate.'

'Excuse me Ali I'm in love, did you two know that, well it's true, I'm in love with Kate, don't look at other girls anymore, don't even want to.'

'Really Rex, in love, out of circulation, sure about that, monogamy, won't that get boring.' Ali's being provocative.

'Don't know Ali, time might tell but I don't think so.'

'That's a bit of a bugger Rex, no more sharing it around.'

What am I hearing, what a hell of a thing to say in Jeff's presence, it's embarrassing.

'Ali, do you mind.'

'Don't worry, stop looking so uncomfortable Rex, Jeff here understands don't you dear,' and she gives him a big kiss.

Please ground open up and swallow me!

'Rex, perhaps I should let you off the hook,' it's Jeff. 'I know Ali's been having sex with you, I don't mind that, I think I'm gay, well I thought I was until Whangaroa, and it's been tough on Ali. To be fair I didn't restrain her if she wanted to jump into bed with someone else, I'm not going to come looking with murderous intent.'

Well that's cleared the air thank god, quite an admission on Jeff's part. Why does Ali stay with him, I think Ali can read the question on my face.

'He's a nice man Rex, a very nice man and he's very good to me. It just pees me off that he's got this preference for the fellows, well he had this preference, but things have changed. I've stayed with him hoping to change his ways, haven't I dear, and suddenly it's working.'

'Here let me get you some drinks, what's it to be?'
I escape to the bar; wow that was powerful stuff.

'Rex this might interest you. I've just had a letter from a distant uncle in Germany, he tells me that recently he met a chap from New Zealand in his home town of Fulder and guess what, his name was Rex, been in Fulder recently Rex?'
Tread carefully now, Ali has no idea what you get up to and I'm sure Kate has not enlightened her, as for being in Germany, might as well have been on the moon. I elect to make light of the issue.

'Oh yes, last week I ducked over to Fulder, got this hot chick who wanted a bit, don't tell Kate.'
I get a funny look from Ali, shit, I wonder if she does know something. Another couple of drinks then Jeff and Ali excuse themselves.

'Night night Rex, home alone tonight?' from Ali.
What's that suggest, I don't think Ali knows where my flat is, hope to hell she doesn't.

Ring ring, it's nine that evening, I'm just back from the pub, might be Kate.

'Hello.'

'Rex,' it's Ali, 'can I come over, please Rex.'

'No Ali you cannot come over.'

'But Rex, Kate said she does not mind sharing and right now I want it, I really do.'

'Ali, no, if Kate was here perhaps, but she's not here. I'd love to satisfy you I really would but you've got Jeff now, the reawakened Jeff.'

'Bugger, you are a gentleman Rex, I have to admire that. Kate's a lucky girl, wish I had found you before she did, oh well sleep tight, perhaps I'll give Jeff a big come on and see what happens.'

The next morning, 'Mr Roberts, come in, the pots on, yes I'm on for a pick up from across the border. That's a lot of money for what appears to be a simple job, there must be some fish hooks?'

'Hopefully not, nothing that we've picked up on. I've taken on board what you had to say about Fulder, Americans, not to be trusted.'

'Ok, what do you want me to do this time?'

'It's a pick up from just north of Leipzig, you will use a Chipmunk and operate out of Celle. The actual pick up date has not been finalised yet, security reasons, however we want you in Celle ready to go on Friday next week, that's ten days from now, full details will be given to you at Celle.'

'By you?'

'That's irrelevant Rex. Here's an envelope, $75,000. I suggest the same travel deal, you can probably do a repeat of the previous arrangements, that all worked out ok, any questions?'

'No nothing right now, that's a lot of money. You're getting me hooked, hope I stick around long enough to enjoy it.'

'You're not a worrier Rex, you can handle it. So far we're pleased with what you've done. The Fulder thing was a bit more than we expected and I apologise for that; Americans.'

'Yes Americans.'

'One more thing Rex, here's a set of topographical maps of the whole of Germany, I want you to spend some time studying everything between Celle and Leipzig. There are hills, water features, wooded areas, numerous villages, small towns, and quite some distance for you to fly. Don't mark anything on the maps and destroy them before you leave for Germany, we'll give you some more charts that cover the actual area between Celle and Leipzig when you get to Celle. Take your time, study the maps carefully, plan your route, and try to memorise as much as possible. Don't let anyone else see them, I cannot emphasise it enough, nobody must see these maps. The opposition's not stupid, not even the STASI. If they ever get wind that you are one of our operatives then you could come under their surveillance, even here in Auckland.'

'Ok Mr Roberts, you've raised my awareness, occupational hazard.'

He hands over a big envelope containing some maps.

'Keep these in a safe place, could be your future well-being depends on it. Normally I would not divulge this much information until you were in Germany ready to go however in this case it would be advantageous to put in plenty of study time. That's about it Rex, our next contact will be in Schapers Hotel.'

'Our next contact? am I going to see you in Celle?'

'Perhaps.'

Mr Roberts is gone, time to reflect. A set of maps that I have to keep quiet about and an envelope containing $75,000 that I should also keep quiet about, tax, bank accounts, money laundering, I've not given those sorts of things any thought at all, perhaps I should. A person of interest, me, the DGSE for one, possibly the STASI, shit I'm getting in deep, is this really for me? the money, all that money.

Go for a walk, fresh air, enjoy the better things of life. I do enjoy the better things of life but there's a downside, the career path I've embarked on. Different, rewarding, but good future prospects? that's what people look for, are there good long term prospects? no, I'm there now, I'm enjoying the long term prospects right now, it does not get any better, it stays the same. It could end abruptly as well. Go for that walk Rex you're getting melancholy, what I need right now is Kate.

A couple of lonely days, no Kate. Poring over Mr Roberts's maps, sorting out how I am going to fly low level from Celle to Leipzig. My circumstances are not comforting, my career, so called career, is not the greatest, Kate is the one ray of sunshine. Kate loves me and I love her so why the hell am I risking my life making a bob when I have Kate. Perhaps I should be looking elsewhere, Cathay for instance, right now I feel locked in.

I've done the bookings. Germany, Celle, Schapers. Leave on Wednesday, Celle on Friday, arse shot off on Saturday, is this what I want?

'Kate,' I surprise myself shouting out in the airport arrival hall.

'Rex,' she throws herself at me, jumps up wrapping her legs around my body kissing me furiously, it attracts attention.

'Whose the lucky fellow that gorgeous girl's going ape over.'
Home to Kate's place, into the sack, we just can't restrain ourselves.

'Dinner Kate? our favourite Parnell restaurant? just us? no Ali, no Jeff.'

'Yes please, I love you.'

It's a bang up meal, no expense barred, my dubious career choice does have its benefits. I don't mention my impending *out of town for a while,* don't want to spoil the moment. Back to Kate's flat, into bed, we can't get enough of each other. There's a lockable door on Kate's bedroom, do I lock it, don't want Ali appearing on the scene, not tonight, will it offend her?

Coffee in the morning sunshine on the little terrace outside the kitchen, just the two of us, no sign of Ali. Perhaps she did not come home last night, good, she might have taken offence if I had locked the door. Ali, she really does need to find herself a real man. She's a spectacular creature I would have thought they'd be lining up, why does she stay with Jeff? what's the attraction? I ask Kate.

'She likes the guy, he likes her a lot as well. He's good to her, very attentive, it's a pity about the sex thing but it looks like that might be coming right. Ali's a sexy girl as you know Rex, she needs satisfaction, demands it.'

'What's with Jeff's boat, the big Riv?'

'Wealthy family.'

'Oh well I guess it's for Ali to deal with but I would like to see her with a real man, I really would.'

'Sure about that Rex, no more Ali hoping into our bed, I thought that was a real turn on for you, it is for me.'

'You're a devil Kate, a sexy devil and I love you, now there's something I have to tell you.'

'Bugger, *out of town for a while* again?'

'Very perceptive Kate, yes, I'm off on Wednesday, three days from now, be away for five or six days.'

'Ok, I've got a couple of days off then I'll be busy for a while as well so that will work out great. Two days in bed with you then some serious work, we could get meals on wheels.'

'Come on get dressed, we'll go for a walk.'

Kate was not wearing anything under her dressing gown, it was not done up at the front either, the glimpses it afforded of her naked body were getting me aroused. A walk in the park, now, make an effort, try and keep away from that bedroom for a bit.

We're on a park bench holding hands, sounds a bit corny but that's what we're doing. A couple of people in love, it's a lovely feeling. We wander along the waterfront to the Viaduct Basin and have a cold beer, then on further to Westhaven Marina.

'Jeff's boat is here, somewhere.'

'Yep, somewhere.'

There are a zillion boats at Westhaven, it's a popular place.

'How about a late lunch at Swashbucklers Kate, it's a great restaurant, best fish in town.'

'Whatever you say dear, I'm putty in your hands, ready to do anything you might ask, satisfy your every wish.'

Kate's being provocative, there's a cheeky smile on her lovely face, god I love this girl. Swashbucklers and it's crayfish, why not, top of the line, I like my new found affluence. I like sharing it with Kate even more, an expensive sav blanc to round it out.

'Is it sausage and sauerkraut again Rex? want to tell me about it?'

'Yes, but I can't and it hurts that I can't, it's not fair on you Kate.'

'That's ok, well not really, but I understand, I'll try not to pry.'

'Thank you Kate, when I can I will, promise, now what about another bottle of this excellent sav, this one's got itself empty.'

'Great then we can go home to my place, only got a few days. Ali won't be there, she's *out of town for a while* in Wellington, will you miss her?'

'What, what did you say?'

'Will you miss her? I know you like fucking her and I like you fucking her as well, it really turns me on, however she's out of town so we'll just have to make do.'

'Make do? Kate what are you saying? I don't need Ali to get me going, believe me, you are the only thing I need.'

Two days together. The mornings I devote to some serious work on Mr Roberts's maps, the rest of the day, and the nights, ah yes the nights, with Kate, it's a pleasant interlude dampened a little by the thought of what I'm about to do for Mr Roberts.

The map thing. I'd found on the two previous excursions across the border that reading the hand held map at night did not work so well, difficult to see the detail, little time to be looking inside the cockpit anyway. This time I'm going to try to memorise everything, well as much as I can, not have to rely on the map. There's quite a bit of variation along the route I intend to follow. Flat open country with water features, wooded areas, some hills, larger wooded areas, plenty of villages and small towns, best avoided, too much risk of detection. I commit it all to memory. The one thing that does worry me, power transmission lines, the cables and pylons. There are several marked on the chart along the route I have decided on, I'm happy in my mind that I can deal with them, it's the unmarked ones that are the worry, how to deal with that problem. The only real way is to be above the pylons that means being up around seven to eight hundred feet exposed to possible radar detection, the alternative, stay low and risk it. Not knowing where, or even if, an encounter with an unmarked transmission line might occur meant being high for the whole flight, not practical, potentially more dangerous than risking it down low, *big money, high risk!* I'll go low, chances are that all the transmission lines are marked. If there is an unmarked one along the route well I guess I'll just have to chance it. Ok, I'm happy in my mind now, prepared for my next big money making venture into danger, the only downer, the nagging thought in the back of my mind, *is this really a good career choice?*

Wednesday, I drive out to the airport with Kate, she's close to tears. At the check in she cracks up completely. She's been thinking too much about my *out of town for a while.* Kate's a smart girl, she's worked out that what I do is dangerous and carries big rewards, my new found affluence is a bit obvious perhaps, she's not asked about that but she must have noticed.

'*Sniff, sniff,* come back in one piece darling please, I love you, I'll die if I lose you.'

'Kate, you're not going to lose me, what are you thinking.'

'I'm trying hard to believe you Rex but ....'

'Kate, you are not going to lose me, I'll be back in a week's time, honestly I will.'

Sure about that Rex, not your first lie is it, remember no lies.

We hug each other for what seems an eternity. Kate is crying, what am I putting this lovely girl through, is this career of mine fair on a girl who's crazy about me, bugger, I just don't know.

Friday afternoon, Schapers Hotel.

'Herr Macare, welcome back, all the way from New Zealand to stay with us again, a fine choice, you are a man of taste.'

This is nice, rolling out the good English for my benefit, what a good hotel.

'Herr Macare, what do we owe the pleasure to this time?'

Careful Rex, what's the cover story again, what was it last time, I don't think I had to give a reason last time, sure I didn't.

'Some acquaintances from a few years ago. I used to be in the Air Force here, thought it's time I caught up with them.'

Will the nosy receptionist buy it I wonder?

'That's nice, friendship's a lovely thing, by the way you might like to know that not long after you left us last time a gentleman turned up here inquiring about you, he wanted to know your name. Apparently all he knew was that you arrived out of the blue, stayed a few days and left. He did not know your name, however,' he thought you might have come from New Zealand and that you might be a pilot.'

Shit, alarm bells, whoever could that have been.

'That's interesting, wonder who it could have been. What did you tell him.'

'Nothing Herr Macare we have a very strict privacy policy here at Schapers, details about our guests are never divulged.'

'That's nice to know, tell me what did this fellow look like?'

'Well dressed, nondescript, I think he was German, but I'm not

sure, could have been French, that's all I can tell you.'
This could be trouble, who would be interested in a pilot from New Zealand? who? It could only be the East Germans. How would they get on to me and so soon after my first venture across their border? Perhaps I've underrated the STASI? the DGSE perhaps?

Saturday morning, 'Herr Macare, there's a lady to see you.'
   'A lady?'
   'Yes a Miss Nicole Townsend, she's in the lobby.'
A lady, Townsend, sounds English, no Mr Roberts?

   'Miss Townsend, I'm Rex Macare.'
She's a real looker, different.
   'Nicole, call me Nicole. Mr Roberts is busy elsewhere, perhaps we can go along to your room, bit of privacy.'
   'Yes, yes, and call me Rex, here it's along the hall, this way.'
She's stunning, far too attractive to be a spook. Careful Rex this is business, serious business, don't even think about it, think about Kate.
   'Rex, my understanding is that Mr Roberts has provided you with some maps that you will have studied and then destroyed, right?'
   'Yes Nicole I've done some homework, as far as Leipzig, that's all I know so far.'
   'Ok, it's a pick up in the Leipzig area. We want you to land, collect someone and bring them back here to Celle. The pickup point is on the eastern side of the Werbeliner See, that's a lake a little to the north of Leipzig. Here's another set of maps, don't mark anything on them and destroy them when they're no longer required.'
   'Ok, got that. I've planned how I'll get to Leipzig, the Werbeliner See you say.'
   'Yes, the eastern side. We want you to plan it so you arrive there

as close to 11pm tomorrow night as you can, there will be a single white light at the southern end of a landing strip, it's an open field. Touch down right on this light heading 020 degrees, there will be a second white light at the northern end of the strip that should be directly in front of you as you land. Keep the engine running and turn the aircraft around so that it's pointed south in the opposite direction. Our people will be there. They will put your passenger into the back seat of your Chipmunk. Take off immediately towards the south. Got all that?'

'Yes Nicole, got it. This person is important?'

'Come on Rex, you know the rules, don't need to know.'

'Ok, yes I know, just curious.'

Curious all right, and curious about how I can get your phone number. Nicole is a real knockout but hang on Rex, remember you're no longer a single young chap chasing everything in a skirt that catches your attention, there's Kate, remember, my beautiful Kate, she's even more spectacular than Nicole here. What am I thinking? lust, it's lust clouding my judgment, something that's clouded my judgment for most of my life.

'One more thing Rex, the field you'll be using is half way along the side of the lake in a relatively dark area so it should not be too difficult to spot the two lights marking the ends of the intended landing strip, now how's all that? any questions?'

'Nope, I think I've got it all, when do I get to see you again?'

'You don't.'

'Well in that case what about morning coffee?'

'No fraternising with the clients, house rules, sorry Rex, you'll just have to think about your lovely Kate and don't look so gobsmacked, we know a lot about you.'

'Nicole, here's something you may not know, it could be significant.' I tell her about the well dressed fellow who came inquiring about me. She looks concerned but gives nothing away.

'I'll pass that on, now I'll be off, good luck Rex.'
Tomorrow night, across the border again. Sounds like I've not been lied to this time. Danger, what's the danger, only thing apparent, the power lines, should not be any guns. Now go for a walk, enjoy the natural world. The weather, nothing's been said about tomorrow's weather. I find a newspaper in the hotel lobby and look at the weather forecast. Sunday, overcast, possible light rain in the evening, bugger, not what I want, visibility could be a problem. Will I be able to do what's required of me? what if I can't?

I walk into Celle, it's overcast, I find the pub I'd had a drink in on my last visit, perhaps one beer, relax me.

'Hallo, Englisch?

It's an old fellow having a beer at a small seat next to me.

'Yes I am, speak English?'

'A little.'

The old chap is friendly, wants to talk, a mixture of English and German. I'll ask him about the weather, he's a local, will probably know a bit about the local weather and besides it's a good way to break the ice.

'Australian?' he asks.

Careful Rex, better be an Australian, that fellow who came asking at the hotel, he was looking for someone from New Zealand, a pilot remember, better not be a pilot.

'Yes, Sydney, tourists, we're driving around Germany, what a lovely country, my first visit.

'Family with you?'

'Yes they are, off somewhere soaking up a bit of the local history, museums, art galleries, me, I'd sooner check the local pub, you sure have lovely pubs.'

Better be careful, don't want to get drinking with this fellow, just one beer remember, clear head tomorrow.

'Bit overcast, looks like rain,' I offer.

'Nein, no rain, a few drops tonight and perhaps in the morning, then it will clear up.'

That's what I want to hear. The old fellow's glass is still pretty full so the question of another drink is some way off.

'Don't get many foreigners up here at Celle, they're missing the best part of Germany and it's not far to go to see that bloody border.' His voice takes on an angry tone.

'The border, that's the DDR border?'

'That bloody big wire fence, a prison, the bastards have most of my family, can't get them out. Those mongrels are not German, they're the scum of the earth, a great big prison run by criminals.'

'Dear me, you paint a grim picture.'

'Yes I do and I apologise, it's just that I get so upset about it. I'm an old man, I want my family around me and it's not going to happen.'

'That's awful, I don't know what to say?'

'That's what happens when you lose a war, it's not you fellows, it the bloody Soviets and their running dogs in the East, bastards. The Americans and the British should have rolled right across Germany, all the way to the Soviet border, but it didn't happen.'

'Where are your family now.'

'Leipzig, there's quite a lot of them, couple of generations, trapped there, no prospect of ever getting to the west and it makes me very angry.'

The old chap is visibly upset, I feel sorry for him, a casualty of war and its aftermath. I'll get him a beer and then take my leave.

Sunday afternoon, the weather's clearing, patches of blue sky. I'd slept in then enjoyed a substantial late breakfast at the hotel. Another walk perhaps then a nana nap, want to get airborne around ten tonight. Light dinner at the hotel then out to the airfield around nine.

It's a different Chipmunk, no camera gear. There's a young British fellow to help me, some unmarked clothes to wear. I leave him with a bag containing my things. The airfield's deserted. Start up, taxi out to the runway. I'm on the local VHF frequency but there's no radio contact, off I go into the night. I wonder what's going to unfold in the skies above the DDR, will my life change, will I get to collect that $75,000. Nav lights off. The ugly wire barrier flashes by just to the east of Wolfsburg. I drop down low and start looking for the expected ground features all of which I've committed to memory. There's patchy cloud cover and a waning moon that's not providing much light, no drizzle though, good. Not easy spotting the ground features I'm looking for, but I'm managing. Memorizing everything was a good idea, don't have to 'come inside' and try to read the map. The transmission lines; there are three that cross my route, they are the danger. Got the first one. There's a pylon clearly visible out on my right that means there will be cables across my path, probably at about 200 feet, I'm around 500, can't see any cables. The pylon's behind me now, two to go, next one in about eight minutes. There's a town all lit up over on the left, that's about right, memorising everything's working well. I continue on, spot the remaining two transmission lines and manage to get by them, constantly looking for any that might be there that I don't know about. Getting close now, happy with where I am, have not had to refer to the map at all, been able to stay low and not hit anything. There it is, a large mass of water, the Werbeliner See. Fly down to the southern end, turn north, fly up the eastern side, what's the time? eleven, how good is that. There it is, a single white light and a second one up ahead. Ok, now land on the field that you can't really see, touch down on that light pointing at the second light, compass should read 020, it is. Bump, rumble rumble, I'm down. Taxi along a bit towards the light up ahead and turn the Chipmunk around pointing back towards the first light, keep the engine running. There's movement outside, the canopy's opened, someone is climbing into the rear seat, the canopy is slammed shut.

'Go go go,' a voice from the back.

Bang the throttle open, we're off.

CRASH-KEERUMPH, total blackness!

A terrible pain in my head, where, what? I'm lying on a bed in the dark, what's going on? where am I? what the hell has happened? what's gone wrong? horribly wrong?

'Hello, anyone there?'

A door opens, daylight floods the room.

'Ah, you're awake Herr pilot.'

'Yes I am, where am I?'

'Don't worry you're in safe hands, we are your friends.'

Friends, I don't have any friends in the DDR, I'm probably in unfriendly hands and in deep shit, ouch my head, it hurts like hell.

'Safe hands, friends?' I ask.

'Yes, we are your friends, honestly, we're not the STASI, we are friends of the west. You are in a safe house in Liepzig, please believe me Herr pilot.'

Oh shit, my worst fears, this is the *high risk* part. Whatever could have happened? My head, it's hurting, really hurting. The fellow doing the talking is a middle aged man, his English is good.

'Any chance of a coffee, my head is hurting, I need a coffee.'

'Coming right up Herr pilot.'

Wake up Rex, sort yourself out, you're in trouble, how much trouble you don't know but it could be a whole lot of trouble, what has happened?

'Here we are, hot coffee. You've had a whack on the head, there's a big lump, you've been unconscious for several hours.'

'What happened?'

'Well you crashed on takeoff. There was a hole in the field we were using and you found it, a wheel dropped into the hole, one undercarriage leg was torn off, the aeroplane spun around, the propeller hit the ground, and you were knocked unconscious.'

'Where's my passenger?'

'In the next room, he has a broken arm.'

'How did we get here?'

'My my, a lot of questions Herr pilot.'

'Well hell, I'm supposed to be delivering my passenger to the West and here I am in a house in Liepzig without my aeroplane.'

'You're in safe hands I promise, we are the people who were trying to get your passenger out of the DDR, now we have to try and get you out as well.'

'What's happened to the Chipmunk?'

'It is no more, completely burnt out with your bones amongst the ashes.'

'What?'

'Well we don't want to make it too easy for the STASI, want to throw them a curly one if we can. You crashed and were killed while carrying out an illegal spy mission inside the DDR, your body and your aeroplane were burnt beyond recognition in the subsequent fire.'

'Excuse me, how is that possible?'

'One of our people operates a mortuary, he has access to dead bodies, it was not difficult to arrange your demise. The idea is to throw the STASI off the trail, don't want them looking for a pilot on the run.'

'Well what can I say, I guess I'm completely reliant on you, what do you have in mind.'

'Give us a couple of days and we will come up with a plan for you and your passenger in the meantime you are safe here, however, I ask you to keep away from the windows. Everything you might want is in the house, we will bring you meals, good meals.'

Well it's happened, it's turned to worms. I guess something untoward was bound to happen sooner or later, the thing now is to try and recover the situation, complete the job I've been entrusted with. Will Mr Roberts know what the situation is I wonder, are these people in contact with the West, they must be, they arranged the pick up that I have gone and stuffed up. Perhaps I should get up off this bed, try my legs, do they work, christ my head hurts, wonder if they have Panadol in the DDR? Yep I'm up and running, just the sore head, try a walkabout, check out the accommodations. I gingerly cross the room and try the door, it opens into a lounge, there are a couple of people sitting there, one of them has his arm in a sling.

'Hello, are you our good pilot,' it's the fellow with his arm in a sling.

'Yes, I'm your pilot, not so sure about the good bit, name's Rex, my German's not the greatest.'

'Not a problem, I'm part Brit, I'm your client, call me Ted.'

'Hello Ted, I'm supposed to get you across the border, not doing very well so far, I think we might be rather reliant on these good folks to get the job done.'

'Looks a bit that way, just plain bad luck that pothole, however, I think these people have done a pretty smart job covering things up.'

'Rex, let me fill you in, not too much information, you know the ropes, don't know can't tell. I need to get across the border as soon as possible, we will be relying on the organisation here in Liepzig to arrange something, I'm sure you don't want to stick around here either so you could say we are a couple. This arm's not too bad, should not be a problem and I'm sure that big lump on your head will go away. I guess the plan will be to lie low until our friends get something organised. They will have got word out that we are both alive and kicking. The burnt out plane and the human remains are purely for the benefit of the STASI.'

'Ok Ted, guess we are a couple, let's hope these people come up with something, just as well they've got us, not sure how I would go by myself.'

'I'm not that worried, from what I've seen they're pretty capable.' Ted's take on the situation.

Well here I am, hiding out in the DDR, didn't plan on this. I think I told Kate it would be five or six days, it's going to be a bit longer than that, that's a worry. I wonder how Mr Roberts will handle it? Will he let Kate know I'll be a bit late home? will he tell her anything? There's just Ted and myself living in the house. A few people come and go, most of the liaising is done with Ted. His German is perfect, I think he lives in the DDR but I don't know, and no one's telling. I don't need to know. I don't think Ted is Ted, that's just for my benefit, I think his name is Otto, that's how the people who come and go refer to him. Ted does not talk much, I don't think he wants me to know anything. His broken arm's not a big worry. Keep away from the windows, no going outside, it's a prison. Need to do something, can't just sit and vegetate. Cooking, that's it, do some cooking, I quite enjoy cooking and there's plenty of food in the house.

'Ted how about I cook us a big pasta, keep me occupied, take my mind off our predicament, could invite our minders to dinner perhaps.'

'Good idea, you do a pasta and I'll do us a good German dish, sausage and sauerkraut perhaps.'

Is this a coincidence or what, Ted mentioning sausage and sauerkraut, Kate's little joke. What psychic forces are at work here? It happens, I spend a couple of enjoyable hours in the kitchen creating my signature tomato pasta, a big one, the hope being that perhaps we might have guests for dinner. It doesn't happen, our minders tactfully advise us, thanks but no, not too much fraternising allowed. They don't want to know too much about us and likewise they don't want us to know too much about them, *don't know can't tell,* pity. I feel I owe these people but that's the way it is in this business. So Ted and myself dine alone on my excellent tomato pasta, the very big tomato pasta. Conversation is a bit difficult, Ted obviously does not want to divulge anything to me and I try not to ask questions but my curiosity gets the better of me, I can't help myself.

'Ted, had enough of life in the peoples paradise, the DDR?'

'Not allowed to say Rex, you might dob me in to the STASI, not allowed to be dissatisfied. Yes I've had a real gutsful, life here is terrible, no freedoms, everyone is suspicious. I've lived here for quite a few years, it's not nice, there's a lot more to life than this miserable existence.'

'What's kept you here, why have you not cleared out long ago?'

'Come on Rex, you're not supposed to ask that question let me just say that suddenly I need to get out if I want to continue living.'

'Ok Ted got the picture, I apologise for the stuff up, for not getting you across the border, putting you at further risk, what can I say, just bad luck.'

We enjoy the pasta and we find a bottle of red in one of the cupboards, we down that as well.

'Ted tell me, what do you know about the STASI?'

'Why do you want to know Rex?'

'Well I think they have a file on me.'

'Really, how could that be?'

I tell Ted about my being in the Air Force and how we had been made aware of the STASI's penchant for keeping files on potential enemies, this included NATO pilots. We were people who could possibly fall into their hands, any information they had about us could be used to extract information; well that was the story our masters gave us.

'Could be some truth in that Rex, I don't really know, I doubt if they would have the nous to be able to do that. There are some bright people in the STASI's ranks but most of them are real low life, dangerous, criminal types, to be avoided.'

The following day it's Ted's turn in the kitchen, his signature dish, sausage and sauerkraut is superb. German sausage, they do know how to make it. We dine alone again, can't convince our minders to join us, pity.

Day three, action, we're being moved. I'm given an East German passport and some other papers, it's a car trip to Bernburg, a village some distance to the north of Liepzig. The trip goes off without incident and we find ourselves in another safe house in Bernburg. Another day, then a fellow comes and gives us some detail about how we are going to get across the DDR border.

There's an extensive area of woodland to the west of Bernburg that extends across the border into West Germany, it's going to be deep in these woods that the actual border crossing will take place, and it's dangerous. The fellow telling us this emphasises the dangerous bit. The border is heavily patrolled and the border guards are trigger happy. The plan is to cross at a controlled point where local farmers are allowed over. The locals have an arrangement with the border guards that allows them to do a bit of cross border trading in farm produce, it's strictly controlled and a there's a fair bit of bribery. We will be under a load of hay. Once across we will crawl out from under and disappear into the woods without the fellow driving the truck knowing. He will not be aware we are on his truck. There's a high degree of risk involved. The guards search the farm trucks occasionally and it's not unknown for potential escapees, if caught, to be summarily shot. The farmers involved in this cross border trading are not to be trusted either. They don't know when someone is concealed on their truck. Hmm, do I want to be hearing this? what's the alternative? Let's face it there is no alternative. The aeroplane's probably the best bet, that's why the Chipmunk had been laid on for Ted however that's long gone, this is plan B and it's dangerous. The fellow telling us this adds that their contacts in the West will be aware we are coming, there will be someone in the woods to meet us. It will be a daylight operation, that's when the farmers do there trading. The dangerous part will be slipping out from under the hay, probably best done once we are some distance from the border while the truck's still moving. You will be on the western side of the border however the locals there are not to be trusted either. The operation is set to go tomorrow morning. We'll be picked up early, around five, and smuggled into the hay before sunrise.

I do not sleep well, bad dreams, the STASI, fingernails, brute of a fellow in a black uniform, they've got Kate, they're raping her, shit! I'm awake, bathed in sweat, settle down, it will all be over inside twenty four hours, I hope!

It's dark, we are rattling along in an old car.

'Ok, out, into that load of hay on the truck there, quick as you can, don't make a sound and try not to move about too much. You'll know when the border is being crossed, there'll be some talking with the border guards. Give it about ten minutes then slip out from under the hay while the truck's still moving and roll into the ditch on the righthand side of the road, don't move. Our people will have spotted you, they'll get you out of the ditch when the coast is clear. Remember that although you'll be on the right side of the border it's still dangerous.'

Buried in hay, not the greatest, dust, don't sneeze.

'How's the arm Ted?'

'Ok, It's not a bad break.'

About an hour or more and there's movement, sound, talking. Thump, something is tossed on top of the hay, something heavy, bit of wriggling to get comfortable again then the truck starts up, we're off. Ted is beside me, can't see him, can't see anything, complete blackness. It's very uncomfortable under the hay rattling along on what feels like an unsealed road, there's dust, we must be in the woods, a back road. Voices, we've stopped, the border, the dangerous DDR border, the death strip. A lot of people have been shot trying to get across this border. The voices move around to the back of the truck, there's talk about the load.

'Hay nichts anderes', ziemlich sicher', 'ja ziemlich sicher'.

('Hay nothing else,' 'quite sure,' 'yes quite sure.')

A short silence then suddenly an explosion of sound very close, its gunfire, an AK47. The bastards are firing into the hay, shit, shit! An excruciating pain in my right arm, the firing stops, must have been four or five shots. Shut up, not a sound, how's Ted, can't see him.

'Ok, auf dem Weg.'

The truck rumbles into motion and we are on our way, shit, my arm! There's blood, my hand works, fingers move, raise my arm a little, yep it works, feel up and down with my left hand, shirts torn, can't feel any great gaping wound, shit!

'That must be about ten minutes.'

'Ted, you ok?'

'Yes, I think we might get off now.'

'Good idea, let's do that.'

We push through the hay towards the back of the truck and get up. There's a shallow wound the full length of my upper right arm, my luck's in. Don't make a sound, don't rock the truck, the driver must not know we are here, yeah right, there's blood on the truck bed.

'Right, out, into the ditch.'

We both drop off the back and scuttle into the ditch at the side of the road. Fortunately the truck's moving slowly, however, I still manage to fall over onto the damaged arm, , the pain. Safe, I think, at the bottom of a ditch and it's on the right side of the border, now let's have a look at the arm. There's a shallow gouge in the flesh along the full length of the upper right arm, looks like a bullet has grazed it, bleeding quite a bit, guess I'll just have to wear it for the time being. There's no sound, no movement, I don't think we've been detected.

'So far so good eh Ted.'

'Got to get lucky sometime. I did like plan A though.'

We lie in the ditch for about an hour, nothing happens, no movement, no sound. I would have thought the truck might have returned by now, but nothing.

'Rex, Otto,' a voice from the undergrowth a bit further off the road.

'Crawl over here.'

We do, there's a fellow skulking in the trees.

'Come with me, keep it quiet, stay in the undergrowth as much as you can, the idea is to avoid being seen by the locals. We walk and crawl behind this chap for quite a while and eventually come to another back road in the forest, there's an old car there, it's for us.

'We off the hook yet?'

'Yes, relax, we're in friendly territory.'

Our guide is a young German chap, excellent English.'

'Well congratulations, you made it. Now the idea is to get you both up to Hanover, that's all I know, all I'm allowed to know, but I hear on the grapevine that you crashed and burned, burned to death a few days ago, what do you think about that?'

'Misinformation.'

'I'll drive you to Bad Lauterberg, it's not far from here, someone else will take you to Hanover.'

'I'd like to get a bandage or something onto this arm, it's starting to give me grief, any chance in Bad Lauterberg?'

The arm was giving me a lot of grief, it was starting to hurt like hell.

'Yes, I know the doc for you, no questions asked, he's done things like this before.'

The doctor was good, a knowing look on his face, his only remark.

'AK47, don't find those in the West, can leave a nasty wound but this is just a graze, nasty one though. I'll put a dressing on it, here are some antibiotics, try and change the dressing every two days.'
And that was it, now Hanover. It was a big Mercedes, a late model and very comfortable. The driver was about thirty, his name was Kurt.

'Kurt, we need to eat, it's been a while and guess what, we've got no money, well I don't think we have, you got any deutschmarks Ted?'

'No, got some of the other stuff but I don't think it will work here.'

'Stop worrying you two, I've got a contingency fund, a substantial contingency fund, where would you like to eat?'

'We're in your hands Kurt.'
He pulls into a big restaurant, part of a large complex just off the road to Hanover. It was good, we both ate up large, I was really hungry. There were several shops in the complex and I was able to find a shirt, Kurt's contingency fund again. My bloodstained shirt was not a good look. A couple of hours driving, very pleasant in the big Merc. It had been an eventful few days and I was feeling the strain, the dangerous side of my chosen career. Eventually Hanover. Kurt advises that his instructions are to drop us at no:6 Stiftstrasse. It's a big grey building with a rather grand entrance. We present ourselves to the girl in the information kiosk not knowing what to expect, or who to ask for. I guess we did not look the greatest. Scruffy, dragged backwards through a hedge, well we had, me showing bloodstains and Ted's arm in a grubby sling.

'I think we are expected, not sure by who?' I offer.
A knowing look from the receptionist and in perfect English.

'Ah yes, just a minute,' and she's on the phone.

'Rex Macare,' it's Nicole Townsend, 'good to see you, very good indeed, come up to my office. Otto, someone will be down to see you in just a minute.'

'Well goodbye Ted, or is it Otto, might not have the pleasure again, I apologise for the rough trip, not meant to be this way, oh well.'

'By Rex, it was a pleasure, I think, all the best.'
I follow Nicole Townsend up a flight of stairs to an office.

'Well Rex, not quite according to plan however here you are and you have delivered your charge, well done, pity about the plane and your untimely death.'

'Well yes Nicole, that's worrying me, my death, who knows about it.'

'No one, the East Germans are very secretive about most things particularly sensitive happenings like this, I doubt if the world will ever hear about you demise.'

'About New Zealand, I was expected back in Auckland a few days ago, people will be worrying about my failure to appear.'

'You mean Kate will be wondering?'

'Yes Kate, has anything been done to let her know I will be a bit late home?'

'No, and the reason is we don't know how much Kate knows, how much you have let slip, we thought we would let you tell her, keep whatever story you have spun intact, we can arrange a phone call from an untraceable source, you can talk to her yourself, how will that fit?'

'Yes I'd like that, will need to be around seven in the morning Auckland time, can that be arranged?

'Yes, that means ten this evening here, I will set it up.'

'Have you got her number?'

'Yes we have Rex.'

'Is it bugged?'

'You have a suspicious mind. We know quite a bit about you but you know all that. Now then I'll book you into a hotel for two days here in Hanover, come back to this office tonight and we'll call Kate, how's that sound?'

'One more thing, I've got no money, all my things are in a bag at Celle airfield, perhaps it can be arranged to get them down here for me Nicole.'

'Not a problem,' she produces my bag from behind her desk. 'We checked you out of Schapers as well, now get some rest. I'll see you tonight, we can make that call, Kurt will drop you off at your new hotel.'

'Well thank you Nicole, look forward to seeing you tonight.'

'Me too.' There's a suggestive look on Nicole's face or is it my imagination.

'Morning Kate.'

'Rex? is that you Rex?'

'Yes Kate it's me, I'll be a bit late getting home, sorry.'

'What? where? I've been worried sick about you and nobody to turn to, nobody to ask, where are you darling? what part of the world are you calling from? please tell me it's the airport here, please!'

'Ah no it's not Auckland but it will be Auckland in a couple of days, got held up, things out of my control but I've got a handle on it now and I'll be right home dear.'

'Where are you?'

'Rather not say Kate.'

'Ok, I'll guess, but you don't have to confirm or deny my darling, it's been sausage and sauerkraut again I'll bet!'

'If you say so dear. I'll be home in about three days. I'll let you know the exact time and date when I've settled a couple of things, love you Kate.'

'Alright my darling, I think I can contain myself until then, I've been imagining all sorts of terrible things but now it's ok, love you.'

'Well Rex, that's tidied that up, I see you've managed to keep Kate in the dark about your activities when you are *out of town for a while,* very good, I compliment you, but, and it's a big but, you will have to confide in Kate sooner rather than later otherwise she could unintentionally make waves and we would not want that to happen.'

'That brings up something Nicole that you might be able to shed a little light on, who exactly am I working for?'

'You know the rules Rex, you only get to know what you need to know, what you don't know you can't tell, that's the way it is.'

'Ok, then what I don't know I can't tell Kate however in the interests of domestic peace perhaps I can divulge a little of what I do know, which is not very much. What's your take on that?'

'You are asking me for an answer?'

'Put it this way, I figure you are closer to, shall we say head office, than Mr Roberts, your man in the field, so perhaps you may be in a better position to sanction just how much I can divulge to Kate. I need to give her something, she's curious. At the moment we have an understanding that she will not ask about what it is that I do but this is not a satisfactory situation and not good for a relationship.'

'Tell me what you know Rex, what you actually do know, not what you've assumed?'

'Ok, these flying tasks I've been carrying out are for the British Government, via an agency, it's clandestine and nobody knows about it. If it turns to worms I will be disowned, the British Government will deny all knowledge. For this I am substantially reimbursed and that's the sum total of my knowledge.'

'How do you know that the ultimate employer is the British Government?'

'Mr Roberts told me it was the Government via an agency.'

'Hmm, naughty. Rex forget the British Government bit. You're employed by an agency, you do not know anything about them except the money is attractive, got that.'

'Ok, got it, I never heard about the British Government being involved, but it's not rocket science to see the connection. I mean Air Force Bases, a Chipmunk, and a lovely girl like you Nicole, the James Bond touch.'

'Kate's a lucky girl, having a charmer like you. Now seriously Rex, yes you can tell her what you know, and I must emphasise only what you actually know, delete the British Government bit, you never heard that. You will need to get Kate to promise never to mention any of this to anyone, the information is for her ears only and it's to give her a little peace of mind, do you think you can handle that?'

'Thank you Nicole, I'll tell Kate only what I actually know, one more thing, when I do a job for you people can I tell Kate about it because that will then be something that I actually know?'

'That's a hard one. The answer is no, but if you really have to then be vague and only after the event. Whatever you do don't divulge anything before being *out of town for a while.'*

'Nicole, you've used the term *out of town for a while,* where did you get that from?'

'I'm a Bond girl, you said so yourself.'

'In that case Nicole, as we've concluded our business here, where's the nearest cocktail bar?'

'Not to be Rex, no fraternising with the hired help. I don't think Kate would approve either, however, I am sorely tempted; another time perhaps.'

Easy Rex, don't poo in your own nest, Kate's your girl now but this Nicole has not exactly slammed the door has she!

I'm in the big jet heading home, very tired, the last few days, the last week, has left me drained and I've got a wounded arm for my troubles. I've been shot, could be dead, and all for money. Is this what I want? I don't know, I don't think so, certainly not long term. Perhaps I need to consider the Cathay thing, a better option. Trouble is I'll get home, the nasty memory will dim a little, I will be enjoying all the money, leading the high life, sharing it with Kate, and it will be great. A career change would restrict me a little, have to tone things down, unable to spend up big whenever I feel like it, a balancing act, big money, the high life, showing Kate a good time, the excitement, the adrenaline rush, the risk, the danger, and the prospect of an early grave, against the more mundane career choice, the airline thing, reduced money, security, relative boredom, living in Hong Kong, that's a big downer. I'll leave the question open, put it off, enjoy the moment. Trouble is I'll just keep putting it off. Right now you need to come up with a story about how you picked up that nasty wound, what are you going to tell Kate? No lies remember, bugger. It's just too hard, try sleeping, have a beer that might help.

CRASH-KEERUMPH, the aircraft ground loops, the propeller flies to bits, the engine stops, dust and smoke everywhere, and suddenly everything goes black.

I come to with a start, must have been dozing, what's happened, I've crashed, no that was several days ago, where am I? It's a big jet, taking me home to Kate, she's going to ask.

'What have you done to your arm?'

'Good heavens it seems to be damaged, how could that have happened, don't know.'

'Don't know! rubbish.'

Wide awake now, cramped airline seat, go for a walk, time for a pee, the beer, what am I going to tell Kate? Try the truth, no lies remember, but she will flip if I tell her a DDR border guard shot me with an AK47, he would probably have killed me if he knew I was there under the hay. Kate will just not accept that, she will freak out and that will be the end of my career as a mercenary, end of the big money, think of something Rex, think real hard. Meal time, there's an exciting in flight meal on offer, yes please. No lies now, perhaps I can be a bit devious with the truth, get away from the gun thing, be vague, no lies, well this is an extreme situation, a potentially life changing one, perhaps a little white one, a little white lie, crap Rex, a lie is a lie, they don't come in different hues. Bugger, enjoy the meal, snooze some more, read a book, do something, but you need to come up with a story for Kate. You did get that message to her about your arrival time, Nicole said she would make sure the message was delivered. That Nicole, she's not bad, imagine her running around in black stockings and a tiny suspender belt. Get a hold on yourself Rex you're fantasizing, but she would look very sexy in black underwear.

Auckland, early morning, busy terminal, immigration, customs, what am I going to tell Kate?

'Reeexx,' Kate's beside herself, she's all over me crying, really crying, kissing me frantically, arms wrapped around me, and my right arm is killing me, the pain, but I daren't say anything.

'Kate I love you, let's go home.'

Wellington

We drive back to Kate's place, my arm, she's going to notice and I've not got a story. There's a bandage covering the whole of my upper right arm, Kate's going to notice the moment our cloths come off.

I sense she's aroused, I'm not wrong. We're barely through the door when Kate starts shedding her clothes right down to those tiny lace knickers, she's teasing me, getting me aroused, it works, the little knickers are incredibly sexy, my erection is immediate. I have trouble getting my pants off and this seems to arouse Kate's desire even more.

'What's this? what's the bandage for Rex?'

'Later Kate, I'll tell you later, right now it's not important.'
We tumble into her big bed, it does not take long, her moaning becomes quite intense and she has a huge orgasm.

'It's been too long Rex, I just have to have it, I even went and bought a vibrator while you were away, what does that tell you. It's something I never thought I would do, not in my wildest dreams, but then you arrived in my life and suddenly sex loomed large in my psyche. I really enjoy it Rex. I've even taken to carrying the vibrator around with me just in case, in case desire becomes unbearable, and you are not here.'

'I don't have a problem with that Kate, sex is the most fantastic thing, something to be nurtured, protected, I love you Kate, I really love you. I had time to reflect this time while I was *out of town for a while,* I discovered feelings I had never experienced before, it's love Kate, I'm in love.'

Perhaps I should be moving in with Kate, perhaps not, not sure about my survival in my chosen career.

'Rex, the bandage?'

'Kate let's have coffee out on the terrace and I'll tell you all about it. Time I let you in on what I do, you've been left wondering too long.'

'Are you sure Rex, I don't want to pry.'

'Very sure Kate, there's this bandage, do you think I should simply not mention it?'

'Ah, well that would be pushing it, am I going to be shocked?'

'Yes.'

'Do I want to know, do I really want to know?'

'Probably not, however you need to know otherwise how can we have a meaningful relationship and I want us to have a meaningful relationship. I love you Kate, I think you know that, we cannot have little secrets.'

'Alright Rex, tell me all, it goes without saying that it's privileged information, for my ears only, not to be repeated, ever!'

I tell Kate about the Liepzig operation, bit skimpy on some of the detail and I don't mention anything about the shooting. The arm wound was inflicted when we were on the back of the truck. When we slid off my arm must have scrapped along something, then I fell on it as well. What I was telling Kate was the truth, the wound was inflicted on the back of the truck, and I did fall on it. I do not want to frighten her with any mention of shooting, that would cause her unnecessary worry.

'It's worse than I'd imagined Rex, your life is in danger when you are *out of town for a while,* that's a bit hard to take in, and it's all for money?'

'Yes, money, big money Kate,' and I tell her just how big the money is.

'I see, now I understand why you do it, I'm at a loss for words, cannot quite get my head around it, the danger, the risk.'

'It's the business I'm in Kate, how long I will be doing it for I don't know. The risk element appeals. I've been taking risks ever since I left home. I'm not sure I could settle into something that did not involve risk, was not exciting, did not give an adrenaline rush, that's the way it is.'

'Ok. I can live with that and thank you for being up front and honest. I do sense you've downplayed the danger bit though, that arm, back of a truck? I'm not going to pry Rex, I love you, I can live with you doing what you want to do. I'm a big girl now, learning fast about what goes on in the real world.'

A package from the Flint Agency arrives the following morning.

I'd been home a few days enjoying a normal life, taking Kate out to dinner, spending a lot of time around at her flat in the evenings, a lot of time in her bed. She was away from Auckland frequently on modelling assignments, it was then that I missed her, realised just how much I loved her, then one evening she comes home from the agency all excited.

'Rex, do I have the deal for you. How about you take Ali and myself down to Wellington for a few days, we'll stay at a flash hotel all expenses paid, plus something extra for you, money that is.'
She says this last bit with that wry look on her face, that look that's invariably linked to something sexual.

'Tell me more Kate, money?'

'It's an agency job, they will pay you for it, chaperoning.'

'Chaperoning?'

'Yes, you look out for us, make sure we don't go off the rails. It's a fashion show, an important one, all the major players will be exhibiting, the agency wants Ali and myself to be there.'

'You mean there will be other girls like you there?'

'Yes Rex, a lot of very attractive girls, you'll love it. It'll be us keeping you on the straight and narrow.'

'How come they want me?'

'At these shows the better agencies always use chaperones, they really do need to keep an eye on their models and they are pretty picky about who they employ as chaperones, there are plenty of sleezy characters in the business.'

'Yes, but why me, I've not done that sort of thing before.'

'They asked me if I had any preferences, the models usually know who they prefer, who to avoid, it was 'no contest.' Ali had a say in it too. We decided that getting you all to ourselves in such a sex charged environment could be, well stimulating!'

'What do you say Rex? oh by the way we'll be the only girls from our agency, just the two of us to look after, to keep happy.'
That wry smile again.

'Sounds great, when do we go, just the three of us?'

'Yep just the three of us, can you manage that, think you can keep us both happy?'

We fly down to Wellington on an early flight and check in to the hotel the agency has booked. A four room suite, quite up market, three bedrooms and a lounge, fully stocked bar, plenty of champagne, big and comfortable.

Three bedrooms? the chaperone sharing with the models? Perhaps the agency thought the girls needed close protection, or did Kate have a hand in this, what mischief does she have in mind?

We get a cab along to the show venue, a big auditorium. This is a big event for the industry, all the major fashion houses will be exhibiting.

'Rex, probably best if you drop us off, nothing really of interest for you here, just a room full of naked ladies. We'll be busy preparing for the two show days.'

'Tell you what why don't I come back around midday and take you both out for lunch, I'd like to do that.'

'Great idea, come in and ask for me, don't know how we'll be fixed but I'm sure it will be alright.'

'Done deal, see you around midday.'

I give Kate a big hug and a kiss. Ali hugs me as well then kisses me passionately her tongue going all the way into my mouth, hmmm! I kill a couple of hours having a look around the city, take the cable car up to the Botanic Gardens, have not done that since I was a kid, a cup of coffee and it's time to get back to the girls.

'Kate Fontaine?'

'Just a minute, I'll find her.'

What a sight, girls everywhere, beautiful girls, all in various stages of undress, some had no cloths on at all. I could feel a swelling in my pants. My presence did not appear to fazz them in the least, this was their normal working environment, the world of the fashion model.

'Rex, there you are,' Kate gives me a kiss, a passionate kiss, her tongue going right into my mouth, what does it mean, did Ali have anything to do with it.

'Rex, this is my friend Tara, Tara Lemaire.'

It stopped me dead in my tracks, there, right there in front of me was this spectacular creature. She did not have much on, lacy little knickers and a fluffy, diaphanous blouse partly open at the front, it did little to conceal her voluptuous breasts, her skin was a light brown, Tahitian was my guess.

'Well hello Tara!'

I choke over my words, I was experiencing a huge erection, my pants were bulging. This is embarrassing, I hope they don't notice, Kate does notice, she gives me a knowing smile.

'Ah, about lunch. Kate why don't you let me take you, Ali, and perhaps Tara, to lunch. I've sorted out a place not far from here, I'm told it's very good. I stopped by just now and booked a table.'

'Great, are you a starter Tara? please say yes, it will give you a chance to meet my man.'

'Yes, I like the look of your man Kate. Perhaps I'd better put on something a little more modest, might get arrested if I'm seen in public like this, give me a minute, I'll be right back.'

'Was that for real Kate, she's really something.'

'Yes she is, top of the line in the modelling world, still on the way up, a real character, wild party girl as well. Give me a minute and I'll find Ali.'

I'm left alone surrounded by all these models with a huge bulge in my pants. Perhaps if I sit down, there's nowhere to sit down, close my eyes, no, just enjoy the sight, it's not every day you're going to find yourself trapped in a room full of beautiful girls with not much on, some with nothing on. This doesn't happen every day now does it!

'Rex,' it's Ali, 'what are you doing standing there perving, you'll get yourself all worked up and be in trouble.'

'Ali, I'm in trouble now.'

She pushes up against me, gives me another one of those passionate kisses. Her hand brushes against the bulge in my pants, she whispers in my ear.

'I want you to fuck me, if only?'

Kate and Tara appear; something more modest? Tara had pulled on a pair of shorts, very brief shorts, she looks even sexier.

The lunch is interesting. An upmarket restaurant, a bang up meal, nothing but the best. My mercenary life style is paying off, I'm flush with cash, able to enjoy the rewards, no longer having to count the pennies and what nicer way to spend it than buying lunch for three beautiful models. I did have a moment of doubt though, would they let Tara be seated? did they have a dress code? She did not have much on in the way of clothes. What she did have on was sensational and she knew it, knew how to present herself. Ali and Kate were right up with the play, provocatively brief shorts and skimpy blouses they looked sensational as well. The outfits were some of the things the girls would be modelling the next day, next summer's fashions.

A superb meal and Dom Perignon, it attracted a bit of attention.

'Who is that fellow spending up big on those beautiful girls?'

He's a mercenary, a fellow who puts his life on the line, gets his arse shot off, makes huge sums of money and gets to screw gorgeous fashion models, that's who he is; eat your heart out!

Lunch was quite a long affair, another bottle of Dom, Irish coffees.

'We had better get back, don't want to get offside.'

'When would you like your chaperone to pick you up?'

'Not sure? I've got an idea. We've only got a couple of hours left here, why don't you make use of the sponsors bar Rex, it's well set up, meant to get the buyers into a good frame of mind, get them to spend up big. The models are encouraged to use the bar, entertain the clients, make them happy, there are no rules and I'm not sure what does go on in there, perhaps you can find out?'

'Sounds a good idea, I'll do that, you'll know where to find me when you're through.'

Not really a good idea Rex, a free bar and unlimited drinks, something I do not really need just now. There's another fellow in the bar, he strikes up a conversation.

'Hello there, I'm Mark Mayland and you're …?'

'Rex, Rex Macare, bit of time to kill, this appears to be a good spot.'

'Yep it is, amazing what can happen at some of these shows, not a chaperone are you?'

'Well I am looking after a couple of girls, a first for me, how about yourself?'

'Same thing, Christchurch Agency, three girls to lookout for, your first time? let me brief you, a few clues to what goes on. Chaperones need to keep an eye on their charges, pressure is put on the models occasionally by some of the less reputable fashion houses, 'be nice to the buyers, encourage sales.' Sometimes the girls go a bit overboard with their favours, someone needs to keep an eye on things.'

Interesting. Kate had not mentioned any of this, not mentioned that I was meant to police their behaviour, keep them on the straight and level not drag them into bed for uninhibited sex, oh well!

'Cast your eye over there Rex.'

Two attractive well dressed women in their mid-thirties had come in and seated themselves at the bar, 'champagne please,' it was that sort of place.

'See that, keep an eye on those two.'

It was just a few minutes before an inviting glance was directed in our direction.

'They're on the hunt. We see this quite often, probably buyers visiting Wellington, they want a bit of action.'

'Really?'

'Yes really, believe me.'

'They can be very generous with their favours, willing to pay for it as well, and it's usually great sex.'

'You're kidding me Mark, you know about these things?'

'Well yes I do, but right now I'm not a starter, I've got my hands full, but feel free, you'll find them quite willing, on for anything.'

I was astonished, naïve me, unaware of what went on in the big world of fashion.

'Ah, not now, I'm tied up as well, but you've got me looking at things in a whole new light.'

The two ladies at the bar sense we are not starters, they finish their drinks and leave. I chat with Mark for an hour or so and enjoy another couple of drinks then suddenly Tara bursts in, her personality dominating the room, a commanding presence, the X factor. Tara does not just come into a room, she *arrives*. The shorts are gone, it's the tiny lace knickers and diaphanous blouse open at the front again.

Christ Tara it's not the girls changing room it's the sponsor's bar.

She comes over and plants a kiss on me, just a little kiss, my erection roars into life.

'Finished for the day, Kate and Ali will be along a little later, how about we have some Dom, they've got it here,' she spots Mark.

'Hello Mark,' her voice goes cold, icy.

'Tara, not seen you for some time.'

'No you haven't, not since that time you got me drunk and tried to get into my knickers.'

Mark looks taken aback, wishing the ground would open up and swallow him.

'Why don't you drink up and piss off.'

Wow ah, strong words, Tara is fired up. I think she might be feeling the effects of our earlier drinking, she was certainly rearing to go.

'Goodbye Mark, don't come back, I fancy Rex here, he's got what I want.'

My erection is now straining my pants, will it be noticed? It is.

'Oohh Rex, what's that down there?'

Tara presses up close and puts a hand firmly on the bulge in my pants. There are only two other people in the bar, fortunately they're not looking in our direction. I can't help myself, I slide a hand up the inside of her thigh, right up to the tiny lace knickers, her eyes close and she lets out a little moan.

'That feels so great Rex,' she's squeezing the bulge in my pants.

'No wonder Kate's such a happy girl these days. I wonder if she'd mind you sharing it around, I reckon you do already. Ali seems to be happy, she get a bit of this as well?'

Tara is looking straight at me as she says it, a final squeeze and she takes her hand away.

'Another time perhaps Rex.'

Kate arrives and shortly after, Ali, 'another bottle of Dom.' Quite a bit of Dom goes down, the four of us are enjoying the moment. People come and go the men unable to take their eyes off the three girl, they certainly look stunning in their skimpy clothing. After a while Tara excuses herself.

'Got a date, have to go, hope he's up to it. I'd rather come home to your place though, how would you like that Rex?'

Whatever does she mean, the wildest thoughts rush through my head, my erection remains rock hard, the girls notice it.

'She's a devil that Tara, what's she done to you Rex? You'll just have to stay on that bar stool till your lust subsides, can't walk around like that.'

'Thanks Kate, it's nice that someone's looking after me, I appreciate it.'

'Mind you we could smuggle you out like that, rush you off, take advantage of it before you fade, what do you reckon Ali?'

'That's not a silly idea, shall we?'

'Christ, what do you think I am, some sort of tame stallion? here have another drink and perhaps we should think about dinner and a decent night's sleep, you two need to be on your game tomorrow.'

'You're right Rex, perhaps we should give it a rest, we've got another two days here.'

'Down the hatch, let me be the good chaperone and see you both home.'

The morning sun is pouring in, Kate's still asleep. I roll over and tickle her nipples with my tongue. I take one lovely breast into my mouth. Kate lets out a little moan, her eyes still shut. I move my mouth to her other breast and slide a hand down over her belly onto her pubic mound. Stroking it gently I slip my fingers inside, she lets out a little moan and opens her eyes. Both her hands grasp my hand and start thrusting it in and out, arousal comes quickly. I throw the sheets off, spread her legs and push my burgeoning erection deep inside thrusting gently.

'Morning darling' she mumbles as she arches her back pushing up into me.

'Morning Kate, sleep well?'

I continue thrusting gently and her arousal intensifies, her panting gets faster, she starts to moan and squirm about on the bed, I find myself thrusting deeper and faster. I'm now mightily aroused, suddenly an orgasm. We both climax at the same time, it's wonderful, a wonderful way to start a day.

'I'll wake Ali, big day coming up.' I look in on Ali's bedroom, she's appears to be sound asleep.

'Wakey wakey Ali, you're working today, remember.'

I go over to the bed and shake her gently, a drowsy eye opens.

'Rex, fuck me.'

I'm not expecting that response and it revives my fading erection.

'Ali, what can I do, your insatiable.'

'You can fuck me right now, that's what you can do. I could hear you two in the next room a little while ago, I thought I was dreaming. It's got me aroused, made me desperate, I've got myself all worked up, please Rex, do it now, fuck me.'

My erection is now rock hard and sticking out the front of my briefs. She gasps, takes it in both hands, pushes the bedclothes away and drags me onto her pushing it all the way in, her back arches and she thrusts upwards, it's lovely. The intensity increases and she starts thrashing about on the bed moaning loudly.

'Now get up Ali, you're working today, that was magnificent. I'm supposed to be chaperoning you two girls, remember, not fucking you, but that was really nice.'

I step into the lounge that's part of the suite, Kate's fixing something for breakfast.

'That took a while Rex, Ali a little slow to climax?' a wry smile on her face.

She presses up against me, hand down inside my briefs squeezing what's left of my erection.

'I want it again Rex, you're screwing Ali in there has turned me right on.'

Day one of the fashion show, next summer's sports wear, what will I do?

'Rex, I've got you a front row seat, right in there with the sharp ender's, a whole new experience for you.'

'Thank you Kate, there have been a lot of new experiences since I met you, a lot of lovely new experiences, thank you again.'

'My pleasure Rex, you can repay the favour sometime, in bed perhaps, sooner rather than later.'

'Easy Kate, I can't go around all day with a bulge in my pants and I can't deal to you here, well perhaps I can, what's in this little side room?'

'Settle Rex, yes you're right, it's not fair of me to get you going now, I can wait a while, I think!'

I seek out my front row seat, a prime position, in amongst the movers and shakers. Kate has done well, but how am I going to relate to these people, we move in different worlds. Theirs is one of design and fashion, affectation and posturing. Gays, a lot of gay people, probably why the models don't seem to be overly concerned by males in the dressing rooms, their nakedness fails to arouse much response. It certainly aroused a response in me, my brief exposure to it yesterday was mightily arousing.

I strike up a conversation with the fellow seated next to me, a buyer from a major Sydney department store, he's after the latest from New Zealand. He tells me New Zealand designers are highly regarded in Australia. He's a regular visitor to these New Zealand events.

The show gets underway, first out, Tara. They are making use of her spectacular body and strong personality, that X factor, to set the tone, it certainly succeeds. Tara's wearing the same outfit she had on the day before, those little shorts and that blouse, it's open at the front again. There's some comment from the front rowers. I think they're impressed, Tara really is a spectacular sight. She stops in front of me, pirouettes around a couple of times and pokes her bottom out provocatively. Those legs, those thighs, the thighs I'd run my hand up, all the way up! I'm squirming in my seat, Tara's incredibly sexy. A string of attractive models follow. Next year's summer sports outfits are all rather brief, rather provocative, could be a difficult summer for the boys. Kate appears, she targets me, or am I so blinded by lust that I'm losing it. Kate's modelling brief little shorts and a completely see through top, her lovely breasts right there for all to see, the breasts I'd had in my mouth just a short time ago. Kate oozes sex appeal her body looking quite spectacular. Perhaps having sex just before a show gives a girl an edge, a certain radiance. I wonder if Tara had sex this morning? Next year's summer fashions appear to be all about the 'sexy look.' Ali comes out, she's also modelling a pair of shorts, a little more modest than the other girls, and a cheeky top that's quite loose fitting giving glimpses of her ample breasts, the overall image is very sexy. Ali's also looking radiant, she too targets me. My buyer friend turns to me.

'You know these girls?'

'Ah yes, I do,' *and I screwed a couple of them before breakfast this morning.*

The show continues, there's certainly plenty for the buyers to mull over. Eventually the compère announces the final offering, something a little different, something for the privacy of the bedroom.

Ali appears, there are gasps from the audience, sexy, the word takes on a whole new meaning. Ali has a superb body, something I am all too familiar with and having enjoyed sex not long before the show she's definitely quite radiant, but it's what she's wearing that's raised the tempo and what's causing me considerable discomfort. I'm squirming in my seat just about bursting out of my pants. All Ali has on is a G string and a pair of braces that only just cover her nipples, how can this possibly be a fashion garment? The girl is practically naked and looks sexier than when she's got no cloths on at all It's definitely a bedroom only offering. I think the show organisers have included it purely to test buyer reaction. How they convinced Ali to model it, well who knows, perhaps she has an erotic side to her that I have not seen yet. She stops in front of me and thrusts her pelvis, her perfectly formed pubic mound, right at me. I'm beside myself with lust and I sense a wetness in my pants; lay off Ali, it's too much! She spins around and struts off along the catwalk. There's a murmur from the audience, I don't think many of them had seen anything quite like Ali before. My buyer friend turns to me again.

'Very sexy; you *do* know this girl?'

'Yes I *do* know her.' *I know her very well, I fucked her this morning.*

He didn't seem to be uncomfortable, Ali's outfit had not aroused him, definitely gay. Any red blooded male would be beside himself by now, I was.

The models were all incredibly attractive, top of the line, but as far as I was concerned my two charges, and Tara, had stolen it.

Ali you are just the most erotic creature, perhaps you can hang onto that creation and we'll have a private viewing later, I'm fantasising.

It's been a long day for the girls and an interesting one for me, no it's been more than that, *Ali in that G string*, the world of the high end fashion model. A couple of drinks in the hotel cocktail bar, then dinner. We decide to retire early, The girls were both tired and tomorrow is the main show day. The latest lingerie was to be the highlight, the models would be required to really strut their stuff, impress the buyers. Kate and Ali had been chosen to model some of the more skimpy designs and this had them rather excited, apparently it was a sought after role. When they told me this it had me excited as well. Could be I might find it a bit too much; again! Two beautiful girls with next to nothing on, two girls who I have enjoyed incredible sex with, running around in their knickers in front of me, *don't touch*!

'Rex, you will enjoy tomorrow, we'll be up there wearing very little, something I know you have trouble with, but this time, no touching. We will not be alone, there'll be other girls, gorgeous girls, and knowing you as intimately as we both do, we think you just might have a hard time, a *very hard* time.'

A hard time alright, I've been rock hard most of the day, I wonder if they've noticed. The reference to we, what did that suggest. I had enjoyed sex with Ali on three occasions and it had been great but it was not as if we were doing it on a regular basis. Ali did not comment, her expression gave nothing away, I wonder what she's thinking, desiring, is she becoming aroused by the conversation, I certainly am. We are seated at a small table in the hotel cocktail lounge, suddenly I'm aware of a hand under the table fiddling with the bulge in my pants, it was Ali. This could be a problem I'm not sure I can contain myself, the stimulation's becoming too much, am I going to ejaculate and embarrass myself. There's another hand geez they're both at it, I'm definitely going to embarrass myself. Both girls are giving me sly looks.

'Rex, you had better duck into the men's room before we go for dinner, don't want to make a mess now do we.'

'Yes, I think I will, you devils.'
Both girls are smiling, knowing looks on their lovely faces.

Dinner is great, a couple of bottles of red. The girls are being provocative, the conversation sexy, they are getting their chaperone aroused even more. I'm in trouble, the trip to the toilet had done little to reduce the bulge in my pants. We did not linger in the dining room, we told each other that sleep was required, tomorrow was going to be a big day, I don't think any of us quite believed ourselves. Off to our suite, our separate rooms.

I was in the bathroom facing the mirror when Kate came in and placed both arms around my body, both hands on my erection. She had shed all her cloths, quite naked, a magnificent sight, I felt faint with lust, I had to have her. We stumbled over to the bed and she went down on me immediately, I could feel a climax approaching. There was movement at the bedroom door, it was Ali, naked, beautiful in the dim light. When she saw Kate down on me she gasped, I'm not sure she had seen this before and I think she was totally overcame with desire. She came over to the bed, pushed Kate off, and went down on me herself taking what was now a huge erection deep into her mouth. She was in a frenzy, gasping and moaning, sucking, licking, her head going up and down, the sensation was unbelievable, I found myself thrusting up into her mouth, she was in a real state, suddenly she rolls off me onto her tummy.

'Fuck me, fuck me now Rex, from behind; please!'
I take her thighs in both hands and draw her back onto my bulging penis, she pushes back vigorously absolutely carried away, we go at it like there's no tomorrow, her whole body moving back and forth, me thrusting deeply, where is this going, what's happened to Ali? It does not take long, we both reach an explosive climax and collapse

in a heap, she's crying pitifully.

'What's wrong with me, why am I like this, why am I so desperate for sex?'

Her sobbing increases, she's really crying her eyes out now. The mood changes, the sexually charged atmosphere gives way to one of compassion, compassion for Ali. I suspect our fucking has turned Kate on, she will be desperate for sex, but now everything has changed, we have a problem. My erection fades, suddenly sex is not so important, we need to comfort Ali, she's in a mess and she has to be at the top of her game in the morning.

Breakfast, Ali is ok, embarrassed but ok. Kate and I had spent some time calming her down, pointing out that very physical sex was ok, enjoyable, nothing to be ashamed of, satisfying a pent up desire is a good thing.

'Sex is good for you Ali, it's just a pity you don't have a man who can give you this satisfaction.'

'Well he does give me quite a lot of satisfaction Rex, since Whangaroa he's a different man, a lover, a real lover, but he's just not in the same league. I've tried all the provocative things, the little knickers, the tiny singlet, all those things that make you, Rex, want to rape me, why doesn't it work with Jeff?'

'You're right there Ali, the sight of you in your skimpy underwear really does bring me on, there's definitely something odd about Jeff though. Stop worrying, there's nothing wrong with you Ali, believe me, I know. Whenever the desire becomes too much I'm available, it's incredible having sex with you.' I'm looking straight at Kate as I say this.

'That's right Ali, I don't have a problem sharing Rex in fact there are advantages, I find it extremely arousing seeing you two doing it and when Rex takes me immediately after it's an incredible sensation, what we have going here is something wonderful and it gives you satisfaction as well Ali.'

What am I hearing, a commitment to a threesome, two beautiful women who want unbridled sex with me, frequently.

It's the last day of the show, this will be hard. Watching two lovely girls who I've been fucking parading in front of me in the latest lingerie.

The show is spectacular, Kate, Ali, and Tara, all model skimpy little numbers. They go out of their way to flaunt themselves right in front of me, it's more than I can take. Show's over, now the promoter's party for all those involved in the industry.

Until now my life has been far removed from anything to do with fashion, however, since taking up with Kate, a whole new world has opened up. All sorts of people, buyers, promoters, designers, manufacturers, sales people, and a fair sprinkling of models will be at the party. It seems only the better looking girls have been invited, better looking being very subjective, they are all spectacular. Kate, and Ali are there, with their chaperone.

Have to keep an eye on my girls, definitely my girls.
The posing and posturing, the 'look at me' types, some big egos on display, a uniquely trendy crowd, and me. I had nothing in common with this lot, they inhabit a different world.

'Rex,' it's Tara.'

'You look like little boy lost, here let me take you by the hand and show you around, show you off you handsome beast, they'll think you're my man, I'd better watch my back.'
Tara takes me over to a girl standing alone.

'Rex this is Erika, we're both with the same agency.'
Erika is a knockout, a fiery looking brunette in her mid-twenties.

'Well hello Rex. Tara, where did you find this one and are there any more?'

'This one's Kate's, she found him first.'

'So you are Rex, I've heard about you.'

'Really,' where's this leading? 'Where could you possibly have heard about me.'

'The smile on Kate's face tells all Rex, better than words.'

'That's very perceptive Erika, here, some champagne perhaps.' A girl with a loaded tray is nearby, I take two glasses for the girls and one for myself.

'Well here's to whatever,' I offer.

'To mischief,' it's Tara.

'Definitely mischief,' from Erika.

'That's enough, times up Erika, I'm moving this hunk on, come with me Rex.' Tara steers me away from Erika.

'She's a maneater that one, a party girl. Let's go over here, there are some nice girls I'll introduce you to, safer.' We are moving through the crowd when suddenly I feel Tara stiffen.

'Shit, there's that asshole Mayland, your drinking mate Rex.' It's Mark from the sponsor's bar, the fellow Tara had been so abrupt with. He's with a group of girls who appear to be quite young.

'That prick will be screwing all of them, they'll be young innocent kids from Christchurch, he'll be the chaperone and he'll be right into their pants, beats me why that agency tolerate him, probably screwing one of the principles.' We avoid Mark and spot Kate, she's talking to the fellow she'd been with in the pub that first time I'd laid eyes on her.

'Rex, do you know about Brian, Kate's ex,' Tara asks.

'No, Kate's never mentioned him.'

'Oh, well Brian's quite a talented designer, works for one of the majors, nice guy but never quite lit Kate's fire, unlike you, you sexy man, you've turned her into an inferno. They were together for about a year until you swept her away.'

'Oh well what can I say, do I want to talk to Brian?'

'No, you don't want to talk with Brian, come over here and talk to Jenna.'

Jenna is another knockout. I don't think I've been amongst such a collection of stunning girls in all my life. Jenna also works for the same Auckland agency as Tara.

'Rex, found you,' it's Kate, she throws herself at me and plants a kiss smack on my lips hugging me lovingly.

'All this temptation, thought I'd lost you, have to watch out for that Tara,' she gives Tara a wink.

'It did cross my mind Kate, thought I might rush him off while I had him, but you'd have killed me.'

'I would.'

'I think this girl loves you Rex, bugger, guess I'll have to look elsewhere.'

'Tara, you telling me there's no man, I don't believe it.'

'Not at the moment, the last one took off to France, shot through for big money in Paris, bit of a bugger, we had a great thing going.'

I spot Ali talking to a fellow nearby, she looks uncomfortable. I go over and take her arm.

'Over here Ali.'

'Rex, you've saved me, that Marty is a pain, jumped up little pipsqueak.'

'Was that Marty? I encountered him at the party in Auckland a while back, I agree with you, jumped up little pipsqueak.'

'He had the gall to proposition me, the cheek of the fellow, should have told him I'd get my minder to deal to him.'

'Your minder? oh yes, that's me, right. I'll go right over and whack him.'

'No no Rex, this is a nice party, not some back ally pub, why don't you just go over and have a quiet word with him.'

'A quiet word? yes right, a quiet word.'

Another new experience coming up, a quiet word! Hmmm!

'Right, excuse me for a few moments girls I need to earn my keep, carry out my chaperone duties.'

The girls are looking at me a little apprehensively.

'Rex, what are you going to do, don't make a scene, please.' Kate's rather concerned.

'Just a quiet word Kate, promise.'

How will I deal with this, ah I know, suddenly I've got a crafty plan. I pick up a couple of drinks from one of the girls circulating with trays of champagne and go over to Marty.

'Marty, how are you, not seen you since that party in Auckland.'

'It's Rex isn't it, Rex Macare the contract pilot.'

'You've got it, I'm the fellow who doesn't dabble in drug running, well not unless it's worthwhile.'

'Really is that right, I was only joking about the meth thing.'

'No no, you hit the nail on the head, running meth is big business; here have a drink, I think it's Dom, the good stuff.'

'Thanks Rex, cheers.'

'Cheers Marty, and oh yes, there is something, that girl in the G string yesterday, Ali, a real sex fiend.'

'Is she, really, that outfit was the sexiest thing I think I've ever seen, boy would I ever like a piece of her ass.'

'So she tells me.'

Marty stares at me startled, his drink spilling down his front.

'And if you ever so much as go near her again or make improper suggestions I'll tear your bloody throat out, now piss off you've outlived your welcome.'

He starts to shake, puts his glass down, and vanishes.

'What did you say, he literally fled the room, can't see any blood on the floor, how did you do it?'

'Well girls, I told him that you're both my private property, that I keep you under very close supervision, particularly in bed, and that if he ever shows his face again I'll get the Mongrel Mob to gang rape him.'

'You didn't.'

'I did so, now then some more of this lovely Dom Perignon.'

'You're a darling Rex.'

They're both kissing me, I wonder if this could be a career path, professional chaperone.

We go back to the hotel in a limousine that the show organisers have provided, Tara comes with us, she's staying at the same hotel.

'Where's your minder Tara?'

'Don't know, I think he's more interested in getting into Erika's pants. He's supposed to be chaperoning her, Jenna, and myself, haven't seen a sign of him, anyway I don't want him around cramping my style, I'd rather have some fun with you people.'

What does she mean? what is Tara hinting at? We are in the back of the big limo all a bit tipsy, too much to drink, any reservations we may have had are well gone, the atmosphere is charged. There's some kissing and cuddling and I'm being groped, it's Tara, Tara? What's she up to? 'just having some fun?' what will Kate and Ali think? Tara has a hand inside my pants and is fiddling with my rapidly hardening erection, it's a lovely sensation. Kate is kissing me passionately and her hand too slips inside my pants. Ali is on the seat beside me, I sense she wants in on the action so I slide my hand under her dress and up her thigh, she's got that G string on again. I push it aside and stroke her vagina slipping my fingers inside, she moans with pleasure. Her moaning becomes louder and she starts writhing about on the seat. Tara is down on the limo floor, down on her knees, she'd unzipped my fly and has my huge erection in her mouth, I cannot believe it, what will Kate be thinking. Tara's head is moving up and down, the sensation is beyond anything I could ever imagine. We get to the hotel, up to the suit, and into Kate's room. It has a super king size bed, a really big one, *a party bed.* The tops come off a couple of champagne bottles. Tara's taking her clothes off, there's not much to take off. In no time she's down to her panties, her ample breasts thrust out, a stunning sight. I'm aroused even more, what had just happened in the limo fresh in my mind. Kate and Ali are standing there slightly in awe of what Tara is doing. I go over to Kate, press up against her and run my hand up her thigh, right up, and stroke the soft velvety bulge under her knickers, she gives a little moan and starts to take her clothes off. Ali intervenes, grabs my head with both hands and kisses me. She's quite aroused, her tongue goes deep into my mouth, she's making a gasping noise. Ali is wearing an outfit from the show, a lacy top and a short belted dress, next summer's fashion. I undo the belt and the little dress drops to the floor, she's wearing that G string, that incredibly sexy G string. I can't help myself, I push the G string down around her thighs and cup my hand over her pubic mound stroking it gently. Ali responds immediately, pulls my pants down with both hands and grasps my mighty erection, she rubs it over her belly and tries to push it into herself. The girls, beautiful in there nakedness, crowd around, their lovely bodies pressed against me. The rest of my clothes come off. It's an erotic scene, they all want a part of me, stroking my erection, rubbing it against their bodies, pressing it hard against their tummies. We move to the bed. They are rubbing my erection over their breasts, their nipples in particular, it seems to give them great pleasure. Tara's naked body is quite spectacular, her light brown skin shining. I don't feel at all embarrassed, my monstrous erection, three naked girls, their hands all over it, arousing themselves, wanting it, all breathing heavily, all pressing their bodies hard against it. I feel a huge desire to have Tara, to really have her, she arouses an incredible feeling in me, straight out lust. I want to bury my head between those magnificent breasts, to thrust my erection deep into her, fuck her senseless. What's happening to me?

I'm losing it, descending into extreme crudity, I can't restrain myself any longer. Tara must want it, that business in the limo, she really went for me, I think it would have been a lot more had there been time, well there's time now. I push Tara onto her back, she responds enthusiastically grabs my huge erection and pushes it all the way in arching her back, pushing up at me, obviously enjoying every moment. I'm beside myself with lust and pleasure. Kate and Ali are watching, a little incredulous at the intensity of our love making, it's aroused them both; it's an erotic atmosphere, Tara and me fucking, Kate and Ali masturbating. It continues on for quite a while, I just can't get enough of Tara, she's a whole new experience, I've not had it this good ever. Eventually we tire, the intensity subsides. Kate and Ali have got themselves into quite a state, they both want me, both want what Tara has just enjoyed, both want to be fucked.

It's sometime later, I've been able to satisfy Kate and Ali, Tara had set me on fire. I was able to really give it to the two girls and they loved it. Both finished up thrashing about on the bed moaning with pleasure. We are spread around the big bed tangled in the sheets, all naked, enjoying some of the champagne that the girls had hi-jacked from the party. Kate is on her back beside me, an erotic sight, glowing, the aftermath of sex. I was pouring champagne onto her lovely breasts, It was running down her front and pooling in her navel, then on down to her pelvis. I was licking it up with my tongue, sucking on her nipples, following the trail down, a brief stop at her navel, and on down to her pubic mound. I buried my face between her thighs and penetrated her with my tongue, she cried out with pleasure, clutched my head and pushed it hard against herself. Kate shrieked with extasy, extreme arousal, grabbed my swollen penis, spread her legs and pushed it deep inside herself, she was in quite a state. I glanced over to where Tara and Ali were playing around on the edge of the bed, pouring champagne over each other and licking it off; the party was degenerating. The girls had Kate's vibrator. Tara was using it at the same time she had her head down between Ali's thighs, her tongue inside her. Ali was moaning with pleasure.

It went on well into the night. We became increasingly intoxicated, pouring champagne over each other, licking it off, masturbating, oral sex, a lot of fucking. Eventually the intensity slowed and we dropped off to sleep, my last fuzzy memory, an unconscious Kate and me trying to enter her for the umteenth time with an erection that had died.

Sunshine is streaming through the window onto the big bed. We are all naked, lying around amongst the sheets. I feel a hand on my tummy, it slides down and starts to fiddle with my penis, it's Tara. I catch her eye and she silently mouths the words *fuck me*. My erection's immediate, I roll onto my back and she goes down on me. It's something quite special. Tara's body is spectacular all the curves, the bumps, the breasts, everything's perfect. Kate and Ali are asleep, exhausted by last night's activities. Tara keeps at it, I can feel a climax not far away. She gives a little moan, raises her head, and mounts me her lovely body rising and falling, I thrust up into her. She starts moaning with pleasure, it wakes Kate and Ali. They lie there watching. I know this will arouse Kate, not sure about Ali. Tara's moaning gets louder, she's writhing about enjoying the moment. I explode into her just as she reaches orgasm and collapses on top of me. There's a moment of silence, then Kate rolls over and pushes Tara away. Kate's lying on her tummy, her bottom, her beautiful bottom, raised a little, it was a very provocative sight.

'Fuck me Rex right now, I love it this way.'

'Coffee, tea?' We're on a plane for Auckland, going home from what has been an incredible Wellington experience. Tara is on the same flight, apparently the agency she works for is Auckland based. We might be seeing some more of Tara Lemaire, a lot more perhaps.

The French Job

'Monsieur Macare?'

'Yes.'

'My name is Pierre Brodeur. I believe you are a freelance pilot, would that be correct?'

It's early morning in Auckland, a phone call, out of the blue.

'Perhaps.'

'Monsieur I am inquiring whether or not you might be interested in doing some flying for us in a Piper Cherokee Six aircraft.'

'Possibly, depends what's involved, can you tell me a bit more?'

'I would like to talk to you face to face, somewhere in the city perhaps, or I can call around to your place. I don't want to discuss it over the phone.'

'My place, later today, I'll be at home.'

'That would be good. I'll be there around midday.'

'Ok, see you then.'

French, well he sounded French, what could the French want with me? Club Med, Monsieur Jacques Joubeit perhaps? He appears to know where I live.

Knock knock, Monsieur Brodeur. A French version of Mr Roberts, oh shit! 'We understand you take on flying jobs that can involve some risk, you do this for money, am I correct?'

'Possibly, but tell me how did you find this out?'

'I'm not at liberty to divulge that but people who have used your services speak highly of you.'

I'll hit him right between the eyes, see how he reacts.

'That would be the DGSE right?'

His face gives nothing away.

'No, we have no dealings with the DGSE we are a private

organisation.'

Yeah right, this fellow's got DGSE written all over him. Don't push it, don't antagonise him, you don't know anything about him yet, could be something right out of left field, something interesting, something where you don't get your arse shot off. Hear what he has to say.

'We would like to offer you some flying in North Africa, we are prepared to pay handsomely for your services.'

'Interesting, who are *we*, and why are you way out here in New Zealand seeking me out?'

'We have our reasons. You are good at what you do, night flying in light aircraft, low level.'

'You mean you want an unknown for this, a completely unknown, someone from the other end of the earth and you think I could be this person.'

'Something like that.'

'How sure are you that I'm completely unknown?'

I am known, the fellow making inquiries at Schapers Hotel in Celle, who was he? and the DGSE, they know about me.

'We are quite sure.'

Easy Rex, either they really don't know as much as they would have you believe, or there's a game of bluff being played out here.'

'Ok, you've got me interested, but who are *we* and what exactly would you be asking me to do?'

'We are a private company with interests in Algeria. As you know there's a war going on in that country, France against the FLN. We want you to fly one of our agents into Algeria and fly him out again three days later. It will be a private aircraft, a Piper Cherokee. We will give you return tickets to Paris where you will pick up the aircraft and fly it to Gibraltar. It will be a night-time operation out of Gibraltar. When it's completed you will fly the aircraft back to Paris.

We will deposit 150,000 Swiss Francs into a numbered account in a Zurich bank, half before you leave New Zealand, the remainder when you arrive back in New Zealand.'

'When do you want this to happen?'

'Three weeks from now. I will give you three days to think it over then I will contact you for your answer.'

'You've got me interested, can I contact you.'

'Yes, here's a number to call, a girl will answer, she will pass on any message you may have.'

'Tell me, why the aeroplane, what's wrong with a boat, Algeria's got a long coastline.'

'Yes they have however the FLN's got the coastline pretty well covered, the coastal people cannot be trusted.'

'Ok, that all sounds pretty interesting, see you in three days.'

150,000 Swiss Francs, that's about 245,000 New Zealand dollars, that's a shit load of money, how can I not do this? Numbered Swiss bank account, real James Bond stuff, tax free, money laundering, profits from crime, I'm getting in deep, what the hell, I do like the money.

The FLN, I've heard the stories, seen some pictures, not a nice lot, if they get their hands on me it would be goodbye nurse big time and it would be a very unpleasant goodbye. The money, that's well over a year's salary in an airline, and in just a few days, bit of a no brainer really. I'm getting sucked in further, further into my chosen career.

Kate's down in Wellington doing a photo shoot, it'll be three days without her, three days to decide if I'm going to sell my soul to the French for mega bucks, bit of a no brainer. Yes I will take up their offer, I mean 150,000 francs in an anonymous account, could be I won't have to work for the rest of the year, won't have to risk getting my arse shot off for Mr Roberts, Kate would like that.

The following day I get a call from an old Air Force mate, Russ Horsley. Russ was the fellow who had flown that Cessna in Vietnam. He had given it all away, too dangerous. Came back to New Zealand in search of something else, bit like myself.

'Rex, not seen you for a while, how about we catch up, the Paddington in Parnell, this afternoon.'

'Good timing Russ, I'm at a loose end, say around two.'

'Done, look forward to it.'

It will be good to catch up with Russ, find out how he's been going in the mercenary world, see if he's rich and famous yet.

'Rex, great to see you.'

It was Russ, shit, he was missing part of an arm.

'You're staring Rex, bit short on the left side eh, lucky I'm right handed.'

'What the hell Russ, what's life dealt to you?'

'A shit hand that's what, restricted my career options.'

'A beer, quick, let me, what's your preference Russ?'

'Monteiths Black draught, great stuff, puts hair on your chest.'

My current favourite as well. I get a couple of Monteith's, but Russ's arm what's happened?

'Ok Russ, give it to me, looks like you've been dealt to, big time.'

'Well I managed to get onto the mercenary world of flying. The very first job my number came up. A shell took my lower arm clean off, lucky to get out of it alive, a real bugger. Career prospects not good at the moment, in fact right now I'm contemplating a career change, but what? I don't know, perhaps a tin arm and get back into flying, but tell me how have you been doing?'

'Well Russ I'm donkey deep in the mercenary business in Europe. I commute from Auckland for each assignment, well I've done all of three so far with another in the works. So far luck's been on my side but, and it's a big but, how long will it last?'

'Yeah, I got into it here in Auckland as well. I was approached by a fellow offering good money, really good money, for a bit of dodgy flying in Germany. I took him up on it. In no time he had me flying into the DDR at night doing a bit of photography. I think I was set up, don't really know, but the so called picture taking put me right into a highly defended area, big calibre radar controlled automatic cannon fire, bloody lucky to get out of it with my life.'

Gütersloh, the shot up Chipmunk that Scruff had seen, could that have been Russ?

'Russ, let me run this past you. Mr Roberts, a lot of money, a Chipmunk fitted with camera gear operating out of Gütersloh at night into the DDR. Photography of some building or other but really a live target to assess the capability of the Soviet's latest weaponry for shooting down a low flying aircraft.'

'How in hell do you know all that Rex?'

'I work for Mr Roberts as well and a buddy of mine saw you on the tarmac at Gütersloh after you got back on that night about four months ago, not a pretty sight, small world eh Russ.'

'Geezz Wayne, very small world. I guess you had no idea that I worked for Mr Roberts, well I've not seen you for several months in fact the last time we met was just after you got back from that big OE of yours. This is just incredible, unbelievable, who else has Mr Roberts got on his payroll and what's the New Zealand connection?'

'Don't know Russ but Mr Roberts is not to be believed, well put it this way, he's not all that truthful. He's MI6 I'm certain of it. They have little respect for the lives of their operatives perhaps that's why they use us colonials, expendable.'

'Expendable?'

'Well it appears that way. I was set up at Fulder in Germany, a live target for the Soviet's upgraded SA-3, bloody lucky to survive. When I tackled Roberts about it he did not exactly say as much but he did not deny it either. So there you are Russ, mercenaries are expendable. Perhaps there's a bright side to your unfortunate episode, you're no longer in the firing line.'

'The bastard. I did suspect that all that high tech automatic gunfire was a bit over the top just to defend some nondescript building and now, after hearing your story, I'm pretty certain I was a target, the bastards.'

We talked on, downed several more Monteith's. Russ's arm was still pretty tender however it had been shot off cleanly and the healing process was pretty straight forward. He still had the elbow and he reckoned a tin arm should not be a problem. Flying, not sure about that, can't imagine the licensing bureaucracy wearing it, but I don't recall my current employer inquiring about the state of my pilot's license. I told Russ all about my experiences doing Mr Roberts's bidding, there was no point in holding anything back, Russ was not exactly going to be a security risk, did it matter anyway?

'Here's a suggestion Russ, get a tin arm, get it working, then take yourself off to the local aero club with a mate, like me, I've got a license, and we'll see if you've still got it, if you still have the passion, if you still want the adrenaline pumping thrill of getting your arse shot off for big bucks. I doubt that Mr Roberts will be too concerned about a pilot's license, how about it? Give you something to aim for, give your life a sense of purpose, bloody sight better than selling life insurance.'

'Rex, you're an inspiration, I'll do it, after all I've had my serving of shit luck, another Monteiths?'

We had several more, in fact we got pretty full, however, I thought it would be good for Russ. The poor bugger must have been to hell and back, losing an arm when you're a pilot, that's about as bad as it gets, he definitely needs cheering up.

'Rex.'
It's a loud voice, it's Tara Lemaire's. She's with another girl, it's

Erika, Tara's friend from that Wellington fashion show, the show I will never ever forget.

'Rex we're looking for a couple of hunks and guess what we've just found them.'

'Well hello Tara and you're Erika, right, I met you briefly in Wellington.'

'Yes I'm Erika, pity our previous meeting was so brief, I wish I had been around for the after party.'

Hmm, interesting, has Tara been telling tales, she did mention that her friend Erika was a party animal.

'Girls, this is my buddy Russ and yes he is single. Russ, meet Tara and Erika.'

The two girls are glancing at Russ' 'short' left arm, Russ, being a sharp lad and rather full of beer, quips.

'Think this is bad, you don't want to see the other fellow.'

There's a moment of embarrassment, the girls are lost for words, Russ comes to the rescue.

'Please, don't be embarrassed girls, the bloody thing got shot off in the war, but the right hand still does all the necessary. Now then, what's it to be?'

The awkward moment passes, the girls relax, Russ gets some drinks.

'Four months ago, wrong place, wrong time, lost a bit of arm, bugger!' Russ makes light of his injury.

'Rex, out with the boys, where's your loved one?'

'Working, out of town Tara.'

'Oohh, no one in your bed to-night.'

'Just me Tara, why do you ask?'

'Well there's no one in my bed tonight either, perhaps we should talk about this.'

'Russ, let me explain. Tara's a party animal, aren't you Tara, she eats men, don't you Tara, and I think she's the girl for you Russ.'

The conversation gets more and more provocative, the girls seem to be enjoying the sexual overtones, us, well we're just full of beer. The afternoon has now turned into evening.

'Tell you what, why don't you let me take you all to dinner, my shout, I'd like to do this.'
Tara's first to respond.

'That's very generous of you Rex, I'm sure Erika will be a starter and after dinner you can all come around to my place, how about that? Russ, you too, please.'

'Ah yes, be delighted,' from Russ.
What have I done, it's the beer talking. Take them all to dinner, party at Tara's place. Erika? if she's anything like Tara, this could develop into who knows? what about Kate, this is cheating isn't it?

I get some more drinks for the girls, more beers for us, don't need them but I still get them and the atmosphere gets really friendly. Erika takes a shine to Russ and Tara is all over me, memories of Wellington flood into my head. I'm getting a hard on, I don't need this, what will Tara get up to, the girl knows no limits. Perhaps I had better let Russ know what these girls are like, well what Tara is like, don't know about Erika but I'm pretty sure she's another Tara.

Kate, come on Rex no secrets remember, what are you going to do here. Tara's got her eye on you, probably wants a repeat of Wellington, let's face it she's a man eater and she's set her sights on you. Play along, try and extricate yourself later, in the meantime enjoy the moment, dinner with a couple of real knockouts. It will be good therapy for Russ I mean how would you cope with losing a bit of arm and your primary source of income, probably needs a bit of cheering up. Tara can certainly do that, probably Erika as well, would not surprise me.

'Ok folks what say I take you all along to Le Paris in Elliott Street, it's good, my shout.'
It's a nice feeling having money in my pocket, lots of it.

It's a bang up meal with some excellent wines, to hell with the expense. I'm loaded these days remember, or am I just so full of beer that my judgment's clouded, probably the latter, but what the hell it's not every day you get to take out such beautiful girls. Well I can take out a beautiful girl any day I like, Kate, my Kate, she's all mine remember Rex, don't go and stuff it up?

'My place for the night,' it's a positive statement from Tara. We're all pretty full, I'm very full, judgments are getting clouded, *don't stuff it up*, I keep reminding myself. We pile into a taxi and it's all on. It's a big taxi and we are all in the back seat. Tara is at me immediately and Erika is groping Russ, yes, she is another Tara.

Tara's place, a house in Epsom, a big house. There's no mucking about, Tara pushes us all into a bedroom and the biggest bed I've ever seen, shit I'm in trouble. Russ looks a bit stunned but he's not objecting to what Erika is doing, pulling his trousers off. I get Tara to one side.

'Look Tara I'd love to, another Wellington, but I won't. Kate's not here and I'm in love with the girl, I don't want to ruin it, sorry but I'm going to bale right now. Give Russ something to cheer him up, he's a bit down right now, the arm, it's quite recent.'

'Rex you surprise me, why is it that a good looking fellow like you, someone whose so good in bed, can also be faithful to his loved one, I admire you for that but bugger, I really want you to fuck me, right now.'

As she says this her cloths are coming off, it's an arousing sight, I'm rock hard and Tara has noticed, her hand is on the bulge in my trousers.

'A quicky, I won't tell, promise.'

'Don't get me wrong Tara I'd love to but no, Russ will do it I'm sure, that's if you can get him away from Erika.' As I say this Russ is already on top of Erika and the two of them are writhing about on the enormous bed.

I give Tara a big kiss and make a break for the door. She says nothing, does not attempt to stop me. I'm out the door onto the street and I'm still rock hard. Flashback, when did this last happen, fleeing a girl's bed with my trousers around my ankles, it was way back when I was a callow youth and her dad had caught us out.

The next day I have mixed feelings, my conscience is clear, I've managed to remain faithful to Kate, but it had been a hell of a temptation. The beer had come close to tipping me over into unfaithfulness, if that's what it would have been. But I had fucked Tara, really fucked her, Wellington, but Kate had been there on that occasion a willing participant in the sexual frenzy. Does that mean I can have sex with others as long as Kate is a participant? Russ had called a little earlier.

'Rex where in hell did you find those two, I didn't get out of there until after breakfast and only because they both had to go to work, they just kept at me, it was heaven on steroids. That Tara wants more, she's already phoned suggesting another pub meeting.'

'Russ it's all yours, fill your boots, I won't be a participant. I'm in love, sounds corny I know but wait until I introduce you to Kate, you'll understand.'

'Lucky you Rex, me, well I just might have another drink with Erika, or perhaps Tara, or perhaps both, don't come across a set up like this every day.'

A couple of days later.
'Ok if I call around in an hour?' it's Pierre Brodeur.
'Yes that will be fine.'

'Monsieur Brodeur, good morning.'
'Monsieur Rex, I can call you Rex? please call me Pierre. Rex, have you come to a decision?'
'Pierre the amount of money on offer makes it a bit of a no

brainer. I assume, because the money is so tempting, there must be a fair degree of danger, am I correct?'

'Well I can't comment on that, my job is to make you this offer, it's up to you to decide, but I do need a decision.'

'Ok Pierre I accept.'

'Good, now the detail.'

He goes into considerable detail about airline tickets, all prepaid by his organisation, a hotel booking in Paris, another in La Linea just across the Spanish border from Gibraltar. The Piper Cherokee Six will be at Beauvais, an airport north west of Paris. The airline booking has me leaving New Zealand in two weeks time and back in Auckland two weeks after that. When I get to Paris I am to contact a Monsieur Robier, he gives me a Paris address and phone number. Monsieur Robier will give me the final details of the mission.

'Ok got all that, tell me about the Swiss bank account?'

'There will be a code word and number, the idea is to commit them to memory. Access can only be gained by using the code word and number. It's not completely secure but the best we can do and still comply with various countries monetary regulations. I'll give you the code and number in a couple of days.'

Bit different to Mr Roberts and his cash under the bed operation.

'That's about it for now, I'll courier the tickets to you. You have our phone number for any questions, good luck. If this goes well there could be more.'

More? I might have struck the mother lode here, but hang on, *big money big risk,* how big is the risk?

'Rex, dearest, let me cuddle you to pieces, I've missed you.'

We're at the airport, I'm picking up Kate from her Wellington flight.

'How was it in Wellington?'

'Cold and boring, very boring in the evenings, far removed from our earlier visit. Perhaps I should take you and Tara along in future, spice it up a bit.'

'You think so, really, Tara?'

'Yes Tara, Ali's not available these days now that Jeff has rediscovered his manhood.'

What am I hearing, does Kate have ideas about a threesome, make it a feature of our lovemaking, there's a lot about Kate that I've yet to discover.

'Tara, sure about that?'

'Come on Rex, stop being so coy you just loved screwing her in Wellington, you were a man possessed, you really went at it. I loved every minute, a huge turn on for me, I think we should do that again.'

What, and here's me running a mile from Tara, wanting to stay faithful to Kate. I could have indulged my every sexual fantasy with Tara the other night, she certainly wanted it, missed opportunity. And I thought I was doing the right thing. Perhaps we might get her around, I'm sure she will jump at the opportunity.

'Home Rex, a bit of catching up to do, that dildo is no match for the real thing, well not your mighty manhood that's for sure.'

It's two weeks before the French job, I'll break it to Kate in a couple of days in the meantime we just revel in each other's company broken only by Kate having to work. She comes home one afternoon with a bemused look on her face.

'Tara tells me you are the perfect gentleman, the faithful lover, a good man, that's nice Rex. I'm not sure how I would react if she told me you had fucked her while I was away, not really thought about that one, could you?'

'No I could not Kate, well not without you being present, bit strange isn't it, we can enjoy group sex but it's a no no if one of us is not there, well that's how it seems, what do you think?'

'Don't know, perhaps we need to find out?'

'What does that mean Kate, you want me to fuck Tara when you're not around just to see if it pisses you off?'

'I don't know, I just don't, let's not dwell on it.'

I wait for an opportunity to tell Kate about the French offer then one evening in bed, when we've exhausted ourselves, I break it to her. I don't tell her too much, just that it's a job for the French in Europe and it's serious money. No mention of Algeria or the FLN, why would I? She would worry herself sick if she knew. It was a bit of a worry to me as well and I'm supposed to be the one who's beyond that, the tough mercenary. Kate does not say anything at first, then in a reflective mood she speaks her mind.

'You're going to do this aren't you, I can tell, you've made up your mind. I guess this is our life now, the money has got you, I understand that, it's huge money and that's nice. I can live with it. My fear is that sometime your luck will run out and I'll lose you, I'm not sure I could handle that, I love you Rex, if I ever lose you it will be the end of me.'

'I'm at a loss for words Kate, it could be construed as selfishness, my blind addiction to money but I find myself deeply immersed in this life now, I can handle the risk, well the risk factors that I have some control over. I'm a mercenary Kate, that's the way it is.'

'Here's my take on it Rex, why don't we give it a year then have a rethink. My career is going well right now and as you know it's taking up a lot of my time, it's going to take up even more in the future. Is that a good or a bad thing, well depends how you look at it. The French have approached me, yes those Frogs are intruding into our lives, the ghosts of centuries past. Paris Vogue have been inquiring, they are interested in a cover shoot, that's as good as it gets Rex. How long it will last for me I don't know, could go on for some time or could just be a short term thing. Perhaps we should let things play out for say another year then have a big rethink.

Attitudes and circumstances may change, I might tire of being *a body* and you might tire of getting you bum shot off. We could even settle down together, lead a quieter life, perhaps start a family, sounds a bit boring right now I know but people do change with time.

'Come here *body* I want to ravish you again.'

'And I want to grab you bum while you still have one.'

Another long flight jammed in a little seat, should think about first class with my new found wealth. This one's paid for by others so no choice, could upgrade, no, stay anonymous, stay below the radar, don't squander your chances, nine lives and all that.

Algeria, FLN, different. Do the British know about this, is there collaboration, is Mr Roberts aware that I'm off to Europe, would he be pissed off if he did know. Of course he knows, he knows my every move it seems, perhaps he recommended me. Unlikely, the Brits and the Frogs never did get on. But Mr Roberts is not to be trusted remember, Fulder. The money for this Algerian one is extraordinary, why? The Brits will know about it. I'm going to operate out of Gibraltar that's as good as telling them in writing, they're not stupid. Whose side are they on in this Algerian business. Last time I got involved the Brits were certainly not on the Frogs side. Are the Brits accommodating the French knowing that it's going to go badly for them, cause embarrassment, sacrifice a rogue colonial to give the Frogs a black eye. No Rex, you're reading far too much into it, you've sold your soul for a lot of money, just do it and stop torturing yourself with all the what ifs and maybes, Kate, think about Kate.

Yes indeed the lovely Kate, the very sexy Kate, the girl I'm completely in love with, the girl with the rather unusual sexual cravings. This threesome business, Tara, done nothing about it but Kate has indicated that perhaps we should invite Tara into our bed.

Tara and Kate naked in bed with me, both wanting it, dream on, but the erotic dream could well become reality.

Immigration, Orly, Paris. The officer eyeballs my New Zealand passport and gets on his computer, he's on it for rather a long time, noticeably longer than he was for the fellow immediately ahead of me. It's a red flag, DGSE I'll bet. It happened at Faa'a in Tahiti, well I'm pretty sure it did, so I am of interest to the DGSE, long memory the French. If it's the DGSE who I'm doing this job for I wonder if it's going to have a bearing on whatever's about to happen now, could be a *black ops* division of the DGSE, nobody knows about it. The officer hands my passport back and I'm waved through.

The hotel, yes I'm expected, there's a booking. Monsieur Robier, there's a number, I call it.

'Monsieur Macare for Monsieur Robier.'

'One moment please monsieur, I'll see if he's in.'

'Mr Macare, Pierre Robier, I've been expecting your call, I need to talk to you face to face. How about tomorrow morning at ten,' you have my address.

'Yes that will be fine, look forward to it,' and that was it, end of call.

What can I expect from Monsieur Robier, the detail for a covert operation into the FLN's Algeria, a dangerous place by all accounts. A drop off, a later pick up, what does that suggest. Is my charge going to do something dangerous? probably. Sabotage, assassination, it's a lot of money, it must be dangerous, what have I let myself in for?

It's a nondescript building in the heart of Paris, room 202, ten o'clock.

'Monsieur Macare, good morning, we'll use English, you live in New Zealand, how would you get to use French? Macare, French, Huguenot yes? please do not worry I'm not a Catholic.'

'No I'm not worried, nothing could be further from my mind than Huguenot persecution in fact it's only in recent years that I even heard about it, no my focus is only on the business in hand.'

'Good, let's get down to the detail.'

'Before we start I do have one question. You may not be at liberty to answer but I'm going to ask anyway, are you DGSE?'

'You are correct in your assumption, I'm not at liberty to answer.'

'Ok, I don't need to know, just curiosity.'

'A word of warning, but I probably don't need to tell you, don't be too curious, knowledge can be dangerous.'

Monsieur Robier proceeds to brief me about the operation. I am to go up to Beauvais to the north west of Paris. A car will pick me up from my hotel at nine the following morning. There's a Piper Cherokee Six at Beauvais airfield, the driver will drop me at the aircraft. I am to fly it down to Gibraltar, a flight plan has already been lodged with French Air Traffic. Park it at the airfield then go across the Spanish border to La Linea, it's just a short walk, check into the Villa Corales. The following evening I am to go back to the airfield at eight. There will be two people at the aircraft, one my passenger, the other fellow will help me get airborne for some night flying in the local area. Normal radio communication with Gibraltar will be observed, however, I am to head for the Moroccan coast, drop down to low level and switch off the navigation lights. Gibraltar radar will be observing all this and when I disappear from their screen, not to worry, they have been briefed.

'You mean the British are in on this?'

'No questions, you don't need to know.'

I am to fly east along the coast to a small port just across the Algerian border, Ghazaouet. Just past the port are two small headlands then a much larger one. Between the last small headland and the larger one the countryside by the coast is wooded. There is a landing strip in this wooded area. Monsieur Robier gives me a chart showing just where this strip is. The strip has rudimentary airfield lighting, it will be switched on when they hear your aircraft. Land, drop off your passenger, and take off again immediately for Gibraltar. Back at Gibraltar switch your navigation lights on and establish normal radio communication. Your *night flying in the local area* will have lasted about three hours however Air Traffic will not be asking questions about the lack of radar or radio contact. Leave the aircraft parked on the airfield and go back across the border to La Linea. Two days to amuse yourself then back to Gibraltar. Be at the aircraft at nine in the evening on the third day, the same fellow will be there to assist you. Same procedure, airborne, across to the Moroccan coast, lights off, down to low level, along to Ghazaouet. Same procedure, keep the engine running, take off as soon as your charge is in the aircraft. When you get back to Gibraltar there will be people to take care of your passenger, do not concern yourself with what goes on. Leave the aircraft there and the following morning fly it back to Beauvais.

'Ok got all that.'

'Good, then there's no more to tell you, if you do have any questions you have my number here, good luck.'

I leave Mosieur Robier's apartment and seek out a coffee shop, there's a lot to think about. Low flying does not appear to be a factor, I doubt the FLN have any radar capability but staying low out off the coastline reduces the possibility of being spotted. An airstrip in the trees by the coast. I thought the coastal people were not to be trusted. There is obviously a ground organisation looking after that end of things. I will be in and out inside a few minutes so there's little time for anyone who's not in the know to react. The aircraft, a Piper Cherokee Six, not flown one, however, if it's anything like other Piper aircraft it should not be a problem. I wonder just who I am doing this for, got to be the DGSE, but I wonder how they could get the British to co-operate? Could it be a British operation, but then they would not be using French facilities. Last time I did something like this it was British and not exactly in the best interest of France. The DGSE know about it, their man in Tahiti gave that away. Got to be the DGSE, but the reality for me? does it matter?

Ok, got the rest of the day to take in the sights of Paris, tomorrow, off to Gibraltar. I've been there before in my Air Force days. Interesting place. The airfield runway runs the full length of the only flat ground available, the main road to Spain runs across the middle of the runway. Traffic lights close the road when there are aircraft movements so there are no clandestine, radio silence operations at night. I enjoy a wander around La ville de l'amour, an early dinner at a local café and into bed for a good night's sleep, tomorrow will be busy.

Mosieur Robier's man picks me up from the hotel and we drive to Beauvais. It's an easy flight to Gibraltar, I get there in the early afternoon. I'm expected, a French fellow meets me and I'm driven across the border to the Villa Corales in La Linea. The same fellow advises he will pick me up at seven thirty the following evening and drive me to the aircraft.

'You could walk, it's not far, quite a pleasant walk as well but it's easier this way, avoids any possible difficulties at the Spanish border. There have been problems with New Zealand passport holders in the past.'

How would this fellow know that, how would he know I had a New Zealand passport? this operation appears to be well organised, got to be DGSE, they're drawing me further into their net, why?

An afternoon and evening in La Linea. I had been here several years ago and the place then was Dirty Dick's, a well known pub run by Dick, a larger than life Spanish fellow. Dick had got offside with Franco in the 1930s and been sentenced to internal detention, not allowed to leave La Linea for the rest of his life, so he opened a bar.

'The world will come to me.' It did.

A long bar with a long line of bar stools; a flamenco guitarist at the far end added a really Spanish touch. Along the wall behind the bar protruded the ends of numerous wine casks. The idea was to drink your way along this line. It was ridiculously cheap, just a few pesetas for a glass, but caution was required, very easy to overindulge. I had done this before and on that occasion it had been disastrous, it was only the intervention of my Air Force mates that had saved me from myself, this time just a glass or two, bit of nostalgia.

The following evening my French driver delivers me to the airfield. There are two people at the aircraft, my helper, and a second person, presumably my passenger. Not much conversation, I do not really determine the nationality of my passenger and I would not be finding out much during the flight either. The aircraft had been modified for freight. Behind the two pilots seats was a partition that sealed off the rear part of the cabin, this is where my passenger was seated, not much was said at all. I established contact with air traffic control and was cleared for a couple of hours of local night flying which I thought was a bit unusual, local flying at night, and for two hours or more. I got the feeling I was just a small part of a greater plan. Across to the Moroccan coast, lights off, drop down low, start crawling along the coast towards the Algerian border. It's all overwater so no problem about banging into things. There's no real requirement for low flying, what's the point, who or what is going to detect me. Ghazaouet, there it is, brightly illuminated, bit different to my previous assignments, the dull drabness of East Germany. There's the headland and bingo, the large wooded area. Fly inland a bit to where the landing strip is marked on the map that Monsieur Robier had given me and there it is, some dull lights that appear to form a landing strip in amongst the trees. How high are the trees? better do a steep approach just to be on the safe side. No landing lights, don't want to advertise my presence. Not the easiest, doing a steep approach without good ground definition, not to worry, I can do it, I hope. Thump, rumble rumble, I'm down unbroken, roll to a standstill, several figures materialize out of the darkness, I feel the rear cabin door open then thump shut, a voice shouts, alla alla, I turn the aircraft around and takeoff. The trees are small stunted coastal ones, not a hazard at all. Back to Gibraltar, navigation lights on, establish radio contact, get a landing clearance, first part of this mission done. I'm sure Air Traffic know a lot more about what I have been up to but I *don't need to know*. My French driver is waiting and he delivers me back to the Villa Corales.

'Tell me what are your instructions regarding me,' I ask my driver.

'English not good, monsieur, don't know how to tell you.'
That means he's been instructed to say nothing so I won't press the point.

'Thanks for the lift, when do I see you again?'

'Same time three nights from now,' he says in perfect English.

A couple of days to fill in, what to do. I get a bus over to Algeciras, just across the bay from Gibraltar. There's a bull fighting ring there, Las Palomas, it's on 'the circuit,' that's all the notable bull fighting rings in Spain. Don't know much about bull fighting, it's a peculiarly Spanish thing. It's huge, Las Palomos, and it's deserted, the season in Algeciras is June. It's now August, the bull fighting circuit has moved along the coast to Malaga. I talk my way into the bull ring. What an impressive sight, seats thousands. I let my imagination flow, the bulls and the matadors doing their thing, all very Spanish. I walk through the town, it's a big port Algeciras, one of Europe's busiest. I seek out a restaurant on the waterfront. An excellent meal, then a bus back to La Linea.

Next morning, *ring ring*, 'Señor Macare, there's someone to see you.'
It's the receptionist. I go along to reception, there's a Mediterranean

looking fellow there.

'Bonjour Monsieur Macare, my name's is Lucien, is there somewhere we can talk in private.'

'Come along to my room Lucien we can talk there, what is it you want to see me about?'

'Not in public, your room.'

Who in hell is this fellow, how does he know who I am and where I'm staying?

'Here we are, now what can I do for you?'

'Monsieur I understand that Monsieur Pierre Robier, has got you doing some work for him, bit of flying.'

'Perhaps, but that's a private matter between myself and Monsieur Robier.'

'Ah, not so private. I understand you made a night-time flight into Algeria recently and you have another one planned. I would advise you not to do this, there are people who do not want to see it happen.'

'Excuse me, what business is this of yours, I'm not sure you've got your facts correct, a flight into Algeria?'

'Yes monsieur, a night-time flight, and I'm very sure of my facts.'

'Well that may be however as far as I am concerned it's nobodies business but mine and if you don't mind I have things to attend to.'

'Very well Monsieur Macare, however, let me say it again, I would advise you not to continue with this business. Good day sir, I will be off.'

Shit, I was shaking, what was that all about, what have I got myself into, *big money big risk,* yeah right! What do I do, what can I do? I'm obligated to follow through with what I've agreed to, can't just change my mind and back out, cut and run is not an option. The word would get out, unreliable, it would be the end of my mercenary career, no more big money. On the other hand it could become known that I was a fellow who followed through, was not deterred by threats, could be relied upon, it could even *up* my asking price, does that make me feel better? No, I'm shit scarred, what am I going to do?

You're going to do what you agreed to do, remember you are doing it for the money and if you fail to do the job then whoever it is who's paying might come looking for you. It's the world of the mercenary remember, you don't have many friends in this business. So Rex tomorrow you will fly back to Algeria and pick up your charge, just as you agreed to do, ok!

It was a terrible night, no sleep, worried senseless, who was that fellow and what did he mean, *I would advise you not to do this.* Should I phone Pierre Robier in Paris, no, not a good idea, he does not want to know about my operational difficulties, he's paying for a job to be done, not for excuses, just go ahead and do it. That fellow was probably just trying to scare me off, what do you mean trying, he's done a good job, I'm bloody scarred. The bad night is followed by a bad day. I go for a long walk and try not to think about what could go wrong? well what could go wrong? I'm going to do just what I did the other night. I know the way, I know the landing strip, stop worrying, go along to Dirty Dick's and have a vino, have several!

'Señor Macare your driver's here.' It's the receptionist, I'm on my way. It's eight thirty in the evening, what will befall me before I return to the Villa Corales. The aircraft is where I left it three days earlier, the French fellow who is there to assist assures me it has been refuelled. Nothing else to do, just get airborne and follow the same routine as before, over to the coast, lights off, drop down low and follow the coastline along to Ghazaouet, it's about two hundred miles. There's the wooded area, where's the landing strip, can't see any lights, damn, they are supposed to switch the lights on when they hear the aircraft. I fly around the wooded area for several minutes, don't like this, all I'm doing is advertising my presence.

There it is, some lights appear close by on the right side, yes it's the landing strip. I make another steep approach and land, roll to a stop, keep the engine running. Several figures materialize out of the darkness, I feel the rear cabin door open, a short delay, then thump shut, a voice shouts, alla alla, I turn the aircraft around and take off. That was all pretty simple. Not a sound from the rear compartment. An hour later we are back at Gibraltar, navigation lights on, make radio contact and land. The controller directs me to a parking spot on the far side of the airfield. There's a car waiting there and several people standing around. I guess this is the reception committee for my passenger. I shut down the engine and get out keen to see who it is I have risked my life for. The rear compartment door has been opened, there appears to be a disturbance, I push forward to see what's going on, the sight that greets me shocks me to the core. There's a headless body in the rear compartment. I feel sick, there's blood all over the place, the fellows head is lying on the floor, there's something else that's even more gruesome, protruding from its mouth are the victim's genitals. It's the FLNs calling card, this is how they deal to their enemies. There's a note pinned to the victim's chest.

n'envoyez plus d'assassins - (don't send any more assassins)
I'm sick in the stomach, dizzy from the horror of it all, what happens now. The reception committee appear to be doing a clean up job. The body has disappeared into the car. There are people cleaning out the rear compartment of the aircraft, me, well I'm just standing there shocked, don't know what to do.

'Monsieur Macare, perhaps you should come over here and sit down for a bit, you don't look the best.'
It's an important looking chap and he's got a big black car.

'Don't feel great either.'
The reality? I feel terrible, sick and dizzy, what in hell am I involved in? I could have been dragged from my plane and murdered in that

Algerian woodland. It would appear the people at the airstrip were FLN and they were sending a message to whoever it was who had infiltrated an agent into Algeria. Would not work if they killed the messenger.

'Perhaps you can tell me everything that happened from when you took on this contract up to the present, in your own time, and when you are ready.'
Who is this fellow, is he on my side? I am sworn to secrecy remember, do not divulge anything.

'Sir, I'm not at liberty to talk, to anyone, that's my understanding so I'm afraid I can't tell you anything.'

'Ok, I understand, actually I'm impressed, you're playing by the rules so here's what I will do. I'll get Pierre Robier in Paris on the phone and you can talk to him first, we'll need to drive over to the administration building to do this, nearest secure phone.'

It happens, this fellow is kosher. Pierre Robier who I speak to authorises me to disclose everything. I also give him all the detail I can about the fellow who warned me off at Villa Corales.

'That's all I know sir; about the fellow who warned me off, what's your take on that?'

'I don't know, obviously we have been compromised and it's cost us one of our operatives, no fault of yours however. We are satisfied with what you have done for us albeit it ended so disastrously, thank you.'
I can't help myself, this chap's obviously DGSE so it's with tongue in cheek that I ask him.

'Tell me, if you can, this is obviously a DGSE operation, well I think so, I also think your organisation has a long memory. You have not forgiven me for what I got up to for Her Majesty's Government a few years ago. Should I not be agreeable to any proposals you might put to me from time to time then it's not beyond the realms of possibility that you might apply a little pressure, what's your take on that?'

'Your very perceptive however no comment.'

'Ok, I understand. What happens now, the aeroplane? do you want it back in Paris?

'Things have changed. I'll drop you off at Villa Corales, we will let you know tomorrow what the plan is, we might want you to fly the Piper back to Paris. Right now I'll get you out of here, not a very nice experience for you. The honourable thing throughout history has been not to kill the messenger, does that make you feel better?'

'No, this was the FLN right, they are not known to be honourable.'

'You are only assuming it was the FLN, we have not divulged who our operation was directed against.'

'Victim's genitalia in the mouth, the FLNs trademark, pretty obvious.'

'Ok Monsieur Macare let's not think too much about it, time you jumped into bed, we will talk in the morning,'

It was a long night, what was left of it, little sleep, terrible nightmares, headless horsemen galloping about, drowning in rivers of blood, kill the messenger, dismember him, off with his genitals, Kate rescue me please, Kate I'm desperate.

In fact it was not a long night, there were only a few hours left when I got into bed and I was wide awake again when the sun flooded into my room, that's better, morning. Did all that really happen last night? yes it did, shit! I don't want this, I think a big reassessment of my future is in order. The money, a lot of money for this brush with the FLN, is it worth it? Will the French tempt me again? Will they apply a little pressure perhaps? Possible prosecution for activities not in the best interests of the Republic? Come off it Rex you're a New Zealand citizen, the French have no sway over you. Hang on, I'm almost on French soil right now, will be on French soil possibly later to-day, they can grab me anytime.

But I was only carrying out orders, failing to obey was court-martial stuff just as it is in the French military, come on, how can they use that against me, Rex you're becoming paranoid.

'Gentleman to see you Monsieur Macare,' the receptionist.
It's the fellow from last night, I don't know his name.

'Morning Rex, I can call you Rex? sleep well?

'No, anything but, bloody awful few hours. Last night was too much for me, not my scene, any future offers had better be more civilised than that.'

'Can't say I disagree, it was pretty awful, we did not expect that. We've been compromised and by the way thank you for the information about the fellow who threatened you, we think we know who he is, we should be talking to him soon, he will not be getting very far.'

'Sir you keep giving your identity away, DGSE for sure.'

'You do have an inquiring mind Rex, no comment.'

'No comment required, by the way I did not catch your name?'

'I have not given it but you can call me Louis. Now about your movements Rex. We want you to fly the Piper back to Beauvais tomorrow morning then you can pick up on your travel arrangements back to New Zealand, our man will pick you up here at nine tomorrow morning. A flight plan has been lodged with air traffic for tomorrow's flight.'

'Ok, about the Piper, been cleaned up?'

'Yes, you would never know what it's been involved in.'

'About the FLN, it must have been them who put that corpse in the back compartment and who chose not to murder the messenger, what happened to your ground organisation?'

'We don't know yet and you don't need to know, it will be appreciated if you say absolutely nothing about this unfortunate business to anyone, absolutely no one, understood.'

'Yes Louis, understood. If you want to use me again then I will be wanting to know a little more about just what the dangers are. This episode has been an eye opener for me and I'm not sure I want to be involved in this sort of thing again.'

'Understood Rex, I will pass it on.'

The flight home was not enjoyable, I've got serious doubts about my occupation. The glamorous life of the mercenary, the big money, the pretty girls, well there are some pretty girls in my life, not sure it's anything to do with the mercenary thing but the risk, that's very real. In the past few weeks I've been shot at, wounded, had SAMs fired at me, and now I'm lucky to have escaped the murderous attentions of the FLN, how much luck do I have, how long will it hold out? I've had mysterious people snooping around. The fellow asking questions in Celle, the fellow warning me off in La Linea. It seems these flying jobs I get are known to others, it could be that sometime someone might 'neutralize' me, take me off the market, do I want to continue with this? The money, how much have I made in the last few days? how long would it take to make that much in some other line of work, remember your line of work is flying aeroplanes, high paying flying jobs are not easy to come by. Anyway put it out of my mind, I'm going home to Kate, think ahead, Kate, forget Algeria and everything French. At the next airport transit lounge I get a message to Kate, let her know when I'm arriving in Auckland.

New Caledonia

'Rex!' Kate throws herself at me. It's so lovely coming home.

'Got you back in one piece, Rex I love you, don't go away again, please.'

What am I hearing, Kate is worried. I thought we had come to some sort of agreement, let things roll for a year, what's changed?

Later that afternoon when we had exhausted ourselves in bed we get to talking. It had not been a good week for Kate, she had been having nightmares, headless horsemen, bodies piling up in rivers, crashed aeroplanes, horrible things.

'Kate, what's the trouble? what's brought this on?'

'I wish I knew, I keep thinking about you, these nightmares torment me. I'm scarred to go to sleep, want to stay awake all night, sleep is patchy and when I do sleep it's awful, perhaps tonight will be different, sleeping with you, it's always nice sleeping with you.

Next morning, 'hmm, that's lovely dear, what a nice way to be woken up.'

'How were the dreams Kate?'

'There weren't any.'

'Ah the cure.'

We continue making love for quite a while, Kate's enjoying every moment.

'It's therapeutic darling, don't stop, I need a lot of healing'

A little later, 'that was so nice, thank you. I find it very difficult you being away.'

'Kate, I think you need a break, see if you can get a week off and we'll go somewhere together, just the two of us.'

'Yes please, somewhere warm and quiet, just you and me, that would be so nice Rex.'

'Any suggestions.'

'An island, a Pacific island. Tahiti was nice, very nice, what about New Caledonia?'

'Yes, good one Kate, let's see what we can find out about the place, not a regular holiday spot for Kiwis, don't know why?'

Breakfast on the balcony in the morning sun then some homework, yes, a week in New Caledonia, good therapy. My need is probably greater than Kate's. I've not told her anything about the French job, don't want to, would only upset her, it's got me pretty upset. The horror, that headless body, it's haunting me. How in hell did I get involved? How was I to know it would turn out like that? Perhaps the size of the payment should have been a clue. Perhaps I need to be more selective in what I take on, not be blinded by the money.

'Kate, what about Le Meridien Noumea Resort and Spa, it's on the coast just south of Noumea. The glossy brochures paint a good picture, there's a magnificent beach and plenty of restaurants nearby.'

'Yes, let's do it, a week in the south seas with my loved one.'

A few days off. We go out to dinner one evening with Ali and Jeff, what a change. Jeff's the doting boyfriend and it's real, Ali's, absolutely blooming. We don't see Ali at the flat very much, she's around at Jeff's place most nights.

Our South Seas holiday. I organise some bookings. New Caledonia is not well served by the airlines. TEAL operate a once a week service with an Electra to Tontouta airport near Noumea. I try out my numbered Swiss bank account, it works, there's a lot of money there, blood money!

'Let's go first class, what the hell, what's money for. I've heard first class on the Electra is good.'

Our holiday is set to start in ten days, a week in Noumea doing nothing in particular. There are a lot of fine restaurants in Noumea so eating will feature large and that beach, some serious sleeping on the warm sand. There are numerous day trips on boats on offer, actually there's quite a lot to do, or we could just be lazy, sleep in, eat, lie in the sun, drink some of those fine French wines, play around in bed, all good therapy.

Ring, ring, 'Roberts here Rex, how are you this morning?' Shit, I'm not ready for this, I'm trying to distance myself from my dodgy career for a while, that last episode has killed my enthusiasm. I don't want Mr Roberts right now.

'Hello Mr Roberts, I really don't want to be hearing from you just now, I'm off on holiday for a while.'

'That's nice, yes I guess you do need a bit of time off after that Algerian business.'

'Shit, what don't you know, that had nothing to do with you.'

'We keep an eye on the people who work for us, taking on that French job was not the wisest thing to do as you have probably concluded.'

'Yes, easy to be wise after the event but there was not exactly a wealth of information available to me before I took it on. If you knew about it then perhaps you could have said something.'

'Come on Rex, we can't interfere with someone else's operation, it's got nothing to do with us, you're an independent operator, you make your own decisions.'

'You mean you don't want the Frogs to find out that you've got access to their DGSE operations.'

'Rex you're entitled to your own opinions and I'm certainly not going to comment on what you might think.'

'Ok, let it drop, now what did you really phone me for?'

'Another job, Germany.'

'I'm off on holiday with Kate, you probably know that already, won't be available for three weeks. Not sure I want another job from you, still smarting about Fulder. The grapevine tells me you pulled a similar stunt with another fellow from Auckland, Russ Horsley.'

Silence, perhaps I've caught him out. How do I know that he set up Russ Horsley as a target.

'Ok Rex, I'll contact you when you get back from New Caledonia.'

Must have hit him where it hurts, my guess is he did not know or could not figure out how I knew about Russ, he had not made the connection. Wonder how long it will take him to find out, and will I ever know.

It's a morning flight in a TEAL Electra to Tontouta, first class and it's good, really good. Kate's at ease, enjoying being fussed over and the cabin crew are really fussing, I think someone has recognised her, one of New Zealand's top models. Immigration at Tontouta, I'll bet there's a delay, a red flag in Paris and sure enough there is. I guess this will stay with me for life, long memories, oh well that's the way it is, stop worrying, nothing I can do about it.

Le Meridien Noumea Resort and Spa, luxurious, good choice, chilled bubbles in the room, huge bed, total privacy. We shed our travelling cloths, open the bubbles and sit out on the very private balcony, me in my boxers and Kate, knickers only. Champagne in the afternoon sunshine. It does not take long, we can't help ourselves, we're on the bed and I'm pouring champagne onto Kate's lovely breasts.

Late afternoon, we've sated our sexual appetite, for a while, let's check happy hour at Le Meridien, yes there is a happy hour. The bar is quite exotic, full of tropical vegetation spilling out onto a big veranda overlooking the water. There's another couple there about our age, she's beautiful, has to be a model for sure, if she's not she should be, definitely French, honeymooners perhaps? An interested glance in our direction and in no time we get to talking, excellent English which is just as well. Usual Kiwi cultural cringe, one language only and that's not the greatest, apart from my German, well that's not the greatest either. She is a model, Paris based, and yes they are honeymooners. Talk about coincidences, he's a pilot, a jet jock in the French Air Force, the Armée de L'Air Française. The conversation gets interesting. The two girls, the two gorgeous girls, have a common interest as have the two boys. Eloise and Alain Dubois, they have been married for just two weeks. Alain tells me he flies Mirage fighters based at Creil just north of Paris and that's all he's allowed to tell. I tell him a little about what I used to get up to in Germany when I was in the RAF, and that's all I can say as well, touché, a drink to secrecy. Alain has a good sense of humour. The conversation gets around to the present and when Kate indicates that she has been approached by Paris Vogue Eloise is mightily impressed.

'That's top of the line Kate, something every model aspires to, you are very lucky.'

'Nothing definite, just an initial approach to see if I would be interested? would I what?'

Alain asks me about what I get up to these days, suddenly I have to be a bit circumspect about what I say.

'Contract flying Alain, I can't tell you too much about it, most of the flying is covert stuff, quite rewarding though.'

'I'm interested Rex, my air force contract has two years to go then I too will be looking for something. Eloise wants me to get into the airlines, me, not so sure at this stage.'

'Alain, go for the airlines, seriously, if you go the contract way you will get sucked in ever deeper blindsided by the money on offer.'

'Big money? so I've heard, that sounds attractive. As you know the military are not good payers.'

'Alain, *big money big risk,* believe me, and I'm not so sure it's a good idea.'

We talk on for quite a while and several drinks later I suggest we have dinner together, perhaps one of the restaurants along on the waterfront.

'Good idea, Eloise and I would love to join you.'

It develops into a great evening. We wander along the waterfront, quite an elegant waterfront, with plenty of what appear to be quite upmarket restaurants. We settle for one that looks good and it is. There's French onion soup, superb, escargot, if you want to, not quite my taste but Eloise and Alain are right into it. Kate dithers a bit then tentatively tries one, 'uumm not sure, not very adventurous are we.' Steak tartare, a favourite of mine, duck à l'orange, absolutely fabulous, filet mignon to die for, it's a great meal, desserts? no room. The wine, some fine French reds, several bottles in fact. We become rather friendly, intoxicated would be a better description. Back to Le Meridien, a pleasant walk, into their cocktail bar. We're getting on famously with Eloise and Alain. I'm particularly taken with Eloise, a classic French beauty, blue eyed brunette and beautiful. Kate is quite impressed with Alain, the handsome French fighter pilot. Eventually we go off to bed promising to meet again at breakfast. Into our rather luxurious room where we both crash, far too much wine, but what a delightful evening and that Eloise, I rather fancy her. Careful Rex that's the wine talking, take a look right next to you, there's a really beautiful girl, perhaps I'll make a play right now, yeah right, Kate's unconscious.

Breakfast on the restaurant balcony, continental, just as well. After last night's big meal there's little room. Alain and Eloise join us, Eloise looking particularly attractive in a very skimpy outfit. Kate's up with the play and looking like a million dollars, definitely a Vogue front page, Alain is giving her a lot of attention.

'Tomorrow Eloise and I are going to Ouvéa for a few days, it's one of the Loyalty islands just off the east coast, Hotel Paradis D'Ouvéa, apparently it's top of the line, right on a white sand beach, why don't you two come along?'

'We're booked in here for a few days, didn't consider the outer islands.'

'You should of, from what we've gathered Ouvéa is the place for love birds and the Paradis is the place.'

I glance at Kate, 'what do you think Kate, Alain makes it sound like a lovers nirvana, shall we?'

'We could, spend a few days with these lovely people from Paris, get up to all sorts of mischief perhaps.'

What's Kate hinting at, I'm getting a hard on and Eloise in her skimpy outfit is not helping.

'You smooth talking fellow Alain you've talked us into it, let's do that.'

A word with the Le Meridien front desk, they are very accommodating, even do the booking for us. Five days at Ouvéa, the Paradis, fly over there tomorrow morning.

'The beach Kate, let's sack out in the sunshine, relaxing stuff, that's what we came here for.'

'That's a good idea, mind if we join you,' from Alain.

'Of course not, show off the lovely Eloise.'

The lovely Eloise, yes indeed, the very lovely Eloise. Typically French she fronts the beach wearing nothing more than a G string. I thought Kate was being adventurous with a very small bikini, she looked very sexy, but Eloise?

Definitely French the beach, virtually all the girls were topless and there were quite a few G strings. I was having trouble, it was all a bit much and there was a very obvious bulge in my swim trunks.

'Darling it's showing.'

'I know, can't help it, we might have to go back to the room for a quicky.'

'Oohh, yes please, what will we tell Eloise and Alain, perhaps we should restrain ourselves for a bit, what if I take my bikini top off, I feel a bit overdressed.'

'If you want, keep up with the competition, but think about me, I'm in enough trouble already just having Eloise nearby.'

'You're right Rex perhaps I should go and put a tracksuit on, but I won't I'll just shed this top and fawn all over you, see if your swim shorts burst.'

It was a lovely morning on the sand. After a while the sheer sexiness of topless girls all around lost a bit of its novelty, well not that much. I was still in trouble, having to lie on my tummy for most of the time, my hard would not go away. I noticed it had not escaped the attention of Eloise, not sure about that one, she sure gets me aroused.

'Spot of lunch perhaps, a wine or two?'

The girls cover themselves with a couple of see through tops that do nothing for their modesty and we return to the hotel restaurant balcony. Chilled savvy and a light lunch. The girls get to talking about the modelling world, they've struck up quite a friendship. Alain quizzes me about the world of civilian piloting. I tell him about my experiences in the mercenary business. I emphasise that some of the things I am telling him are for his ears only. He's a military pilot well aware of the need to keep his mouth shut. In his case, as he's a current fighter pilot, the Arab states would be fertile ground. Short term contracts flying jet fighters could be very rewarding. The danger level would probably be lower as well, lower than what I'm experiencing. The money? well I don't have any figures but it should not be too hard to find out. There's no long term security though, a contract's just that, a contract for a fixed term. The situation I find myself in is individual flying tasks, no continuity, no security, and high risk, people try to kill me, however, the rewards are very high; I give him some figures. There is one problem however, you have no friends and some of these flying tasks could well be fatal, in fact sometimes the odds appear to be stacked against you. The people employing you are aware of this. I tell him about the Fulder business and Russ Horsley's unfortunate incident in Germany, how we were both set up as live targets so that the interested parties could evaluate the Soviet's latest weaponry. The mercenary world can be deadly but, as I've mentioned, the rewards can be very high. I've also had a go with your outfit, the DGSE, and I tell him about the Algerian business. There's another thing you need to be aware of, the possibility of blackmail, or perhaps I should say coercion. Your DGSE have me on record because of some gun running I did for Queen and Country when I was in the military, it was not in the best interests of the Republic. I would not put it past them to put the pressure on at some future date. Right now I find myself locked in, blindsided by the money, but it's definitely not a good career path. The idea at the moment is to make a killing during the next year or so then get out of the business, could even retire, but more likely I'll go for the airlines. I've got Cathay Pacific lined up.

'Rex, you frighten me. I'd no idea it could be that dangerous, food for thought, a lot of thought, right now we need another bottle of savvy, perhaps two.'

'Okay girls, ready for a little more? wine I mean.'

'Always ready Rex, you know how I am,' from Kate.

Could be a possible problem here, it's hot, we are knocking off quite a lot of wine, and it's nice.

'I think your Kate is suggesting something Rex, do you think we should drag the girls off to bed for a while?'

'Honeymooners, can't help yourselves eh, neither can I. Your Eloise is certainly a very sexy girl, you're a lucky fellow Alain.'

'Yes she is, like to try?'

What the hell, what did Alain just say, must be the wine, the sunshine, surely not, you did not hear that, just ignore it. But I did hear it and suddenly I've got a hell of a hard on, christ!

Another bottle and Alain and I resume our discussion about flying. I'm trying hard to distance myself from what Alain has just said but the sight of Eloise in her see through top and G string is now really causing me a problem, the prospect of bedding her now very real, what's the quid pro quo? I've noticed Alain has been paying a lot of attention to Kate. Not thought about that one. Kate does not have a problem with me bedding another girl but how will I react to another man fucking my Kate? I don't know, I really don't, would it be a turn on for me or would I blow up? The flying, drag your mind away from sex. Tell Alain some more about the world of flying beyond the military.

Airlines, that's the way to go Alain, it's long term, secure, the money is pretty good and no one's going to try to kill you. The downside, bit boring, so the choices are, heaps of money, excitement, danger, and an early grave, against a long and steady job flying airliners around the world, reasonable money and a happy family life with Eloise, that's as I see it so why am I chasing the dangerous option? Good question, no answer, just got sucked into it.

'Thanks for all that Rex, the other option for me is staying in the Air Force, I've been offered a permanent commission but unfortunately once you get past about thirty five to forty there's no more flying and that would be a real bummer, now then what about a swim in the ocean.'

'Swim girls, come on.'

We hit the water and suddenly we're all fooling around with each other, there's a bit of groping going on and nobody's objecting. We've had several bottles of wine and it's showing, where is this leading?

Back in our rooms after the swim. Kate and I have that quicky, well it's a bit more than a quicky and while we're enjoying each other's bodies Kate asks?

'Do you fancy Eloise Rex, I think she fancies you.'

'No, you're wrong there Kate, she's got Alain, they're on their honeymoon, why would she be looking elsewhere?'

'Well Alain put the hard word on me, he's indicated that Eloise is available as a trade-off, she would like to have sex with you, what do you make of that?'

'The bastard, what a nerve and I thought he was a good guy, when did he proposition you?'

'When we were in the water swimming, he wanted to do it right there, bit of a surprise, not ready for that.'

'I'm lost for words, what would you think if I wanted to have sex with Eloise?'

'Rex you know how I am, it would be a turn on for me, but more to the point what would you think if I had sex with Alain?'

'I don't think I would like that at all Kate, no not at all, never thought about it.'

'Well perhaps you should, they call it wife swapping and I hear tell that it can intensify a couple's relationship. I know when I've shared you with Ali and Tara my subsequent feeling for you has certainly intensified, perhaps we should think about it because I think the situation is going to come up.'

'Kate, this is a watershed moment, me sharing you when up till now it's been you sharing me, do you think it's right?'

'What's the difference Rex, the only problem is your acceptance of the situation, the end result could well be heightened sexual pleasure for us both.'

'Well the world has changed, it's possible I could accept it, just don't know. Some awkward situations could develop on this holiday, perhaps the only way to find out is to try it.'

'Ok then we are open to the suggestion when and if they make it, is that where we're at Rex?'

'I guess so, but don't lose sight of the fact that I love you Kate, I really seriously love you, anyone else is just sex.'

'I'm the same Rex, I do love you, no one will ever replace you, it's just sex, the plain enjoyment of sex.'

'Ok, have we got all that straight in our heads. Perhaps I should not think that Alain's a bastard he's just a little ahead of us and now it's just about happy hour. I think the arrangement was to meet in the bar, we'll be seeing each other in a totally different light.'

Different indeed, I catch Eloise's eye, it's a come on look. Alaine is quick to seat himself next to Kate, I notice his hand on her knee. A few drinks and the conversation turns to our move to Ouvéa in the morning. Alaine and Eloise are already booked on the little aeroplane, it's the only way to get to Ouvéa, there's no boat. The Le Meridian has booked a flight for us as well, perhaps it's the same flight.

'Good, that's settled, wonder what the accommodation arrangements will be at the Paradis, perhaps one huge bed?' Alain says this with a provocative edge to his voice.

'Oui s'il vous plait, that would be nice,' from Eloise.

What am I hearing, it's all on, pretty obvious. This island sojourn is going to be different, a whole new experience.

'Dinner, let's try another of those waterfront restaurants perhaps,' I offer.

'Yes let's do that, we'll walk along and pick a likely looking one, last night's was good, shall we try that again?' from Kate.

'No, something different, variety you know, the spice of life,' Alain's contribution.

'Yes variety indeed, always on for something new and different,' this from Eloise, she's looking straight at me with a lascivious look in her eye.

She's a sexy creature Eloise and she's certainly giving me the message. How long will it be before we're all in bed together? The very thought of sex with her is causing a bulge in my trousers.

'Right dinner, we're getting sidetracked here with mischievous thoughts and I like it, but seriously, let's have dinner.' Alain's take on the developing situation, a pretty clear indication of what's going to happen somewhere down the line.

It's a different restaurant and every bit as good, another superb meal and a lot of fine red wine. The conversation is heavy with sexual inuendo, there's no doubt in our minds that it's all on once we get to the Hotel Paradis.

Back at Le Meridian, Kate and I enjoy a long and loving sexual session, the realisation that we may be having sex with Alain and Eloise in the next day or so proves to be surprisingly stimulating. Just thinking about Eloise gets me highly aroused, not sure what Kate is thinking or how I am going to react to Kate having sex with Alain.

It's a spectacular sight from the air, Ouvéa and its huge lagoon, a world heritage site. Fayaoue Beach, miles and miles of uninhabited white sand and crystal clear water, what a great choice, the Hotel Paradis D' Ouvéa right on the beach. It is indeed a honeymooners dream, the four of us are going to revel in all of this for several days, who knows what will happen, how relationships will develop, how will I react.

Check in. 'Messieurs you are two couples, our farés are single bedroom, we do have some that are connected, suitable for groups of four like yourselves, what would you prefer?'
We look at each other not quite sure of our ground yet, do we want the rather close intimate relationship of connected bedrooms or do we want our privacy? Eloise breaks the awkward silence.

'Connected,' and she's staring straight at me. Kate looks a little unsure of herself but this changes to a look of relief when Eloise makes the decision, the tone is set, where to from here?

The farés are magnificent, very upmarket, ultra modern, and right on the beach. They are separate units with a large interconnecting door, fully stocked bar, lots of luxurious beach towels, and the bed, well what can I say, it would have to be the biggest I've ever seen. I catch Kate's eye.'

'Shall we?'

'Yes, right now, that bed looks irresistible.'

We're deep into each other and loving it when the interconnecting door opens, Eloise and Alain, they've got no clothes on.

'Can we join you?'

I'm lost for words, Eloise looks incredibly sexy and Alain is sporting a huge erection. The situation is bizarre. I look into Kate's face and she mouths a silent *yes*. Eloise and Alain need no prompting they get right into the bed. It's unbelievably sensual. In no time at all I'm fucking Eloise and Alain is fucking Kate, how am I going to react? Surprisingly I'm not upset but then I'm so deep into Eloise and she's responding so vigorously that I'm totally distracted by lust. It goes on for some time, both girls are moaning with pleasure. Eloise is extraordinary, I roll her over, raise her bottom and draw her back onto my bulging erection, this sends her right off, her moaning becomes quite loud and she's thrashing around quite out of control. Eventually we tire and finish up all lying on the huge bed wondering what's just happened.

'We need a drink, a toast to new found freedoms, to our partnership, our sexual adventure.'

It's Alain and while he's making his little speech Eloise is pulling the cork off a bottle of champagne. Are we going to drink it, pour it over each other, or both? Eloise is doing the honours. Having the naked Eloise pouring champagne while standing beside the bed is a bit more than I can take, I run my hand up her thigh, all the way up.

'To us.'

We're lying on the bed as we toast each other. It's not long before champagne is being pored over the girls, this leads to another flurry of sexual activity. This time I'm with Kate and it really is something, she may have a point about being turned on by sharing.

Mid afternoon, we're lying on the one big bed reflecting on what's happened. It's been a new experience for Kate and myself, well not completely new, there had been Wellington. I suspect Eloise and Alain are no strangers to this sort of activity. What did I think? Well it was extraordinarily enjoyable. Eloise was quite a revelation, obviously enjoys sex, certainly gave me huge satisfaction. Kate, what did she make of it?

'I enjoyed that Rex, it was a turn on for me but you're still my man, no one can replace you, with Alain it's just sex and there could be more to come, what do you think about that?'

'Strangely Kate I did not get upset seeing you and Alain together, mind you that Eloise was giving me such an incredible experience that I don't think anything could have got me upset but it's you I love, I want. Eloise is just sex.'

While Kate and I are reflecting Alain and Eloise are stroking and touching each other in a very intimate way, next thing he's mounting her and they are away thrashing about on the bed.

'Let's leave them to it, what about a swim, that magnificent beach?'

'Good idea let's do that.'

We leave Alain and Eloise, deep into each other on our bed, and go out onto the beautiful white sand and what a beach it is. Fine warm powdery sand, and the water, it's almost body temperature and crystal clear. We swim around for a while, it's just so nice, beaches don't get any better than this one. It's all ours, there's not a sign of anyone else just miles and miles of perfect beach. We have swimming costumes on, Kate a bikini bottom and me in swim shorts, why are we so overdressed? off they come. We swim around for a bit with nothing on it's rather stimulating, next thing we're at it, Kate's legs are wrapped around me and I'm driving into her standing in the shallows, it's quite erotic.

'What are you two doing?'
It's Alain and Eloise wading into the water, naked.

'Want to swap.'

'Why not.'
Where is this going to finish up, we've only just arrived at Hotel Paradis and already we are an active foursome, it appears to be working and it's nice.

Out of the water and onto a couple of big beach towels the hotel has provided. We're lying in the sun naked and it's lovely, all inhibitions well and truly gone. Suddenly nakedness seems to be quite normal. I'm in trouble though, the sight of the naked girls causes me to have a mighty erection, it cannot be hidden when you have no clothes on. The sight seems to fascinate Eloise, she moves a little closer to me on the big beach towel and takes my erection in her hand. Strangely this does not seem to be out of place in this environment. She appears to be fascinated and strokes it gently and of course this causes it to enlarge even more. Kate is watching with a bemused look. I am becoming mightily aroused, I don't need this, we've just about exhausted our sexual appetite for the day. Eloise keeps at it and I'm transported to heaven but the thing that is causing me some concern is the climax I can feel coming on, could be a bit embarrassing. Next thing Eloise has taken my erection into her mouth right there in full view of Kate and Alain. It's too much for me and I ejaculate right into her mouth. It does not appear to fazz Eloise in the least, she appears to just swallow it all. I'm flabbergasted. I've heard about this but to actually experience it, and in such a public way. My sexual horizons are being expanded. What else are our French friends going to come up with? What is Kate thinking, what is Kate doing, it's obviously arousing her. Alain is also sporting a mighty erection and Kate is fiddling around with it, next thing she too has taken Alain's erection into her mouth, her head is moving around and she's making little moaning sounds, then she's on top of Alain pushing his erection right inside her and in no time she's writhing around, moaning loudly, approaching climax.

This whole situation is spinning out of control, all inhibitions are completely gone, anything goes.

It's now late afternoon, we've left the beach and are back in our rooms, our two separate rooms.

'Do you think we should lock the door Kate, need a break.'

'Good point, I think we've got a tiger by the tail here, what do you think?'

'A whole new experience, have not encountered anything quite like this before, it's nice and I think we are both enjoying it but really the pace, there's no let up.'

'Yes, I am enjoying the situation, how are you reacting to me having sex with Alain, not getting annoyed or jealous are you Rex, could be a lot more to come and Eloise will be wanting more of you as well, think we can handle it?'

'I think we've got it sorted dear, a foursome, a whole new experience.'

'Ok, now what about a drink out on our deck with our clothes on, see if our neighbours want to do the same.'

'Good idea, I'll just pop through the door and suggest it, if I'm not back in two minutes break in and save me from myself, from the insatiable Eloise.'

'Done, you're right though, we really do need to try and limit the sex, bit hard, no self control.'

It happens, we gather on our deck fully clothed, best behaviour, and enjoy a wine or two in the late afternoon sunshine. The intimate familiarity that we now have puts us completely at ease. There's that knowledge in the back of our minds that if we want to have sex with whoever then just go ahead and do it, makes for a relaxed atmosphere, very different, rather enjoyable.

'This is nice, why don't we have a couple of drinks here then go along to the house bar for a sundowner, it looks like a good spot, I noticed it when we arrived, not seen much of the hotel so far, got a bit sidetracked.'

'Yes we did.'

'Dinner later?' I ask, 'we're limited, there's the Paradis's restaurant and not much else, bit isolated here but my information is that the Paradis is seriously good, no need to go elsewhere.'

'Right that's settled, now a little more of this chardonnay, I found it in our bar.'

The conversation turns to the following day, what shall we do. We need to get out and about, can't spend all our time in the sack playing with each other. Apparently the hotel has a small yacht that guests can use and the huge lagoon is the perfect place. It's a self-sail set up. I can sail and it turns out that Eloise is an experienced yachtie as well so we're well qualified. That settled we go along to the house bar.

'I'll talk to reception, see if we can corner the yacht for tomorrow.'

Reception is very helpful, the yacht for the day, packed lunch, wine, a chart showing the good beaches around the lagoon and the places where there's interesting marine life, masks and snorkels are on board.

'All done, the yacht's ours when we want it. I suggest we get up reasonably early and enjoy a full day's sailing, that ok with everyone?'

It's picture postcard stuff, the view from the hotel bar balcony out over what must be the most spectacular lagoon around, shimmering white sand beaches, tall palms, ridiculously crystal clear water, a gentle breeze, and a spectacular setting sun, does not get any better than this.

Thank you Alain and Eloise for telling us about this place and thank you for all the other things you've introduced us to as well. We're here for five days and it's only day one, how good does it get.

Dinner, it's a top of the line affair. This place is not cheap, it caters for guests who can afford to pay a bit more, *like mercenary pilots with lots of cash and numbered Swiss bank accounts.* The meal is superb, real Michelin five star stuff. It gets me reflecting on my life. I'm able to afford this and with a girl like Kate, could I ever settle for less, I don't think so, not now, I'm far too deep in to just give it all away, bit of a worry.

A warm sunny morning, they're all warm sunny mornings. We're sailing across the magnificent Ouvéa lagoon, it's huge, surrounded by numerous motus, small corral islets. We're heading for one that's been marked on the chart the hotel has given us, a good spot for a picnic. There's a lunch hamper and several bottles of wine on the yacht. Eloise is an excellent sailor, a girl of many talents, we have appointed her 'Captain' for the day. The lagoon is quite shallow, fine white corral sand covers the bottom and reflects the sunlight, bathes everything in a shimmering white light, it's quite spectacular. There are a lot of fish clearly visible. Every sort of small coloured tropical fish you can imagine, small black tip sharks, numerous big turtles, rays of every description, patches of colourful corral and some giant clams, really big ones. Hanging over the side and gazing into the water is just fascinating. We sail over to a spot marked on the chart where the hotel suggested we should do some snorkelling, perhaps see the resident Giant Trevally, masks and fins on, over we go. It's wonderland, colourful fish everywhere, a lot of bright corral, rays, they just appear, very friendly, I think they expect to be fed but we don't have anything for them. Apparently the locals feed the rays, they're a good tourist attraction. Black tips, small sharks with a black tipped dorsal fin, harmless, 'the man said so,' about twenty of them just swimming around amongst us, bit spooky until we get used to it. The Giant Trevally, where is it? bingo there it is, seriously big, over a meter long. Difficult to see, same colour as the sandy bottom, merges right in, apparently it's been around for several years, same spot, the locals feed it to keep it there. We hang in the water for a long time, just hang there, not moving, the fish and the sharks all around, it's a surreal experience.

'Ok, everyone out, lets picnic.'
The motu is small, walk right 'round in ten minutes, idyllic. We go ashore with our hamper and spread the big beach towels out under some coconut palms, I wonder how this will develop?

'A wine perhaps?'

'Good idea, there's ice, the chilly bin's full of it.'
We get to talking. Alain and Eloise have been married for two weeks. Ouvéa's been their dream spot for a honeymoon and what a good choice. They've been living together for a year. The idea was to get away from their life in France and just enjoy each other for a week or so, then they came across us and that idea has sort of foundered. They are an active couple back in France, swapping partners was common amongst their friends, now they don't seem to be able to break the habit.

'We were going to try and go the monogamous way during our honeymoon then we met you two and it was too much of a temptation, oh well that's life, however, we are glad we did meet you, you've added real spice to our honeymoon, you're a great couple to share with, believe us, we know.'

'Yes, Alain is right Kate, you are very lucky.'

'Well some frank admissions here,' I venture. 'Kate and I are not completely new to this, we have shared a little.'
What am I admitting to, should I be saying these things, will Kate take offence. Kate catches my eye, there's an understanding look there.

'It's a bit new to me, I've not really been involved in partner swapping until now but Alain you've been a very enjoyable first experience, thank you for that. You've been instrumental in Rex being able to accept that I can enjoy sex with another man and still retain my love for him, in fact it intensifies my feelings and that's a good thing.'

'Thank you Kate, Rex is a lucky man. You are an extremely good sex partner, perhaps we'll be able to further our mutual experiences soon.'

'This is heady stuff, enough for now, perhaps a toast to our continuing relationships and then a swim, there's a lot of food here as well.'

A swim, yes well we're far away from anywhere so it's everything off and into the water, trouble is Eloise is just such a sex bomb that all I can focus on is fucking her so I do. I grab her, she responds immediately, wraps her legs around me and I thrust into her standing in the shallows, right next to me Kate is doing the same thing with Alain, where will this all end?

We come out of the water and settle on the big beach towels, no need for clothes, nakedness seems so natural now. The hotel's hamper is excellent, cold meats, salads, cheeses, fruit, and several bottles of wine. Eating and drinking in the warm sun on a tropical beach, the beautiful people, naked, knowing that at any time our sexual fantasies can be indulged, just do it, no embarrassment, no restrictions, it's incredibly erotic. Time passes, it's just so delightful on this little motu, the sun warming our bodies, life is complete. So glad we came here, so glad we met Eloise and Alain. Do I have to go back to that other world? the one where I get all that money, the money that enables me to be here on this motu, able to enjoy unlimited sex with two beautiful females just whenever I want, two eager partners. Yes I will have to go back, I'm inextricably involved, unable to give it away now, the money has got me and I'm revelling in the lifestyle that the money can buy, what else would allow me to do these things? How long can it last? I don't want to answer that question, don't want to face reality, am I living in a fool's paradise? probably!

Stop thinking like this Rex, live for the moment, that's the way your life is now, don't let the downside spoil your enjoyment. You've been lucky with your life so far, there's no reason why it won't continue. You make your own luck, the psychiatrists tell you that but hang on how do I reconcile that with Fulder? Inexperience in the business that's what. It was probably luck that saved my ass on that occasion. In the mercenary world you have to assess the risk, no one else will do it for you, the amount of money on offer should be an indication, Algeria was an example. So what's the score so far? You've done four jobs, what's the risk factor been? Brandenburg, well I don't know, my first job, reasonable money but I did get shot at. Fulder, bloody high risk, unacceptably high, and I've let Mr Roberts know. The money was not that great either considering the risk. Sucked in I reckon and it might well have been an early grave. The pick up from Leipzig? quite a lot of money for that, should have been an indication there was risk involved, however, in the event the only risk that manifested itself was that bloody hole in the field, probably just unlucky. I don't know what the real risk was. The classic example was the French job. Algeria, big money and very high risk but I could not see it, did not think it through. The people who put that corpse into my little aeroplane were obviously FLN.

I'm thankful they did not choose to kill the messenger. So what have I learnt? Well it's not easy assessing risk. The money on offer for the Algerian job should have been an indication however the Fulder business was misleading and the Leipzig pick up is a bit of an unknown. Make your own luck, it's not that easy in the mercenary world, people don't tell the truth. Is it worth it? Yes, all things considered. Look at my present circumstances on this motu right now, yes it is worth it.

'Another swim.'

I'm awoken from my dream world, it's Alain, he's heading for the water with the girls in tow, wonder if we can resist the temptation this time?

'We'll sail the yacht around the edge of the lagoon and check another couple of motus on the way, good idea?'

There are several and we stop off at one of them, a small corral outcrop that's formed a sand island complete with coconut palms and small bushes. A lot of sea birds. The motus are breeding grounds, there are chicks in amongst the small bushes, they show no fear, not used to humans. We go ashore and have a wander amongst the birds and chicks, it's quite something. There's a coconut on the ground that's been colonised by hermit crabs, little fellows each with a small shell on their back for a home, they've hollowed out the coconut and taken up residence inside, fascinating.

Another swim, more fooling around in the warm water, then we sail back across the lagoon to the Paradis, what a great day.

Our holiday falls into a pattern, we take the yacht out several times and enjoy picnics on the outer motus. The evening meals, the quite magnificent evening meals, all taken at the hotel, there's not really anywhere else to go, why would we. The Paradis dining room is top class. Our relationships strengthen, we are frequent sex partners with Eloise and Alain and it appears to be working. The interconnecting door is open all the time. I find myself fucking

Eloise frequently, all sorts of times, day and night. Kate too is getting a lot of attention from Alain. How are we going to behave back in Auckland? The sharing arrangement here is really good, how will we get on back home? will we want to share? It could work for me, there's Ali and probably Tara, but how will Kate get on? I doubt Jeff will be into this sort of thing and Kate will probably have pretty strong preferences.

Our last day, back to Noumea tomorrow, not looking forward to it. No more Eloise, she's been such a magnificent sex partner. I detect Kate too is a little remorseful, no more Alain, he's certainly lit Kate's fire. She's become quite insatiable in bed, well she always has been but now even more so, and I love it.

Our last dinner at the Paradis, another gourmet experience, meals are just never going to be good enough after this, the bar has been set very high. We order up big, champagne, lots of it, damn the expense. Does not seem to worry Alaine and Eloise. Alaine's in the military and they are not good payers, me, well I'm flush, there's that numbered Swiss account as well, yes I'm definitely hooked, it's the mercenary life for me. We toast ourselves numerous times and make promises to see each other in Paris. Kate could be visiting that city soon, the Vogue thing, and if Pierre Brodeur calls on me in Auckland I too could go there again, could bed Eloise. Not sure about Pierre Brodeur though, don't want any more of his Algerian ventures.

'Let's have a jacuzzi,' it's Alaine.

There's a spa pool set into the deck of each faré, we have used our one a couple of times.

'Yes, let's do that.'

Off we go, out of the restaurant, bit tipsy, a lot of Dom has gone down, both girls start shedding their clothes. It's become a bit of a habit not wearing clothes, enjoying each other's naked bodies.

Makes it a bit easier as well when temptation becomes too much, but hang on this is the hotel, not some remote spot out in the lagoon, oh what the hell, it's our last night, who cares. We arrive at our two farés and all our clothes have come off, into the jacuzzi.

'Get some Dom, there's a bottle in our fridge.'

It becomes straight out debauchery, sitting in a jacuzzi naked, Kate on my lap, my monstrous erection deep inside her, drinking Dom out under the stars, it's the most sensual thing, our last night, what a way to go, 'let's swap.'

It's a very torrid night. After the jacuzzi it's the big beds, we cannot get enough of each other. There's quite a bit of swapping, could be some time before we experience this again. Eloise is quite carried away, her love making has a frantic edge to it and I'm loving it. Kate too is really turned on, we experience beautiful sex together, the best yet.

Scruff

Auckland, our erotic holiday over, our French friends are back in Paris. The memories, incredible memories, did all that actually happen? Will Kate and I be able to maintain a monogamous relationship, well almost a monogamous one, in the future, the immediate future, here in Auckland, or have we experienced something that we liked, will not want to let go, the next few weeks will tell.

Ring, ring, not Mr Roberts, please no, I'm not ready for him yet, can't be, I'm not at my place, it's Tara, Tara Lemaire. A quickening of the pulse, my imagination kicks in, imagine Tara at Ouvéa, that would have been something else.

'Rex, what are you doing answering Kate's phone, you're in her bed I bet, good holiday? I bet she's smiling from ear to ear. Good news, my man's returned, back from Paris for a while, a long while I hope, just thought I would let you people know, we must get together soon, you'll like him Rex, he's a sexy devil, bit like you.'

'Great news Tara, keep you on the straight and level for a bit, possibly.'

'Yes possibly, I'll have to break it to Russ, I've been seeing a bit of him recently.'

'Really Tara, you're quick off the mark, how's Russ getting along?'

'Well he was seeing quite a bit of Erika then I got involved and it's been sort of a threesome recently, sexy beast that Russ. He's got a tin arm organised and he's getting back into flying, seems you gave his life a new sense of direction Rex, you're an angel, I must reward you sometime.'

'Sounds interesting Tara, I'll look forward to the reward, how about we meet your lover from Paris, what about a foursome for dinner?'

'A foursome, yes please, dinner would be nice as well.'
She's a devil that Tara, wonder what the boyfriend's like. Kate had told me he's French, had been living in New Zealand for several years, a talented fashion designer with one of the majors. Went back to France to further his career about a year ago. I think his name's Marciel Fournier. The girls had been all over him, a good looking fellow apparently but when he took up with Tara it was no contest although I did hear they had been into sharing, now there's a thought.

Kate's been fixing breakfast during my conversation with Tara, I fill her in on the latest over coffee.

'Hmm, interesting, the possibilities are boundless, what do you take out of this, could be the start of something new in our lives, I mean what we experienced with Alain and Eloise was quite extraordinary, I liked it, what are your thoughts Rex?'

'Well what can I say, yes I did like it, liked it a lot, but do we want to make sharing part of our relationship in the future? will it work out in the long term, or will we find it too stressful?'

'Don't know, perhaps we should give it a try, we've already broken the ice, I mean there's Ali, then there was Wellington. Tara's obviously a starter, perhaps her man as well, there's your friend Russ, and perhaps Erika, what do we do?'

'Don't know Kate, how do you initiate a thing like this?'

Later the same day, Kate's gone to work and I'm at my place.

Ring, ring, bugger it will be Mr Roberts.

'Welcome back Rex, Kate well? good holiday? recovered from that Algerian business?'

'Ok Mr Roberts no need to rub it in. The French paid well for my services, made your offers look a bit ordinary and don't pull the risk thing, there was Fulder, hardly worth the money.'

'Alright Rex let's not get confrontational, you're learning.'

'Yes, indeed I am, now what's the purpose of your call this fine morning Mr Roberts?'

'I've got something for you, perhaps tea an hour from now?'

'I'll put the jug on.'

On the dot, *knock knock,* 'Mr Roberts, come on in.'

'It's another operation in Germany, out of Gütersloh this time.'

'Oh, what happened to Celle, I rather liked going there, good place to operate from, well I think so.'

'No comment, you don't need to know our reasons.'

'Something to do with the mysterious fellow asking questions at Schapers Hotel perhaps?' Mr Roberts ignores my pointed remark and continues on.

'This time we want you to drop a fellow inside the DDR, there will be people on the ground to meet him, then you will fly back to Gütersloh.'

'Sounds simple, low risk perhaps, but I doubt it, seems to me nothing is low risk, perhaps the money you are about to offer will give me an idea. I keep thinking about Fulder, your offer for that was what appears to be your standard payment and the job turned out to be damn near terminal. The Americans topped it up a bit but perhaps you don't know about that, whatever; how much for this one?'

'One hundred and fifty.'

'Ummm, let me think about it, call me tomorrow, ok! Oh, hang on, how rude of me, the tea.' I pour the tea. Mr Roberts seems in no hurry to leave.

'Rex, let me give you some advice. We are interested in your welfare, in your survival. You are turning into a good operative and we would like to keep you on, take an interest in your survival, so please have a little faith. What I offer in future will not be that dangerous, well as far as we can tell, there's always going to be an element of danger but that's the nature of the beast, I apologise for Fulder but we were in the dark ourselves on that occasion, Americans! This one is moderate risk.'

'Thank you for that Mr Roberts and I've made up my mind, I'll do it, you smooth talking fellow, you've talked me into it.'

'Good, the Flint agency will drop around tomorrow with 75,000, the balance on completion.'

'Just a question, what happens if I fail to complete a job, what happens to the outstanding balance?'

'It would be paid, just who would be the beneficiaries would depend on the circumstances.'

'Wow stop right there Mr Roberts, I'm not talking about my demise, just about my failure to complete the task satisfactorily, the Leipzig job for instance. What if I had got back across the border without my charge, would you have still paid up?'

'Yes, it's a risk we take.'

'Thanks for that, I won't ask for it in writing; joke!'

'Nothing's in writing in this business, you realise that.'

'I had noticed, now what exactly do you want me to do for this one?'

'Get yourself to Gütersloh, arrive there on Friday week and book yourself home the following Friday, there will be a room in the mess booked for you and keep your mouth shut, no confiding with Scruffy Jacobs. I know he's your mate, I also know he can be trusted, but, no confiding, is that understood?'

'Yep, done. How in hell do you know I told Scruff anything, you're guessing, I never told him a thing.'

I could almost be breaking my own rules here, never tell a lie, but I never told Scruff anything of importance, and how would Mr Roberts know anyway.

'You're bluffing Mr Roberts.'

'No comment, now then the details of exactly what we want you to do will be advised at Gütersloh and that's about it, so I'll be off.'
I had the feeling I was one up, he was bluffing. I had not told Scruff anything relevant to the Fulder operation and even if I had Scruff would not have said anything. There's no way Mr Roberts could know, definitely bluffing, what else is bluff? it's a murky world I'm moving in.

Having committed I got straight onto making the necessary travel arrangements, familiar territory now, well perhaps not that familiar. This time I elect to use a different travel agency, just a precaution. Could be the people who don't want me doing these things are keeping tabs on my movements, the DGSE for instance? unlikely, but a certain sense of self preservation was entering my thinking these days. All done, now a little social life before I re-enter my murky mercenary world.

'How about we ask Tara and her man out for dinner to-night?'
'Yes, that would be nice, do you want to give her a call or shall I do it.'
'Might be better coming from you Kate, if I call she might get ideas, not sure we want that just yet.'

He's quite a hunk Tara's man, Kate's impressed. Dinner at our favourite Parnell restaurant is great, always is. We talk a bit about our holiday, particularly the Ouvéa episode.
'Bet you got up to mischief there,' from Tara.
She had opened the door a little, an opportunity to hint at what might be.
'Yes we did, Alaine and Eloise were a great couple, we got up to all sorts of tricks,' this from Kate, not quite what I expected to hear.
'Kate, you didn't, not you, surely,' from Tara.
'Yes we did Tara and it was great.'

'Well, well, that's interesting, what did you think about it Rex?'

'Yep, great, Eloise was quite something.'

What am I saying, practically admitting to Tara that we had been sharing partners during our holiday, what will this lead to, nothing right now I hope, we need time before we get into anything like that again.

'A toast to changing circumstances,' Tara offers.

I think our relationship has just changed, changed to what? time will tell.

During all of this Tara's man, Marciel, says nothing but I sense he is taking it all in, all the subtleties, his English is excellent. I wonder what his take on it is?

Breakfast; we made it home without complications. We're on Kate's deck in the morning sunshine reflecting on what had transpired at dinner.

'Well it's out in the open now, I think we've made it pretty clear we're open to suggestion.'

'You're right Rex, Tara's in the picture and her man, Marciel, the look in his eye, he's a starter, nice fellow too.'

'We'll leave it to them to make the first move. Knowing Tara, well the little that I do know about her, it won't be long.'

'Have we messed up Rex, do we really want this thing to progress, not sure I'm ready. Ouvéa was different, holiday mode, anything goes and it was short term, here it's different. If we start something it could go on and on, do we want that?'

'Not sure, not sure at all, perhaps we should play it down a bit, try and put Tara off, that might be difficult, perhaps a heart to heart. Yes we think we would like to but not right now.'

Fortunately we don't hear from Tara and I tell Kate about the latest offer from Mr Roberts.

'*Out of town for a while* again Rex, sausage and sauerkraut?'

'Something like that Kate, well yes I can tell you, it's Germany again, off on Friday.'

'Rex please, don't come back with bullet holes in you, please, I can't handle that.'

'Kate I haven't come back with bullet holes in me.'

'Come on now, that arm, scratched it on the back of a truck, I don't think so, but you don't have to tell me, I don't want to force you into any little white lies.'

I have not told Kate a lie, it was not a bullet hole. Shit it could have been a fatal hole through the heart but it wasn't, it was a scratch suffered on the back of a truck, a scratch made by an AK47 bullet. Bugger, my occupation is causing Kate distress, intruding into our relationship, this is not good.

Gütersloh, it's mid afternoon when I front the main gate, the sentry is expecting me, Mr Roberts is certainly efficient. I'm directed to the Officers Mess and the first person I run into is Scruff.

'Rex, here again, delivering Chipmunks? Where have you been since I last saw you?'

'Scruff a lot has happened, an awful lot, my life has been very busy. I've been home in New Zealand, around the Pacific, and now back here, what have you been up to?'

'Still flying a Javelin, still spending a lot of time patrolling the border, quite a bit of activity these days, don't know what's going on but then we never do. Airwork's Chipmunk delivery pilots probably know all about it eh Rex, I did notice a Chipmunk on the tarmac today, yours?'

'Could be Scruff but I'm not telling and please don't voice your suspicions either, I'd appreciate that.'

'My lip is zipped but come on what are you up to?'

'Can't say because I don't know yet.'

'Don't know, can't tell?'

'Something like that Scruff.'

'Rex you need to tell me a bit about this mercenary stuff. I've figured out you're donkey deep, I intend to get into it as well. I'll be leaving the Air Force at the end of this Javelin posting, entering the civil world. I'm lining up a contract with, guess who, Airwork. They're agents for the Saudis and there're employing qualified fighter pilots, three year contracts, based in Saudi Arabia flying F16s, big money.'

'Sounds great Scruff, go for it.'

'Come on Rex, what exactly do you do, I mean a Chipmunk, pretty obvious you're across the DDR border. I think we're flying cover for you guys in Chipmunks, it's been going on for a while.'

'As they say in this business Scruff, no comment and please don't ask, now what about a beer in that excellent cellar bar.'

'Rex just one more question, are you making money?'

'Shit loads Scruff, like you would never believe.' Poor Scruff, he looked like a stunned mullet.

Next morning, *ring, ring,* 'Mr Macare there's a lady to see you.'

'A lady! bit early, I'm still in bed, can you give her a coffee perhaps and I'll be right down.'

'Just a minute; no she says she will come up to your room, is that alright?'

'Well eh yes I guess so.'

Knock, knock, Nicole Townsend and she looks ravishing.

'Caught you with your pants down Rex, ummm!'

'Cheeky, I could pull your pants down, interested?'

'Now then this is not New Caledonia this is business, serious business.'

Shit, these people know my every move, absolutely no secrets. Nicole apparently knows about the holiday, I wonder how much she knows, would it be inappropriate to make a pass. She's gorgeous, I would not put it past her to be agreeable, we'll see how things pan out.

'Would you like a coffee Nicole, I've got the makings here somewhere.'

'That would be nice, thank you. Now then I've got everything you need to enable you to do this task for us, we are assured there are no pot holes in the field you will use.'

'That sounds good, don't want a repeat of Leipzig.'

'No, no more bad luck, no more nasty experiences, your last two jobs have been rather unfortunate, that Algerian business, not nice.'

'Tell me Nicole, what do you know about the Algerian business, what has your mole in the DGSE reported?'

'No comment, you have a suspicious mind Rex. A word of advice. It's not a good idea to be asking questions, you should know that by now.'

'Ok, naughty boy me, should know better.'

'Yes you are a very naughty boy, and Kate's a naughty girl, I would have enjoyed being along on that holiday with you two, particularly the Ouvéa bit, I've never been to New Caledonia.'

What is she saying, is this a come on or what, how can I tell, better just stick with the briefing for now.

'Let's not get side tracked, let's get to the briefing. Here are some charts, it's near Brandenburg, you are familiar with the terrain. There's a spot marked on the chart, you figure out the best way to get there. It will be low level at night, a fairly full moon and hopefully little cloud so visibility should not be a problem. You will have a passenger. The idea is to drop him off at this spot then return here. The place selected is a large open field. When the people on the ground hear your engine they will switch on a light, it will be in the middle of the field. The suggestion is you land on the light, there's plenty of open field all around so the actual direction of landing is irrelevant. After you've landed turn around and take off in the direction from which you've landed, how does all that sound?'

'Yep, got it all Nicole, I assume the usual things apply, leave everything behind, some nice new designer clothes provided, some East German currency. When do you want me to be at this spot?'

'Midnight tomorrow.'

'Right, good as done, now coffee, I've been remiss, make an offer and fail to follow through.'

'Alright, I'll have that coffee with you here in your room, live a little dangerously.'

'Nicole you're tempting me, you're not supposed to fraternise with the hired help isn't that the way it is?'

'Unfortunately yes, but who would know?'
Careful Rex, Nicole could be testing you here, you just don't know, better play it cool, bide your time, opportunity will present itself again, bound to.

'Not now Nicole but how about dinner with me when I get back, I'd like that.'

'Alright, it's a date, thanks for the coffee, I'll be on my way.' She stands up and gives me a kiss, just a peck on the lips, but it tells me heaps.

I've got today and tomorrow, I need to be on the ball tomorrow night. The charts, put some time in, sort out a route and commit to memory, all the map reading features, wooded area, little lakes, roads, streams, and the dreaded transmission lines. There are two on my chosen route, one rather close to the spot where I'm required to land, better watch it.

'You're beyond the pale Rex.'
It's Scruff. I'm in the dining room enjoying an excellent late breakfast when he confronts me with this accusatory statement.

'I just don't believe it, my eyes deceive me, here's this gorgeous creature snucking out of your room this morning. Rex how in hell do you do it?'

'Eat your heart out Scruff, there are certain advantages that come with the job.'

'Come on Rex how in hell did you smuggle a squeeze like that into your room, the Mess Manager will do his block.'

'Different rules Scruff, you'll find out when you leave the service and become a *pilot for sale*, there are fringe benefits.'

It's a sunny morning, I take a walk into town, into Gütersloh, seek out the same pub on the banks of the Dalke, enjoy a stein sitting in the midday sun, it's very pleasant, I feel like I belong. I've only been here once before but there's this feeling of belonging. I get to reflecting, the contrasts in my life, the things that have happened since I last enjoyed a beer sitting at this very same spot. The missiles at Fulder, my life on the line. Kate, the Club Med and their île d'amour. Getting shot at on the back of a truck down by Leipzig. A night of debauchery in Wellington. Algeria, that frightening experience. Ouvéa, all that uninhibited sex with Eloise. There's been a lot of water under the bridge, what does the future hold?

The following evening, a light dinner in the mess then I walk along to where my little Chippie is parked. It looks like a new one, no registration markings. I reckon it will take me about an hour to fly to the designated field across the border. There's plenty of time so I get in and familiarise myself again with all the controls, well there's not that much to familiarise yourself with in a Chipmunk. While I'm doing this there's a loud roar as two pairs of Javelins get airborne, wonder what they are up to? Memories from the past come surging back, roaring off into the night in a B(I)8, the big jet was very noisy but it was a lot safer blasting around in that than what I'm doing now, sneaking about in a little Chipmunk. After a while a groundcrew chap shows up, he's got some clothes for me, I give him my bag of things and change into my nice new labelless designer gear. I wonder if Kate has noticed my nice new clothes when I come home from these *out of town for a while* ventures. A car arrives with my passenger, no introductions, *I don't need to know.* His minders strap him into the rear seat. From what I can see he appears to be a middle aged man, bound to be a spook of some kind but it's not my business, I'm just the delivery boy, the well paid delivery boy, the delivery boy who's probably putting his life on the line, but I don't know that.

Airborne, radio silence. It's quite a long way to the border, wonder why they picked Gütersloh for this operation. Somewhere closer to the border would have involved a lot less flying, perhaps it's a security requirement, who knows. The reality is it's an easy flight for me, most of it in friendly air space, no requirement to stay low. I cross the border near Magdeburg, nav lights off, get down low, real low, enemy territory. The map reading goes well. I pick up the first transmission line and then we are getting close to where this open field is supposed to be. There's the second set of cables, real close now, look for the field, not easy to see an open field at night. There's a light, it's in the middle of nowhere, that's it, yep, I can see the outline of a large field. Land on the light, well not right on it, a bit to one side, depth perception is not easy at night, really need a bit of light; thump, we've arrived. People appear, my passenger is whisked out of the rear seat, *go, go.* I spin the Chipmunk around, open the throttles, hold my breath, no pot holes please. Airborne, back the way I've just come, same landmarks, yes they all appear as ordered and in no time I'm nearing the border, that did not hurt at all.

Boom, a huge flash in the sky above and behind, what the hell's that, not my concern just keep going. Across the border, relax, nav lights on, up to a respectable height, enjoy the rest of the flight back to Gütersloh, if only they were all that easy. Land, park on the tarmac, not a soul around, but then it's around three in the morning. I walk back to the mess and crawl into bed for a few hours sleep, not much night left.

Knock, knock, what the hell, I've only just got to sleep, the bedside clock says seven. I get out of bed and open the door, there's an RAF Wing Commander standing there.

'Morning Mr Macare, sorry to wake you, can I come in, it's a matter of urgency.'

'Yes of course, come in.'

'We need your services right now.'

'Really, what's up?'

'I'm Wing Commander Jenkins, Commanding Officer of the Javelin Squadron here and I need your help.'

'My help?'

'Last night we had two aircraft up covering your flight, you're probably aware we've been doing this sort of thing. Well last night it turned bad, it appears a Mig got lucky and got one of our aircraft right on the border with a missile. We've been in contact with our agents over there, they've got one of the crew members from the aircraft, he managed to eject, our people got to him before the STASI. We want you to go across the border and pick him up.'

'Ah, well yes of course, why me?'

'You're experienced in this type of operation and your Johnny-on-the-spot, we want to do this right now.'

'Well yes, of course, but what about the people who employ me, and the aircraft?'

'I appreciate there could be problems but we must act quickly, we want our man back and I'm asking you to go and get him, we'll sort out the mess later, I don't think there will be any issues but there's no time to even think about that.'

'Okay, let's do it, where is he?'

'Good question, he's just across the border near Magdeburg, our people are going to get him to an open field, they'll give us a location shortly. We want you to fly in and snatch him. We'll put up some Hunters. If needs be they'll cross the border and deal with any threat from Migs, ready, I'll drive you to the dispersal.'

I'm strapped in ready to go. The Wing Commander comes running across the tarmac map in hand and points out an area of open ground that's not far across the border, the problem in my mind is the time it will take me to get there, it's quite a long way to the border from Gütersloh. Map in hand I'm off, full throttle due east. It's almost a pleasure flying in bright sunlight, map reading is dead easy. I've figured out how I'll get from the border to the open ground marked on the map and being daylight I'll be able to get seriously low, flying around the trees not over them, they'll never see me coming. The Chipmunk's ideal for this, real seat of the pants flying, I'm loving it. Those nasty bastards with their AK47s will be hard pushed to get a shot off. There it is, the open ground I'm looking for but there's no one in sight, probably hiding. I land, several people appear, a flurry of activity, someone is bundled into the back seat, *go, go,* I do, take off straight ahead, there's plenty of room, a Chipmunk does not need much space. Suddenly gun fire, muzzle flashes, not very distinctive in the sunlight, probably AK47s, ping, ping, shit we're taking hits. A misfire, the engine's misfiring, bugger. Full throttle straight for the border, it's not that far, forget the low flying bit just get away from here. There it is, a long straight fence not far in front of us, the engine's starting to make terrible noises, shit, don't stop now, *bang,* it stops.

'Hang on, were going to land straight ahead, crash straight ahead,' I shout to my back seat passenger.
The border is very close, we should be able to reach it, we do. The little Chipmunk crashes right through the ugly wire fence.

'Get out, run.'
There's a tremendous roar and a Hunter jet fighter thunders right over us, really low, going east. I'm out and running, so is my passenger, the Hunter will deal with any pursuit. We're on the right

side of the border fence, we run like hell then collapse in a heap, exhausted.

'Scruff'

'Rex'

Small world!

We're in the cellar bar at the Officers Mess at Gütersloh, Scruff and myself, we've already had far too much beer but the circumstances are extraordinary. Wing Commander Jenkins is with us, he too has had quite a bit. It's mid-afternoon and other members of Scruff's squadron are trickling in, this could, will, develop into quite a drinking session. Scruff's radar operator, the other member of the Javelin crew? no news. What had happened? Well two Javelins had been flying cover for me, something I was not aware of, *don't need to know.* The East Germans must have become a bit fed up with the border incursions by the little Chipmunks. Unable to down a Chipmunk they had gone for a Javelin instead, it must have been just a bit over the border and thus open to attack. The bright flash I saw as I came back from my insertion was Scruff's Javelin being hit by a missile.

'Scruff you will be forever in my debt, just think about those finger nail extractions the STASI specialise in, think about what I've saved you from, now you know first-hand how I'm becoming rich and famous, well rich anyway.'

'Thank you Rex, I owe you my life and thank you for the insight into what it's like out there in the civilian world of flying but tell me, how in hell did you get that squeeze into your room the other night?'

'Goes with the job Scruff, about your radar operator, any news?'

'Nothing yet, he did eject but I never saw him on the ground, big worry, don't want to lose him, he's my mate, been together for a couple of years, he's a good chap and a skilled operator.'

The drinking session intensifies as more of Scruff's squadron show up, this sort of thing needs to be celebrated. I think back to my own squadron days, did not take much of an excuse to have a real bender, quite a common occurrence.

About eight in the evening Wing Commander Jenkins jumps onto the bar, taps his glass for attention, and announces that Scruff's radar operator has been found by some friendlies, he's in safe hands albeit on the wrong side of the border. There's an eruption of cheering and a rush on the bar, some serious drinking now. My thoughts turn to my part in all this, will I be called upon again or will I simply return home to Auckland as planned, guess things will sort themselves out in the next day or so.

Ring, ring, next morning. I've got a splitting headache, a severe hangover and fond memories of how this was almost the norm when I was at Geilenkirchen in my Air Force days.

'Morning Rex, Nicole here, how's the head?'

'Well it's on my shoulders but it's very tender.'

'Congratulations for what you did yesterday, it's all been approved, a good outcome, well apart from losing a Chipmunk. Mr Roberts will be making an adjustment to your remuneration, that'll be an upwards adjustment, we won't be deducting the cost of the Chipmunk but that's the second one now and another shot up.'

'Thanks for that Nicole, where are you calling from, not downstairs are you?'

'Yes I am, I'll be having breakfast in your dining room shortly, why don't you join me?'

'Well yes I'd like that, give me a few moments to rejoin the world, bit slow at the moment, say thirty minutes.'

'I'll wait for you in the lobby, look forward to it.'

Sounds promising, Nicole obviously wants a bit more contact otherwise things would have been dealt with over the phone. I race under the shower, all cleaned up, down to the lobby.

'Nicole.'

'Morning again Rex,' and she gives me a little peck on the lips just as Scruff walks into the lobby.

'Jeezz Rex, how in hell do you do it.'

'I've told you Scruff, perks of the job.' I catch Nicole's eye as I say this and give her a wink, she catches on immediately, sharp girl.

'So this must be Scruff, the fellow you told me about *last night*, the fellow you saved from the finger nail pullers, hello Scruff, I'm Nicole, Rex's friend.'

Poor Scruff, we've got him completely foxed; *told you last night?*

'We're going to have breakfast in the dining room, why don't you join us Scruff.'

There's an incredulous look on his face, not only does he have a girl in his room in the Officers Mess, a no no at the best of times, but he's got the gall to bring her into the dining room as well.

Nicole opens the conversation in the dining room.

'Scruff, your radar operator is in safe hands, you'll be seeing him again, probably within the next few days, it won't be via Chipmunk though, we've overplayed our hand a bit there, need to give it a rest for a while.'

This is news to me, good news. Obviously Nicole's organisation, the people who currently have me in their employ, are well organised and Nicole is being kept fully informed. Sounds like another back of a truck deal. I think back to my own border crossing on the back of a truck, bloody high risk. Scruff looks mystified.

'How do you know this Nicole?'

I intervene. 'Scruff, Nicole is a very perceptive girl, she just knows these things.'

'Yeah right, very perceptive indeed and I thought she was just another girlfriend Rex.'

'Scruff, what's this just another, I am *the girlfriend*.' Nicole is really getting Scruff confused now.

'Now then breakfast, first time I've been invited into an Officers Mess for breakfast, looks like a good selection.' Nicole says this with tongue in cheek.

The organisation, whatever form it may take, and something I don't need to know about, obviously has strong ties to the military establishment, Nicole has access to a lot of things.

It is a good breakfast the Air Force look after their jet jocks at Gütersloh. Scruff is still unhappy, he can't quite figure out my relationship with Nicole but he's starting to get it. Scruff's been given some time off from flying, the last couple of days have been stressful, very stressful. Shot out of the sky, ejecting, then getting snatched from under the noses of the bad guys by me.

'Why don't we all go for a walk after breakfast, into Gütersloh.' I suggest.

'Good idea,' from Nicole, 'I'm staying in Gütersloh. I'd like to get you two handsome guys a beer.'

So Nicole has been in the area during the insertion operation, interesting. My masters obviously keep a close eye on their operatives in the field. It also explains how the Air Force was able to get authorisation so quickly for me to rescue Scruff. Nicole must be quite senior in the system, whatever it is. Perhaps she's just staying around so she can keep that dinner date she promised a few days ago.

A couple of hours later we're in *my* pub on the banks of the Dalke enjoying a beer, Scruff gets to questioning Nicole.

'Nicole, you don't have to, as they say in your business, confirm or deny, but you've just got to be Rex's controller in the murky business you two are involved in and I just want to take the opportunity to make a pitch for the future, get myself on the record. I'm out of the Air Force in eighteen months and I wouldn't mind following in Rex's footsteps. At the moment I'm looking at a contract with the Saudis then I see what Rex is up to. His current employment seems to involve pretty girls, well there's yourself, who else is there?'

This conversation is getting awkward, better introduce a bit of levity, throw Scruff off a bit.

'Pretty girls you say, you don't know the half of it.'

'Rex is right, he's got more pretty girls in his life than he can handle, he's just come over to Germany to see me, his European girlfriend, get away from his Auckland hareem.'

Nicole is something else, she's come to my rescue, I wonder what she's really thinking, what she really knows, probably an awful lot. Scruff looks thoroughly confused.

'His girlfriend? sure about that Nicole, I don't think so.'

'Oh well, not to worry Scruff and on the subject of girlfriends why don't you and Carrol join Rex and myself for dinner tonight at my hotel here, they have an excellent dining room.'

Well that's right out of left field, who's Carrol?

'How do you know about Carrol?'

'Scruff you've got a crush on Carrol, the schoolteacher who lives in the Officers Mess, she would love you to invite her out to dinner, you just ask.'

Yet again I'm amazed at the depth of knowledge that these covert organisations have about people, poor Scruff, he's looking like a stunned mullet again.

'I'm in awe of you Nicole, you are all knowing, definitely Rex's controller, yes I'll do that, ask Carrol out, I'm sure she'll say yes.'

It's a great dinner; Carrol is an attractive blue eyed blond who Scruff's rather smitten with, he's been dating her for several months. We avoid anything to do with what's happened during the last few days, way outside Carrol's comprehension, far removed from the world of school teaching and not something we want to become common knowledge. Nicole plays the part of the girlfriend, plays it a bit too well, she's getting me aroused and she knows it, doing it deliberately perhaps? After dinner we adjourn to the hotel's cocktail bar, quite an elegant affair and enjoy a couple of Baileys, by then it's quite late.

'Ah well perhaps it's time to go home, that was a lovely dinner Nicole, nice to get to know you, remember my name now, get me on the record. I'll just call a cab, Carrol and myself will be off. Rex want a lift back to the mess?'

'No, Rex does not need a lift, he's staying here with me tonight.'

Vietnam

The long flight home, that was quite a mission. Shot at again, crashed a plane, how long is my luck going to hold? Nicole, a revelation. That one night in her bed confirmed everything I had imagined, my wildest fantasies, she was incredible.

'Breakfast sir,' it's the hostess, another airline meal, not too bad, not too good either. Not long now? Auckland and the normal world, the world where people don't try to kill me. Kate, my Kate, guilt, Nicole, does that count? It was business, Nicole was just business, would not want to dissatisfy my masters. Can I believe myself, am I trying to justify something?

'Sorry Nicole I can't hop into your bed just now, it's not right, I know you're my boss and it will cost me my job, but sorry, not tonight.' Yeah right!

Get a message to Kate at the next transit lounge, there seem to be a lot of transit lounges these days, it's a long way to Germany, too far, need something closer to home. I'll suggest it to Mr Roberts, perhaps the French have something but hang on they're dangerous, big money though, puts Mr Roberts to shame. Do I want to continue in this business, yes I do, I like the money, give it that year we agreed on.

What will the scene be back in Auckland, how will relationships be developing, what will Tara be up to, how long before she's in our bed, and the boyfriend, Marciel, what will Kate make of him? I wonder if Ali's still fooling around or has Jeff taken her out of play? Different life to being *out of town for a while.* We're back at my place, the airport pick up, the onlookers gawking at Kate's wild welcome. It's a wet morning, not one of Auckland's best, we're straight into bed, best place on a day like this, there's some catching up to do. Kate's searching my body for war wounds, all she succeeds in doing is bringing on a mighty erection that gives her, gives us both, extreme pleasure.

Next morning, breakfast, delivery from the Flint Agency, this could be interesting. There's $175,000 in the package, big notes. I'm going to have to do something about all this cash, can't just keep it under the bed. $100,000 extra for Scruffs rescue, interesting, how has it been calculated? A highly skilled and experienced night fighter pilot saved, does not need to be replaced, what's that worth? how much to train a replacement? to acquire the experience, the skills, probably millions, how would you cost it? I've just made a quarter of a million for a week's work, that's incredible, and I got to bed Nicole. I think I will continue in my chosen career for a bit longer. It's got to the stage where I can't give it away, not now.

Still raining, breakfast in the kitchen, the delivery has really brightened up the day. I tell Kate, all this cash and how I earnt it, she's lost for words. We decide to open several bank accounts, several accounts each, disperse the cash a little, it's a nice problem to have and, 'look Kate, no bullet holes, not even a scratch,' ummm, is this a fool's paradise I'm living in? Well I'm committed so stop thinking about it, worrying achieves nothing, enjoy the moment.

'What shall we do with the day Kate, you don't have to work do you?'

'Not today, got a shoot tomorrow afternoon, a full day after that, then a day off.'

'How about something ordinary like going to a movie, popcorn and chocolate tops, cuddle in the back row, back to our teenage years.'

'Yes, keep us out of the bedroom for a while, where's the paper, what's on?'

That evening we're back at Kate's flat, Ali and Jeff come 'round. Ali's spending all her time at Jeff's place these days. The big announcement, she's moving in with him and wants to relinquish her share of the flat. Well now, how about that, should I move in with Kate, I would certainly like to but how will it impact on her developing modelling career?

'Not a problem darling, I'm probably one of the few models who is not living with their man, shall we go and get your things right now?'

'Come here, I love you, love you to bits. Quick Ali, gather up your things, oh, most of your stuff's already at Jeff's place, well let's all celebrate, a momentous day.'

Some quiet time in Auckland, I've moved in, relinquished my flat. Kate's tied up with work but we still manage plenty of time together, it's nice. This life I'm leading is a bit disorganised though, I never know when there'll be a phone call, an offer too good to refuse and I'll be off, *out of town for a while.* There's no stability, cannot plan anything, no goals, and I find myself asking for the umpteenth time, is this what I want to be doing and getting the same answer every time, I just don't know. What I do know, the one certain thing, the money, where else am I going to be able to generate wealth this quickly? What I can do, and what I have done, is make it easier for Kate, take her away for some serious rest time. I have the wherewithal to do this, to do it in style, compensate her for what must be some serious worrying.

Been back a few days now, not heard from anyone, no phone calls, no Tara, bit scarred she might call, no Mr Roberts, no Pierre Brodeur, not seen anything of Ali either apart from that first night when she made the big announcement, and then it happens, a call from Mr Roberts.

'I see you've changed your address Rex, cup of tea in an hour.'
It's bad news. Mr Roberts felt he had to tell me face to face. Apparently Scruff's radar operator was being smuggled back across

the border on the same truck that had been used for my border crossing when it all went wrong. He had been dragged out from under the hay by the East German border guards, badly beaten, and shot dead. Apparently the smuggling operation had been compromised and the whole covert organisation in that part of the DDR had now been closed down. Unlikely to be any more Chipmunk operations for a while.

'How's that going to impact on me Mr Roberts?'

'At this stage there will be no more of what you have been doing in the foreseeable future, no more German operations, but don't despair Rex we have other irons in the fire that could involve you.'

Bugger, poor Scruff, he was pretty close to his radar operator. Casualty of the Cold War, the war where no one gets killed, well that's the public perception. I guess the demise of Scruff's mate will never be made public and when you think it through it could be construed that some of the blame for this could be laid on me, after all it was me he was protecting.

'Rex, put it out of your mind, don't go and get all upset by this, it's the reality of the business we're in, these things happen, a fact of life. I won't be calling on your services for a little while, take a break, enjoy some time with Kate. I believe there will be an offer from Vogue soon, you might perhaps get to go to Paris, catch up with your French holiday friends.'

'Mr Roberts you should write a book, *The Man Who Knows Everything*.'

'That's a thought Rex, have to wait for retirement. I'll be off now, sorry to have to give you the bad news but please try and put it out of your mind.'

Ring, ring, can't be Mr Roberts again surely; it's not.

'Russ Horsley, hello, not seen you for a while, well I've been out of town for a bit.'

'Rex what about a beer, I've got something I want to talk to you about, the Paddington in an hour?'

'Done.'

It's a good spot the Paddington, the last time I had a beer there with Russ it developed, Erika, and a near miss with Tara.

'What's with the arm Russ, appears you've grown a new one, let's have a look.'

It's a very high tech piece of arm indeed, fingers that worked, able to hold a beer glass, probably wipe his bum as well.

'That looks pretty smart Russ, what won't it do?'

'Can't feel things, no sensory ability but it's really good in every other department, now what I want to find out, will it fly an aeroplane. I've tackled the Aero Club, they are a bit reluctant which I thought was pretty poor so I thought I would lay it on you to take me up, see if I still have it.'

'A Monteiths Black while we plan the campaign. Of course you'll still have it, what are you talking about. The hard bit will be getting your license back, the department has the understanding of a rock when it comes to things like this.'

'I want to find out if I can still fly, a licence is not really a requirement in the mercenary business but people like Mr Roberts might baulk at the idea of a pilot with a tin arm.'

'Why don't we tackle the aero club, fly with me, have nothing to do with their training organisation. I wonder how they would react if we told them we are sharpening up our act so we can do some covert flying for secret Government agencies, totally beyond their comprehension.'

'Right that's settled, we'll book an aircraft for a few flying sessions. You can do your thing, convince yourself you're still up to getting around the highlands of Vietnam, dodging the bullets, or sneaking along at night over the DDR in a little aeroplane and getting shot at by bigger guns, reckon you can still do it? of course you can, have faith.'

'Thanks Rex, let's get right on to it, what about tomorrow.'

'Done, you do the booking, no hang on, I will, the license, yours has bullet holes in it.'

'Yeah, the license thing is a problem, can't see me getting it back without a fight, do I want it back, do Mr Roberts and his kind worry about things like that, let that one lie for the time being, could be a long term project.'

'Now then Russ, change of subject, how's your love life, or more correctly, your sex life?'

'Well what can I say, up until recently I've been keeping both Erika and Tara happy and that's been pretty full on, then Tara's man reappeared and took some of the pressure off, now we've got a foursome going, it's a really erotic set up.'

'Well you are a dark horse Russ, Tara *and* Erika.'

'It's changed a bit with Tara's man back on the scene. I'm taking Erika out, quite keen on her actually, but Tara and Marciel keep crashing the scene, they love the group sex thing, can't complain though, it's a great set up at the moment.'

'You're a sexy devil Russ, something about a man with a tin arm eh!'

I'm thinking, hope Tara's satisfied with the current arrangement, does not come after Kate and myself, not sure we want to be involved here in Auckland. Let it lie for the time being, see what time brings.

A couple of days later Russ and myself front the aero club. We hire a small Cessna, use my license, and off we go. I let Russ do it all, that's what we're here for. It's a no brainer, he's right up with the play, could be buzzing along at night over Germany right down on the deck, not a problem.

'Well that's laid the bogey to rest Russ, the tin arm's no handicap at all, could be advantages, less body parts to get shot off. What happens now, we get onto Mr Roberts and convince him you're available again, see how he responds, how do we contact him?'

'I've got a number.'

'Well that's it, what are we waiting for? Bit short of work in Germany at the moment Russ.' I tell him about my last job and the unfortunate aftermath.

So that's Russ sorted, just got to convince Mr Roberts to take him on again, see how he reacts.

A few days later, a phone call, it's Pierre Brodeur.

'Monsieur Macare, I would like to talk.'

'Ok, but I'm still having nightmares about that Algerian business. If you've got something for me it will need to be lower risk than that one.'

'Perhaps I can call around, you've changed your address I see.'

'Yes you are seeing correctly monsieur, say an hour from now, is that ok.'

Knock, knock, Monsieur Brodeur.

'Good morning Rex, I've got something that might interest you, Vietnam.'

'Vietnam, different.'

'We have a situation where some big French owned rubber plantations are having an access problem. The Viet Cong control most of the roads in the countryside and they have taken to kidnapping French nationals for ransom and extracting taxes for use of the roads. Normal road traffic for the transport of provisions and rubber are not that big a problem, the South Vietnamese Government has been providing armed escorts, it's people, it's become quite dangerous for Europeans to travel by road. The only safe way now is by air. This has deprived the Viet Cong of one of their sources of income. They have been taking pot shots at some of the light aircraft we've been using, probably trying to deter us. We are interested in employing freelance pilots to do this flying. There are some big numbers involved. The biggest rubber plantation in Vietnam, the Michelin owned Dâu Tiêng plantation in Binh Duong province, covers 15,000 hectares and employs 40,000 people. There are dozens of smaller ones. The total area involved in rubber production is huge in Binh Duong province.'

'You say we, who exactly are the people employing these pilots?'

'It's a French Government agency. These plantations are supported by the French Government and they are prepared to pay handsomely for your services.'

'Sounds like a long term thing, would that be correct?'

'Yes and no, we are flexible, we can offer long or short term, depends on who's involved and what our requirements are. A two week contract would be the minimum period, longer term could be available.'

'Ok, what sort of money are we talking?'

'A two week contract averaging two flights per day, 2000 Swiss Francs per flight, paid into your numbered Swiss account.'
That's not bad money, two thousand Swiss francs is about $3,200, two flights a day, $6,400, two week contract, almost $90,000.

'What's the deal, would there be two flights every day.'

'It will vary, two would be the average, weather and actual requirements determine the number. Payment is for flights completed.'

'Ok' where will this operation be based and where are the plantations involved.'

Pierre Brodeur produces a map of South Vietnam and we get down to details. The flying is based at Quy Nhon airfield which is on the coast about half way between Saigon and the border with North Vietnam. There are several rubber plantations in the area inland from

Quy Nhon, the biggest being the Michelin one. The flying will involve several plantations in the area so there's plenty of work.

'Danger level?'

'At this stage it appears to be low. It's not in the best interests of either of the opposing sides in Vietnam to have these plantations cease production and there's a lot of political will on both sides to ensure their viability. The only threat is from local militias who are annoyed that one of their revenue sources is being compromised.'

'Sounds interesting, what are the accommodation arrangements in Quy Nhon and when do you want my answer?'

'We will put you up at one of our hotels, a good one, and secure. We will also give you return airline tickets to Saigon and supply secure road transport to Quy Nhon. The aircraft involved will be a Piper Cherokee Six carrying up to five passengers, you are familiar with the Piper?'

'Indeed I am. I do not have happy memories.'

'I would like your decision in the next day or two, that ok? Here's a number that will get me.'

'Ok Pierre, I think I'm interested. I've got a mate who's also a pilot, similar circumstances to myself, he's already done contract flying in Vietnam, he might be interested in what you are offering me, shall I put you onto him?'

'Yes, give me his details, we will check him out.'

I give Pierre Russ's contact information. He's probably not on the DGSE's radar so they will probably want to do some background checking.

'Well that about wraps it up for now, call me when you make up your mind. If you're on we would want you in Vietnam in two weeks' time.'

'Russ, the Paddington in an hour, I've got something for you.'

Along to the Paddington.

'Might have some flying for you Russ; might!'

I fill Russ in on what has just transpired with Pierre Brodeur.

'The DGSE probably don't know you, not crossed the Frogs at any stage have you Russ?'

'Not that I'm aware of, wonder how they'll react to my tin arm, guess we'll be finding out. Vietnam, my experience there was not the greatest but this sounds relatively safe. Both opposing sides on our side, odd things happen in war. Just the rogue militias to worry about, should be ok. I'd take a punt on this one, good money for the risk involved. I'm certainly interested, if I'm acceptable that is.'

'Monteiths Black?'

'Why not, how's Erika Russ?'

'She's good, pretty demanding in the sack though, not that I'm complaining.'

'And the license, pushed that one along yet?'

'Yes, I got right onto it after our Aero Club session, the first response from the department was not good, looks like they are going to really lay it on me to prove that my tin arm is absolutely safe to fly with, how they want me to do this they haven't said. Going to be bloody minded by the look of it.'

'I don't know what the Frogs will want in the way of a license, they never asked me for the one and only job I did for them, I suspect a license will not come into this current offer, I'm sure we will find out soon enough.'

We spend the rest of the afternoon in the Paddington, I suggest dinner, myself, Kate, Russ and Erika. I did not really know Erika, just that one night when Russ first met her and I was busy dodging Tara.

'Good idea, you're on, I'll give her a call.'

'I'll sound out Kate.'

We get the girls agreement, dinner at our favourite restaurant, that's settled. Perhaps I'll give Pierre Brodeur a call, tell him I'm on for his Vietnam offer, Russ in keen as well.

Another good dinner, they're all good dinners at our favourite restaurant and the service gets better with every visit.

Big spender that Rex and his girlfriend, we like them using our restaurant, wonder where he gets all his money, always picks up the tab. They're with another couple this time, she's a real beauty, probably another model. He seems to have an in on the modelling world. The fellow with her, got a prosthetic arm by the look of it, not your ordinary everyday diners, definitely the beautiful people.

Erika is a real live wire, she's got that *party girl* something about her, Russ has confirmed it, she's a real party girl. They've been into the foursome thing as well, not sure we want to get involved in that right now, not ready for it, if we were it would have to be with Tara. Kate and I have already been there with Tara. She's got the boyfriend from Paris now, Kate would have to make up her mind there.

'Baileys perhaps?
It's starting to rain, good Auckland weather, we'll get a taxi home in a little while.'
We drop Russ and Erika off.

'Come in for a night cap.'

'Ah, thanks but no, not tonight Erika.'

'Come on you two don't be spoil sports, come in and we'll have some fun.'

'I'm sure we would but not tonight, another time perhaps Erika.'

'Alright then but is that a promise, another time, promise, say it Rex.'

'Goodnight Erika, great getting to know you, goodnight Russ.'
Was that a come on or what, a blatant invitation to who knows what, I catch Kat's eye.

'Need to tread carefully there eh Kate, she's a wild one that Erika, real character though.'

'Yes she's got a bit of a reputation, very good model though, true professional, but yes, she absolutely eats men, hope your buddy Russ has got what it takes.'

'Russ will be ok, he'll handle Erika, but the question right now is, do we want to get involved in a foursome.'

'Don't know Rex but I do know I want to be involved in a twosome and right now, could be in the back of this taxi. When did you last do it in the back of a taxi Rex and don't tell me you never have.'

We're dropped off at our place, the flat that Kate and I now share, straight into bed, a twosome, it's so nice.

A couple of days later Pierre Brodeur calls 'round, he's got tickets and some Vietnamese currency, it's called the dong and it's not worth much. Huge denomination notes, some are for 500,000, worth around $30, better off with US dollars, you can get some in Saigon on your way through. The booking puts me in Saigon in eight days time, one night in a hotel, then a chauffeur driven car to Quy Nhon.

Seven days in Auckland before I'm off to ply my trade in South East Asia, different, very different. Russ has not heard from Pierre Brodeur, I guess the French will be checking his background, his flying experience. These organisations who employ mercenaries seem to be quite careful about who they take on. Russ should have no trouble, apart from his tin arm. Don't think the lack of a license will trouble Pierre Brodeur. Kate and I keep to ourselves during this period, not overkeen to socialise, could lead to compromising situations that we don't want just now.

Ali calls around one evening, Jeff is out of town and she's at a loose end. She stays for dinner, seems reluctant to leave.

'Perhaps I could stay the night with you two?'

'Come on Ali, you're Jeff's squeeze now, you're supposed to stay faithful to him.'

'No, that's not the arrangement, well I've not really discussed it with him but he's never objected in the past and besides I want to have sex with you Rex, , Kate will be on for it, isn't that right Kate?' Kate stares straight at me and comes out with it.

'Yes Ali you're on, it'll get me going, we can get Rex all worked up, what do you say Rex? want two girls to work you over?'

There's no stopping them, the clothes come off and they've got me on the bed doing all sorts of things, delightful things, it culminates in some serious fucking, particularly with Ali, she's just about out of control. I don't think Jeff's been giving it to her as much as she would like.

Eventually our desires are sated and there's some sleeping but when the morning sun comes in through the bedroom window the sight of two naked girls in the bed sets me off, it's all on again, both girls are more than willing.

'Morning girls, great night eh, satisfied?'

'No Rex, again please,' from Ali.

'Do you think I could take to coming around here whenever I want in the future, would that be alright with you two?'

'Don't know about that Ali, Jeff would not be impressed, it would not be a very nice thing to confront him with either, not now that you two are a couple.'

'Perhaps you're right, I should not be jumping into your bed like this, just can't help myself.'

'Ok that's settled, breakfast, then a walk in the park, you come too Ali, don't have to work do you?'

'This afternoon, I've got a shoot, I think Kate's in it as well.'

'Yep I am, we can take our shared lover for a walk though, keep him fit and healthy, he's good for our wellbeing, need to look after him.'

What am I hearing, is Kate letting me know that she's partial to having Ali drop in for sex whenever she feels the urge, christ, is this what I want, sounds like it's what Kate wants, mind you I have no problem giving it to Ali, she's a very willing partner and she's good at it, a real delight.

Saigon, hot, humid, and it smells. I'm in a hotel, The Rex, must be a good hotel, got a great name! The room is huge, high ceiling, big fan, a real blast from the past, very comfortable. I've got a day here then a drive up the coast to Quy Nhon. I need to get out and about, explore this famous old Asian city, a first for me, not been to Vietnam. I wander out onto the bustling street and hail a cyclo, a three wheel adaption of a bicycle, two passengers sit in the wide seat at the front, the 'peddler' sits behind them.

'Ben Than Market,' we're off.

I've been told it's a 'must,' a huge covered market, very old, in the centre of the city. What an experience, wall to wall traffic, total bedlam, hundreds of cyclos, mopeds, taxis, cars, a lot of old Citroëns, the noise, constant toot toot, from a huge variety of horns, ring ring, from hundreds of bicycle bells, mopeds accelerating past dangerously close, people shouting, it's a surreal experience. I'm there, a huge sprawling covered market, one of the biggest in the Orient. Everything's on sale here, absolutely everything and the place is jammed with people all jabbering away, it's a noisy place. I wander around the jungle of aisles and alleyways awed by the huge selection, the variety, the sheer volume of things available for purchase and right down at the back of the place I come across a food court and butchers area. Bit different to my concept of a food court. It's a charnel house, blood and guts everywhere and there are people eating there, the smell. I'm out of here, not sure my stomach can handle it. I hail another cyclo and get him to take me around the city, I want to soak up the sights and sounds, it's just so fascinating. Back to the Rex and a beer in their bar, a step back in time.

Somerset Maugham, pink gin, liveried barmen, overstuffed sofas, spit and polish, real colonial atmosphere, the French have created something here.

My thoughts turn to dinner. I've heard of a place, La Bibliothèque de Madame Dai, commonly known as Madam Dai's, another 'must do' in Saigon.

'Sir, you must book, it's very popular, I'll do it for you, just one is it?' the hotel receptionist is very helpful.

Another cyclo and I'm there. It's impressive, high ceiling, almost a medieval atmosphere, quite small, not many tables. Apparently the place used to be a museum. There are all sorts of artifacts on the walls, some of them seriously old. There are signed photos of famous people as well, the place just oozes character. The menu, here's a challenge, French Vietnamese, I need help and help is on hand. The waitress, an attractive Vietnamese girl, excellent English. She soon has me sorted and orders some dishes she knows I will like, not wrong, the combination of French and Vietnamese cuisine is something else, no idea what I'm eating but it's good. I'm seated at a small table that allows me a view into the bowels of the kitchen each time the door opens, a dark and threatening place with a high ceiling, devils and dragons and all things spooky, another wine perhaps, Rex your imagination is running riot, but the food that comes through that door is great.

Outside, I'm besieged by youngsters hawking things, cards, cigarettes, biro pens, cigarette lighters, small flags, everything's 'a dollar, one dollar mister.' They are persistent, won't leave me alone, follow me along the street, 'one dollar mister, one dollar.' Eventually I hail a cyclo, 'The Rex please.' The youngsters run after the cyclo, 'only a dollar mister, one dollar.'

'Monsieur Macare, I'm your driver.' It was an ageing Citroën, one of those ones with the gear shift poking out of the dash, there are hundreds of them in Saigon. Off we go, next stop Quy Nhon and my next flying job, something a little different in my chosen career. The drive through the outskirts of Saigon is fascinating. The traffic, total bedlam, mopeds, cyclos, cars, noise, toot toot, ring ring, shouting, squealing brakes and apparently no accidents, it all works. The traffic thins and we are out in the countryside driving up the coast road. The city traffic is replaced by country traffic, farm vehicles being drawn by water buffalo, old tractors, a lot of bicycles, people walking, coolie hats, everyone seems to be wearing one, still the old Citroëns, how many of these things are there in Vietnam? The traffic is still quite heavy. Everyone seems to be driving in the centre of the road moving over just a little when there's conflict. Amazingly there do not seem to be any accidents, an interesting drive. We arrive at the Villa Hy in Quy Nhon, an old four story French Colonial building. I'm expected and shown to a pretty comfortable room.

'Gentleman to see you Monsieur Macare.' There's a French fellow waiting in the lobby.

'Bonjour, I'm Lois Couture your contact here in Quy Nhon, I'll be briefing you on what we require of you while you are here, perhaps we can go up to your room.'

'Now then Monsieur Macare, by the way please call me Louis, some background. There are several French owned rubber plantations that we service, all inland from here in Binh Duong province in the Central Highlands. Dau Tieng is the biggest, owned by the Michelin company. There are more around Pleiku in Gia Lai province, the rubber capital of Vietnam. Rubber is huge business in this country, their major industry and the biggest money maker. What we want you to do is fly people into and out of these plantations. Road travel has become hazardous, local rogue militias have been kidnapping people for ransom, particularly Europeans, the safest way now is to use an aeroplane. Operations are conducted from the airfield here and there is another airfield at Pleiku but that is a very active military base, we don't use it unless there's an emergency. The plantations are not troubled by the sporadic fighting in the area, both sides realise the value of the plantations and don't want to disturb rubber production. Bit of a strange situation but then everything about this war is a bit strange.'

'What's the threat level, like how dangerous is this flying?'

'There's little danger, the odd pot shot from rogue militia, that's about all, if there are any major military operations in the area then we suspend flying.'

'And the workload?'

'Ok, each morning I will brief you on what we want done each day, it will probably involve two or more return flights to various plantations, there are quite a lot of them. Around 200,000 people work on these plantations mostly Vietnamese, however, there are several thousand French nationals as well. You will be busy for the two weeks you are here, and that's a point, how come you are only here for two weeks?'

'That was the contract offered in New Zealand, it was suggested a longer period might be available.'

'Odd, most of the pilots who come here stay a month or more, they have all been French, you're from New Zealand, different.'

'I think your Government, specifically the DGSE, are not sure about me so they are easing me in gently.'

'Really monsieur, sounds rather strange, what's the problem?'

'I think I got offside with your people some years ago, not my fault, however they appear to be a little suspicious, quite unfounded I assure you, I hope you will find me satisfactory, just another fellow who flies aeroplanes for money, in this case rather good money, that's why I'm here, oh yes, please call me Rex.'

'Well that's interesting, the DGSE you say, we are not DGSE, we're a Government agency but you do have a point, the DGSE have their sticky fingers into everything. What did you do to attract their attention?'

'Should not really be saying but it was something I was involved in while I was it the Royal Air Force when I was a young chap, doing what I was told, your people saw it as not being in the best interests of The Republic.'

'Well we all have a past, now then what about a drink down in the hotel bar, I will be seeing quite a lot of you during your short stay here, daily briefings and anything else that might come up. Have you done work for us before?'

'Once, this is my second flying job for French interests. The first was high risk, bit too high for my liking and I let it be known so now your people have come up with this, supposedly low risk.'

'Yes the risk factor is low but tell me, what was it that was high risk?'

'Algeria.'

'Enough said, that's a bloody dangerous place, perhaps they were testing you.'

'Testing me, bloody nearly killed me.'

'Enough, let's have that drink.'

Louis Couture was a good guy, a nice Frenchman. We had several beers in the hotel bar then he took his leave saying he would be around at eight in the morning to brief me on tomorrow's flying task.

'Morning Rex, sleep well, good breakfast? I've got some interesting flying lined up for you today, a couple of trips for our biggest client Michelin, some people they want flown into Dau Tieng and some more they want brought out, probably a couple of trips at least, I don't have the actual numbers. Here's a map of the area, all the plantations we service are marked on it, you'll need to familiarise yourself with the area. It's pretty straight forward. Dau Tieng is easy to find and there's a good strip there. A Vietnamese chap will service your Piper at Dau Tieng, he's good, been doing it for quite a while and there's another one of our people who will look after you here at Quy Nhon. I'll drop you off at the airfield now.'

Four men and a lady are waiting at the aeroplane.

'Bonjour, I'm the new chap, just give me a minute to get my bearings and I'll be right with you.'

Thrown in at the deep end, quick, let's have a look at that map, where's Dau Tieng.

'Hello I'm Tung you crewman.' It's a Vietnamese fellow, an intelligent looking chap.

'Need a hand,' Tung offers.

'Ah yes Tung, where's Dau Tieng?'

'Right there, can't miss it, big strip, easy to find.' Tung points it out on my map.

'Thanks Tung, bit new, learning fast.'

'You'll be ok, it's easy flying around here, just be aware of the weather, rain can close the place down at times otherwise there are no problems.'

I'm studying the map, don't want my passengers to see this, not confidence inspiring, however it's pretty plain sailing. The route to Dau Tieng is obvious, map reading will be easy, damn sight easier than doing it at night at ground level.

'Mesdames et messieurs we're ready, hop aboard please.'

Into the pilot's seat and I've got the lady in the seat beside me.

'Bonjour Monsieur, my name is Michelle, and yours?'

'Ah, Rex, call me Rex,'

'Rex, you are not French?'

'New Zealand.'

'Ah from Nouvelle-Zélande, a handsome man from Nouvelle-Zélande.'

She's a looker, early-thirties, grey eyed brunette and cheeky. I busy myself with the business in hand, refamiliarizing myself with the Piper, trying to make it look like I do this every day, Michelle is watching me closely.

'You have done this before Rex?'

'Yes, but it was a little while ago, just refamiliarizing myself, we'll be off in just a minute.'

'Ah Rex, I know the feeling, I am a pilot, I have flown this Piper several times, just ask me if you want.'

There's a cheeky tone to her voice and I feel myself warming to Michelle, a bulging in the pants. Bugger, no time for that, this is serious business. I glance at Michelle, she's looking at me with what I interpret as a provocative look.

'If I want? about this Piper you mean?'

'About whatever you want Rex.'

I try and ignore her remark, it's a come on if ever there was but I'm not exactly in a position to take advantage right now. I get the Piper started under Michelle's watchful eye and we're off. It's pretty straightforward flying to the big Michelin plantation, Michelle wants to talk.

'What are you doing flying me around Vietnam Rex, you live in Nouvelle-Zélande'

'Michelle I fly all over the world, go where the money is.'

'A pilot for hire, you hire out your body to fly aeroplanes, anything else you hire it out for?' the look on her face, she's really pulling my leg now and she knows it.

'Michelle I think you're trouble.'

'Yes I am, life's too short to be anything else. Not stopping over at Dau Tieng by any chance, I live there with my family.'

'Family?'

'Well my two brothers, we are part of the Michelin dynasty, been here for a long time.'

'Husband, children?'

'Unfortunately no, still looking for him, not too many around in this part of the world, perhaps I should go to Nouvelle-Zélande.'

There's a road down below going in the same direction as us, I'm following it on the map, it appears to be going to Dau Tieng, Michelle notices.

'Yes you can follow that road, it goes all the way to Dau Tieng. We used to use it, however, it's become quite dangerous. My brother was snatched there six months ago and we had to pay a ransom to a Viet Cong faction. All air travel now and even this attracts attention occasionally, the odd pot shot from an AK47, gives life an edge.'

'Yes I have been briefed about what goes on, what to expect.'

'What to expect, how could they possibly brief you on what to expect, no one has asked me what I would do with a pilot from Nouvelle-Zélande if I got my hands on him.'

This lady is something else, I wonder if stop overs at Dau Tieng are on the cards? Michelle reads my mind.

'Rex occasionally a pilot has to overnight with us at our place, you should organise something like that, could be a bit of fun.'

We arrive without further provocation from Michelle, she gives me a peck on the cheek as she gets off and adds.

'Organise a stop over Rex, I'll be here.'

There are five passengers to take back to Quy Nhon, all French men, no ladies. I wonder if Vietnam does something to French women, that Michelle! The fellow who looks after me at Dau Tieng makes himself known and in no time I am off back to Quy Nhon. This is easy money, where are the fish hooks?

Back at Quy Nhon it's raining, visibility is not good, the only navigation aid is an NDB, non directional beacon, a basic aid found all over the world. I don't have any approach charts however I manage to get in visually, just. Better get the NDB let down chart for Quy Nhon before I do another trip. I lay it on Tung our groundcrew man and in no time he comes up with a let down chart, 'thank you Tung.' Some more people want to get to Dau Tieng, I'm a little concerned about the rain. If it's raining at Dau Tieng I may not be able to land, they will not have any landing aids. Tung manages to phone Dau Tieng, it's fine, no rain and does not look like rain either, 'thank you again Tung.' Three French men and two Vietnamese, no ladies, another full load, off we go. Getting airborne in the rain is not a problem, it's the landing bit. The road I had used earlier is below us for about two thirds of the trip, it's not difficult seeing it through the rain. As we get closer to Dau Tieng the rain clears and the sun breaks through. I land and offload my passengers, there's no return load at this stage. The groundcrew man who I met briefly on the first trip makes himself known, he's Eurasian, part Vietnamese, part French, a handsome fellow who calls himself Benny. He tells me there will probably be some people wanting to go to Quy Nhon in about an hour so why don't I make myself comfortable at the local restaurant, a company affair located at the edge of the airstrip, Benny will give me a shout when my passengers turn up.

It's well set up this little restaurant, good menu. I'm feeling a bit peckish, perhaps a steak, go the French way, entrecôte avec frites, wine perhaps, no, don't be tempted Rex, don't drop your standards, you might be a mercenary but don't let yourself fall into a hole. It's an excellent meal, the French influence. Wherever the French go the good cuisine is sure to follow. I'm enjoying a coffee when Benny shows up.

'Four passengers in about half an hour, I'll join you for a coffee, get to know the new boy.'

He's a mine of information, Benny. Apparently there have been quite a few pilots who have done this job, it's been going on for a couple of years, ever since the roads started to get dangerous. Mostly French nationals but there have been others as well. I'm the first they've had from New Zealand.

'Bit of a mixed bag so far, everything from real professionals to out and out rat bags, some stay for several months, others are gone the next day, how long will you be here?'

'Two weeks, that's all I was offered back in New Zealand. It was suggested longer term might be available.'

'Two weeks, bit short, you'll only just be getting the hang of it.'

'Yes, you're right there Benny, perhaps I should negotiate a longer stay, see how these first few days pan out first.'

Benny wants to talk, I let him go, could learn a lot. Apparently the various Viet Cong militias in the area are not very well controlled by their masters, rogue elements have been imposing their own local rules, extortion has become a problem. The vast quantities of latex produced by the plantation is shipped to Saigon by road and these shipments have been getting held up by armed Viet Cong demanded taxes. The plantation owners consider this just another cost to doing business. Rubber is dominated by the French, it's incredibly profitable. The Saigon Government are in on the act as well. They impose their own taxes on rubber passing through Saigon, it's in their interest to ensure the industry survives. To this end they provide armed escorts for the shipments. Kidnapping is the big problem hence the aeroplane for moving people around. There have been attacks on the plantation as well. Both sides are actively discouraging this, don't kick the gift horse in the mouth. In spite of all this the industry remains viable and very profitable. The rubber produced here in Vietnam is high quality, much in demand on the world market.

Recently there's been an increase in hostile activity, more attacks on the outskirts of the plantation and shots being fired at the Piper, nothing that cannot be handled, but it is causing concern. The other plantations in Binh Long province, and the ones further inland in Gia Lai province around Pleiku are having the same problems.

'Thanks for that Benny, interesting place, I knew very little about Vietnam until now, thanks for filling me in. I see some people have arrived, must be my passengers.'

Three French and one Vietnamese, all men. I get them aboard and we're off, weather remains fine, no sign of rain. I'm following the road again, makes it pretty simple having this road. I notice a bit of traffic congestion, some trucks stopped.

'Les salauds,' from one of the French men, 'the bastards are extracting tax again.'

What's happening down on the road is one of the things that's become a problem. A group of armed Viet Cong has held up a convoy and are demanding tax.

'Don't get too close, they can be trigger happy.'
The words were hardly out of his mouth when I notice what appear to be muzzle flashes, shit, we're out of here.

Back to Quy Nhon, land and offload my passengers. I have a good look around the aircraft, any bullet holes, none that I can see. It's starting to appear that being a mercenary means that people shoot at you with AK47s, seems to go with the job, this is the fourth time I've been shot at. Kate must never know, she would flip, hard enough explaining away the scratch on my arm after Leipzig. If I came home with a real bullet hole, well who knows. Perhaps it would not be a silly idea to fly a bit higher here in Vietnam, not my usual style though. I mention it to Tung, the groundcrew man, and he tells me that yes the Piper has been hit, one hole from an AK47 about four months ago, perhaps following the road to Dau Tieng may not be such a good idea after all.

Back in the Villa Hy I reflect on my first day, very different to Germany. Michelle, now there's a thought. The money, six and a half thousand dollars for the days flying, nowhere near what the German jobs returned, need to fly for fifteen days or more to get into the same league, but wait a minute, was that 2000 Swiss francs for a single flight or a return one, not clear on that, better wait and check the Swiss account before I ask questions. I think it must be for a return one. The risk? not great. Hang on, you've just been shot at on day one, what do you mean little risk! Ok true, but people are not really out to get me here.

'Monsieur Macare, Louis Couture to see you.'

'Evening Louis, that was an interesting day, drink in the bar perhaps?'

'Oui, Rex that would be nice.'

We discuss the day's activities, getting shot at included. I tell him I'm quite happy with the set-up, what's he got for tomorrow.

'Some people for Hoàng Anh plantation in Gia Lai province, it's a bit further inland than Dau Tieng, then I want you to stop at Dau Tieng, pick up some people and bring them back here, after that I'm not sure at the moment, there may be something else, I'll know tomorrow.'

'Sounds straight forward, what's the strip like at Hoàng Anh?'

'Ok, not as good as Dau Tieng, but ok for our operation, they will have their own man there as well, not one of our fellows but that should not be a problem, here I'll show you just where the place is, got the chart there?'

We spend a bit of time with the map, he shows me where Hoàng Anh is and points out some other useful landmarks.

'You met Michelle I hear, now there's a real woman, heir to a big chunk of the Michelin empire as well, she's a catch for some lucky man.'

'Really? yes I thought she was a bit of a character.'

'Bit of a character, that's an understatement, she's a maneater, a real handful.'

We have another couple of drinks and Louis Couture takes his leave.

Five of them, all Vietnamese, for Hoàng Anh. Quite a long way to Hoàng Anh in Gia Lai province near Pleiku in the Central Highlands. As we get further inland the terrain becomes hilly and the weather closes in, rain and low cloud, not the greatest, this could be testing. It's all map reading and there are not many distinctive features, just a lot of jungle, but I'm managing, have to manage, can't just stop, can't just change channels. Luck is on my side, it should not be luck though, I'm supposed to be master of the situation. There it is, the strip at Hoàng Anh. There's light rain and it's hot and humid when we land. My passengers get off and I take off almost straight away for Dau Tieng. The rain eases as I head out to the east and there's it is, the strip I was at yesterday, the place where I dropped off Michelle, wonder if I'll ever see her again. Another five men, all French, there's certainly a lot of traffic moving around these plantations but then there are a lot of people involved in the rubber business. This sort of flying could be an ongoing thing. Back to Quy Nhon, up to 3000 feet, avoid the road. Tung meets me and advises there will be three for Dau Tieng, about an hour from now.

This could get a bit monotonous, same old, same old, safer perhaps, no hairy low flying, pity. Being up at 3000 feet could still be dangerous though, those rogue fellows with AK47s, even at very low level in Germany they still got me a couple of times. I've got this feeling no matter what I do I still get shot at, bugger! I think the ploy here in Vietnam is to stay up, 3000 feet at least, I doubt if an AK47 would be a worry at that height.

Three Frenchmen turn up, passengers for Dau Tieng.

'You must be Rex, my sister told me about some chap she rather fancied from Nouvelle-Zélande, a pilot.'
He was a good looking fellow, late thirties, Michelle's brother, another of the Michelin clan.

'Really, your sister said that, I'm flattered.'

'Oh yes my sister has very strong preferences in men, if she decides you're it, then believe me, you are it.'

'Well that's nice to know, I'd like to meet her again sometime apart from just taking her to and from Dau Tieng.'

'She'll probably seek you out, are you here for very long Rex?'

'Afraid not, twelve days then I'm back to New Zealand.'

'Michelle will not be happy when she hears that, pity.'

'Could be back again, don't know at this stage.'

'By the way I'm Raoul.'

I'm thinking, could have some fun around here but wait a bit, what about Kate, don't go cheating on Kate, put Michelle out of your mind. But there was Nicole, thinking about Kate did not stop you when she invited you into her bed! Stop thinking about these things, concentrate on flying, you're being paid handsomely to fly so fly. We get airborne, Raoul is in the seat next to me, he too has flown this aeroplane.

'Why am I here flying you people around, you are all qualified to do what I am doing, how come?'

'Company policy, only professional pilots are allowed to fly our people around Vietnam however that policy has its shortcomings. We've had a couple of fellows we had to get rid of, hard getting good help sometimes.'

I'm at 3000 feet off to the south of the road but still following it, makes it easy.

'Dangerous that road, I got nabbed around six months ago. I was with one of our truck convoys, we got held up by some Viet Cong, they wanted tax as they call their extortion racket, we always pay, it's the easiest way out, the only way out. They spotted me, a Frenchman, I was dragged off, ransom, cost the firm quite a bit, no more road travel.'

'Sounds dodgy Raoul and I thought flying could be risky sometimes.'

I told him about the convoy being held up on this road the day before, the muzzle flashes, probably AK47s, he was aware of it.

'Yes, that cost us quite a bit as well, it was a big convoy, they appeared to know about it. Can be hard doing business here but the world needs rubber and all the warring parties know it. Just a matter of how much they think they can squeeze out of us without wrecking the whole industry.'

We are now quite close to Dau Tieng, I can see the strip and I'm lining it up when there's a loud 'clunk' and the engine stops, just stops. Shit, can still reach the strip, straight ahead, we make it, just, touching down on the very end and roll to a stop.

Appears to be a mechanical failure inside the engine, the Piper could be out of action for a while.

'Rex, looks like you're stuck here, come up to the house with me. The firm will probably get another plane from Saigon if this one can't be fixed quickly, we have to have air transport, the roads are too dangerous.'

'Ok Raoul, thanks, I guess I'll have to wait and see what Louis Couture comes up with.'

It's huge, an old French colonial mansion, something out of a movie. Big verandas all 'round, vast gardens immaculately manicured, Vietnamese servants everywhere. The French certainly have a good thing going here, a very good thing.

'Well Rex, something to eat after that little drama? you've been flying all day, a glass of wine perhaps? no more flying for you today.'

We move out to the veranda and one of the servants produces a chilled savvy in a silver cooler and a plate of sandwiches, it's very comfortable, what a life style, no wonder the French are hanging on to what they have here.

'Cheers Rex, better luck tomorrow. They say you make your own luck, how does that fit with what's just happened? If I was a conspiracy theorist I'd say Michelle had a hand in it.'

'Michelle, is she here?'

'Yes Rex she is, well I think she is, better watch out.'

I get on the phone to Louis Couture in Quy Nhon and fill him in on what's happened. He will have a mechanic here first thing in the morning, charter company in Quy Nhon will fly him in. If it can be fixed here then that's what will happen. There's a big engineering facility on the plantation so the problem can probably be fixed on site.

'Raoul, looks like I may be here for a couple of days.'

'Not a problem, we'll put you up, there's plenty of space, choice of rooms, this place is enormous, a real blast from the past. Been in the family since last century and as you can see it's pretty comfortable. Biggest problem is keeping it all going, everyone seems to want a slice of the pie and the pie is shrinking. Don't know what the future holds, not looking good right now. I'll get one of the staff to show you to one of the guest rooms, I say one because there are quite a few. You're the only guest at the moment so you get the good one. You'll find some clothes in the room, help yourself, back here around five, cocktail hour.'

Good one? an understatement, I have trouble just getting my head around it. The room is huge, high ceiling, big fan, monstrous four poster bed, big bathroom, huge bath, a big wardrobe with a selection of men's clothes and it all opens out onto a veranda, lawn, and more manicured garden. I spread myself around the room, the very big room, and relax. No flying for a few days by the look of it, that means no money coming in, the deal was payment for flights completed. Could argue I'm unable to fly because there's no plane, not my fault. Better play it cool, don't even mention it, enjoy the moment, a few days here could be quite something.

It's cocktail hour, I find my way back to the veranda.

'Hello Raoul.' I'm smartly dressed, there was a very upmarket selection in the wardrobe.

'Ah there you are Rex, just to put you at ease you're our house guest for as long as it takes to get things sorted, take advantage of the situation you find yourself in, enjoy the place.'

'Thank you Raoul, that's very kind of you, certainly a magnificent place you've got here.'

'Yes it is, the Michelin dynasty got onto rubber in Vietnam a long time ago and created all this, kept it going right up to the present day, how much longer though is the question. Not looking good at the moment but it's too big a business to let go, no one wants to see it fail. All the warring parties can see the value of the place. It will probably come down to a question of ownership. The French have all the know-how and connections to keep it going, without us it would probably fail.'

'Uncertain times Raoul.'

'Very uncertain; our current problem, well there are quite a few current problems, but the biggest worry is fighting within the confines of the plantation and the damage it could cause. The place is huge, thousands of hectares, if there is any armed combat within the plantation then that would be very bad. Not happened so far and I think both sides, well there are more than just two sides, realise this.'

'You live here full time Raoul?'

'Yes, pretty much, I manage the place. My younger brother is my offsider, he's away in Paris at the moment, then there's Michelle, she flits in and out, here today, Paris tomorrow.'

'Family?'

'Wife and two young boys, I moved them to Paris nine months ago, schooling for the boys. My wife, Dominique, looks after them, provides a home environment, better than boarding school. This place is becoming too dangerous. I go to Paris frequently, let them know they've still got a Dad.'

'So you're home alone Raoul?'

'Pretty much, there are always people visiting, friends, company people, they all love coming here, we've got friends we never knew we had.'

'I can see why, this place is paradise.'

'Yes it is nice, just hope we can keep it going. Empty at the moment just you and I, not sure where Michelle is.'

Dinner and it's quite an experience, the ultimate in silver service, the finest French cuisine, servants all over us, I can see why the French want to stay in Vietnam.

'Raoul I must compliment you on your hospitality, this is just so good.'

'Thanks Rex, yes it is good but then we can do this here in Vietnam, the old colonial ways, our forebears set the place up rather well, enjoy it while we can.'

'Here try this Châteauneuf-du-Pape, my favourite red, we're well stocked.'

'Châteauneuf, it's a favourite with me as well ever since I discovered it in France, at Châteauneuf-du-Pape itself,' and I tell Raoul about how this came about.

I was in the RAF based in Germany, my contract was about to expire, I was going to leave the RAF and return to New Zealand. A requirement for one of the squadron aircraft to fly out to the Mediterranean to carry out some flying tasks in Libya, Malta, and Gibraltar came up, I put my hand up, my luck was in. It was a week long affair involving a stop over at Luqa in Malta, some low flying over the dessert well inland from Tripoli in Libya, and a few days in Gibraltar. It was a pretty enjoyable interlude the true purpose of which I have no idea, that's the way it was in the military, don't need to know, bit like the business I find myself in now. It was the flight back to Germany from Gibraltar where it got interesting. I was about to discover my love for Châteauneuf-du-Pape. The weather over Germany was not good, widespread fog. When we were approaching the French coast it became apparent that we would not be able to land at Geilenkirchen, the RAF station where I was based, our best course of action would be to divert to the French Air Force base at Orange in the south of France. Orange is next door to Avignon, Châteauneuf-du-Pape territory. The French Air Force liaison officer who met us, our minder, was of the opinion that the Officers Mess at Orange would not be up to the standard required for RAF Officers which I found a little strange however we were in his hands, what did he suggest? A hotel in Avignon was the answer, well ok, if you say so and that's what happened. Talk about lucky, the hotel was a good one and the French Air Force would be picking up the tab. We were stuck there for three days waiting for the fog to lift over Germany. It was during our first meal at this hotel that we discovered Châteauneuf-du-Pape, red. I fell in love on the spot. We consumed a lot of it during the course of our enforced *holiday* and we got to visit a couple of the Châteauneuf vineyards as well. It was a great experience, changed my drinking habits forever. Just why the French put us in this hotel had us thinking. Our aircraft was an English Electric Canberra B(I)8, a specialised low level aircraft. Our role was nuclear strike, a two man crew, pilot and navigator, the aircraft was fitted with some pretty sophisticated LABS equipment, that's *low altitude bombing system.* It crossed our minds that the French Air Force wanted us out of the way so they could have a good look at our aircraft. They would have been disappointed. The computer gear at the heart of the LABS system was always removed whenever the aircraft were away from Geilenkirchen. I've often wondered if this incident incurred some more black marks for me with the DGSE. Eventually the fog cleared over Germany and we were on our way having enjoyed three days in Châteauneuf territory and an enduring love for Châteauneuf-du-Pape, red.

'That's quite a story Rex, I can see you enjoyed your time in the Air Force. I should have chosen that career path myself but *the family* forced this upon me. I would have liked to have been a glamorous jet jock.'

'Yes you probably would Raoul but there's a downside, there's absolutely no money in it. You have a fabulous few years then suddenly it's all over, you're out on the street and there's no money in the bank. There is one thing going for you though, you're well trained. Air force training is the best, it's up to you how you turn this to your advantage.'

It's a pleasant evening dining with Raoul and quite late when I retire to the superb room he's allocated me, full of fine red wine as well.

The mechanic from Quy Nhon, a Frenchman, arrives early. The Piper has been manhandled into a small hanger at the airfield and he's right into it. An hour later he's determined that it's a cam shaft problem, not too bad, can be done here at Dau Tieng, but, and it's a big but, have to get a new cam shaft. It's unlikely there will be one in Vietnam. He's right, it has to come from Lycoming, the engine manufacturer in America, how long?

'Lycoming are pretty good, I'll get onto them right away, air freight, my guess, three to four days, once I get it, just a few hours.'

'Right go for it.'

Looks like four days, possibly more, what to do? I phone Louis Couture in Quy Nhon and put him in the picture, what does he want me to do? Will there be another aeroplane in the interim for me to fly, and earn money, or do I come back to Quy Nhon and cool my heels there?

'Give me a little time Rex, I'll call you back.'

Hanging around for a few days, not earning, away from Kate, not the greatest.

'Ok Rex,' it's Louis, 'we can get along without an aeroplane for a few days, if we do need to move somebody then there's a charter company here at Quy Nhon we can use. We've used them in the past, not the greatest but they are a backstop. Can't get you back here to Quy Nhon, no aeroplane, perhaps you could ask Raoul if you can stay there for the time being, failing that you can try and get back here by road but that's not advisable.'

'Ok, I'll ask Raoul, it's pretty nice here, perhaps a little rest and recuperation.'

And that's what happens, Raoul is only too happy to have me around for a few days.

'Bit of company Rex, that will be nice. You can learn all about the rubber business as well.'

That evening Raoul and myself are on the big veranda having a few drinks, he tells me a little about the aeroplane set up.

'The Piper is owned by a subsidiary company we set up to give us better control of our movements. The charter company we used before was unreliable and they had some dodgy pilots. We carry our own insurance as well, the big insurance companies don't want to know anything about us, Vietnam, too risky. We get our pilots from a French agency that's a branch of Government in France and they are pretty good, not had any problems with pilots since we went with them. Most stay around a month to six weeks, several have returned for another go at it.'

'Interesting, I was only offered a two week contract and that's starting to look a bit wobbly now, be a bit down on the flying and I only get paid for actual flying.'

'That's not so good Rex, don't know why the two weeks, could be they're testing the water, New Zealand pilots, see how they go. We pay the agency a fixed fee for pilots, you fellows are quite expensive, however we have been happy with what they have supplied so far.'

'Who's licensing rules apply to your operation, pilot licensing?'

'Vietnam's rules and they are not very particular. It's another reason we carry our own insurance, I don't think the major companies would be too forthcoming in the event of an accident, well they won't insure us anyway. Now that you mention it I don't recall any of the pilots we've had having to produce a license, why do you ask Rex?'

'I've got a mate back in New Zealand who's interested, he's been in Vietnam before, CIA, supply dropping to the Meo over by the Cambodian border. He gave it away, too dangerous, but now he wants back in, not the CIA stuff, something a little less risky.'

'That CIA operation is indeed dangerous, would not want to be involved there, do you think your friend would be interested in what we have going here? We service a couple of other plantations as well as our own, I think you went to one the other day, Hoàng Anh over by Pleiku.'

'Yes I'm pretty sure he would, there is a problem though. He had his lower left arm shot off over East Germany some months ago. He's got a prosthetic and is back into flying but no license and the New Zealand aviation authority are not being helpful, so he's looking at the mercenary market. Perhaps I should call it the freelance market, where employers do not worry too much about a license. When your agent offered me this job in Auckland he never asked about a license so I would have to assume that a license is not a requirement for flying your Piper. It would only ever be asked for by an insurance company trying to get off the hook over a claim but you carry your own insurance so that potential problem goes away.'

'Arm shot off, sounds horrific.'

'It was, happened in East Germany. He was doing a bit of covert stuff in a light aircraft for the British, I've done some of it myself, I guess he was unlucky.'

'So you've been doing dangerous stuff in Europe Rex?'

'Yep Raoul I have, the money on offer made it very tempting, but you're right, it was dangerous, what you have here is a lot more attractive.'

'Sounds like your mate is pretty experienced, we could use him perhaps. I'll pass his name on, the agency will check him out, they like to do their own background checking.'

'Thanks Raoul, Russ will be grateful for that, I think any flying job will be good for him, restore his confidence.'

'Only too pleased to be of assistance, perhaps we might even see him here sometime. Tomorrow I'll show you around the estate, interested?'

'Am I ever.'

It was another great meal with Raoul, just the two of us, wonder where Michelle is? I don't ask.

It's huge, thousands of hectares, takes us almost an hour just to drive to the southern boundary in a land-rover, a mature beat up land-rover. Rubber trees everywhere you look, stretching to the horizon, or so it seems, hundreds of Vietnamese workers attending to them, tapping the latex, the white gold. The sheer size of the operation, no wonder the French don't want to lose it. Raoul tells me the big worry is the sporadic fighting between Government forces and the Viet Cong that occurs in the area and the harassment of the local villagers by both sides. The plantation is by far the biggest employer of labour in the area, the local villages are totally reliant on it. The security situation is slowly deteriorating and there's evidence of North Vietnamese infiltration as well.

'Not a good scene Raoul.'

'No It's certainly not and I can't see any light at the end of the tunnel, just a black hole. We're just making the best of it while we can but I suspect our time here is limited.'

'And you run the show yourself Raoul?'

'Not all by myself, there's a big staff behind the scenes, you don't see them. A lot of well qualified Vietnamese who've been with us for a long time. The problem now is intimidation by the Viet Cong.

There's no common policy with the Viet Cong, they're not very well controlled. I think their leadership appreciate that it's in their best interests to allow the rubber business to continue and only the French can run it. The trouble is the rogue factions, they've got no brains, violence for the sake of it, they are the people causing us problems. There was a skirmish just outside the plantation a couple of days ago, the local Viet Cong executed a village headman for no particular reason and all the villages took fright, did not come to work, it's that sort of thing that's an ongoing problem. We do have channels that enable us to contact the Viet Cong leadership but as I've said it's the rogue elements.'

We drive around for a couple of hours, Raoul taking the opportunity to let the labour force see *the big boss*, good public relations. We stop frequently and talk to the employees, letting them know that we are the nice people, the Viet Cong are the baddies. But as Raoul tells me it's just about impossible to know what they are thinking.

Around mid-afternoon we get back to the house, standing on the veranda is Michelle.

'The handsome man from Nouvelle-Zélande, a little birdie told me you were here.'

'You've met my sister Rex?'

'Well I met her briefly a few days ago.'

'That's right, Michelle mentioned something about a chap she met on the aeroplane flying in from Quy Nhon the other day, I think she fancied him.'

'Rex, the hunk from Nouvelle-Zélande.' Michelle gives me a big hug and a kiss firmly on the lips; wow there, what's this?

'You will be staying with us, right?'

'Yes Michelle, broken aeroplane, can't go anywhere at the moment.'

'Well how good is that, I've got you all to myself for a while, what mischief can we get up to?'

Raoul gives me a wink, 'you're in trouble Rex.'

It's cocktail time on the veranda again, three of us this time. I could live here, it's so comfortable.

'Michelle my lovely sister where have you been, you were here a couple of days ago, then you vanished.'

'Saigon Raoul, had to go to Saigon.'

'What's his name Michele?'

'Oh what's it matter, just needed a little excitement, but then I heard you had a house guest, the pilot from Nouvelle-Zélande, a no brainer, had to get back here, after all, I did ask Rex to organise himself a stop over at Dau Tieng and he has. The next few days will be fun.' She's looking straight at me as she says this.

'Rex, has Raoul put you in the number one guest room, that's the one with the monster four poster?'

'I think so, certainly a big bed there.'

'Great, that bed's really comfortable, lots of room too, there's only one that's better in this place and that's in my room.'

'Michelle, my dear sister, give our guest a little breathing room, now how about some dinner, see what the kitchen has rustled up for us.'

The kitchen has rustled up another 'out of this world' spread and Raoul produces several bottles of Châteauneuf, yes I could live here, the life style is something else, but how long will it last? Michelle is a real live wire, full of life, she's giving me a lot of attention, she's also extremely attractive. No man in her life, well no serious man as far as I can ascertain, she would be a handful, perhaps she scares them off. Dinner is a lengthy affair, a lot of wine, eventually we adjourn to the veranda, coffee and Baileys out under the stars, it's quite a romantic setting. Raoul asks.

'Rex, do you ride, we have a stable here, four horses, they need attention, need to be ridden.'

'I have done a little, nothing recently.'

'In the morning, why don't you and Michelle give the horses a workout, there are some good trails around the plantation you'll enjoy it, Michelle knows the way.'

'Great idea brother dear, Rex could do with a little riding,' Michelle directs a wicked look in my direction as she says this.

'That's settled then, I'm for bed, early rise for me, few problems to sort.' Raoul disappears, it's just Michelle and myself, we are both rather full of fine wine.

'Rex are you a good lover, are you good in bed?'

'That's a bit direct Michelle, how do I answer a question like that.'

'Well do your partners make comment, express satisfaction, always wanting more, I bet they do.'
This is unreal, she's a beautiful woman and she's asking these intimate questions, it's getting me aroused.

'Michelle you're a devil, another Baileys perhaps.'

'Ok one more, then I want you to come with me to my bedroom.'

It's huge, a massive four poster bed in the middle surrounded by lace curtaining. The room is tastefully decorated and there's a bathroom with a big bath. Michelle is intent on just one thing, she wants me in her bed doing just whatever comes into her head, it's a surreal experience.

She's a remarkable woman with an incredible sexual appetite. I wonder if I have satisfied her, I've certainly sated every desire I could possibly have.

'Morning Rex, my lover from Nouvelle-Zélande, my fantastic lover from Nouvelle-Zélande, that was great.'

Breakfast out on the veranda in the morning sunlight and it's excellent. Michelle looks radiant. I feel a bit the worse for wear, the red wine, quite a bit of red wine and Michelle, the demanding Michelle, this could possibly become a problem, nice problem though.

The horses, today Michelle is going to refamiliarize me with horse riding, it's been a while, not done much horse riding. Michelle will sort me out, sure sorted me out last night. She had this sheer see through nightgown affair, incredibly sexy and when she appeared through the lace curtaining around the bed it was the most sensual thing. Enough Rex, concentrate on horse riding not riding Michelle.

There were trails all through the plantation, Michelle knew them all. Thousands upon thousands of rubber trees all producing white gold and hundreds of Vietnamese working them, collecting the latex, rubber is a huge business. We ride the horses up into a hilly area, into a small valley with a lake at its centre, an idyllic spot, secluded, no rubber trees. We dismount, let the two horses graze, and seat ourselves at the edge of the lake. It's sunny and warm as we lie down on the grass.

'Rex would you consider coming here permanently, be our pilot. I like you, like you a lot, you're different to other men, you're a real man, you know how to satisfy a woman, last night was fantastic, perhaps tonight can be fantastic as well.'

'Sure about the permanent thing or is it you just wanting me in your bed all the time?'

'Well you have a point, perhaps it's me being a little selfish, but there is a requirement for some continuity with our pilots, having our own would make for a smoother operation.'

'No Michelle I don't think it's for me, I have a life in New Zealand that I like. I'm not saying I don't like it here, this is great and you are great too, last night was really something. You're a sexy devil Michelle and yes I am looking forward to another night in your bed.'

'Rex I can't help myself, I can't wait till tonight, I want you now, right here on the grass, please?'

How can I resist, do I want to? It's bliss, sex on the grass in this little secluded valley.

'A swim, the little lake's quite warm, come on Rex.'
We shed what little clothing we still have on and swim around in the warm water, *and she wants me to move here, to Dau Tieng,* it's quite an offer. If I did not have my life in Auckland it would be a no brainer. We swim around for a while playing with each other, then it's out onto the grass and the warm sunshine. The two horses are quite content grazing nearby.

'Rex I really do want you to think about moving here, I need you, I don't think anyone else can satisfy me like you do. Perhaps it is me being selfish but then you fly for money, you go where the money is, we'll pay you well and there's little risk.'

'You're making it hard Michelle but I've got a life in Auckland and I'm not in a position to move right now.'

'It's a girl, right?'

'Right.'

'Lucky girl, the story of my life. When I find a man, a real man, they're always committed elsewhere, oh well, what have we got, another couple of days then you disappear out of my life.'

'Not right out of your life Michelle, I think there could be another offer to fly your Piper and for a longer period as well, this was just a trial I think. The people who have employed me are sounding me out, seeing if someone from Nouvelle-Zélande can hack it.'

'Oui, there's hope, always hope, enjoy the moment. Let's continue the horse riding, that's what we said we were going to do, not fuck each other in some secluded valley.'
We gallop the horses , it's been a long while and it's exhilarating.

'Race you Rex,' she's off, no contest. Michelle is an accomplished horsewoman, leaves me struggling to keep up, struggling just to stay on my horse, but it's great fun. I really like Michelle, that's a worry.

Back at the house, the mansion, and good news, the cam shaft from Lycoming will be here tomorrow afternoon, the Piper should be airworthy the day after.

'That's not good news, it's very bad news,' Michelle's take on it. It's another session on the veranda in the late afternoon sunshine. Raoul has sorted the day's problems and I'm thinking about flying again; Michelle is looking a bit down.

'What's troubling you little sister, not your normal self this evening?'

'I find a man, a real man, and now he's going, going off to fly his aeroplane, going off to his loved one in Nouvelle-Zélande. I'll probably never see him again, that's what's troubling me big brother.'

'Come on Michelle we've been down this track before. It was never the plan for Rex to be here anyway, just the way things happened to turn out and dare I say it, you've got him for another two nights.'

I'm squirming in my seat, this is embarrassing, Michelle's promiscuousness does not seem to concern Raoul.

'Oui, I guess I can handle it, perhaps it's time to visit Paris again, erase my memory of Rex. What an awful thing to say, erase Rex.'

I'm thinking, erase Rex, a few people have tried to do just that in the past few months, I hope Michelle's words do not become fact. Erase Rex, it sends a shudder down my spine.

'Come here Michelle, give me a big kiss, it's good for you, an upper.' I hug her, a real squeeze, Raoul won't be embarrassed, he obviously knows what his sister's like. She latches on and really hugs me, there's a tear in her eye, what have I done to this girl she's quite upset about me leaving.

'Two more knights in your bed,' I whisper in her ear, 'two more knights of sexual excess.'

'Hhmm, that will be nice Rex, I feel better already.'

'What's with the whispering, did the horse riding do something to you two?'

'Like you'd never believe big brother.'

'You're incorrigible little sister.'

'Here have a drink, a sundowner, what's it to be, some of that Châteauneuf perhaps Rex? and Michelle?'

'Yes please, I'll join you. Châteauneuf, it got me into trouble last night, nice trouble.'

Another sumptuous dinner, more Châteauneuf. Raoul is the excellent host again, coffee and Baileys on the veranda then Michelle leads me off to her bedroom. She's quite out of control, almost desperate in her lovemaking, it's great but I'm beginning to wonder where it's leading.

Breakfast, what to do today,

'Michelle what do you suggest?'

She's not quite her bubbly cheeky self, is it because of me, have I become a little too close perhaps, got through her defensive shield, pinged her heartstrings. I'm feeling a bit sorry for her, has her desire to bed me backfired and she's gone and fallen for me, could be a problem. I'm out of here tomorrow, might be awkward.

'What about some tennis, there's a swimming pool as well, you play tennis Rex?'

'Yep, I'm a gun player, and you Michelle?'

'I'm another gun player, this could be good.'

The gauntlet's been laid down, see how it develops. Michelle is good, she plays an excellent game and starts to get the better of me. We thrash ourselves to a standstill then call a halt.

'You are good Rex, tennis that is.'

'Cheeky, you've shown me a thing or two Michelle, your game is very professional.'

'Yes I think I've shown you a thing or two, still got a couple of tricks left, show you tonight.'

'Come on another game, I think you're ahead at the moment.'
We play for quite a while and eventually call it quits.

'The pool, need to cool off.'

'Good idea Michelle, lead me to it.'
It's huge, Olympic size, the French really have it made here in Vietnam. It's a bikini this time, well it's a G string and a tiny top. She's come up with some budgie smugglers for me. The sight of Michelle in a G string causes me some embarrassment, a bulging erection inside a pair of budgie smugglers cannot be concealed.

'Rex, what have you got there, come here, I'll see if I can do something about it.'

'Get real Michelle there's nothing you can do for it apart from some frenzied lovemaking.'

'That's what I had in mind.'

'This is a fairly public place Michelle, get real.'

'Yes it is pity, tell you what, jump in the pool and we'll see what we can do.'

She's at me immediately, legs around my waist, she's ripped the budgie smugglers off and she's pushing my huge erection right inside herself.

'There, that's fixed it, now what about a drink.'

'Michelle, you're unbelievable, but yes, a drink.'

The Piper's repaired and ready to go, there are several people for Quy Nhon, an early start's required. I've been in Michelle's bed all night and she's a bit of a mess this morning, she's crying and I'm feeling bad about leaving. I think she's fallen for me, not a good scene.

Five passengers, all French men, off we go to Quy Nhon. There's another job, four Vietnamese for Hoàng Anh, then back to Quy Nhon and a night in the hotel, the Villa Hy. I give Louis Couture a call, 'what about a drink?'

'Rex, bit of a glitch that cam shaft, these things happen from time to time however I hear you enjoyed your brief stay with Raoul and Michelle. Nice guy that Raoul, and Michelle, well what can I say, she's a real handful.'

'Yes Louis it was great, you can send me back to Dau Tieng anytime you want and if you want the aeroplane to overnight there that's ok with me.'

'It's that Michelle, it's written all over you Rex.'

'Well yes you have a point, Michelle's really nice, pity I have to go back to New Zealand so soon. I think there's only two or three days left for me to earn some money here, that engine failure dented my earnings somewhat.'

'Yes, not good. I'll advise the agency that we are pleased with you and perhaps they might like to make another longer offer, would you like that Rex?'

'Yes Lois, I would, thank you.'

Sure Rex, do you really want to come back, get in deeper with Michelle, she's fallen for you, you do realise that.

It's over, I'm in a plane headed for Auckland. There was some flying out of Quy Nhon, a couple of other plantations, nothing for Dau Tieng. It was a tearful goodbye when I left Dau Tieng that morning. Will I see her again? who knows, do I really want to get involved? an awkward question. It seems the odd casual affair is an occupational hazard in this business, something that could impinge on my real life in Auckland, do I want that? no I don't. What if Pierre Brodeur offers you another contract in Vietnam and for a longer period? Need to seriously think about that because it's a real possibility. Was it worth it moneywise? I completed about ten flights in the two week period that will have put something like 20,000 Swiss francs into my account, that's around twenty to thirty thousand NZ dollars. If the Piper had not broken down it would have been twice as much. Bit far removed from the other jobs I've done but the risk factor was way down and it was easy flying. Do I want to go back to Vietnam? need to give it some serious thought. Do I want to tangle with Michelle again? I don't know the answer to that one. She keen on me and that could become a problem.

'Drink sir,' it's the hostess, 'we'll be serving a meal shortly, here's the menu.'

'A red wine would be nice, any chance of a Châteauneuf?'

'I'll see sir, won't be a minute.'

Pushing it a bit Rex, Châteauneuf on an airline, that's the good stuff, the expensive stuff, you're travelling steerage, get real.

'Here we are sir a glass of Châteauneuf-de-Pape.'

'Really, I was just pulling your leg, being the difficult customer, you have called my bluff, thank you, thank you a lot, I'm impressed.'

'Not a problem sir, I normally work in the first class cabin, I just happened to know there was some Châteauneuf there.'

'Well I'm very impressed, quick where's some paper, I'll write the airline a thank you note, what's your name?'

'No don't do that, could backfire on me, serving first class drinks in economy, but thank you for the thought sir. My name's Monica and I live in Auckland.'

'Well thank you again Monica, you've made my day.'

I think Monica could be a bit pushy. I reckon if I asked she would give me her Auckland address. Careful Rex you seem to have a penchant for getting involved. The meal is excellent, better than the normal airline offering and Monica brings me another glass of

Châteauneuf.

'My pleasure sir.'

She's an attractive girl, come on Rex, get a handle on yourself.

Another Vietnam contract, do I want it? don't know. Can make a lot more money taking on the dodgy stuff but the risk factor, it's a very real consideration. Vietnam is low risk, no one is out to seriously get you, the odd pot shot from an AK47. The other stuff involves some serious shooting, bigger guns, missiles, people with murderous intent, think about it. You've been brought down by gunfire twice, it was just luck that you finished up in friendly territory. Crashed on takeoff and very nearly shot by border guards, and that Algerian business, well your customer had his head cut off. Face fact, you're in a bloody dangerous business. The biggest danger with the Vietnam flying is probably Michelle.

Auckland, wet, windy, and cold, welcome home. Kate's welcome is much nicer, she's all over me, warm and cuddly.

'My darling you're in one piece, no holes, no bits missing, I love you, let's go home.'

Paris

It's great to be back in the fold, my comfortable place, Auckland and Kate, I really love the girl. Will I marry her? too hard basket. Of course I want to marry Kate but how can I ever have a married life while I'm doing what I am? When you are married you have children and that's right out of the question, totally incompatible. Try not to think about such things, put it on the back burner, ignore it, just let it slide for the time being, but you can't fly in the face of reality, you'll have to face it one day Rex!

Kate's very excited and it's not just about rushing into the bedroom, well it is that but there's something more to her excitement this time.

'What is it Kate, what's raised the tempo?'

'Guess what, Paris Vogue have been in contact, they want me to do a cover shoot.'

'You're kidding me, the most beautiful girl in New Zealand and you've landed the top job, the top job in the world Kate, Paris Vogue is *it*, you've arrived.'

'They want me in two weeks time, how about that!'

'Two weeks, that's not far off, this could change your life.'

We're in bed when Kate breaks this news. I've been home a couple of hours and we've been *catching up*.

'Celebration, what's in the fridge, yes, there's a bottle of the good stuff.'

I pull the cork on the bottle of Dom and we drink a toast sitting up in bed.

'It's the big time Kate, exposure on the world stage, you'll be a name, a recognised name in the fashion business, fame and fortune.'

'Vogue's Auckland agent has been to see me, they want me to go to Paris. The deal is first class travel to be there by the 20th, it's now the 7th. I'm allowed a chaperone, same first class travel. I've been wracking my brains about who I should ask.'
Kate's looking me straight in the eye as she says this and gives a big wink.

'I was wondering if you would be available after all you are an experienced chaperone, Wellington and all that.' Kate grabs me, the champagne glasses go flying.

It's wet and windy outside, we spend the whole day in bed, it reinforces my love for this girl, she really is the one for me and now it looks like we are off to Paris together, this could be interesting.

'Eloise and Alain, they live in Paris, I think they gave us their address and phone number, got them written down somewhere.' Kate says this with some enthusiasm, hmm!

'How long do they want you for Kate?'

'I think the Vogue fellow mentioned something about a week, he'll be around tomorrow with the details. Just think darling a week together in the city of love, oh yes, another thing, apparently there's a big fat cheque involved.'

Big money, no risk. I'm in the wrong business.

Next morning the man from Vogue phones, can he come around. It's first class return air fares for two to Paris, seven days in a first class hotel and as your chaperone is also your partner it will be one big double room. Vogue will require Kate for six half day sessions. He hands Kate a cheque, an advance payment, twenty-five thousand dollars. Depending on how the shoot goes this amount will be doubled. Kate is mightily impressed, it's the biggest fee she's earnt yet, *welcome to the big money club Kate*. The airline tickets have us leaving Paris to return to Auckland on the 28th, we ask the Vogue man. 'Can we alter the return date, or better still leave it open, it would be nice to have a short holiday in Paris at the end of the shoot.'

'Not a problem, they are first class tickets, you can vary the dates according to your wishes, the hotel booking however will end on the 28th.'

'That's great, thank you, now what else is required from us.'

'That's it, all pretty straight forward, here's the hotel name and address. When you have checked in call this number, the Paris team will take over and look after you, good luck, enjoy, and congratulation Kate. Vogue are very choosy about who they take on. They are impressed with you.' That was it, the man from Vogue was gone.

'Geez Kate you've struck the mother lode, it does not get any better than this. Congratulations dear, you're not just another body, you're *the body* now, a very beautiful body too. We need to celebrate, let our friends know the good news. How about I shout them all dinner at our favourite restaurant. Who would you like along, what about Ali and Jeff, Russ and Erika, Tara, and her man from Paris, Marciel I think his name is.'

'Yes let's do that, we can make it a surprise party, don't tell them what it's for, that will get the tongues wagging, see what wild guesses they come up with.'

'I'll get onto it, what about tomorrow night, will that fit?'

'Yep, I'm not working at all tomorrow, took a few days off to welcome you home Rex. We should try and contact Eloise and Alain, would be good to see them again, I know you'd like to bed Eloise.'

'You're a devil Kate, I reckon you have a hankering for that Alain, right?'

We're gathered in our favourite Parnell restaurant, eight of us, the tongues are indeed wagging.

'What's the big news, don't tell us you two are going to ---?'

'Surprise folks, I know you're all wondering why the dinner invite? what's it all about? Well we have something to celebrate, something none of you will have picked, not in your wildest dreams.'

'The lovely Kate here has just topped the modelling world, the big one, the cover of Paris Vogue.'

There's a hush, how can this be, a stunned silence, then an eruption of congratulations, pandemonium. The press arrive, I think Kate's agency must have leaked something, flashbulbs, reporters. The other restaurant customers enter into the spirit of it all, the place becomes one big party. In amongst it there's dinner, a seriously good dinner, the restaurant have gone out of their way for this one, for their celebrity guest, their regular diner who lives just down the road. It's a great evening, Kate is absolutely radiant. I think the other girls are envious, understandable, I mean the cover of Paris Vogue, it does not get any better than this.

'How did you crack it Kate?'

'No idea, out of the blue.'

Kate is one of New Zealand's leading models, possibly *the* leading model and Vogue have talent scouts everywhere. Well she's done it and we're off to Paris. The after party, Tara's right onto us.

'My place, all of us, Jeff's on for it?'

'No Tara, not tonight, not quite psyched for an orgy.'

'Rex, don't be a killjoy, a night of sexual excess, a real celebration, you're on for that.'

I have a word with Kate, no, she's not ready for that perhaps another time but not tonight, it's all a bit much right now. She just wants to curl up in bed with me I think she's not quite come to grips with the magnitude of what she's been offered.

Next morning, it's all over the Herald, front page pictures, lengthy articles from the columnists, all the armchair experts. Kate Fontaine has put New Zealand on the map, how did it happen? how did a girl from New Zealand make it to the very top of the world's fashion industry?

'Heady stuff Kate, your famous.'

We're in bed, sleeping in, it was a great night at the restaurant. We managed to dodge Tara's 'after party' that on reflection was probably the right thing to do, after all Kate's private life will be scrutinised now, that's what happens in New Zealand, tall poppy syndrome, just a whiff of sexual shenanigans would not be good.

Ring, ring, it's Russ. 'Rex, you missed a good one. Tara really aced it this time, she had five couples at her after party and it descended into absolute debauchery. There was quite a bit of cocaine and Ali went right off her trolly, had sex with every male present. The big surprise was Jeff, screwed every girl in sight. Not sure it would have been Kate's scene. You were a wise lad keeping your famous girlfriend away from such goings on but shit, it was a lot of fun.'

'Good one Russ, put a big smile on your face by the sound of it, by the way, I might have some flying lined up for you, the Vietnam thing. I've passed your details on to a Pierre Brodeur the French guy here in Auckland who recruited me, I've also put a word in for you with the outfit I worked for in Vietnam, it's based at Quy Nhon, you probably know the place. The flying is low risk, to and from French rubber plantations in the Central Highlands. Money's not bad, not in the same league as the German deal but there's very little risk involved, with any luck they'll be in touch. A word of advice, perhaps a warning, if you encounter a fiery French bird called Michelle watch out, she's lovely, but an absolute maneater.

'Thanks for that Rex, yep I'm all set to get back into it, even the department in Wellington are being a bit more co-operative, might even get to be New Zealand's first licensed bionic pilot.'

Well that's nice, Russ is up and running again, having the time of his life by the sound of it.

'Kate, what about breakfast out on the balcony, we, or perhaps I should say you, can soak up the flattering words in the morning's paper, enjoy the moment, the fame, the nice feeling.'

Ring, ring, 'Pierre Brodeur Rex, congratulations to the lovely Kate, that's quite an honour believe me, Paris Vogue. No doubt you'll be going to Paris with Kate, would that be right?'

'Perhaps, why do you ask?'

'We could have a job for you in Europe, perhaps after the Vogue thing, interested?'

'You know my thoughts on the jobs you put in my direction, no more of that Algerian horror.'

'Qui, qui Rex, I understand, this would not be as risky as that, nothing to do with the FLN. The money would be good, a lot better than Vietnam.'

'Let me have a think about it Pierre, come and see me in a couple of days with some detail, ok?'

'Qui Rex, when will you be finished with Vogue in Paris?'

'The 28th of this month, however, we are planning on having a few free days in Paris before coming home, perhaps after that, say anytime after the 2nd of next month.'

'Good, I'll contact you in two days time.'

'Kate we've got ten days before we pack our bags for Paris, excited?'

'Very, this will be me being *out of town for a while,* different.'

'You've got a phone number for Eloise and Alain in Paris right, perhaps we should give them a call, let them know we are coming and will have a few free days after the Vogue thing.'

'Good idea I'll do that right now.'

It is a good idea. Eloise answers the phone, her excitement is palpable. Eloise suggests we come and stay with them for a few days, they can introduce us to their circle of friends, Eloise would love to see me again. Alain has talked about Kate quite a lot since they've been back in Paris, sounds like we might find ourselves involved in some serious partner swapping. Could be interesting, short term as well.

The next few days are different, everyone wants to interview Kate, she's in huge demand, New Zealand's wonder model. All the women's magazines want a piece of her, it's quite something, totally unexpected. Poor Kate, all very nice but tiring.

'The trappings of fame Kate, *big money, no risk, very tiring.*'

'I wish they would back off and leave me alone with you Rex but that's not going to happen. The pressure will be off once we board that plane for Paris, how long now, six days?'

'Come on, let's sneak out for dinner at our favourite, no one will spot you, big scarf.'

It was different, we were spotted, the staff were in awe of Kate, almost embarrassing, the manager fronts, we have a nodding acquaintance with him, George, nice guy.

'Miss Fontaine we are honoured that you still choose to dine with us, tonight is on the house, it's our pleasure, our sincere hope is that it may continue.'

'This is embarrassing George, you're just too nice, thank you. I'm still Kate, nothing's changed, just the public's perception. Of course we will continue, it's a no brainer, why would we go anywhere else?'

'Well Miss Fontaine it's going to be the finest dining in Paris, wish I could be there with you, you'll love it. We'll have to up our act before you return, your expectations may change, we'll have to keep up.'

'George, you're a charmer, no way are we going to change our favourite restaurant, you worry unnecessarily.'

'One final thing Miss Fontaine, can we take some pictures, for the restaurant wall, signed perhaps.'

Kate is now famous, well in Auckland, how far will it spread who knows. A Paris Vogue cover will put her in the world's fashion spotlight, her life could well change, change a lot. There are a couple of farewell parties and I'm hard pushed keeping Tara under control, she's very persistent, wants to turn them into something a bit more salacious.

Finally the big jet, we're off, first class. There's no respite, the cabin crew are onto Kate, she's treated like royalty, particularly the hostesses, they are in awe of her but she's just Kate, nothing has changed but it is nice; me? I'm savouring the reflected glory. It's a long way to Europe, something I know all too well. As we get further away from New Zealand and onto another airline we become just another couple of passengers, albeit first class ones. It's nice returning to the ordinary world, somewhere where we are not famous. Travelling first class gets me thinking. It's a lot more relaxing than economy, or steerage as it's called, I should be using it. I can afford to these days but ingrained habits, perceptions, are difficult to shake, can't afford it, but I can afford it, and first class, certainly is nice. Pierre Brodeur had called as arranged, he had given me a contact in Paris, Monsieur Robier again, same address and phone number. He will have something for me, probably North Africa, not what I wanted to hear, however, I will give him a call when we are finished with Vogue.

Paris finally, Charles de Gaulle airport and another red flag on the immigration computer, has to be. Kate goes straight through, me? the now usual delay while the immigration officer consults his computer at length, sucks his breath a couple of times and eventually stamps my passport. They know I'm on French soil again. A hair raising taxi ride to the Hotel de Crillon near the centre of Paris, what a place. The man did say a first class hotel, he certainly got that right, the place is fabulous, very up market and ridiculously expensive. We check in and it becomes obvious we are getting VIP treatment. Paris Vogue, it means something in the city of love. The Concierge lets us know discreetly that Vogue will be picking up the bill for everything we utilize within the hotel, restaurants, bars, room service, etc, everything, how good does it get. The room, it's enormous, big windows looking out across the city, fully stocked bar, monstrous bathroom, a study, giant TV screen.

'The trappings of wealth Kate, good eh!'

'Oh Rex this is so good, see if there's some Dom in that bar there. It's a first for me, I've not experienced anything like this before, it doesn't get this good in New Zealand. We need to toast our new found circumstances.'

There is some Dom Perignon in the bar's fridge, we pull the cork.

'To us Kate, or perhaps I should say, to you Kate, it's all your doing, I've not had a hand in it at all.'

'We need to consummate our newly found circumstances Rex, this monster bed, send me off to that happy place as only you can do.'

It's late in the afternoon, we've well and truly sated our desires, and in such luxurious surroundings. Perhaps we should be thinking about what we need to do.

'I'll call this Vogue number, see what they require from us?'

It's a pick up in the morning. Kate and her minder will be required at the Vogue studio for the whole of the morning, the chauffeur will be outside the Crillon at eight thirty.

'Let's freshen up and go for a walk Kate, it's Paris, can you imagine? and we've got money in our pockets, it's a nice feeling.'

It is lovely, there's an atmosphere, the city has a unique something about it. We stop at a sidewalk café and enjoy a wine, the prices are outrageous but who cares, it's the city of love and we are in love. It's now early evening, something to eat would be an idea, but where? There are a couple seated at the next table about our age, I think they have picked up on our English, our New Zealand, accents. The girl, the attractive girl, catches my eye.

'Nouvelle-Zélande monsieur?'

'Oui, and no French I'm afraid.'

'Not a problem, we all speak English here, well we can all speak it but some French people, the language snobs, choose not to.'

'Wow, that's a bit harsh, but really we should be speaking your language. What we want to know is where there's a good restaurant, we've just arrived in your lovely city and we're a bit lost. I'm sure there are many very good restaurants, perhaps you could suggest one?'

'That's easy monsieur, you are sitting outside one at the moment, it's good, no need to look any further. We will be eating here ourselves a little later, you could join us perhaps?'
I glance at Kate and she nods.

'That would be nice, you're very kind, perhaps we can introduce ourselves. I'm Rex, Rex Macare, and this lovely lady here is the girl I'm in love with, Kate Fontaine.'

'Lovers, and you are in Paris. Those are French names as well, is there a French connection?'

'Yes but it's distant, Huguenots from way back, quite a few in New Zealand.'

'That's interesting, I am Marciel Chastain and this is my wife Maria. Are you just visiting Paris?'

'Yes and no, Kate has a modelling contract to fulfil and we are extending it into a short holiday.'

'A modelling contract here in Paris, and you live in Nouvelle-Zélande?'

'Yes it's with Vogue.'

'Vogue, really, that's serious stuff, what exactly are you going to do for Vogue?'

'Well Paris Vogue have asked Kate to come over here to do a cover shoot for them, completely unexpected, and here we are, our first day.'

'Paris Vogue, a cover shoot, c′est incroyable, you must be famous, only the very best get onto a Vogue cover monsieur.'

'No, not famous, bit of a surprise to us as well. We don't know much about it, Vogue just approached Kate in Auckland and asked if she would be interested.'

'Maria, we are in the company of famous people from Nouvelle-Zélande, it will be an honour to have you dine with us.'

'I don't know about the famous bit Marciel but yes we would like to dine with you.'

Our new found French friends appear to be in awe of us. This adoration that's been heaped upon us recently, well upon Kate, is becoming a bit more than embarrassing, very nice but we've not done anything, it just happened, what else is about to happen in our lives?

The restaurant is an extension of the sidewalk café, it's good, an excellent meal. We get to talking, small world, they both know the Club Med on Moorea, they were GOs there two years ago, it's where they met. Marciel now works in IT and Maria is a personal trainer, they've been married for a year. We reminisce about the Med, what a great place it was, still is, the memories, the île d'amour.

'You remember that, Qui? I bet you do, we both went over there frequently, such a romantic place, it's where I proposed to Maria. It would be nice to go back, we will go back won't we Maria, one day.'

'Another bottle, let me.' I ask the waiter if he can rustle up a bottle of Châteauneuf-du-Pape, he can.

'Cut above the Med's carafes. I've got a particular liking for Châteauneuf but those carafes were great, especially when it rained

at lunchtime.'
Marciel is curious, 'tell us about this Vogue business?'

'Well it's a bit of a mystery to us as well,' and I tell them how it happened back in Auckland.

'Kate, you must be a top of the line model, well I mean just looking at you you're spectacular, Vogue obviously think so too.'
Kate's a bit flustered by Marciel's remarks.

'Thank you Marciel, I think you might be a bit of a charmer, is that right Maria?'

'He's a charmer all right, won my heart at the Med and there was a lot of competition, all those hunky GOs.'

'Rex, what do you get up to when you are not looking after this beautiful girl?'
Here it comes the probing questions that I have to tactfully skirt around.

'I'm a freelance pilot, I go where the money is. I'm not long out of the military, still trying to find my niche in the civil world.'

'That must be interesting Rex, what sort of flying, tourists around beautiful New Zealand, or is it drug running and killing people?' he says this with a provocative tone in his voice.
I decide to jump right in at the deep end and throw him off.

'It's the real bad stuff Marciel, drugs, gun running, nothing under a million bucks.'

'I think you might be pulling my leg Rex.'

'I might.'
Kate comes to my rescue.

'You won't get much out of Rex, Marciel, even I don't know what he gets up to a lot of the time, isn't that right dear? could be a string of girlfriends I don't know about.'

'Could be.'

'Enough of this, Rex has a secret life, if we poke our noses in too far it could be an early grave, isn't that right Rex?' Marciel has a good sense of humour. The awkward conversation turns to something easier. Maria inquires about what we plan on doing for the holiday part of our trip to Paris.

'A couple we know have asked us to stay with them for a few days, Eloise and Alain Dubois.'

A stunned look from both Marciel and Maria.

'You're kidding, they are our good friends, how come you know them?'

'New Caledonia, we met them a couple of months ago, they were holidaying there.'

More stunned looks.

'I don't believe this, Eloise and Alain have told us all about you two, about Ouvéa, the fantastic time you all had at the Paradis D'Ouvea and now we come across you here in Paris and you tell us you are going to stay with them for a while.'

'That's the plan.'

'This is incredible, I think me might be seeing you again, we spend quite a bit of time with Eloise and Alain, they like to party, but I guess you already know that.'

We sure as hell do and I think we have just met a couple of people who probably participate in Eloise and Alain's parties. Suddenly both Kate and I are looking at this couple we have just met in a different light. Maria is attractive, sexy, could be I might get to bed her in the not too distant future, the very thought is stirring an erection. What is Kate thinking, she's certainly having a hard look at Marciel, does she find him attractive, sexy, time will tell.

'What a small world,' from Marciel, 'I'm sure we will be seeing you again soon. You'll enjoy staying with Eloise and Alain, they're a fun couple. Now then I think we need to be off, we live north of Paris, it takes a little while and it's getting a bit late.'

'Good idea, we have to front Vogue in the morning and we have no idea what to expect, so night night, look forward to seeing you again.'

'Well Kate, what did you make of that?'

'I'm lost for words, what are the chances of just running into a couple in a big city like this who know about us, probably know about what we got up to at Ouvéa, and who seem to be keen to involve themselves with us.'

'Some coincidence, could be interesting, what do you think?'

'You're right Rex, I think we may be in for a fun time. I got good vibes from that Marciel, what did you make of Maria?'

'Yes, I warmed to her, I think she could be a little sex bomb, attractive too.'

It's a great night in the Hotel de Crillon's huge four poster bed, Kate really lets herself go.

'We're in the city of love Rex, let's do it justice.'

Up, no sleeping in, a working day. Breakfast, and what a good breakfast, room service and it's top class. Kate is looking radiant. I'm sure a night of sex makes a girl radiant, will it show on a Vogue cover? Eight thirty, there's a limo waiting, a limo, it just keeps getting better, but we are a bit out of our comfort zone. Centre of the city, big building, Paris Vogue headquarters. A minder takes over and shows us to an upstairs office, no waiting, straight in. We are introduced to a fellow who is obviously senior in the hierarchy, he's excellent on the PR, puts us right at ease.

'First let me congratulate you Miss Fontaine, our man in Auckland speaks highly of you. When we scrutinised the pictures he provided we knew we had found a Vogue cover girl. My name is Henri Bessonnet, I decide who we have on our covers. Now this is what will happen. We'll spend the morning taking a lot of pictures of you Kate. Your chaperone here, Rex, who I understand is your fiancé, can be present and observe it all. Rex you are a lucky fellow, Kate here is a true beauty. Now before we start perhaps a coffee.'

We enjoy a coffee, a very good coffee, with Henri Bessonnet, he will be our contact during our stay in Paris.

'Any questions, any problems, I'm your man. After this preliminary session our team of experts will go over the results then plan another shoot for tomorrow. This procedure will continue each morning until we think we have what we want. Locations and outfits will vary. What we do is attempt to capture Kate Fontaine, her real personality, the girl from the South Seas, we want impact, something that jumps out from the cover and right now we think you have what we want.'

It develops from there. We are taken to a studio and during the next few hours hundreds of pictures are taken, Kate in an ever changing selection of outfits from high fashion garments to cheeky little brief outfits. I'd never seen a model at work for a photographer, it was fascinating. They were true professionals, able to bring out Kate's personality, her moods, her character, the resulting pictures covered the whole spectrum, some of them were spectacular and dare I say it, quite flattering. It's early afternoon before it's all over, they want us back, same time tomorrow morning.

'How about that Kate, what did you make of it all?'

'Very professional, cut above the New Zealand scene, what about some lunch?'

We are out on the street in the middle of Paris, cafes and restaurants abound, we pick a likely looking café and seat ourselves.

'How do you think we should play it Kate, do we do a bit of sightseeing, take in a show or two? Need to keep a balance here, you have to be at the top of your game first thing each morning, would not be a good look to turn up tired.'

'Your right Rex, it's quite tiring in front of the camera, perhaps we should just take it easy for the rest of the afternoon, dine at the hotel, definitely the hotel, they've got a top rated restaurant and we've got a free meal ticket, mugs if we don't take advantage.'

'Good idea, now a bite to eat right here.'
We spend a good part of the afternoon seated at that little café, a bite to eat, several coffees, a wine or two and an outrageous bill, well it is Paris and we are tourists.

The dining room in the Hotel de Crillon is as good as it gets, we splurge, really spoil ourselves, everything is just so good. The wine list is seriously expensive, my favourite Châteauneuf is outrageously priced, but then everything is way upmarket,`` and very well done, fitting for a Vogue cover girl, my Kate. We're not long out of bed, need to play it real easy, don't want to blow this opportunity. Vogue don't come knocking on the door every day, maximise the opportunity we've been presented with.

Similar train of events the next morning, Kate is radiant, again I observe her doing what she does. There are some variations this time, some way out kinky things, she gets right into it. The photographers seem to be able to bring out behavioural traits and play on them, clever stuff. To my untrained eye the pictures are better than yesterday's. Kate is happy with the day's shoot, we reason that taking it easy the previous afternoon and evening has paid off. We'll do that again then the following day we can think about doing a bit of sightseeing, perhaps take in a show, and that's what happens.

Day four and it's outdoors in a park, quite different to the studio sessions. It's fascinating observing the people in the park. Here is this film crew, a beautiful model, numerous helpers, all doing their thing, and the general public just take it in their stride, nothing unusual, nothing to gawk at, bit different to what would happen in Auckland. At the end of five days of shooting we are back in Henri Bessonnet's office, judgment day. I feel like I am back at school in the headmaster's office about to be reprimanded for some misdemeanour, odd, why should I feel like this. Kate is visibly nervous, understandable. Henri Bessonnet is a PR master.

'Relax, you have passed.'
Kate bursts into tears, the tension has been too much.

'Kate you are allowed to cry, let it all out. I know it's been stressful for you, however, you have presented us with a problem.'
I tense up, a problem, it's not going to turn sour on us, surely not.

'Kate you have given us so many good pictures, now we have a problem, which one do we use? You will be on the cover of Vogue's next issue, Henri Bessonnet says this in a very firm voice.

I feel a little faint, that crude expression, stunned mullet, springs to mind.

'Our problem, which picture, you have presented us with so many. We will probably include something in the body of the magazine as well, not probably, definitely, there are just so many good pictures. Congratulations Kate we are very pleased with what you have given us, we will be knocking on your door again.'

What did he say, they want to use Kate again, this is incredible, life changing, the big time, the seriously big time. Kate is still looking rather stunned. I feel so proud of her, she's being rewarded for putting up with the uncertainties of the life I have imposed on her.

'Now then we will celebrate our new cover girl,' and Henri Bessonnet produces a bottle of Dom.

'Kate, this is for you,' he hands her an envelope, 'there's a substantial cheque in there, I predict there could be more in the future, congratulation.'

What a day, Kate's finally able to relax, it's over, no more stress, she's made it onto the cover of Paris Vogue, she's famous. The parting comment from Henri Bessonnet.

'Vogue might think about coming to New Zealand, there's talent down there!'

We dine at the hotel again, it's a no brainer, their dining room is as good as it gets, and for us, no charge. The hotel staff appear to be aware of Kate's Vogue connection, they are unusually attentive and it's nice, then the restaurant manager comes to our table and congratulates Kate on her success, how does he know? He offers a toast. It's all just great, Kate is beaming, she's so happy. Later in bed we reflect on the past few days. It's been a roller coaster culminating in the ultimate for a model, Kate's reached the top of the modelling world, where to from here? Our love making that night is possibly the most fulfilling we have experienced.

'I'll drive down and pick you up,' we're on the phone to Eloise.

'Alain is out at the base today, he'll be here this evening, see you in about two hours.'

Our commitments to Vogue have been fulfilled, we are now free to do whatever with Eloise and Alain and that could be just about anything. I can feel a stirring already and I think Kate is getting a bit aroused as well. Suddenly a very different atmosphere to that of the past few days.

'What do you think Kate, will we be straight into it or will things be a little more restrained here in their home environment?'

'Hard to know, what I do know is that I am starting to feel very sexy, looking forward to whatever they might want to get up to.'

'Me too, that Eloise gets to me and I know you are itching to have Alain get into your pants, don't deny it.'

'No I won't deny it and while we have some time to kill before Eloise gets here why don't you get into my pants, make use of this monster bed for a final time.'

Eloise has a classic Peugeot cabriolet sports car, a two seater with two small seats in the back. Top down, we squeeze in with our bags and we're off. She's a demon driver, a hair raising experience. About an hour with our heads stuck up in the slipstream. Eloise and Alain live in Creil, a town to the north of Paris, close to the air base of the same name where Alain is stationed.

'We've got a spa, a big one, we'll use it when we get home, you'll be able to shed the wind blown look.'

It is a big spa, as soon as we arrive we're into it, everything off, that pretty much sets the tone. Eloise is looking very provocative in her nakedness, I think back to all that sex at Ouvéa, how long will I be able to restrain myself. There's a roar overhead and a Super Mystère jet fighter thunders by heading for the nearby Creil Air Base.

'My loved one perhaps, should be home soon. Kate you'll be pleased to see him, right?'

I'm starting to wonder just how fast the pace is going to be, Eloise is certainly giving out the come on. Shall I make a move now or wait until Alain gets here? better wait, we could be here for three days perhaps, plenty of time. We fool around in the warm water, I feel Eloise's hands on me, not really the time, Alain needs to be here. Perhaps Kate's thinking if I take Eloise right now it could stimulate her the same way my screwing Ali does, I wonder. It does not get any easier, I've now got a mighty erection and it's plainly obvious to both girls, Eloise has her hand on it, Kate gets in on the act as well, it's too much, how long can I hold out.

'Bonjour ladies,' a handsome Armée de L'Air Française officer in uniform. Alain does not waste any time, his uniform goes flying and he's into the pool and straight on to Kate.

'Let's adjourn to the pool house, a lot more comfortable, some big sun lounges,' Alain's suggestion.

It's all on, just like Ouvéa. I'm into Eloise, Alain is right into Kate, and it's wonderful, we just let ourselves go, as much sex as you want, four willing participants. A great start to our visit. Eloise is a terrific sex partner and I think Kate is enjoying Alain fucking her again.

'Well now hello you two from far away, welcome to our place and thank you Kate, you are a lucky man Rex.'

'Speak for yourself Alaine, you've got Eloise here, she's really good at it, right Eloise?' I'm still inside her and I give her a big thrust, it brings forth a moan and she starts thrashing about on the sun lounger, god where's this going to end up, three days!

'Now then let's go into Creil for dinner this evening, we've got a favourite restaurant, we can invite *your* friends from Paris to join us.' It's Alain making the suggestion.

'When Marciel and Maria told us they had met you well, we had trouble believing them, small world, what are the chances of that happening?'

'Blew us away as well Alain, lovely couple, we enjoyed their company.'

'Oh yes they are indeed a lovely couple, we enjoy their company quite often, I'm sure you will too while you're here with us.'
Well Alain's practically telling us, Marciel and Maria are into the group sex thing. I thought Maria had something sexy about her, I wonder how Kate will react to Marciel?

It's another good restaurant, Marciel and Maria are surprised to see us.

'We meet again so soon, perhaps we can get to know you a little better this time.'

I'll bet we can, could be fucking you before the night's over.

We enjoy an excellent meal and several bottles of red.

'Tell us about the Vogue shoot,' it's Maria asking the question.

'Vogue shoot?' Eloise asks, 'tell us more, this is news to my ears.'

Eloise and Alain did not know about the Vogue thing and when I think about it, we had not told them. We fill them in on the details, they are impressed. Eloise is a model and fully appreciates what it means to be a Paris Vogue cover girl.

'Kate that is so good and all the way from Nouvelle-Zélande, congratulations. Alain, if he was the boastful type, which thank god he's not, would really have something to boast about, screwed a Vogue cover girl!'

'Eloise, please not in front of your friends.'

'Don't worry Kate, we are intimate with Marciel and Maria quite often, no secrets here, we could all get it on tonight, what do you think folks?'

There are slightly embarrassed looks all 'round, we are all aware of what might happen but to actually come out and talk about it is a little awkward.

More wine, coffees, and then it's time to go home. What happens now? Alain takes the lead.

'Marciel, Maria, come back to our place, Rex and Kate are staying with us, we have no secrets, we can all get right into it.'

I have a bit of a problem reconciling myself to what's about to happen, I think Kate is a little unsure as well but the die is cast. It's going to be a group thing with six people. Eloise and Alain have set up their lounge with some big soft rugs on the floor and we are no sooner through the door when Alain is cracking a bottle of Dom. Champagne all round and the clothes come off, all the clothes. It's an erotic scene, we are all lying around on these big soft rugs naked, the idea is to just take whoever you want. I find myself alongside Maria and I can't help myself. I'm into her almost immediately and she's fantastic, a real sex bomb. After a bit I roll her onto her tummy and take her from the rear drawing her buttocks back onto my huge erection and this sends her right off thrashing about on the big soft rugs. It continues on, there's a bit of partner changing and I find myself with Eloise, she really goes at it. I think the close proximity of other couples fucking, really fucking, is a big turn on for the girls. It must have been about an hour later when we had all pretty much exhausted ourselves and are lying about naked when Alain sums up the evening.

'That was great, welcome to our guests from Nouvelle-Zélande. You are a great couple, we should do it again before you leave us, would you all be starters say in a couple of days?'

There's general agreement, yes, we all liked it, a repeat in a couple of days would be good.

Marciel and Maria rummage around, find their clothes and start to get dressed. Maria makes getting dressed as sexy as she can, the devil, she's brought a hard on, I might have to fuck her again before she goes. It happens, I tear her knickers off and really give it to her. 'Maria you're just too sexy.'

Breakfast; 'that was a great night,' I offer, Kate adds, 'yes it was, I really enjoyed it, is this a regular thing with you two?'

'Not a regular thing but it does happen, we find it stimulating, it brings us closer together, there's no temptation to stray, all the sex you could possibly want is readably available. There are two other couples we interact with, you could possibly meet them while you're here.'

'Now then what to do with today? I suggest that Rex comes out to the base with me, I'm pretty sure I can get him in, ex-military, interested Rex?'

'Am I ever.'

'Eloise you could take Kate into the city, you've got a shoot this afternoon right, Kate might like to see how it all works here in Paris, well she's already seen how it really works, but I'm sure she'll be interested, that right Kate?'

'Very interested.'

'There's a fast train service into Paris that we normally use, better than a car.'

And that's what happens. I go out to Creil Air Base with Alain and Kate goes into the city with Eloise. I dig around in the back of my wallet and bingo, I've still got my RAF ID card, a 1250, it works. Security at Creil are familiar with an RAF 1250. The details go into a computer and I come up clean, I am what I say I am.

Bet it flashes on the DGSE's computer as well. What's he doing at an Armée de L'Air Française base?

Alaine takes me along to his squadron's dispersal and introduces me to his commanding officer. His boss is very interested, ex RAF strike pilot, LABS, Germany. He had been involved with LABS a couple of years earlier, before he took on this current role running a Super Mystère fighter squadron. He had been a flight commander on a Mirage 4 squadron that specialised in LABS bombing, an advanced under the radar bombing technique that I had been involved with on B(I)8 Canberra's in Germany, so we had something in common. It was hard watching the hot French jets roaring around, tugged at the heart strings, seemed like it was just yesterday that I was doing this sort of thing, now it's just a little toy aeroplane. Could still come to grief though, even get yourself killed in the little toy aeroplane. Alain was not scheduled to fly so he was able to show me around. A squadron of the latest French supersonic jet fighters. The squadron had a two seat trainer version of the Mystère, now there's a thought, if only. Forget it Rex, that was yesteryear. We had lunch in the Officers Mess. My mind went back to that diversion into Orange on our way back to Geilenkirchen from Gibraltar, quite a while ago now, where the French Air Force Officer we dealt with advised that their Officers Mess would not be up to the required standard for RAF Officers. I thought at the time, rubbish, you have ulterior motives. The mess at Creil was very comfortable, the dining room excellent, definitely up to the required standard. Later in the afternoon we went back to Alain and Eloise's place and hopped into the spa. It was a warm afternoon, we cracked a bottle of savvy and were sitting in the spa enjoying a glass when the girls arrived home. Kate was full of enthusiasm about her day with Eloise immersed in the Paris modelling scene, different to Auckland, a lot more professional and very competitive. When they heard about Kate's involvement with Vogue she was suddenly royalty, embarrassing but very nice.

It's not long before the clothes come off and we are naked in the spa, almost felt like old times like we had been doing this for ages, total familiarity with each other's bodies, no awkwardness whatsoever. The only problem was me, the sight of the naked Eloise brought on this mighty erection, couldn't help it, I just had to have her. Eloise could not help but notice, she led me out of the spa, into the pool house, onto a sun lounger and went down on it. Almost immediately Alain is fucking Kate right alongside. It was certainly a different environment, this casual approach to sex, just whenever you felt like it, do what you want with whoever you want.

We dined at home that evening, Eloise and Alain were both good cooks and we enjoyed an excellent meal, the clothes stayed on, rather comfortable having clothes on but there was this underlying feeling that if you want to, feel free. Some fine reds, they had quite a cellar, it was an enjoyable evening. The following day Alain is required at the base, he was off into the wild blue yonder, the handsome jet fighter jock. Eloise has the day off, she will look after us. Eventually after a pleasant evening, bedtime.

'Interested in swapping for the night?' from Alain, Eloise has an expectant look on her face as well.

I glance at Kate, 'why not' is her response. This will be a first, I don't have a problem with the idea, a night in the sack with Eloise will be heaven, the girl is just so sexy, I can't get enough of her, it happens. Eloise is all over me, her penchant for going down on my erection, bringing me to orgasm, and then apparently swallowing it all is incredibly erotic. We spend a good part of the night fucking each other every which way. Eventually there's some sleeping and as the room brightens in the morning I'm awoken by this incredible sensation, Eloise is down there again.

Breakfast, another excellent breakfast.

'How was it Kate,' I ask.

'Rex it was good, really good, made me realise how good you are. Did you satisfy Eloise dear, she certainly appears to be happy, did he satisfy you Eloise?'

'Qui Kate your Rex knows how to give a lady great pleasure, you're a lucky girl Kate.'

Alain goes off to fly his hot jet and I'm left with two sexy girls for the day. I'll give Pierre Robier a call, see what he has for me.

'Rex, can you come and see me, perhaps tomorrow.'

'Yes I can do that, I have your address, would two in the afternoon be suitable.'

'That will fit, I have a job in North Africa that will suit you, it will be out of Gibraltar and will tie you up for three days.'

'Not Algeria?'

'No not Algeria, I'll give you the detail tomorrow.'

Right that's settled. What will I do with these girls for the day and I had better think about asking if we can stay a bit longer. If Pierre Robiers's job is going to take me away for three days then perhaps Kate can stay here with Eloise and Alain. Is that a good idea, leaving my lovely Kate alone with Alain. I raise the matter with Eloise, she's sure there will not be a problem.

'Of course Alain will be agreeable, three more nights with your Kate, will that be ok with you Rex? Right now you've got all today with the two of us, Alain won't be back till late, what mischief can we get up to?'

What is this girl suggesting, a day of casual sex perhaps, that would be nice, or perhaps we could go into Creil village and have a look around.

'Shall I give Marciel and Maria a call, suggest dinner tonight or shall we leave that for another day and just enjoy each other for a while, what do you two think?'

'Another time perhaps Eloise, looks like we are going to have a few more days here, a few more days of casual sex.'

'Casual sex, I like that idea Rex, lets adjourn to a bedroom and do that.'

The conversation seems to have got both girls quite worked up. Eloise leads the way, off come the clothes and Eloise goes down on me again and does what French girls seem to like to do. Kate observes this and sure enough the sight becomes too much. She pushes Eloise away, mounts me and it's not long before she's moaning with pleasure. Here goes the day, casual sex with two lovely girls, as much as we all want. They both seem to want a lot, how nice is that.

'Eloise, how about we take a break and go into Creil for lunch, show us around your lovely village, good idea?'

'Good idea Rex, let's do that, need to save ourselves for later, there will just be the four of us tonight.'

Creil is a lovely town, we find a café, have a light lunch and finish up sitting outside in the sunshine with a bottle of savvy, we get to talking.

'Eloise tell me, do you two have a grand plan for your life?'

'I wish, it's day to day at the moment. We think about it occasionally but then with Alain being in the Armée de L'Air Française he does not get a say in where we go next. He likes being a fighter pilot and I like the modelling, right now we are pretty much just enjoying the moment. How about you two, you're not married are you?'

'No we're not, have not even discussed it. We've only been together for a few months but I'm pretty sure I've found my soul mate, I just hope Kate feels the same way.' I give Kate a long look as I say this.

'Yes I do, stop worrying Rex, you're the man I love, the man I want to marry, but when? The problem is the way we lead our lives, not exactly conducive to marriage and children. I could keep the modelling thing going, in fact right now I will definitely keep it going. It seems I've reached some sort of pinnacle, people want me, but Rex? he goes off doing his mercenary thing and it worries the hell out of me, it's dangerous. We've talked about a change of direction, something that's not so risky, and that's about all we've done, talk about it. I guess we are a bit like you and Alain, living from day to day.'

'Two couples adrift on the sea of life but at the moment the trip is very enjoyable and since meeting you Eloise, and Alain, and coming over here to France, well more of the same please. The Vogue thing could bring us here again. They did indicate they will be wanting Kate and my chosen career will continue taking me all over the place. Marriage? well right now it just would not fit however it is there, in the future somewhere, right Kate?'

'Yes Rex it is but as you say, not right now, but definitely one day. You are, will always be, the man I love, the man I want to father my children.'

'This is stirring stuff girls but we should have plans, goals. We're doing things that we like but are there long term goals. Flying is flying. I've done the exciting stuff and Alain's doing it right now. When the apprenticeship is over, when he leaves the military, the idea is to get into some long term flying business that supports a comfortable life style. I'm not sure I've got that bit right. Certainly able to afford an extravagant life style, but long term? not sure about that. The modelling world, how does it work there? what's an ideal career path? Kate here appears to have fast tracked hers, I mean a Paris Vogue cover, that's the pinnacle isn't it? where to from here, how long does it last? What's your thinking Eloise?'

'Alain is going to be out of the Armée de L'Air Française in eighteen months and right now he's not sure which way to go. I think he discussed it briefly with you Rex at Ouvéa, you suggested flying fighters for the Saudis in the Middle East in the short term, make some real money, then look at the airlines. Me, well as you know Kate where does modelling take you and how long does it last? These questions don't have answers, anything can happen. In your case Kate something did happen, you're set up now, you are *known*. Me, still hoping, but I love the job and I'll keep it going until life demands a change.'

'Well now, have we sorted out our lives? No, just itemised all the uncertainties. Let's reconvene this meeting in two years time and review progress, that's my summing up and this bottle has got itself empty, another perhaps.'

We continue siting in the sun in Creil, it's very pleasant. Eventually we wander back to Eloise and Alain's place and get into the spa again, the usual problem, the sight of Eloise and Kate naked causing me another erection problem, how long can I hold off this time?

Ring, ring, It's Alain, he won't be home this evening. His squadron has been playing war games and he's diverted into Orange in the south of France with an engine problem, probably be sometime tomorrow before he can fly back to Creil. *Wonder if the Officers Mess will be up to scratch?* Looks like I'm going to spend the night alone with these two girls, could be interesting. I have to meet Pierre Robier in Paris at two tomorrow, I'll take the train into the city.

'Let me take you girls out for dinner this evening, that restaurant we went to with Marciel and Maria perhaps.'

'That's kind of you Rex, yes, that's a good one, perhaps we can repay you in bed later.' Eloise again, she unstoppable.

It's quite a night, both girls are all over me in Alain and Eloise's big bed. They're competing to see who can bring me to orgasm the fastest, me? well how good does it get, raped by two beautiful girls.

The train into Paris, it's a fast modern affair, very comfortable. I seek out Pierre Robier's building and room 202. Bzzzz, I press the doorbell, 'Monsieur Robier,' no response, I knock, 'Monsieur Robier,' still no response, have I made a mistake, I'm sure it was two this afternoon, room 202. I push the door, it swings open and I recoil in horror, the place is a charnel house, blood everywhere. There's a body on the floor, throat slashed open, I feel faint, want to throw up, it's worse than a horror movie. I look closer, the body has been mutilated, clothing torn open, blood all over the place, it's Monsieur Robier. There's something on his chest, a note.
　　Rentrez chez vous Monsieur Rex, ne plaisante pas avec nous.
　　Go home Mister Rex, don't mess with us.
French, English, my name, it's meant for me, shit! There's something else, his genitals have been torn off and stuffed into his mouth, the FLN's brutal calling card.

Shit, I panic, what do I do, get out of here, get as far away as you can. I literally flee the building. Will I attract attention, I don't care, I'm terrified. I rush down the street, there's a small park, an oasis of green, I crash onto a park seat. I'm shaking uncontrollably. Am I safe, is my life in danger, I want to throw up. I sit on this park seat for a long time. Whatever have I got myself into, my tunnel vision, money, and now murder, brutality. My life is screwed up, change it, change it now. Go back to New Zealand, give up this mercenary business, marry Kate, settle down, get a boring job and learn to live with it. A little old lady sits down beside me.

'Ça va monsieur, tu n'as pas l'air trop beau.'

'Yes yes, I'm all right thank you. I do not speak French though.'

'Oh, silly me, I speak English, you do not look well monsieur, are you sure you are all right, you are very pale.'

'You are very kind but yes I am ok, just a little tummy upset.'
I think the best thing to do is get back to Creil then get out of France, go back to Auckland and don't leave the place.

The train journey is a nightmare, I'm terrified, feeling sick and shaking uncontrollably, it attracts some curious looks, not good.

'Rex, what's wrong?' Kate looks worried.

'Let me lie down for a bit, get my brain sorted, I've had a terrible experience, I need to rest for a while.'
Alain is back in the house, he has a word with me.

'What's happened Rex, come on no secrets, what's gone wrong?'
I think about it for a while and decide to level with him, after all he is considering this mercenary business. I would be remiss if I did not enlighten him with the reality of just what can, and does happen.

'Get Eloise and Kate in here, I'll let you all know the reality of the business I'm in, the business you are considering getting into Alain.'

It's late afternoon, I'm lying on a bed, Kate, Eloise, and Alain are gathered around. My gut feeling is that I can let it all come out, reveal everything. I don't owe anyone any allegiance and anyway I don't care anymore.

My story goes on into the night. I relate everything that's happened to me since embarking on my mercenary career path, the huge money involved, the dangerous bits, the brushes with death, the grisly Algerian business. My audience is spellbound, having difficulty comprehending. Then I tell them about what I suspect has happened in this case, just how dangerous this business can be, the forces at work, things you may never know about. My take on what's just happened? Well the DGSE know I'm in France, I mean the immigration delays. There's obviously a mole in the DGSE, information is being leaked to the FLN. The Algerian job was compromised, the FLN knew about it and made the connection to the New Zealand pilot being employed. When I popped up on the DGSE's computer the other day the FLN would have been alerted, if they made the connection with Pierre Robier as well then I guess they must have assumed I was about to do something that was not in their best interests and decided to warn me off. I don't know what the job was going to be. I had made it very clear that anything involving Algeria was not for me. It's not rocket science to see that continuing with my present lucrative career could well come to an abrupt end.

My audience of three were silent, Kate looked shocked and suddenly I felt sorry for what I had put her through with my *out of town for a while*. I was now feeling a bit better, getting it off my chest was therapeutic. Alain and Eloise were looking very apprehensive, they probably had no idea of what went on out there in the mercenary world, how would they, I had no idea myself, it's been a shocking awakening.

'Alain, I don't think you want to get involved in this, the Saudi deal is probably the thing for you, then the airlines.'

It was a terrible night's sleep, or lack of it, sex was farthest from my mind, I think Kate stayed awake as well worrying. I figured the quicker we get out of France the better, perhaps tomorrow, our first class tickets are open ended. No big money for this one, no money at all.

We have breakfast with Eloise and Alain, the conversation is stilted, not sure what to talk about. After breakfast Alain goes off to the base, he's rostered to fly to-day, lucky devil, he'll spend the day blasting holes in the sky in his hot jet, if only!

Knock, knock, there's a fellow at the door, he's smartly dressed with a look of authority.

'Bonjour Madame Dubois, je suis l'inspector Jean Naudin de la police métropolitaine de Paris, je suis à la recherche du'n autre néo-zélandais, Rex Macare.'

'Rex Macare, yes he's here,' Eloise answers, 'can we speak English, Rex Macare does not speak French, might I ask what this is about?'

'Murder madame Dubois, I need to speak with Rex Macare.'
Eloise looks shocked, 'murder you say?'

'Yes murder most foul, yesterday in the city, but relax madame, monsieur Macare is not a suspect however we think he may have all the clues about who did this, may I come in?'
I'm in the room and hear what's been said.

'Hello Inspector, I'm Rex Macare, I had a feeling you people might come calling, how can I help you?'

'Well monsieur Macare we know who you are and what you do but we don't think you did this, however, we do think it was what you were about to do that caused the demise of Pierre Robier.'

'Well I don't know what Pierre Robier was about to offer me, that was the purpose of my going to see him yesterday. When I got there I found that appalling scene in his office.'

'Why did you not call the police right away?'

'No reason, I was so shocked I just wanted to get as far away as possible, I came straight back here, I did not know what else to do. Perhaps I was remiss in not contacting the authorities.'

'I understand monsieur Macare, I too viewed Pierre Robier's office, it was one of the most horrific murder scenes I have ever seen, I understand you revulsion. We are pretty sure it was the FLN and that indicates to us that you were going to be offered something that was not in the best interests of the FLN.'

'Well if that was the case Pierre Robier would have been disappointed. I had let him know in no uncertain terms that I was not interested in anything involving Algeria. The one job I did do for him also culminated in murder, but I'm sure you know all about that Inspector Naudin.'

'Yes we know quite a lot about your involvement. Perhaps you can tell me everything you actually know about Pierre Robier and how you came to be working for him.'

The next hour is interesting. I tell the Inspector everything about my mercenary activities that involve the French. Mr Roberts's side of things I do not divulge, no need for the French to know, it appears that any information the French may have is not secure. I voice my suspicions about a mole in their DGSE, I mean how else would the FLN know I was in France, and I suggest that Pierre Robier's telephone was not secure either. How was it that my visit to his office was known, I only made one phone call to him. Inspector Naudin did suggest that my suspicions about the DGSE were unfounded, that this business had nothing to do with the DGSE, however, he went a bit quiet on that when I pointed out how I always seemed to run into a delay when I encountered French immigration at their border.

'Now then Inspector, how about a coffee, perhaps Eloise can do the honours.'

Eloise and Kate are party to this conversation. I'm not able to read their expressions, a strange mixture of incredulity, shock, disbelief. Revelations about the real world, things that regular law abiding citizens would not have a clue about. Their eyes had been opened the previous evening when I poured my heart out.

'Yes of course, coffee, coffee and a biscuit, coming right up.'

'Now then Inspector we're thinking about returning to New Zealand immediately, quite frankly I'm scarred and I don't think I want to be on French soil any longer than necessary. The FLN have told me to go home in the most gruesome way imaginable, I think I just might comply.'

'Monsieur, at this stage we would like you to stay for another two days, I want to pick your brains again, see if there's anything more you can help us with, could you do that?'

'That's ok Rex,' Eloise adds, 'Alain and I would be only too pleased to have you stay on for a bit.'

'Now tell me Inspector, if you can, what's your take on this murder? We'll keep it to ourselves of course, after all we, or perhaps I, already know just about everything anyway.'

'The FLN, as you are aware, are a murderous adversary, take no prisoners, make the message clear, don't mess with us. Rex, you have been the recipient of such a message. You would be wise not to undertake any more flying jobs involving French interests in Africa. You are known to them, how they identified you I cannot say, but they have.'

'Well it's pretty obvious Inspector. I've got a red flag against my name on the DGSE's computer because of something I was involved in with the military years ago. Whenever I cross a French border the DGSE are alerted, the mole just passes the information on. Why don't you find the mole? If he passes on low level information about the movements of a pilot what more serious stuff is being leaked?'

'Monsieur Macare you have a suspicious mind.'

'I don't think so Inspector, being involved in two murders does focus the mind. I think I've got it sorted. Now then let's get away from this serious stuff and enjoy Eloise's coffee and by the way this is my partner Kate. Kate is also from New Zealand and shortly you will be seeing her on the bookstalls around your lovely city. Kate is the cover girl on next month's Paris Vogue.'

'Really, well hello Kate, I've never had the pleasure of meeting a Vogue cover girl.'

We enjoy Eloise's coffee and bikky and Inspector Naudin takes his leave, he'll be wanting to talk with me again, probably in two days' time.

'Well girls, that was different and not particularly enjoyable, the underbelly of society, the world we live in. Eloise I think Kate and I should rebook our departure for New Zealand for three days from now, how does that fit with you and Alain?'

'Yes, but if you can we would like you to stay for longer.'

'You're a temptress Eloise but I've been threatened, it was very real, I just want to do what they've suggested, go back to New Zealand.'

We rebook our flights, Eloise looks a little down when I tell her, she really wants us to stay on.

The next couple of days are enjoyable, more high jinks with Eloise and Alain, more hopping in and out of each other's beds but the fun's gone out of it for me, deep down I'm just plain scarred. Inspector Dubois phones and requests a further meeting. He comes out to Creil and picks my brains on the detail, anything that may even remotely be connected to the dreadful business and I tackle him on my suspicions about a mole in the DGSE. He's non-committal, but he does not dismiss my suggestions either which tells me that *I've got it right.*

Our last night with Alain and Eloise, I'm still finding it hard to work up any enthusiasm about anything.

'Rex you need cheering up,' it's Eloise, 'how about we have dinner at our favourite and then come back here and jump in the spa, perhaps a few more wines than usual might help.'

We do have more wine than we should and it starts to show. An excellent meal and we stumble back to Eloise and Alain's place. The clothes come off and we're into the spa. It's does not take long, the urge returns and we're all trying to do it in the spa.

'Better in the pool house, those big sun loungers,' Alain's suggestion.

It develops into a bit of an orgy, too much wine has got the better of us and things become a little depraved, eventually it's decided bed's the story.

'Let's swap for the night, or what's left of it,' our last night in France.

It's all behind us, we're on our way back to Auckland, drifting in and out of sleep in our very comfortable first class seats. It's been two weeks since we left and our world has changed. Events in France have forced a rethink about how we lead our lives. Kate's world has suddenly opened right up, her career possibilities limitless. She's about to be known around the world, a sought after commodity with a price to match. I feel so pleased for her. Not sure she's got her head around the enormity of it yet. Me? quite the opposite. My chosen career has turned to worms. I've only carried out a handful of flying jobs for big money. Two of them have involved murder, another two came close to getting me killed, and the rest have all been high risk. People have been shooting at me. Only the Vietnam one was relatively low risk but there was still risk involved, how much luck do I have? Do I want to continue like this or do I need to change direction completely. Put the thought away for a while, think about the nice things and there are some very nice things to think about. Kate could well be going back to Paris again, perhaps more than once. I can go with her, why not, be the chaperone, spend time up at Creil. Eloise and Alain will be only too happy to accommodate us. Have nothing to do with any flying the French may offer. Really I need to get right out of the mercenary business, the risk is too high.

Auckland, a bright sunny morning, makes coming home much more enjoyable. Home to the flat, coffee on the balcony.

'Well Kate, where to from here? You were the big earner on that trip, me, nix, I need a serious rethink.'

Amongst the mail waiting for us there's a letter from Australia, from an old mate who's been over there for several years. He's heard I was back in New Zealand and on the lookout for some flying, small world.

Australia

My mate in Australia runs an aerial agricultural business in Griffith. He's on the lookout for pilots and is wondering if I would be interested. Is this coincidence or what, I am very susceptible to just about anything right now, anything where people don't try to kill me. Ray Welland; apparently he's well established in Griffith in the Riverina, a rich pastoral and farming area in New South Wales, there's a phone number. I give him a call keen to find out what else there is out there in the flying world, anything that's safer than what I'm doing at the moment. Ray's surprised to hear from me. He'd tracked me down via the New Zealand licensing authority and written on the off chance that I might be interested, might respond. His company, Air Ag, has ten Piper Pawnee aircraft converted for agricultural work, he is a part owner. The business has been going for several years. Fifteen pilots, however, they are always on the lookout for more, there's some staff turnover, pilot poaching is a problem. If I'm interested perhaps I could come over and stay with him for a few days, see how the business operates, get a feeling for it, see if it's me. Well food for thought, not a silly idea, but the money? be a different league altogether. Life expectancy will be better, so will peace of mind. I'll think about it for a while then broach the subject with Kate.

It's not long before the news media are onto Kate. She's a celebrity, big news on the New Zealand scene, picture in the paper, knowledgeable articles by all the columnists, all the women's magazines want her story, there are offers.

'Kate your story is a saleable commodity, you need an agent, something a cut above the agency you work for at the moment.'

Kate's no slug, she soon tracks down a hard-nosed fellow who has a good reputation for getting the best possible deal for people in the public eye. The better the deal, the bigger his commission. Kate's happy with the arrangement and some of the cheques that start coming in are substantial. Then out of the blue a call from Pierre Brodeur.

'Pierre here Rex, what can I say, I guess you will not want anything to do with me, right?'

'Don't be too hard on yourself Pierre, how would you know the DGSE had been compromised to such an extent? Don't deny it, don't try and tell me you're not one of their agents. I've figured it out, I've also found out a bit from the Paris police as well, let's just let it rest. What I do want you to be quite clear on, I don't want you to offer me anything that involves Africa, perhaps not anything that involves French interests in Europe either, it's just too dangerous.'

'Vietnam perhaps Rex?'

'Perhaps, but I am seriously considering giving it away altogether.'

'That's sad to hear but understandable and by the way we have made a deposit into you Swiss account, we feel we owe you for the trauma you experienced, 10,000 Swiss francs.

'Thank you Pierre, I was thinking the whole dreadful business was going to return me zilch. I do have one question, but you may not know the answer. I thought I made it clear I did not want any flying involving Algeria, just too dangerous, the FLN. The flying I went to see Pierre Robier about in Paris was to be out of Gibraltar and that's all I know. Subsequent events, specifically his brutal murder, suggests the flying job was going to involve the FLN, what other reason would they have to send such a horrific message?'

'I can't help you there Rex, I too do not know the details.'

'Ok, I forgive you, no Algeria is that clear, Vietnam perhaps and by the way have you given anything to my mate Russ Horsley?'

'Yes we have, we've offered him something in Vietnam, not heard back yet.'

'Good, Russ will like that. Well thanks for the call and thanks for the cash, no rush to offer me anything, as I mentioned I'm thinking about a career change.'

Paris Vogue hits the newsstands around the world, Kate is famous, the super model from New Zealand. In Auckland she's elevated to stardom, the first model from New Zealand to really hit the big time.

'Well Kate, what now, you are going to be swamped with lucrative modelling offers, me, well I'm thinking about going over to Australia to see a mate who's involved in the aerial topdressing business, could be a safer way to earn a bob, there's that Cathay offer on the table as well. I'm seriously thinking about a change of direction.'

'Australia, topdressing, different, that would mean living there Rex.'

'Guess it would, not sure about that, right now I like Auckland. I wonder if you will remain here? Vogue are interested in you now that could mean Paris possibly. Lot of variables at the moment, perhaps we just do nothing for a bit, see what pops up.'

'You could go over to Australia and get a fix on what's on offer. What would that involve, a week away, perhaps sooner rather than later Rex, what do you think?'

'Yep good idea, want to come?'

'Not at the moment, too many people want a piece of me, best if I stay here.'

Griffith in the Riverina in New South Wales, a predominately Italian town with a history of Italian settlement going way back. It's at the centre of a huge agricultural area, vast crop growing operations that support several aerial farming companies operating a variety of agricultural aircraft. One of these is Air Ag partly owned by Ray Welland, it's Ray I have come to see.

'Come and stay at the house Rex, I'll show you how we work, let you try your hand perhaps, see if we can get you onto the payroll. Good to see you, must be eight or nine years since we were knocking around Auckland together, what have you been up to? I came over here and finished up in Griffith flying for Air Ag. They're a good crowd, I became quite involved, married the boss's daughter, became a part owner of the business. I think I'll be here for the rest of my life, why would I move away?'

'You're a happy man Ray, settled, career path spelt out, me? well the best way I can put it is unsettled and rather confused. I'm making shitloads of money but I think I want out.'

I tell Ray what I've been doing since getting out of the Air Force in Europe, he's impressed.

'Why do you want out?'

'The very real prospect of an early grave, believe me, what I'm doing is bloody dangerous. I don't think I want to risk it anymore. There's a girl involved as well. I'm in love and I think I want to get married, settle down, have kids, all those ordinary things that ordinary people do.'

'Well not the Rex Macare I used to know, there's been a seismic change. So you are looking at other career options, right? Well I can show you what it's like in the aerial agricultural business. Tomorrow we'll be doing some spraying up at a place called Goolgowi north of here. I'll take you along and you can see for yourself in the meantime come home with me, you can meet my lovely wife and we'll down a few middies, sundowners on the veranda.'

Ray's wife is an attractive brown eyed brunette, Lydia, there are three young boys. The house, a big rambling farmhouse with a veranda that goes right 'round. We sit in the late afternoon sunshine enjoying some middies and the conversation turns to what life is like in the aerial agricultural business here in Australia.

'A bloody roller coaster, very dependant on the climate and that's totally unpredictable. One year you are up, making serious money, the next you can be on the bones of your arse, there's no continuity, no certainty, very difficult to plan too far ahead. It should be a stable industry able to absorb the fluctuations but that's not the case and Government is not particularly helpful when times are bad. Overall it is viable and it will always be here. Farming would not be practical in the Riverina were it not for us. You could say it's good for the long term but it can be very testing, very testing indeed. Air Ag is quite well capitalised, not totally dependent on the banks, it puts us at quite an advantage when times are tough. I'm pretty sure we are going to be here for a long time.'

'That's quite an insight Ray, very different to what I'm doing right now. It has appeal but really to make it work long term you would need to be an owner not just a salaried pilot, right?'

'You're dead right there, when there's a bad season the pilots are the first to go, there's little security of employment.'

'No security in the business I'm in either but the money involved means I can go for months without flying and not have to worry about it.'

Lydia asks, 'What do you do Rex?'
I give her a *sanitised* account of what I do, I doubt she would comprehend if I gave her all the rather unpleasant detail.

'That sounds fascinating why would you want to do anything else? the money? Sounds like early retirement could be on the cards.'

If only, an early grave is more likely, richest corpse in the cemetery.

'Lydia it's not all beer and skittles, I'm afraid there's an element of danger involved. I want out, don't want to push my luck, looking at other options at the moment. Ray here is going to twist my arm, try and get me to fly for him, right Ray?'

'Well we can certainly use you. We have a turnover in pilots, as I mentioned, there's a bit of poaching going on. Now then I think Lydia might have cooked up a feast for us, right dear?'

It's a lovely family dinner, me, Ray, Lydia, and their three young sons, far removed from the sort of thing that's dominated my life in recent months. No sexual inuendoes, no hints at bedroom activities to follow, totally the opposite, a lovely normal family dinner and it's nice.

'Rex in the morning you can come up to Goolgowi with me, we've got a big spraying job to do that will probably take a couple of days. Aerial spraying is a big part of our operation, we have two aircraft modified for spraying and they are fully utilized for most of the year. That's the good years, they're not all good years though. Tomorrow's job is fungicide onto a large area of maize.'

'Sounds interesting Ray, tell me what variation do you get in your operations, it's not all spraying, right?'

'No it's not, depends on what the farmers see as the best cash crop for the coming year, there's a lot of crystal ball gazing involved. Weather is the big unknown, wet, dry, drought, flood, we get the lot and the crops vary accordingly, rice, cotton, maize, barley, wheat, all depends what the cockies think will get the best cash return. Every crop has different pest control and fertilizer requirements, demand for our services can vary enormously. Not easy for us, we need a crystal ball as well, but a good year, that's one where the cockies get it right, can be very profitable, likewise a bad year can be very bad.'

'I guess your pilots don't have any security of employment then?'

'You've got it, there's no security at all and that's not good for the industry. When we lay off pilots we give them the right of return when things pick up, however, there are plenty of young fellows out there fresh out of the aero clubs who will do anything to get into the business, will work for peanuts just to get the flying. Trouble is experience, or lack of it. Employing these young fellows can be costly for the employer but when he goes looking for the experienced pilots he's had to lay off they're not there anymore.'

'Hmm, not sure it's my thing, you really need to be an owner not an employee, right Ray?'

'You've got it, and you need to be a well capitalized owner, not one at the mercy of the banks. Starting up around here would not be easy. The industry is well served by several well run companies, a new boy would have a hard time, a very hard time.'

'Hmm, you're putting me off Ray, but I'm keen to see what's involved in a day's spraying.'

It's huge, there's maize as far as the eye can see, stretches to the horizon and it's all got to be sprayed with a fungicide. Both of Air Ag's spray aircraft are involved, Piper PA25 Pawnees. The fungicide being used is nasty stuff, there's a lot of protective clothing and some breathing gear involved, quite a complicated operation. The two pilots are long term employees of Rays', spraying is not for beginners, these two are very experienced.

It's an interesting day for me, these fellows work long hard hours for *ordinary money* and there's no real job security although Ray would be very reluctant to let either of them go when times were tough, would he be able to get them back again? Very different to what I'm involved in. Do I want to get into this sort of thing? not really, I've been well and truly spoilt by the big money. Let's face reality, nowhere else am I going to get the sort of money I'm getting now. If I want out then I'm just going to have to lower my expectations. Perhaps the best option, all things considered, are the airlines, but having to live in Hong Kong does not appeal. What about New Zealand? there's TEAL, they're based in Auckland, perhaps I should sound them out.

That evening back at Ray's place we enjoy a roast dinner Lydia has prepared. The three boys, Ray, myself, and Lydia. It's the normal domestic environment again, something that most people enjoy and it's nice, I could get used to this.

'Well Rex, what did you make of that, a day in the life of an aerial sprayer, when do you want to start?'

'Thanks for the offer Ray but I'm not sure it's for me. I've got this girl and she will not be wanting to live here in the Riverina, at the moment Paris is a more likely place for her.'

'Really Rex, what does she do?'
I give Ray and Lydia a run down on Kate, her modelling career, and the Vogue thing.'

'Wow, that's really something,' from Lydia, 'I'm going into town tomorrow, see if the bookshop has got the latest Paris Vogue, see what this love of your life looks like.'

'Rex you might end up living in Paris, ply your trade from there.' Ray's take on my situation.

'Could be Ray but I think the airlines are looking more attractive as time goes on. I'm definitely going to give the mercenary thing away, not sure how much luck I've got. The insight into your business was interesting not sure it's for me though, I'd want to be an owner not an employee and that's not on the cards. I do like the lifestyle you've got here, domestic bliss, kids, a normal life, I'm envious.'

Another day up at Goolgowi, Ray offers to let me try my hand. It's seriously low level stuff, but it's in bright sunshine over vast flat fields. The idea is to have the wheels of the Piper just above the top of the maize, almost touching. There's a lever to pull when you want the fungicide to flow. Pretty simple operation really but it could become very boring, not for me. We finish the job and go back to Ray's place in the late afternoon, middies on the veranda again.

'Well Rex what do you think, is it for you, can I sign you on?

'Thanks but no thanks Ray, it's not me, however, it's been instrumental in making up my mind, definitely the airlines. My mercenary days are drawing to a close and I have you to thank Ray. An insight into a normal family life, your family life, that's for me. Now let me take you and Lydia out to dinner this evening, Limones, I hear it's rather good.'

'Good, it's the best around, sure you want to do this Rex?'

'Yes very sure, I owe you, you've made me decide my future. I've been living day to day recently, no clear direction, that's not good. My lovely Kate doesn't like it either and now an insight into real domestic life, with kids, your life.' It's decided me, time to settle down. I thank you both for sorting me out.'

'Well a watershed moment, a very different Rex to the tear away I used to know in Auckland. We need to meet your Kate, she's obviously caused you to take your life a little more seriously.'

'Yes she has and that's a good thing, probably prolonged it as well. Tomorrow I'll organise getting back to Auckland. I cannot thank you two enough for removing the blinkers from my eyes, there's a lot more to life than money.'

Limones is good, very good, an excellent meal, Ray and Lydia appreciate it. I don't think they are in the habit of eating out, well three young boys, bit limiting. Will this be my future with Kate?

It's a TEAL Electra, Sydney to Auckland.

'Any chance of a flight deck visit,' I ask the hostess, 'I do a bit of flying, I'm interested.'

'I'll ask, what did you say your name was?'

'Rex,' it's the co-pilot, a mate from the air force, another Kiwi who had been in the Royal Air Force.

'Not seen you for a while, Geilenkirchen I think, what are you doing here?'

'Looking for a job, what are the chances?'

'You're kidding me, a little birdie told me you were into the naughty stuff, becoming rich and famous.'

'Misinformation, but tell me what are you doing here?'

'I'm brand new. My good Captain here has been charged with trying to turn me into a competent airline pilot, he's very good, patience of Job.'

'I'm interested in becoming an airline pilot, how come you have made it into TEAL, I've heard it's a closed shop, no chance. I've been talking to Cathay, they're very interested. They've made me an offer but what I would like, in a perfect world, is to fly for TEAL.'

'Allow me to introduce myself, I'm Captain Clarke, Nobby, and yes I'm trying to knock the rough edges off your mate here, turn him into an airline pilot; you are from the Royal Air Force?'

'Yes, I was at Geilenkirchen in Germany with this fellow, we were both based there, different squadrons.'

'And you say you would like to join TEAL?'

'Would I ever, but it's a closed shop I hear.'

'Well it has been however times are changing, there's some expansion planned and there will be a requirement for more pilots. Your mate here is the first, he got lucky, presented himself at just the right time, what experience do you have?'

I give Nobby a brief run down on my air force career and he calls a halt.

'I've heard enough, TEAL could use you. Get along to our Auckland office as quick as you can, tell the Ops Manager I have interviewed you and I said you are the right stuff, how does that sound?'

'It sounds incredible, thank you, I think you might have changed the course of my life.'

'You tin bum,' from my air force mate, 'I had to fight and struggle to get into this seat and you just slide in here and charm

Nobby, just like that.'

'There's got to be some luck in this world, I need a bit of luck, right now I'm running on borrowed time.'

I'm ecstatic, how lucky can you get? a real opportunity to get into TEAL.

'Thank you Captain, thank you a lot, yes I will be along to your office first thing.'

I go back to my seat in a daze, my life *will change* I've decided. What's just been offered is perfect, well it's not in the bag yet but it looks promising. Airline flying with TEAL, the ideal choice. Auckland based long term, well for the rest of my flying career, no more danger, no more people trying to kill me, Kate will be over the moon. The money? it will be ordinary, bit above ordinary, airline pilots are well paid but I won't be getting a quarter mill tax free for a couple of days flying, kiss that goodbye, it will take well over a year to earn that much, bugger.

'Kate, our lives are about to change.'

'Really Rex, mine's changed already. While you were in Australia I've been swamped, all sorts of offers. Vogue have been in touch, they want me in Paris again soon.'

'Well I'm giving up the mercenary business, I've got an *in* on TEAL, how about that.'

'That's the best news of all Rex, I've been wanting to hear that for some time, but tell me, what happened in Australia?'

I give Kate a rundown on events in Griffith, how I decided it was not for me, what I did discover was how enjoyable normal family life with kids could be, a far cry from our present lifestyle, something I think we would both enjoy.

'A different Rex, life does change.'

'About your going to Paris. I'm not going to be my own master if the TEAL thing happens. Getting time off whenever I want will be a thing of the past. That aspect of our lives will change and not necessarily for the better. I will no longer be flush with funds either.'

'Rex, we'll have peace of mind, well I certainly will, the money, well there's been a huge change of circumstances there, it will be me splashing out.'

'Dinner Kate, our favourite, just the two of us, a celebration, our new lives.'

I front the TEAL office, an interview with the Ops Manager.

'Hello you're Rex Macare. Nobby Clarke has been in touch, all you have to do is sign here; that was easy wasn't it.'
I'm dumbfounded, easy or just lucky? whatever, it's what I want, have always wanted in the back of my mind, and now it's a reality.'

'We won't actually want you until two months from now, then you will be employed as a co-pilot on DC8s. I see you have air force experience on multi jet aircraft, that's just what we want, not many people around here with that sort of experience. We are about to take delivery of three DC8 aircraft. You will do a ground school course here in Auckland, then a simulator course with United in Denver, Colorado, in the meantime you are a free agent as far as we are concerned.'

I'm gobsmacked, big jets, conversion in America. A far cry from skulking around in the dead of night in a Chipmunk getting shot at. It appears I've got a definite airline job so it would be polite to let Cathay know that I'm no longer available. I've got two months before TEAL want me, time to make a bit more money, some serious money, perhaps Vietnam? shall I give Pierre Brodeur a call?

'Rex guess what, Vogue are coming to Auckland. They are sending a crew here specifically to take pictures of me *at home,* they want to have a look at the local scene as well. The agency I'm with has been given the contract to come up with some New Zealand models, that will get the knives out.'

'That's great Kate. I'm thinking a bit more flying for cash, some safer flying, Vietnam perhaps. I've got a couple of months before I'm required here.'

Kate's face clouds over, 'must you Rex, you don't really have to.'

'Well yes but I'd like to, have a final fling at some real flying, make a bit more money before it all changes, before the big income dries up, only two months.'

'You've made up your mind, a final fling, you're going to do it anyway, I can tell.'

'Let's not make a big thing out of this, I'm not going to hang around doing nothing for a couple of months and besides you are going to be busy by the sound of things. Let me do this Kate, this once, then it's all over and well under the year we were going to allow ourselves.'

I give Pierre Brodeur a call, tell him I'm on for another job, preferably Vietnam, got to be low risk. I make no mention about giving it all away, no need for him to know, he will get back to me.

Vogue arrive, quick off the mark. A big team, they really do want to check out the New Zealand scene. Kate is in demand, several photo shoots around Auckland then she's off around New Zealand, all the tourist spots. Vogue are going to run a feature on New Zealand and Kate's going to front it. Other New Zealand models will feature as well, the knives are out. Tara, Ali, and Erika's names have been put forward by the agency but Vogue want to see a wider selection of girls, they have their own ideas about what they want, a Parisian viewpoint. Chaperoning? not been mentioned, I think Vogue do their own *looking after* so my services are not required.

Kate's off down country with the Vogue team, going to be away for a week She's hardly out the door when Pierre Brodeur calls.

'Rex I've got something, Vietnam, can I come around?'

Back To Vietnam

'Morning Rex, I've got something I think you will be interested in, Vietnam, low risk, as requested. This time we want you to take people up country from Saigon. The roads are becoming increasingly dangerous for Europeans, kidnapping for ransom is now widespread. The aeroplane is the only safe way to get around. Most of the business is French nationals involved in the rubber business, they need to be able to get to and from the plantations, interested?'

'Yes.'

'Ok here's the deal. The aeroplane will be a Piper Cherokee Six based at Tan Son Nhat in Saigon. You will be required to fly to several plantations up country in Binh Duong and Binh Long provinces, one of them will be Dau Tieng in Binh Duong province, you are familiar with that one. The other two will be Loc Ninh and Xa Cat in Binh Long province right up on the Cambodian border. You will be accommodated at the Rex Hotel in Saigon. A four week contract and payment will be as before, 2000 Swiss francs into you numbered account for each return flight completed. Four weeks should get you well over 90,000 Swiss francs, well over 130,000 NZ dollars. We will give you return tickets to Saigon and accommodation at the Rex, how's that sound?'

'Sounds ok, I'll take it, when do you want me there?'

'As soon as possible, let me know when you can go and I'll do the bookings.'

'I can go right now, by the way, make that first class.'

'Ok, how about tomorrow provided I can get some bookings, get back to you later today, that alright with you?'

'Yep, fine with me.'

This will work out great, Kate's away for at least a week and when she gets back to Auckland she's going to be busy with the Vogue people. It's not long before Pierre calls back, he's secured bookings all the way to Saigon and the Rex Hotel, leave Auckland tomorrow morning. I track down Kate in Queenstown and bring her up to date; she is not overly impressed.

'You're going to do this Rex anyway, right? Please be careful I want you back in one piece, I love you. By the way Tara is here with me, the Vogue people have taken a shine to her, they think she is suitable for the magazine. The suggestion is they might need her in Paris at some time in the future, interesting.'

'Perhaps we can all go to Paris Kate, now there's a thought.'

'Hmm, Tara in Paris, Alain and Eloise, not sure about that.'

'Is Tara behaving herself Kate, no shenanigans, not leading you astray?'

'Stop worrying Rex, no Tara is not leading me astray, I don't want to be led astray anyhow, remember I'm in love with you. Actually Tara is being remarkably well behaved. I think she realises there could be an opportunity here, does not want to screw it up, just wants to impress the Vogue people.'

'Yes well I'm sure she's capable of impressing them all right and in the proper way, the Vogue people are no slugs, Tara probably realises that.'

'Mr Macare.' I'm in first class, Pierre Brodeur has gone along with my request. It's the hostess, Monica, she had looked after me on a flight home some time ago.

'A glass of Châteauneuf perhaps?'

'Thank you Monica you've got a good memory, it is Monica right? I heard you were back in first class so I changed my booking. I do like Châteauneuf and it makes it easier for you if I'm not down the back.'

'You're a charmer sir, off to Saigon?'

'Yep, be there for a few weeks, the Rex.'

'The Rex Hotel, really, that's where we stay, perhaps I might see you there, I would *like* to see you there.'

'Sounds like a come on Monica, I think I might like to see you there as well.'

'Then it's a date, cocktail bar this evening, eight o'clock.' Monica says this with a very provocative tone to her voice.

Careful Rex, what are you thinking, away from home for five minutes and lust is taking control but this Monica is attractive and sexy. She's pretty well spelt it out that's she's available, available for what?

Check in and there's a message. A Monsieur Henri Purdu will phone, he will be my contact for the operation out of Saigon. The hotel give me a big spacious room, veranda looking out over an internal courtyard, high ceiling, big fan, a nineteenth century feel about the place and it's nice. I get a rum and coke from the complimentary bar fridge and sit out on the veranda.

Ring, ring, 'Monsieur Macare, Henri Purdu, can I come around and see you, now perhaps.'

'Yes that's ok with me, come up to my room, 201.'
Half an hour later a knock on the door.

'Monsieur Macare, I'm Henri Purdu, I will be your contact here in Saigon, anything you need to know, I'm your man.'
Henri is a sharp looking French fellow in his forties.

'Henri, call me Rex, a drink perhaps while you give me the run down on what you require from me.'

'Make it another rum and coke. Now here is what we want you to do, starting tomorrow.'

Henri spends some time briefing me about flying a shuttle service between Tan Son Nhat airport and several French rubber plantations upcountry. The actual destination for a particular flight will not be known until shortly before the people travelling arrive at the aircraft.

I will be busy, there's a lot of traffic. He gives me a chart showing all the plantations involved and I notice one of them is Dau Tieng, Michelle! There will be a shuttle car to transport me between the hotel and Tan Son Nhat as required. He gives me his phone number should I need to contact him.

'That's about it Rex, any questions?'

'No, I think that covers about everything I need to know.'

'Oh yes, you might be interested, your buddy Russ Horsley has just arrived at Quy Nhon, he's going to be doing the same job you were doing up there a while ago.'

Thinks, geez Russ, watch out for Michelle and perhaps it might be a good idea if Michelle does not find out I'm here in Saigon.

'Want to come down to the bar for a bit Henri I'm a stranger in town at the moment.'

'No, not now Rex, got a bit of business to tidy up. You'll find the bar interesting, it's well known, popular with the girls.'

Well known all right, there must have been twenty or more attractive girls there, European and Asian, what goes on?

'Rex, there you are,' it's Monica and she's looking like a million dollars. It was about then that I twigged, these were not just girls out for a drink, these were working girls, probably all available for money.

'Monica, hello, you're looking very seductive to-night.'

'Feeling very seductive too, you might like to try me Rex.'

Shit she's propositioning me, she's a hooker.

'Excuse me, did I hear that right?'

'Yes Rex you did, you can have me for the night, I would like you to have me for the night, you're an attractive man.'

'Come on Monica you've just popped my bubble, I thought you were just a lovely airline hostie, a first class airline hostie.'

'I am, I'm a very good airline hostie and I provide a service for a lot of first class airline customers. Now get a couple of drinks and

I'll tell you about it, might even convince you to spend the night with me.'

I could feel a stirring in my loins, Monica was certainly attractive, very sexy, but a hooker, bugger. People paying her for sex, bit of a put off!

'What can I get you Monica, drink I mean?'

'Gin and tonic Rex and perhaps a night in the sack, for you, no charge!'

I sort the drinks, rum and coke for me. How am I going to handle this, she's set her sights on me, I'm not sure I'm on for it, I mean a hooker, why would I go for that? Because she's a sexy girl that's why and you can't help yourself, yes but a hooker, it's just not me. Paying for sex, but she's already told you no charge, does not change anything, a hooker's a hooker.

'Here we are Monica your drink, you're certainly not backward in letting me know the score.'

'Well it's a lucrative sideline, very lucrative sometimes. I was always having the hard word put on me, first class passengers are shockers for that, so I got to thinking. Most of the men who propositioned me were well heeled and not unattractive, me? well I do have a strong sex drive so why not enjoy what was being offered, make a little money as well. It developed from there. Quite a few men are happy to pay me, and pay handsomely for casual sex. I enjoy it as well which is a big bonus. So there you have it Rex, the airline hooker. I only do this when I'm away from home and all my customers are from the first class cabin. A couple of other girls are onto it as well. I suspect the airline is aware of our activities, however, nothing has ever been said to me. Perhaps it's good for business, the accountant's bottom line.'

'Well what can I say Monica you've opened my eyes, I would not have guessed. Airline hostesses will never be the same, does she or does she not?'

'Here, let me introduce my friend Patty, she's another hostess and yes she's available, but not for you, I've bagged you already, no poaching.'

Patty is very attractive, a classic blue eyed blond.

'Hello Patty, by yourself?'

'Not really I'm meeting a fellow here shortly, an old friend, he's in town for a couple of days, bit of catching up to do.'

Monica chimes in, 'that's a pity, Rex here is being coy, not sure he wants to get me into the sack tonight. I was thinking perhaps you could help, a threesome, we could give Rex here something to think about.'

Christ what am I hearing? two good looking hookers working me over, what tricks would they get up to, would sex ever be the same? There's an out, Patty's got a date, I hope her man turns up, and soon!

'Tell me, what's with this place? there seem to be a lot of pretty girls here, not all doing the same thing surely?'

'Yes they are Rex, it's a popular meeting place for us, however, you can't just walk in and take your pick, everything is prearranged. It's where you meet your date for the night. Casual meetings do occur but it's not the norm; now tell me what brings you to Saigon?'

Careful Rex Monica's not the sort of person you want to know about what you get up to. She does know it's not your first visit to Vietnam. A cover story, and no lies, lies will catch you out so there needs to be an element of truth in what you say. There's no real danger, what you're doing is not covert. There are no bad guys trying to kill you, well there are bad guys with guns but they're not specifically after you so you don't have to deviate too far from the truth, just be vague.

'I'm a pilot, I do some flying for the French.'

'But you're not French, why do they employ you?'

'The rubber business Monica, it's huge here, you probably know that, French owned. They employ people from all over the place including contract pilots from New Zealand, it's quite rewarding.'

'That's different, the only pilots I meet are airline types. They are a mixed bag. Some of them seem to think they have rights to me, others are real gentlemen, never met a contract pilot.'

'Well here's one, a fully formed freshly minted contract pilot chatting up an airline hostess.'

'You're a wag Rex, I want to bed you, how about it?'

'Not to-night Monica, I've got a full day tomorrow, not that I don't find you attractive, it's me. I've got a hang up about you being a part time hooker, not my scene, sorry.'

'That's a shame Rex, we could enjoy wonderous sex, however, I respect you being a gentleman. Perhaps we can have another drink to-morrow evening, I will be here, same time.'

'Perhaps.'

Another Piper Cherokee Six, the French must like them. Bit 'used' this one. It's standing on the commercial tarmac at Tan Son Nhat. There's a lot of noise, jet fighters roaring around, Tan Son Nhat is a major base for the American war effort. A French fellow introduces himself, Gaston, he's my groundcrew man, Mr 'fixit' for the Piper here in Saigon, he also doubles as the organiser at the airfield.

'Gaston, call me Rex, I'm here for four weeks.'

'Only four weeks, most of the pilots stay a couple of months at least, why the four weeks?'

'No idea Gaston, probably because I'm from New Zealand or perhaps your masters are not sure about me, actually it suits me, don't want to be away from my loved one for too long.'

'Rex, you have a loved one back home? that's nice. Tung, remember him from Quy Nhon? he tells me you have another loved one, Michelle.'

Geez, no secrets in Vietnam. If Gaston knows about Michelle then it's probably common knowledge. Michelle's bound to find out

I'm in Saigon, bugger!

'Misinformation Gaston, Michelle is not my loved one, just a friend.'

'I'm sure she is. Rumour has it she's been miserable since you left Quy Nhon however rumour also has it that another fellow from New Zealand has caught her eye, how about that.'

How about that indeed, she's obviously found Russ, wonder how he will handle her, could be a good thing for me, keep her away from Saigon, fingers crossed!

'Now then there are four passengers for, guess where, Dau Tieng. It will be a straight drop off then return with another four, that ok? Don't want to stop over at Dau Tieng?'

'No, don't want to stop over at Dau Tieng just yet, perhaps never.'

'That's not very nice Rex if Michelle hears that she'll scratch your eyes out.'

'Life can be difficult sometimes Gaston.'

We get airborne amongst all the heavy stuff, big military transports, jet fighters, civilian airliners, four Frenchmen and me in a little Piper, we head north at 3000 feet. Dau Tieng, happy memories. It was a lovely interlude staying in the big house with Raoul, those dinners out on the veranda, the wine, the fabulous life style, and Michelle, she was quite something. If it was not for Kate I could imagine myself taking up their offer, moving to Dau Tieng, being their personal pilot, not a silly option. I wonder how Russ is finding it, perhaps I might get to meet up with him while I'm in Vietnam.

There it is, the Dau Tieng airstrip. I land straight ahead and park the Piper by the little restaurant at the edge of the airstrip, Benny is there to meet us.

'Rex, I heard you were back in the country, staying a bit longer this time?'

'Saigon, four weeks Benny.'

'That's not long, what is it with you people from New Zealand. We've got your mate Russ Horsley here at the moment and he's not staying very long either, oh well that's the way it is I guess but I can't understand why. Now then we've got four passengers for you who want to be in Saigon, they're having a meal in the restaurant, will be out in a moment.'

Four Vietnamese men appear, they climb aboard. I'm just pulling the aircraft door shut when there's a commotion outside.

'Rex you devil, open the hatch I'm coming with you.'
Michelle piles into the seat beside me, shit, she's all over me, kissing and caressing.

'Cut it out Michelle, you're upsetting the passengers, get a handle on yourself.'
I'm deliberately harsh in my manner. I don't need this, first day on the job, what the hell do the passengers think, they're all Vietnamese and this sort of behaviour will make them nervous.

'Darling I don't care, what's with you coming back to Vietnam and not telling me, avoiding me, I'm coming to Saigon with you and you can't stop me.'
Oh shit!

We take off and head south, Michelle has calmed down, how is this going to develop. Will Michelle be wanting to stay at the Rex with me? probably, can I say no? I can't, is this going to impact on my daily flying? probably, shit. I don't need this, what are the options? precious few, none.

We are half an hour south of Dau Tieng at 3000 feet over thick jungle when it happens, the engine starts misfiring, misfiring badly. I have radio contact with Saigon. I let them know about my problem. They inquire about what I intend to do. A quick perusal of the chart is not reassuring, no landing strips anywhere, just jungle. The engine is not delivering enough power to maintain level flight and the aircraft is losing height. The Vietnamese passengers start to panic, not really understanding. I can't speak any Vietnamese. Michelle, bless her, does not panic, in fact she remains very calm. She is fluent in Vietnamese and reassures the passengers that the pilot has things under control.

'Michelle you're a darling, we're in the poo and it looks like we're going to end up in the jungle.'

'Rex, you can handle it, you've got to handle it.'
The little Piper continues to lose height. I'm frantically looking for some sort of clearance in the jungle below, somewhere I can attempt to put it down while there's still some engine power available, and there is a clearance, small, but a clearance.

'There you go Rex, just what you are looking for, of course you can handle it.'

'Thank you Michelle I admire your confidence in me.'

'I admire everything about you Rex especially your bedroom capabilities.'
Christ does this girl ever get her mind off sex. I advise Saigon radio that we are going to attempt a landing in a jungle clearance and give them our position as far as I can determine it. The clearing is small and surrounded by big high trees but it should be just big enough. A very steep approach will be required. The engine is still delivering power but it's misfiring badly.

'Michelle perhaps you can make sure our passenger are strapped in and tell them what I'm about to do.'

'Anything you say my darling.'

In the face of hell this girl never gives up, she's something else.

It's doable but it won't be easy, I'll need every bit of skill I can muster. A circling approach and I line the Piper up to take advantage of the longest clear run available. The ground's not level, there are tree stumps and small bushes, no turning back now, brace yourself Michelle. The wheels touch, I try the brakes, all appears to be going ok then *bang,* a big *bang.* The aircraft lurches to the left, the wing drops, the prop hits the ground and disintegrates. We've hit a tree stump and it's torn off the left undercarriage, the little Piper swings around to the left and stops, silence!

'Everyone ok?' Michelle translates, 'yep everyone ok.'
I'm shaking, probably a bit of shock. We clamber out and sit down on the long grass, the Piper's a mess, there's a lot of damage. One undercarriage leg torn off, propellor broken, the left wing is broken as well. I guess its flying days are over, what happens now? Not sure where we are but we're in dense jungle and probably a long way from anywhere, what to do? Saigon know we have attempted a landing in the jungle so it's a fair assumption they will come looking in which case we stay here with the aircraft for a while, how long? Well we'll review that from time to time but at first guess I'd say at least a day. I relay my thoughts to Michelle and ask her to convey it to our passengers. They are very quiet, probably in shock like me. Michele? well she appears to be completely in control of herself, she's a strong personality. We don't have any food or water, just have to tough it out, I'm sure we can handle that. The four Vietnamese men look worried. Michelle is able to determine they're concerned we are in Viet Cong territory and the Viet Cong will come looking, what can we do about that? hope for the best, I can't think of anything else. Perhaps we can occupy ourselves setting up some sort of camp, organise some sleeping arrangements. We could be here for a while before we think about moving, but where to? I have a map but it's not that detailed, intended for aviation, not a great help to us in our present circumstances. If we move then the nearest civilisation appears to be east of here but moving through the jungle could be really difficult. We're in the poo. We could get lucky and be rescued quite quickly or we could be confronted with having to make our own way out, that could be really challenging.

'Ok, here's what I think we should do. If anyone has some ideas then please let's hear them. We'll set up somewhere to sleep using what shelter the aircraft can provide. It's now late afternoon, I don't think Saigon will come looking until the morning.'

We get to work and set up some sleeping spaces under the wing and another inside the aircraft. There are some small rugs in the Piper, these will make do as blankets. It's quite warm so there should not be a problem keeping warm during the night. Michelle is giving me the eye.

'Where are we going to cuddle up Rex, inside the aircraft or are we going to roll around in the grass?'
She never stops, I hope this does not become embarrassing.

One of the Vietnamese men speaks some English, quite good English. He tells us he's pretty sure we're in Viet Cong territory and he thinks they will come looking. This is not necessarily a bad thing, two Europeans can be worth quite a bit, ransom, and if they identify Michelle then the ransom demand could be substantial. Us? well we are involved in running the plantation. If the Viet Cong have any sense they will not want to harm us, just ransom. The problem is some of these Viet Cong factions have got no brains. His suggestion is we stay where we are for tomorrow, then perhaps consider moving east the day after. His suggestion aligns with my thinking, this is a good thing, we are all on the same page. It's now quite late in the day so we settle down for the night. Michelle drags me into the aircraft cabin and cuddles up.

'No sex tonight dear, don't want to upset our fellow survivors.'

Sun is streaming into the aircraft cabin, it's been an uncomfortable night. *Shit,* what's this, we are surrounded by armed Vietnamese, real bad looking dudes, the Viet Cong have found us. Our English speaking fellow is talking to them, it appears to be amicable. Michelle is awake and trying hard to hear what's being said. It appears the armed men are indeed Viet Cong the question in my mind, are they reasonable ones? The fellow who appears to be their leader addresses us in broken English. He orders us to line up alongside the remains of our aircraft facing his heavily armed and menacing men. I'm trying hard not to get the shakes, it's a potentially explosive situation. This job is supposed to be low risk remember. Michelle squeezes my hand.

'Try to relax Rex, it's not all bad. I think they realize they've got some captives who can be held for ransom, there could be money it for them.'

The fellow who appears to be their leader addresses us again. The gist of what he says is that we are now his captives, running dogs of the corrupt imperialist South Vietnamese Government and we do not deserve to live, however, in our case, he will spare us provided our masters pay to get us back. Right now we are to busy ourselves dragging the remains of our aircraft across to the edge of the clearing and in under the tree line. If aircraft come looking then the Piper must not be visible. This is not good, even if Saigon are able to locate the area there will be nothing to see. Any chance of rescue has suddenly disappeared. Our four passengers apply themselves to the task goaded on by the armed Viet Cong, there is an air of hostility. Our passengers are visibly scared, so am I. Michelle is a revelation, she realises we are in a dangerous situation and decides to do something about it. She speaks the language fluently and engages the Viet Cong leader in conversation. I can see she's trying hard to win him over, good girl. The conversation goes on for quite a while and I sense the tension dissipating.

'Rex, this is what I've been able to glean from the boss man. They want money, ransom, failure to get it could put our lives in jeopardy. I've told him who we are and where we come from. He understands the significance of our connection to the rubber business. He also knows that Michelin always pay to get their people back. In the meantime, while he makes his demands known, we are his prisoners, what that involves I don't know.'

'You're an angle Michelle, just one thing, I'm not a Michelin employee.'

'Bugger, we'll have to leave you behind in the fond care of the murderous Viet Cong Rex, pity, I do care for you. Oh well perhaps if you had told me you were coming back to Vietnam I would feel more favourably disposed towards you, bad call!'

'Thanks Michelle, a woman scorned is a fearsome thing indeed.'

'Rex, I'm pulling your leg, I would not let you go for anything, I want to keep you forever. Looks like we are going to be together for a while anyway. I can't see this thing being settled any time soon. Michelin will negotiate a group deal for the six of us, they've done this in the past, it's nothing new.'

While we're talking an aeroplane flies over, the search aeroplane from Saigon. The Viet Cong boss man heard it coming and ordered us all under the trees. The remains of the Piper were already out of sight, bugger, there goes our one and only hope.

'Well Michele, looks like the die is cast, we are the guests of the Viet Cong for a while, not too long a while I hope.'

'Depends how good their contacts are, they don't want us hindering them, they just want money. I've given them the details of who we are and where we're from. Raoul is at the plantation, he will be right onto it. His little sister in danger will fire him right up, the only problem, where are we?'

'We move now.' It's the Viet Cong boss man, he wants to move us away from the clearing, where to, I don't know. Off we go into the jungle. We move along a trail. I guess these fellows know their way around which will be better than us trying to find our way out to the east not knowing about trails. An hour later we come to a village where the Viet Cong fellows are obviously welcome, I think it's their home village. Food, that would be welcome, it's been a while since we ate. Some cold spicy chicken and rice, it's not bad, and some fruit juice, I guess we are going to be looked after. It would be prudent to be grateful for anything that comes our way, not upset our captors. I've heard the stories about how brutal these people can be. It's now midday on day two of our *adventure* if we can call it that, certainly different. Thinks; I'm not making much money here, not meant to be like this, day one on the job and I've not made a dollar. Don't think I'll be making anything for a while, could be quite a while, could go back to New Zealand empty handed, assuming I do get to go back to New Zealand. Oh shit! Kate will not like this, not like it at all, my life on the line again. The boss man approaches and converses with Michelle in Vietnamese, it's easier for him. He's made contact with Dau Tieng. He's got a radio and he's actually spoken to Raoul. The deal is that Raoul needs a few hours to get organised, the required ransom has been demanded. Raoul will get back to him.

'This is the dodgy bit Rex, these initial demands are always outrageous and when these people realize it's not going to work, that negotiation will be required, then they can get a bit testy and threatening. This one could be difficult because of me, part of the Michelin dynasty, they probably know that by now, it gives them a powerful hand to play.'

Around the middle of the afternoon the boss man comes back, he is not happy. His initial demand has been declined and a lesser amount, considerably less, offered. It's not good enough and he tells us that no way is he letting all six of us go for that amount of money, five perhaps, but he will keep Michelle. He wants Michelle to talk directly to Raoul on the radio, she agrees and the upshot is that Michelin will only agree to pay the lesser amount, no further negotiation. I'm shocked, real hard ball is being played here. Michelle conveys this to the boss man. He flies into a rage, this could get dangerous, will get dangerous. He orders his soldiers to get one of our Vietnamese passengers. The fellow is dragged into the hooch where we are talking and hurled onto the floor. The atmosphere is threatening, our man is terrified. We are told that if the ransom offer is not increased they will shoot our passenger. Michelle intervenes and points out that if our man is murdered all deals are off and if she, one of the Michelin dynasty, is harmed, then the forces of the South will obliterate this village and everything related to it. They know where we are, the radio transmissions will have enabled the Government forces to pinpoint this spot. The words are hardly out of Michelle's mouth when there's an ear shattering roar as a jet fighter thunders right over the village. This has a dramatic affect, the boss man is visibly shaken. He realises he's pushing it too hard. I too am impressed. It appears the initial radio contact with Dau Tieng had been picked up by one of the numerous listening posts around the country and its source pinpointed. The information would have been passed to Raoul. He would have requested the Government to assist with some intimidation, it's worked. Michelle asks to talk some more with Raoul, it's quickly arranged. The deal now is Michelin will raise the ransom offer a little, if the boss man does not accept then his village will be attacked, not just attacked, obliterated. I was having trouble comprehending the brinkmanship being played out here, would the village really be destroyed with us still here? Whatever the thoughts and motives, they work, the boss man tells Michelle to advise Raoul the deal is on. I feel a huge surge of relief. Could we all have been annihilated in a flaming mess of napalm, Michelle included, what level of brinkmanship is involved here, bit beyond me.

The atmosphere in the hooch is strained, the boss man is no longer friendly, he has suffered a big loss of face, we will need to be careful, the situation could become dangerous.

'Michelle you are a revelation, your insight into the Vietnamese psyche is incredible, the risk taking!'

'Rex, I was shit scarred the whole time, believe me, but I've been here before, I know a little about how to deal with the Vietnamese, they are not good gamblers, Raoul knows it too.'

'What happens now?'

'We'll be hearing from Raoul, he'll probably send a helicopter.' It's now late in the afternoon, looks like we will be spending the night in the village. Details of the deal will need to be agreed on and that could take a while. We are shown to a couple of hooches, one for the four Vietnamese and one for Michelle and myself, dirt floor, no bed, just a heap of dubious looking blankets.

'This will be a little different, not quite the big bed at Dau Tieng.' I'm thinking, what will Michelle get up to, whatever it is the setting is not the greatest. Our hosts, if that's the right word, provide us with a meal, cold chicken again, more fruit juice. We have a word with our Vietnamese passengers, they are terrified, fearful for their lives. We tell them what has been negotiated but it does little to ease their fear. The Viet Cong can be very brutal to their countrymen who side with the Government the only saving grace for them, it's not the Government they are aligned with it's the French dominated rubber business and that's neutral territory.

Bedtime; 'come my love, into the sack, not the greatest but when will we ever have the opportunity again to fuck each other on the dirt floor of a hooch in a Viet Cong village.'

She's right, it's a whole new experience. Michelle goes at it with a certain desperation and in no time we are both writhing about on the scruffy blankets on the dirt floor, it's wonderful.

Morning, it's not been a comfortable night, Michelle is sound asleep, I think the tension of the previous day has exhausted her. There was the furious love making as well, she's a remarkable woman. What will today bring forth? The boss man pokes his head through the door of the hooch.

'We talk now.'

The ransom deal has been sorted, a helicopter will be here at midday with the cash and the six of us will leave on it. I'm wondering, how much ransom has been agreed? I've no idea what sums of money are involved in this sort of thing but the involvement of Michelle will have raised the price considerably, as Raoul said, it's just another cost of doing business in this country. We are given some fruit for breakfast but are not allowed to leave the hooch, I guess our captors don't want us to see what's in the village, tunnels, hiding places, is it a Viet Cong aligned village? If it is then it's a target. Taking us hostage then making radio contact has revealed the allegiance and location of this village. That will put it on the Government's hit list. I just hope we are out of here before there's any attack. I'm wondering if the boss man has thought about this, has his desire for ransom endangered his village, will he perhaps think about keeping some hostages for the village's protection? *Raoul get us out of here!*

Right on midday there's the thump thump of a helicopter, it puts down in a clearing in the village. They are all Vietnamese on board, no Raoul and when I think about it of course he's not there, he could be nabbed for more ransom. Just one person gets off. I notice there are several armed Vietnamese on the helicopter, they have a military bearing about them. Of course, this will be a highly trained commando unit ready for anything the Viet Cong might try on, there's probably air support as well in case things turn sour. I can feel myself getting the shakes again, this could be dangerous. Vietnam, low risk, remember!

The fellow who gets off the helicopter appears to be a South Vietnamese Officer, he confronts the boss man and there is some discussion. I notice a satchel being handed over, presumably the ransom, I wonder how much cash is in that satchel?

'Come,' the officer is calling to us, 'make it quick.'
We don't need prompting, all six of us are out of our hooches' and scrambling aboard the helicopter, it takes off immediately. I wonder

if the boss man has had time to count the money, was there money in the satchel? I've no idea how this game is played but it seems there's a fair bit of bluff and brinkmanship involved. I can feel myself unwinding, a tremendous relief, the tension of the past forty-eight hours has been enormous. Vietnam, low risk, yeah right! Michelle does not look too good, suddenly she's vomiting, poor girl, the brave front she's been displaying has taken a toll, a severe toll, she's a remarkable woman.

We head north, the officer tells us we are going to the plantation at Dau Tieng. I try to get some answers from him about what has happened but no joy, he's not saying anything. Raoul greets us when we put down alongside the big house.

'Welcome back Rex, the lengths that sister of mine will go to to get what she wants, better watch out.' He says this with a twinkle in his eye.

'Good to be here Raoul, seems my visits to Vietnam, my low risk jobs, are anything but. This one is supposed to be Saigon based and here I am at your place again, much nicer than Saigon though Raoul.'

'Rex, there will be a fellow here later in the day to debrief you, he will want to know everything you can tell him about the people who captured you, and the village, I don't think the authorities are aware that the village is Viet Cong. It may not be, could be the Viet Cong have just imposed themselves, a bit of terror, murder the village headman, they are very good at terrifying the general populace, hopefully that's the case. If the village is Viet Cong there could be consequences,. Let's drop this conversation, how about something to eat, guess your diet's been a bit spartan the last couple of days. By the way you are welcome to stay with us for as long as it takes to get sorted, Michelle will like that Rex.'

We adjourn to the big veranda, Raoul's staff rustle up a magnificent meal.

It's late in the afternoon when the Government man turns up, a smart intelligent fellow. He wants us to detail everything from the moment we went down in the clearing. Apparently these ransom matters are handled by Government in close cooperation with the plantation involved. The South Vietnamese Government has a big stake in rubber and does not want the industry to fail. In this case, being a Michelin plantation and having a Michelin family member involved, then the matter assumed considerable priority hence the rapid response. The one thing that is not clear is whether or not the village involved is Viet Cong or whether the Viet Cong have just imposed themselves. Raoul gets the four Vietnamese fellows who were with us, employees of his, to join us and the Government man really picks their brains, they will be aware of things that we may not have noticed. At the end of it all the Government man has a brandy with us, thanks us, and is off. I notice he is travelling in a jeep, must be locally based.

'Well Raoul what's your take on this?'

'Opportunists, they saw you come down, saw a chance to make some money. I don't think they were hard core Viet Cong, if they were then I think the outcome could have been a bit different, a bit unpleasant even. We try hard not to get offside with the various combatants, and there are quite a few. So far it's paid off for us, no real trouble. In this case because it involved a Michelin plantation and one of the Michelin family there was a rapid response from Government, they took over the operation, probably liaised with the French Government, Michelin has considerable clout in France. I think your captors must have realised they had nabbed someone important. The jet overflying the village so soon would have frightened them. Had they been hard core then things could have been different, unpleasant, hard core Viet Cong are a murderous lot.'

I'm thinking, French Government involvement, DGSE, that Macare fellow again, what's he up to now. They must have quite a file on me by now.

'Tell me Raoul what will happen to the people who nabbed us, and the village?'

'Hard to say, the South Vietnamese intelligence people will analyse the information they have, this incident and anything else they might have, and act as they see appropriate. Anything from a search of the village to determine if it's Viet Cong, to an outright attack and complete annihilation, there's a whole range of possible responses.'

'Serious stuff and all because the little Piper had a crook engine.'

'Let's not think about things like that, you have managed to survive and now we need to know what to do with you Rex, no plane to fly, can't get back to Saigon. Just have to stay here with us for a while, is that ok with you?' it's Michelle and she has a big smile.

The following morning. It's been a great night in Michelle's bed and I'm feeling guilty. Kate, I should not be doing this, what happens now? It's midday when Russ comes calling.

'Rex, heard you were here, I've an hour or so, just came from Quy Nhon, waiting for some passengers. You devil, can't keep out of trouble can you.'

'Russ, good to see you, going well for you? me? it's just more bad luck, not exactly coining it here in Vietnam, right now no aeroplane to fly.'

'Come on Rex, a little birdie tells me you've got it made here at Dau Tieng, what's her name, are yes Michelle, could be you won't come back to Auckland.'

'Cut it out Russ and keep it to yourself. I'm not cheating on Kate, for christ sakes I'm in love with the girl, it's the situation here, it's weird and when you get to meet Michelle you'll see why.'

'Russ, you've arrived.' Michelle appears, 'now I've got both my hunks from Nouvelle-Zélande here.'

Russ gives me a knowing look and just shrugs.

Day two, mid afternoon at Dau Tieng, we are enjoying lunch on the balcony. Russ had to fly off to Quy Nhon with his passengers, after all he's a working mercenary making money, me, an unemployed mercenary living in lust and earning nothing. Michelle is asking me all sorts of questions about Russ, the tin arm for one. I have to be very circumspect in just what I divulge, particularly about his private life in Auckland, I don't want Michelle upsetting things. Not meant to be easy and right now I need to sort myself out. I need to be working not just having a glorious time in Michelle's bed. She has tried again to get me to be the plantation's full-time pilot, to come and live at Dau Tieng, again I've had to let her know it's no deal, I'm attached in Nouvelle-Zélande. It has not gone down too well. Phone call from Saigon, it's Henri Purdue.

'Rex we need you back here, we've acquired another aircraft, another Piper. I've arranged for your mate Russ Horsley to fly some people from Dau Tieng to Saigon tomorrow, you're one of them, is that ok with you?'

'Yes, good, I need to be back earning, that's what I'm here for, thanks Henri.'

Dinner time, another of Raoul's superb offerings, he really is a great host. I'll have to advise them I'm off tomorrow, how is Michelle going to take it? Not well, she's visibly upset.

'Rex just two days here, I thought at least a week, why Saigon, perhaps I can come along with you.'

'Not to be Michelle, I'm a working pilot, all day every day, well that's the idea, so far it's not been working out quite like that.'

'And then you will rush off to your loved one in Nouvelle-Zélande?'

I'm going to have to be a bit harsh here, can't have Michelle tying herself to me like this. It's been great but perhaps I've been a little remiss in allowing myself to become so involved. It seems Michelle has taken a real shine to me, something I did not see coming.

'Michelle I'm in love with my girl in Auckland, really in love. I will be giving away this mercenary flying soon, no more Vietnam. I'm sorry, you were not meant to take such a liking to me, perhaps it's my fault for allowing it to happen, a bit too keen to jump into your bed but Michelle you are a fantastic girl. If circumstances were different then perhaps, but they're not. I will be going back to New Zealand at the end of this contract and that will be it.'

She's devastated, I feel bad, Raoul discretely excuses himself. I suspect he may have seen this scenario played out before. Michelle is an incredible girl, there must have been others.

It's not a great night, a lot of crying, Michell's enthusiasm for sex has noticeably waned.

'Rex, I'm very unhappy, I've fallen for you, you're not like other men. I've fooled myself into thinking that you are the one but that's not going to happen is it? not a chance. You're going back to your loved one, I can't compete with that.'

'Afraid so Michelle and I will probably be staying in Auckland as well, career change, no more pilot for hire, no more Vietnam.'
I feel bad, I should not have let this affair develop in the first place, but it was not meant to be an affair just a short sharp sexual interlude. I mean what man could resist Michelle when she sets her sights on you. Well now it's come to a head and I have to break it off as best I can. I'm off to Saigon in the morning. The best thing I can do is complete my contract and get back to Auckland, distance myself from Michelle. Does not sound very nice but it makes sense. If I'm in Vietnam Michelle will seek me out and that will not be good for either of us.

Morning, Michell has cried herself out.

'Rex, once more and that's it, it's over, I can accept that, I think.'

We make love, it's more than that, Michelle virtually rapes me, she goes at it with a furious passion, then collapses, completely spent.

Breakfast on the veranda, just Michelle and myself, again a magnificent spread.

'Rex, have you seen this?' She has the latest Paris Vogue and there on the cover is Kate.

'It says here the cover girl comes from Nouvelle-Zélande, perhaps you know her?'

'Yes Michelle, I do know her, it's the girl I'm in love with, Kate.' Michelle looks stunned, not quite comprehending.

'But this is Paris Vogue and your Kate lives in Auckland, this is not possible.'

'It is possible Michelle, Vogue head hunted her in New Zealand and this cover is the result.'

'Why did you not tell me, not put me in the picture, your girlfriend is a Vogue model, that's incredible, hard to believe, she's beautiful Rex, how can I hope to compete.'

'This is not a competition Michelle, I've been in love with Kate for some time, this Vogue thing happened recently. I have not mentioned Kate to you, why would I, it's not something you would want to hear, me going on about my girlfriend.'

'Oh Rex, you are so lucky and yes I've fallen for you but it's not going to happen, you are going to fly off to Saigon today and out of my life. It's going to be hard but I will deal with it. Now that I've seen the girl you love I understand, you are a very lucky man. Now your mate Russ will be here around eleven, he is going to fly you to Saigon, and out of my life. I think it's best we say goodbye here at the house, I'm not sure I will be able to control my emotions, down at the airstrip will not be a good place.'

It's emotional all right, Michelle cracks up completely, there are tears, a lot of crying, then she breaks away from me and disappears. I do not see her again.

Right on eleven Russ appears in the Piper and we fly off to Saigon along with four other passengers, two French, two Vietnamese.

'Rex you old devil I hear you've been having a pretty good time at Dau Tieng, what's her name again, oh yes Michelle.'

'It's all over Russ, it was never on in the first place and I'd appreciate it if you made no mention of it to anyone, can I rely on you?'

'Course you can Rex, as they say, what happens in Vietnam stays in Vietnam, right!'

Mid afternoon, Tan Son Nhut airfield in Saigon, Henry Purdue is there to meet me.

'Rex, glad you are back, we need you right away. We've got hold of another Piper and there's a job that needs doing right away. We have some people who want to go to Phnom Penh, it's not far, about thirty minutes across the Cambodian border.'

'Hang on, my contract says flying in Vietnam, nothing about Cambodia.'

'Well that's not strictly correct, we can use you wherever our interests are and right now we need to get these people to Phnom Penh. It will be straight there and straight back, no stopping. The political scene is not good, becoming dangerous. There are several factions, Lon Nol's lot, Prince Sihanouk, the Chinese, and the Khmer Rouge sitting on the sidelines.'

'Ok, guess I'll go along with that, not happy though, when do you want me to go?'

'In thirty minutes, ok!'

They are all French, Michelin people I suspect. We get airborne amongst all the military traffic, very busy place Tan Son Nhut. It's map reading all the way, good visibility, not a problem. We land at Phnom Penh airport and the four Frenchmen disembark immediately. I notice there's an official looking car to meet them. I take off for Saigon, don't want to stick around. Back at Tan Son Nhut I'm directed to a parking space amongst some military aircraft and there lined up right beside me are four Canberras, a blast from the past. They are the American made version, B57s, these ones are reconnaissance aircraft. The Americans are using them for night-time infrared surveillance of the Ho Chi Minh trail that runs along the Cambodian side of the border with Vietnam. Apparently they carry some very sophisticated surveillance gear and the American's are getting good intelligence. The war is hotting up, ever increasing military activity. Vietnam is starting to look like a bad place for a mercenary pilot, too dangerous. Henri Purdue meets me when I land.

'How was it Rex?'

'Not a problem, but what's the Phnom Penh connection Henry?'

'Michelin have interests in Cambodia that are being threatened. Your passengers were a high-powered delegation from France who are going to try and salvage something. The military situation is deteriorating all over South East Asia, the future's not bright. Now then, tomorrow, I've got two jobs lined up, both straight transportation jobs to a couple of plantations up country, that ok?'

'Yes Henry, sounds like what I contracted for. By the way I'd appreciate it if you could keep me away from Dau Tieng if that's possible.'

'Really Rex, has Michelle put the breeze up you.' He says this with a twinkle in his eye. 'She's quite a woman.'

Back to the Rex Hotel.

'Welcome back Monsieur Macare your room is still there for you. We did get a message that you were going to held up for a few days,' then, in a conspiratorial voice she murmurs, 'we also heard you were the guest of the Viet Kong.'

'No secrets in a small town I see.'

'No Monsieur, we get to hear everything. Anyway welcome back and I'm glad you're still in one piece.'

'Thank you for your kind interest, now I think a cold beer in you bar would be in order.'

'Careful Monsieur Macare, that bar's a man trap.'

'I had noticed, I'll just live dangerously.'

Sure enough there are a lot of attractive girls in the bar, Monica is not one of them but her friend Patty is, she locks on immediately.

'Rex Macare, Monica's friend, remember me. I'm the girl who was going to help Monica show you a good time the other night but you were not up to it, how about tonight?'

'Thanks but no thanks Patty, I'm not in the market, should not be a problem for you though there appear to be plenty of likely prospects here, you go for it.'

She gives me a disgusted look and moves away. I order a cold beer and settle into a big padded armchair and observe the scene. It's quite an up market place. The girls are a cut above the average and very discreet. The men, all sorts, business types, military people, and me, the mercenary. I was pretty sure some of these other fellows were adventurers as well, all out for a quick buck, prepared to take risks. Was this really my scene? Sitting in an upmarket bar in Saigon, outside a war that was intensifying, surrounded by hookers, good looking discreet ones, but still hookers, no, this is not my scene. When I get back to Auckland that's it, the TEAL job becomes more inviting by the day but right now I'm here and I need to be making money. This could be, will be, my final fling at the big bucks. I down my beer and head upstairs, bed, out like a light, it's been a while since I had a descent night's sleep.

Morning, out to the airfield, a lot of activity, mainly military, and my little Piper. Gaston is there and advises me I've got four passengers for an airstrip way up north near Hue on the border with Laos, it will take about three hours. Then I am to fly to Quy Nhon where I will overnight. About four hours flying all up, enough for one day. I will spend the night at the Villa Hy.

'You know the place, you've stayed there before. Your mate Russ is based at Quy Nhon, he'll be there tonight as far as I know.'
That will be good, catch up with Russ again, but only the one flying job today, not making much money. Here for three weeks, half of that's gone already, only done two jobs and one of them was a disaster. This one is a long way north, did not know the rubber growing country extended that far. The country inland from Hue is mountainous, would not have thought there would be rubber plantations.

It is a long way north, three hours in the little aeroplane with four Vietnamese. They don't look like Michelin people, more military looking. Map reading all the way but it's not difficult. The weather is kind, bit of rain here and there and that's about all. I find the airstrip, right on the border with Laos. It's a good one, there's no sign of a rubber plantation, more like a military airfield. My passengers thank me, hop out, and I take off for Quy Nhon.

There's a bit of interest during the flight to Quy Nhon, a military operation going on in an area of jungle about half way through the flight. I climb up to eight thousand feet, don't want to get too close to the war. It appears to be an army operation, plenty of big guns in action, several fires on the ground, the occasional explosion. As I'm looking at this a couple of fast jets streak in and drop napalm cannisters. It's horrendous, the jungle is engulfed in fire, everything is torched, a huge fireball erupts skywards. Get out of here Rex, it's not your war. Flying for TEAL gets more inviting by the day.

'Russ, in here.' I'm in the house bar at the Villa Hy, I notice Russ pass by the entrance.

'Rex, small world or are we following each other around? Good to see you again but what are you doing here? I thought you were based in Saigon, well that's when you're not in Michelle's bed.'

'Easy now Russ, you assume too much. They want me here, don't know why. I'm on my way back from up country, way up country. I guess there are people here who want to get to Saigon, would not want to be horning in on your turf now would I.'

'Who cares, what about a beer or two.'
We go out and sit on the small balcony outside the house bar and get talking, reminiscing on our recent lives. I tell Russ about my intention to give it all up and take up a quieter life with Kate back in Auckland flying for TEAL.

'You've got a flying job with TEAL?' Russ looks surprised, 'you tin bum, how did you manage that.'

'Got lucky Russ, people do get lucky sometimes,' and I tell him how I landed the job.

'Definitely a tin bum, I would dearly love to follow you but this tin arm, can't see an airline going along with it, not a good look.'
I tell Russ about Michelle wanting me to move to Vietnam and be Michelin's permanent pilot.

'I think it was for real as well not just Michelle's desire to keep me in her bed, having their own pilot makes sense. That would be you Russ, perhaps you should sound Raoul out; you have met Raoul?'

'Yep, at the big house at Dau Tieng, remember, met Michelle as well, actually I had met Michelle once before, perhaps I will talk to Raoul.'

'Think about it Russ, I think there's an opportunity there, would probably mean living at Dau Tieng, then there's Michelle, not sure how that would go.'

'Thanks for that Rex, I'll give it some thought, but the war, not looking good at the moment, far cry from Auckland. Future's not looking the greatest here in Vietnam right now.'

Next morning up early, out to the airfield where Tung, the Vietnamese groundcrew man, meets me.'

'Five for Saigon this morning. Good to see you back here again Monsieur Rex, been a little while, you going to stick around?'

'Afraid not Tung, I'm Saigon based right now and that's not for much longer either.'

'Saigon eh, can get into trouble down there.'

I load the passengers, three French men and a couple of Vietnamese women, very attractive women, and off we go.

Tan Son Nhut and I'm parked alongside the B57s again.

'Rex,' Henri Purdue meets me on the tarmac, 'change of plan, you're wanted in Germany, urgent. Here hop in my car and I'll give you the details while we drive into the Rex.'

'Germany, not psyched for Germany Henri.'

'You are wanted at Gutersloh, you have been specifically asked for. The other lot you do a bit of flying for have been onto us, apparently you are experienced at what it is they want done.'

'And what's that Henri?'

'Don't know, don't need to know, whatever it is it's urgent.'

Germany, what could it be? It will involve crossing the DDR border, all the German jobs are border crossings. What is it this time? how dangerous? The money will be good, well it should be, better than here, and it could be my final fling as well, go out with a decent pay check, yes perhaps this could work in my favour, but what's all the urgency about.

'Rex I've taken the liberty of booking you all the way to Hanover leaving tonight, is that ok with you? Our masters did ask me to get you to Germany as fast as possible.'

'I guess that's ok Henri, big change of scene though, don't suppose you know what they're offering?'

'Afraid not but reading between the lines it should be good, they definitely want you, no one else.'

Wonder what it could be? why the urgency? my guess it's an extraction, they want someone out, now! Why me? I've done it before, not very successfully, I lost a couple of aeroplanes as well, I guess they know what they're doing. The money, it will be good, something to carry me over while I settle into my new career. Hang on I've already got a heap of money stashed away, numbered accounts, under the bed, there's no shortage of cash at the moment but a decent final cheque would be nice. Kate, what will she think about it, Germany again, sausage and sauerkraut, not sure she will like it, high risk, I promised to keep these final few weeks low risk. I will have to let her know, perhaps I can get her on a secure phone from Gutersloh, my last shot at the big bucks.

'Henri, a question. That job yesterday up on the border with Laos, that was not Michelin, my passengers were military people and that was a military base, that's not my understanding of what I'm meant to be doing here. It's supposed to be civilian flying, nothing to do with the military.'

'Ah, well yes, you are correct, however, there is a grey area between civilian tasks and military ones. I can't tell you much about yesterday, I don't know much about it myself.'

'Ok, I won't take you to task about it, not your decision, but perhaps it's an opportune time to remove myself from the scene, it's not quite what I've been led to believe.'

Indeed it's not, yesterday was an outright military job, nothing to do with the rubber business. If the Viet Cong got to know about it then things could be very different should they ever get their hands on me again. Definitely time to give it away. There is no low risk flying in this business.

We get to the Rex, 'Henri come in for a drink, could be the last time I'll see you.'

'Why do you say that Rex, don't you like us here in Vietnam.'

'No, no, nothing like that but I'm out of here this evening, you've booked it, I may not be back. I'm thinking seriously about a career change, this business is just too dangerous.'

'Ok, one quick one, there's not a great deal of time, your flight's at nine this evening.'

It All Goes Bad

Hanover Airport, bus to Gutersloh, feels like old times, far cry from Vietnam's heat and humidity. It's almost midnight when I front the main gate at Gutersloh, been on the go for over twenty-four hours and I'm buggered. The guard directs me to the Officers Mess, I'm expected, good room, straight into bed, glorious sleep.

Ring, ring, what the, where am I, drugged with sleep, oh yes, I'm in Germany, it's the telephone.

'Hello.'

'Welcome back Rex,' a female voice, sounds vaguely familiar, it's Nicole Townsend's voice.

'Nicole, hello, an unexpected surprise.'

'This is a bonus Rex, getting you back here so soon, perhaps we'll be able to get together again. In the meantime however, there is some urgent business to attend to. Can I come up to your room in half an hour or so.'

'You can come up to my room anytime Nicole, just give me a bit of time to get cleaned up, still a bit scruffy from that long flight.'

I leap out of bed, suddenly I don't feel so tired, the memory of Nicole in the sack has revitalised me, however, I rather doubt there will be time for anything like that right now.

Knock, knock, it's Nicole looking radiant, a peck on the cheek, perhaps an indication of things to come.

'Rex, here's the deal. We need to get someone out from across the border tonight, it's a high value customer and it's urgent. The pick up point is a little to the north of here. Celle would have been closer however we think our operations have been compromised up there so we are giving Celle a miss for the time being. We asked for you specifically because you have demonstrated that you have what it takes and besides I rather fancied the idea of seeing you again. The other thing is the money. We know you have not been doing so well out there in Vietnam so we are offering you NZ$180,000 for this job, how's that sound?

'It sounds great and perhaps dinner with you when it's over?'

'Perhaps.'

'180,000, that's a lot, that means danger, right?'

'I don't know Rex, these amounts are decided by our masters, I'm not party to the risk factor. There have not been any cross border operations for some time. We became aware we'd been compromised and operations have been suspended for a while, apparently this one's important.'

'180,000, that means high risk, believe me I know!'

'Rex I'm not party to the risk factor, only what I need to know, you know how this game is played.'

'Nicole, getting your arse shot off is not a game!'

'There is one thing, I need to talk to Kate in New Zealand, let her know where I am. She has me in Vietnam and will not be impressed to find out I'm in Germany. Can you organise a call, this morning perhaps, catch her in the evening in New Zealand. Not sure where she will be, probably down country, here's her agency's number, they will be able to get hold of her.'

'Oh, by the way Rex, I've seen your Kate, the Vogue cover girl. It's a spectacular cover, you're a lucky lad, now the detail. There's not much time, you need to fully familiarise yourself with what's required. Here are some charts, the pick up point is detailed. Be there at ten tonight. I will leave you to it while I go and try to organise a call to Kate, I'll be back.'

I spend the morning pouring over the charts, selecting the best way in and out, map reading at night again, low level, not done any recently, need to sharpen up my game. The pick up point is an open field about twenty kilometres over the border, there will be a light in the middle of the field but it will not be illuminated until they hear my engine. Hmm, must be worried about the bad guys, 180,000, there must be quite a degree of danger. I'm supposed to keep out of danger for this last bit of my mercenary career, that was the deal with Kate, the reason I picked Vietnam, but that turned out to be bloody dangerous. Let's face it all my mercenary flying has been dangerous, more dangerous than I realized.

Ring, ring, it's Nicole. 'I've got Kate's agency on the line, can't get Kate herself.'

'Hello, this is Rex Macare, Kate's fiancée, I really need to talk to Kate, is that possible?'

'We've been trying Mr Macare but she's somewhere in Queenstown with the Vogue people and we can't get her. We have left messages to contact us as soon as she can, no luck so far.'

'All right, then perhaps I can leave a message. Tell her I've been called over to Germany, Gutersloh, urgently, I expect to be back in Auckland in a few days time, can you do that for me please.'

'Sure can Mr Macare and just to let you know the Vogue people are very impressed with everything New Zealand, I think we might be seeing a bit more of them out here.'

Nicole comes back on the line.

'What about some lunch Rex, dining room, ten minutes.'

We are seated in the dining room when Scruff appears.

'Rex, *and* Nicole,' Scruff appears surprised.

'Hello Scruff, just popped over to see my favourite girlfriend, been a wee while.'

'Yeah right, what are you up to now?'

'Nothing Scruff, nothing at all, just trying to make a bob, life is tough in the civilian world.'

'I have noticed, that's why I want a slice of the action.'

'Bye the way Scruff I heard about your navigator, I'm sorry, in a way I feel responsible.'

'Don't be Rex, it's a war, undeclared, but still a war, people get killed in wars, please don't feel bad about it. You were lucky not to get shot yourself by those trigger happy bastards. Now tell me how long are you planning on being here, we need to have a few drinks and perhaps another dinner with the lovely Nicole here.'

'Great idea, bit tied up for the next day or so, perhaps after that. You on for dinner with Scruff Nicole?'

'Yes Rex I am,' there's a seductive tone in her voice, it's not lost on Scruff.

'You're a tin bum Rex, I think the lovely Nicole here fancies you.'

'Of course she does, she's my favourite girlfriend, I've told you before.'

Lunch over Nicole and I go up to my room, it's all business. We go over how I intend to carry out this job. I've memorised all the ground features that will be useful, and the power lines en route. I'm to leave my clothes with the ground crew man who will give me some nice new gear, mine to keep, no labels, and some east German currency. It's all got a familiar feeling about it.

'Now Rex, I'll leave you for now, see you tomorrow morning when it's all over, look forward to that dinner date, good luck.'
Nicole takes her leave, a peck on the cheek, suggestive of things to come. I would like to drag her into bed right now but come on Rex get a hold on yourself, this is not the time or place. Into bed, get some more sleep, need to be sharp tonight.

Sleep eludes me. I get to thinking and when that happens sleep does not get a chance. This is going to be my last job, Mr Roberts is going to be disappointed. The quiet life has taken centre stage. Settle down, marriage perhaps, kids, the boring life of an airline pilot. From what I've heard it's not really boring, that's a perception some people have. However it turns out it's got to be better than this. The money?

well there's a fair bit stashed away, it will give us a great start in our new life. Mind you the airlines are good payers and Kate is now into the big bucks, life should be pretty comfortable. Life expectancy will be vastly better and Kate will have peace of mind. I just hope she's not too upset that I'm here in Germany. The deal was low risk until I actually give it away and here I am taking on what appears to be a high risk job. Kate does not know that, does not need to know, she would worry. Would have been nice if I could have actually spoken to her. Right sleep, switch the mind off.

A light meal in the Mess around six and then an evening walk finishing up out at the tarmac, and there it is, another Chipmunk. This could well be the last opportunity I get to fly one. I have a look around, appears to be new, no markings. A groundcrew fellow appears and gives me a bag with some nice new clothes, I trade in my current garb. The sky is clear but no moon, quite dark, map reading will not be easy. I get airborne and head north intending to cross the border as close as I can to the pick up point. Lights off, radio silence, turn east into the DDR, the peoples prison, and drop down close to the ground. Map reading is ok, I've memorised all the water features, wooded areas, and the power lines. The flight progresses without incident, it's not far to the pick up point. There it is, I think, the outline of a large field. There's a light near the centre, must be the spot, circle around once and land, careful it's dark, hard to see the ground, little depth perception, it's not a great landing.

A flurry of activity outside the aircraft, there are several people there, keep the engine running and get out of here just as fast as possible. Take off straight ahead, there's enough room, *I hope,* Nicole said so, it's a big paddock. It's dark, can't see much at all, a blind take off at night, dodgy. The rear canopy is opened, somebody jumps in, 'go,' bang the throttles open, we're off.

'Ping, ping, ping,' I'm taking small arms fire, we're airborne, 'ping, ping' and suddenly it's hard to see, oil on the windscreen, a hit on the engine, we're losing oil, shit! The aircraft gains a bit of height then the engine starts to misfire, I manage a quick look inside, no oil pressure, the engine will fail any moment now, put it back on the ground, straight ahead and just hope it's flat ground.

Crash, we're back on the ground and I think the undercarriage might have been torn off, the little Chipmunk comes to a sudden halt.

'Get out, fast as you can.'

I'm shouting at my passenger, no idea who it is, *you don't need to know, remember.* I slide my canopy open, well I try to, it's very stiff and a big effort is required, the aircraft has obviously been damaged when it crashed back onto the ground. I leap out and start running, get away from the aeroplane, people will come looking that's a certainty. Get well away, forget the passenger, you have no idea who it is anyway and you are under no obligation to assist, that was not part of the deal, remember this is a high risk business. I run and run stumbling over what appears to be a ploughed field. After an eternity I stop, need a bit of a rest, it is a ploughed field, hard going. What's happened to my passenger? No idea, he's on his own, with any luck he, well I don't know if it's a he or a she, probably a he, will have taken off in a different direction, draw off the searchers. There will be searchers, someone was firing at us, now they will be looking. Why the shooting, had we been compromised? The aircraft had come down some distance from where we had taken off so there should be a bit of time to take evasive action.

What's happened, why am I suddenly on the run in hostile territory? *Big money, big risk,* you've experienced all this since you've been in this game. Why am I shaking, shaking a lot, and I'm cold, it's shock, of course, I'm in shock, the last few minutes have been a bit too much for the body, better lie down for a bit, no, not yet put some more distance between you and the aeroplane.

Whack, something hits my body, suddenly I'm sprawled in the dust and there's hurt, a lot of hurt.

'What the hell?'

There's blood, a puddle is forming in the dirt beside me, blood, *it's my blood,* what's happened? shit, I'm bleeding, bleeding a lot.

'Help, someone help me.'

Who's going to help, who can even hear me?

Movement, there's someone there, a figure looms above, there's a dog, a snarling vicious looking dog, who is it? a gun, they've got a gun, have I been shot?

There's wetness on the front of my jacket, blood, my blood, and there's a hole, it's in my chest, *shit, I have been shot, I'm in trouble.*

'Beweg dich nicht, wer bist du, was machst du?'

A wave of nausea washes over me, this is not how it's supposed to be, what's gone wrong, it was going to be straight in, pick up, straight out.

'Sprechen Sie, wer sind Sie?'

'Sorry, verstehe nicht, nur Englisch.'

I think this is the best way to go, I do understand German but if I don't let on then perhaps I might be able to figure out what's happening. A savage kick in the ribs, excruciating pain.

'Englander, a filthy Englander,' another savage kick.

Shit, I can't take much of this and that puddle beside me, it's getting bigger, it's my blood, how much is there, only have to lose around four litres and you're done for. There's a second person looking down at me, some conversation in German, they're trying to determine where I've come from.

'Englander.'

This second fellow speaks English.

'You from that little aeroplane? where's your mate?'

'What mate?'

Another vicious kick, if there's much more of this I'm done for, dizzy, lost too much blood, there's a blackness descending. There's more conversation between my two tormentors, they think I'm from the Chipmunk but they're not sure, but they know I'm an Englander and that pretty well gives the show away. The second chap appears to have some authority, he's now giving the orders, it's decided they had better stop treating me badly, keep me alive, see what they can get from me, don't like the sound of that.

The blackness is taking hold, I'm feeling faint, my memory starts to wander, Kate, my lovely Kate, that first night in bed, I'm shot, so what, Kate, I'll be right back, these bastards tormenting me, they'll go away, Kate, Michelle, Kate, Eloise, Ali, confused memories, Kate, Ali, Kate, Kate, Kate, Kate, Kate, blackness.

big money, big risk.

Three weeks later, early morning, Auckland, a knock on the door.

'Delivery, florist's delivery for Miss Fontaine.' Kate comes to the door.

'Interflora, Germany, flowers for a Miss Fontaine.'
The delivery boy has a wreath made entirely from black flowers, the whole thing, completely black, there's no note.

Kate collapses unconscious

NZ Herald – August 27th 1967

Top Fashion Model Dies.

One of New Zealand's leading fashion models died yesterday in a traffic accident on a busy Parnell street. Miss Kate Fontaine, a rising star in the fashion world was killed instantly when she was run over by a bus on Parnell Road. Miss Fontaine was much in demand in the fashion world and had recently appeared on the cover of Paris Vogue. The driver of the Auckland Metro bus that was involved is being counselled. The driver claims that Miss Fontaine was looking straight at him when she stepped out in front of his moving bus.

Kate Fontaine was twenty-seven and considered to be one of the brightest lights on the New Zealand fashion scene. She and her partner, Rex Macare, were a popular couple around Auckland.

NZ Herald – August 31st 1967

Missing in Europe.

Friends of Rex Macare are concerned about his whereabouts, they have not heard from him for over four weeks. A freelance pilot, Rex Macare was visiting friends in the North Rhine - Westphalia area in Germany when he apparently disappeared. Interpol have been advised. Rex Macare was the partner of Kate Fontaine the fashion model killed in a traffic accident last week in Auckland.

NZ Herald –September 5th 1967

Killed in Vietnam.

Russel Horsley, a freelance pilot, has died in South Vietnam. He was shot in the head, apparently by an AK47 fired from the ground while flying into a rubber plantation at Dau Tieng in Binh Duong province. Russ Horsley was well known in Auckland's flying community for his 'tin arm,' the result of a flying accident some time ago.

About The Author

After a lifetime of flying, military and civil, Rex Mangin now lives in a cottage on a beach in Auckland New Zealand with his partner Lynne. He has discovered a love for writing and now spends a lot of time doing just that. There have been some short stories, and a couple of autobiographies, now the first novel, there will be more.

Books By Rex Mangin

These books by Rex Mangin are available as paperbacks and at most e-book outlets worldwide.

Infidelity Gun Running & Other Tales

Fourteen short stories drawn from the author's vast treasure trove of experiences. He spent a lifetime in aviation, both military and civilian, became involved in the Cold War in Europe, nuclear testing at Christmas Island, topdressing in New Zealand, and spent many years flying the Pacific. Now retired, he has turned his hand to writing. His aviation background is reflected in many of these stories.

Set in Europe, North Africa, Hong Kong, New Zealand. Sydney, Honolulu, Christmas Island, Tahiti, Mo'orea, Rangiroa, and Bora Bora it's a diverse and entertaining collection of fact and fiction, all based on the author's real-life experiences.

The dramatic engine failure described in *A Close Call In Tahiti* did occur, July 17th 1980, at Faa'a Airport in Papeete. The *Gun Running* happened back in 1957.

The author flew into Hong Kong's old Kai Tak airport many times. *Remember Kai Tak* describes just what it was like flying into that extraordinary place. The yacht featured in *Andria* is the *Jardilinka*, a well-known vessel in Hong Kong waters. The author was lucky enough to enjoy many cruises on this fine old vessel.

The Jury is a true story as, are *A Curious Business, The Bottle*, and *Christmas Island. A Labs Attack* describes some of the things that went on during the Cold War, all true, these things happened.

Aerial topdressing features in *The Greening Of Northland,* an insight into this unique New Zealand industry.

I'm sure you'll enjoy reading these stories just as much as the author enjoyed writing them.

Flying The Pacific
(a memoir)

After several years in NATO's Second Tactical Air Force on the front line of the Cold War in Germany the author returned to his native New Zealand and joined TEAL, Tasman Empire Airways. During a thirty year career with the airline he was part of the enormous expansion into the present day Air New Zealand. He flew everything from the jet prop Electra to the 747-400. The Pacific, the Orient, America, and during the later part of his career all the way to Europe. It was not a simple process however, there was a lot of angst and heartache.

This book is not just about flying it includes everything else that's involved in an airline pilot's life, the travel, the 'holiday' stopovers, living abroad, interesting experiences, some of them very interesting, the stresses and pressures, the rewards, it's a rather unique lifestyle.

Here's a sample of the first chapter.

Joining TEAL

'Got the checkerboard?'

'Yep, got it' replies the co-pilot.

'Height ok?' I ask.

'Yep, looking good.'

'Ok when that tall building with the mast over on the right is abeam we'll turn.'

'Yep it's coming up now.'

'That wind's picked up, better turn a fraction earlier,' the co-
  pilot offers.
'Yep, thanks.'
'Right; go now.'

We are flying a DC8, it's Hong Kong's notorious checkerboard approach at the old Kai Tak airport. I bank the big jet steeply to the right and peer out looking for the runway, there it is, right on cue. It's a murky evening, there's a strong crosswind blowing us right into the checkerboard, it's bumpy and we're in amongst the tall buildings. This approach is one of the more challenging things in aviation, not for the faint hearted. There's a stiff southerly requiring the use of runway 13, the south easterly one and that necessitates the famous checkerboard approach, the one the passengers love, the one that takes you right in amongst the tall buildings. The downside is that when this approach is required there's always a stiff crosswind on the runway. We complete the turn onto finals, assess the crosswind, kick in some rudder and prepare for the actual touchdown still with quite a bit of drift on. Just before the wheels make contact I kick it straight; the touchdown is quite smooth. Hold the wing down, careful with the reverse that wind is strong. We decelerate and turn off the runway; another adrenaline fuelled Hong Kong arrival. How come I'm doing this? I'm 32 years of age and this is one of aviation's more difficult places to be flying and in a big jet full of people. It's quite a story.

Cold War Warrior
(a memoir)

A true story about a young lad who grew up in Blenheim, New Zealand, during the 1940s and early 50s. He developed an insatiable passion for flying, travelled to England and became a pilot in the Royal Air Force. He soon found himself involved in the United Kingdom's nuclear testing programme in the Pacific. This took him around the world and in just a few short years he found himself on the front line of the Cold War in Germany.

If things had turned ugly this young Kiwi, along with others, was going to unleash nuclear mayhem on Europe and would no doubt have perished in the process. This is his story.

Early Days

'Ok Harry, here we go.' I nosed the big Canberra over and headed for the ground in a steep dive, at about 600 feet with the target firmly in the gun sight I squeezed the trigger. Four 20mm Hispano cannons burst into life and sent a shudder through the aircraft, I could see the shells shredding the canvas target on the ground. When we were ridiculously close I stopped firing, pulled up hard, and climbed away. Harry, my navigator, was jammed up in the nose cone, he must have been terrified. Again! We were at a live firing range in the old West Germany practising air to ground gunnery, I was having a ball, Harry was not! How did I come to be doing this?

Well I was a front line jet jock in the Royal Air Force, actually I was in NATO's Second Tactical Air Force in Germany, how did I get to be there? it's a long story.

In our cottage on a beach in Auckland, amongst all the wine glasses, there's a copper tankard, it's lined with silver and looks old and tarnished. There are some words engraved on it. *IN HAZY MEMORY OF SALISBURY SOUTHERN RHODESIA JUNE 1962.* On closer inspection the engraving's a bit rough, the Os look like Ds, however, the quality of the copper, and the silver lining, appears to be surprisingly good. This tankard is a constant reminder to me about the early part of my life, the part that now seems so very far away when I was involved in the Cold War in Europe. On occasions I ask myself, did all that really happen?

Was that me thundering around Germany in a jet, right down on the deck, eyeballing the East Germans? Was it me out in the Libyan desert amongst the flies, the sand, the heat and the sweat, trying to toss a bomb onto a target from very low level? Did I really shoot up the Larnaca range out in Cyprus with those big 20mm cannons? Did I really fly around those Norwegian Fjords in all that murk, ice and snow? That gun running business in Tunisia, did that actually happen? Was that me flying over the vastness of East Africa, the endless deserts of the Sudan? Did I do that sabre-rattling for Queen and Country in Central Africa? Was I really involved in that nuclear testing in the Pacific in the 1950s? Did I really wander around East Berlin at the height of the Cold War? Yes I did, it was all part of my Big OE, let me explain.

Albert McConachie's Bad Day

A three part tale about the slow decline of Albert McConachie's matrimonial life into total disaster. Albert, however, quite unexpectedly, finds love elsewhere. The three parts of this tale are interspersed with a collection of short stories that you will find entertaining and amusing. The trivial, amusing, and the disastrous, childhood memories that you can probably relate to.

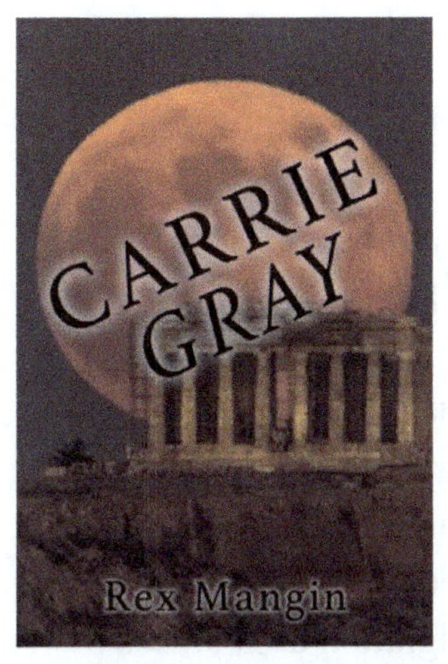

Carrie Gray
(a novel)

A young girl leaves New Zealand for Europe, the big OE. She goes alone, wants to do her own thing, unrestricted by others, experience everything. A skilled boaty she wants to crew on a superyacht; she disappears. Her boyfriend, Michael, becomes concerned at the sudden lack of communication and sets off to find her; he disappears.

Michael's father Frank, a retired detective, becomes alarmed and sets off to find them both. He discovers a frightening underworld of drug smuggling, murder, and prostitution, dominated by several powerful families. It's devouvred these two youngsters from far off New Zealand.

A fast moving story of romance, adventure, and danger set in Paris, Athens, and Istanbul, and spills out into the Pacific.

Travel Bites

'You're under arrest sir.'
'Excuse me?'
'You're under arrest.'
Excuse me indeed; how can this be? I was at the immigration desk at Los Angeles airport, just got off a big jet after flying all the way from Auckland, when I was confronted with this. *I was the Captain!*

A collection of short stories, all travel related. The author spent much of his life travelling the world, and accumulated a mother lode of experiences. Some of these are shared in this book.